THE AGENT AND THE OUTLAW

VAMPIRES IN VERSAILLES
BOOK TWO

LILY RILEY

This is a work of fiction. Unless otherwise indicated, all the names, characters, businesses, places, events and incidents in this book are either the product of the author's imagination or used in a fictitious manner. Any resemblance to actual persons, living or dead, or actual events is purely coincidental.

THE AGENT AND THE OUTLAW

Vampires in Versailles, Book 2

Copyright © 2024 by Lily Riley

Cover design by Covers by Jules

Interior artwork by Calesia

PRAISE FOR LILY RILEY

"Scandal, seduction, and supernatural secrets animate Riley's deliciously decadent debut and Les Dames Dangereuses series launch. Riley brings the heat as the erotically charged animosity between Daphne and Étienne...evolves into a genuine connection. This hits all the right notes."

— PUBLISHER'S WEEKLY

"There's a delightful balance between history, romance, and setting. The love scenes are steamy enough to be enjoyable without reaching an erotic level, still, a fan may be needed! The characters vulnerability in going from hunter/hunted to partners and lovers is well done...*The Assassin and the Libertine* is an excellent start to what promises to be an interesting new series!"

— IND'TALE MAGAZINE

"Get ready for historical hotness in a paranormal world that's sure to sweep you away! Lily Riley sizzles with a passionate debut that transports the reader to a version of 18th-century France where vampires roam among the aristocrats, indulging their dalliances and evading those bent on eliminating them...*The Assassin and the Libertine* is a steamy tale sure to stimulate the imagination that will leave you impatiently anticipating Ms. Riley's next installment in this fabulous series."

— KAT TURNER, AUTHOR OF THE COVEN
DAUGHTERS SERIES

"Bridgerton meets Buffy in this tale of love between two French aristocrats. Étienne is the brooding, misunderstood vampire and Daphne the deadly assassin sent to kill him. This fun, racy romance is a thoroughly enjoyable read."

— GIRL WITH A BOOK

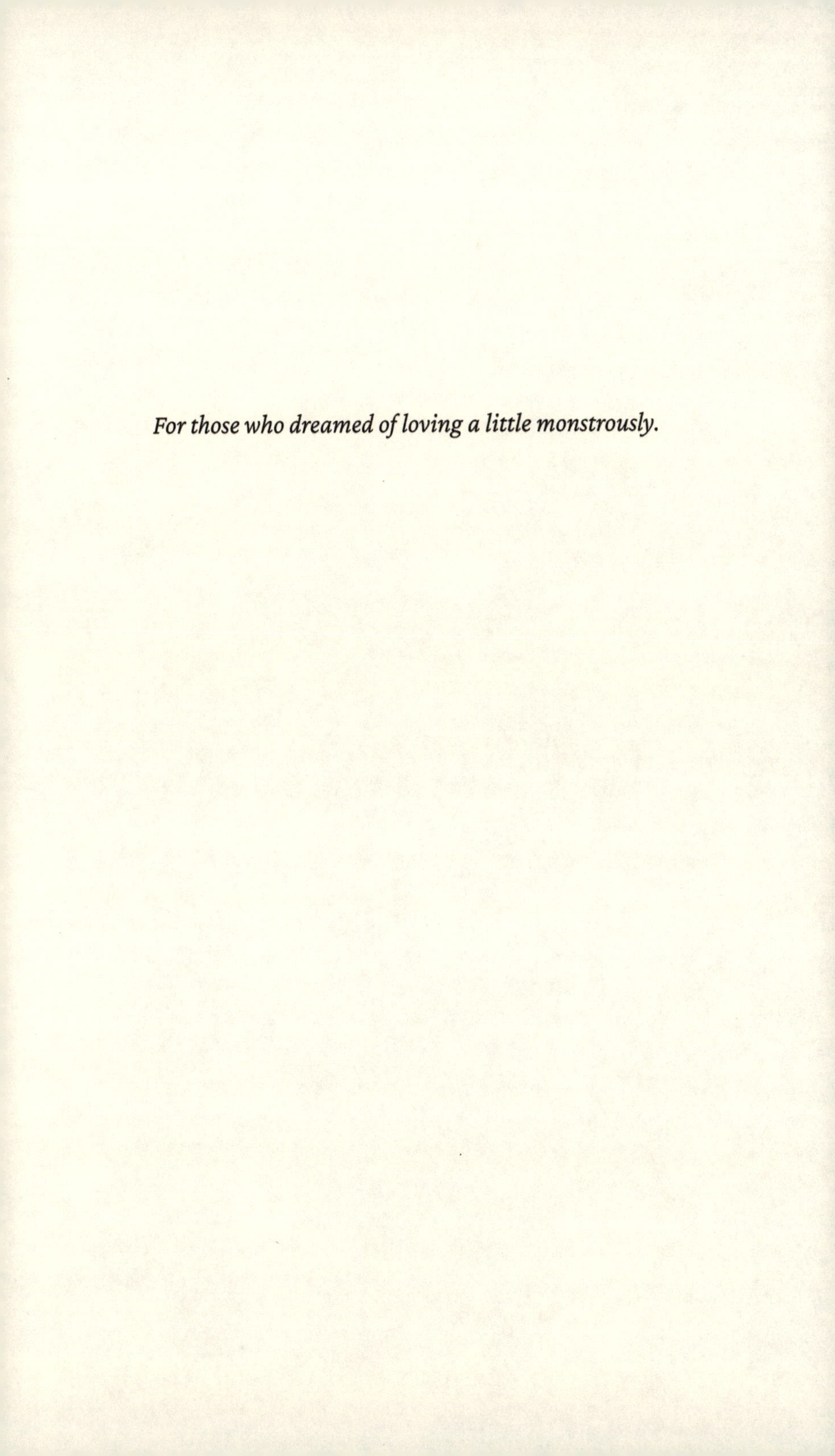

For those who dreamed of loving a little monstrously.

PROLOGUE
CHARLOTTE

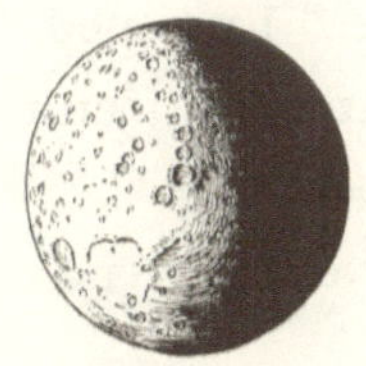

November 15, 1766
Château de Champs-sur-Marne

IT WASN'T OFTEN THAT I DESIRED BLOODSHED. IN FACT, THE ONLY other time I truly *wanted* to murder someone had been a year ago, when my former husband summoned a demon to try to force my cousin to love him. It didn't quite work out for him, and needless to say, it made for a rather awkward evening.

"Do you ever wonder what they do with these reports?" I asked, stamping my seal into the molten wax on a thick sheaf of papers. "Sometimes I think they don't even look at them. They couldn't possibly read them all—every scrap of *occasionally* useful information from every agent. I've half a mind to test the theory and slip in some dirty words to see if anyone says anything."

Firelight flickered around the room, casting an amber glow upon the towering shelves of books that lined the library of my cousin's impressive château. Daphne, Duchesse de Duras, agent of The Order, leader of their women-only sect called *les*

Dames Dangereuses, and my best friend, peered at me over the rim of her champagne glass.

"Charlotte, I've read your reports. There aren't any more filthy words than the ones you already use. I've seen seasoned agents blush beneath their masks while reading them. Perhaps you should consider a career as a writer of erotic novels."

"I would truly excel," I preened. "I know so many good synonyms for male anatomical features. *Quivering rod. Virility spear. Throbbing manhood.*"

Daphne rolled her eyes to cover a smirk.

"Silent flute."

"Speaking of silent..." She looked at me pointedly.

I grinned and handed her the sealed folio—thirty-six pages of tightly scrawled script outlining an avalanche of evidence of the Marquis de Sade's crimes. Treason, blackmail, extortion, sexual abuses, violence against innocents...it had been months of grim and grueling work, and my biggest investigation since joining *les DD*. At court, all the aristocrats knew of the marquis's villainous tendencies, but no one had the temerity to bring charges against him. As a member of court, he was a titled aristocrat. *A peer.* At least, until Daphne and I had come along and forced the issue with The Order—the long-shadowed organization of powerful men in France who tasked themselves with the safety of king and country, but which operated in a sort of gray area just outside the law.

"What is to be done about his associates?" I asked.

She raised a brow at me and drained her glass. "I thought you handled that already." Her displeased tone implied she hadn't approved of my methods.

"Oh, *chérie*, just because I killed a vampire doesn't mean it was an indication of my feelings about the poor souls suffering from the blood plague. You know I'm all for integration of vampires and humans—I have been since the plague took hold of Paris years ago, really—and you know how much I love you and Étienne. Your hematic preferences don't bother me one whit. But truly, that bastard was evil. I mean, *really* evil. Quite possibly as evil as my former husband, may he rot in Hell," I said earnestly.

"Charlotte, he's imprisoned in the Château d'If," she replied. "Not technically dead. Probably mad, but still quite alive."

"Well, it's almost the same thing, isn't it? And The Order gave me his falsified death record after all that *unpleasantness* a year ago," I grumbled.

"Yes," she replied drolly. "'All that *unpleasantness*.' Summoning a demon and murdering several people— including my own awful husband, as well as the king's mistress—is what you would call *unpleasant*." She chuckled. "No, *chérie*, it's not that I disapprove of you staking a vampire who certainly deserved it, it's just that you killed him before he could tell us who Sade's other associate was. We know he had more than one highly placed individual feeding his depraved desires."

"Well, honestly, Daphne, it's not *my* fault a supernatural kidnapper ended up being so frail as to die when he was stabbed a few times—"

"Twenty-seven times."

"Twenty-seven times, then. But really, who's counting?"

"You did. It was in your report!"

"Because I'm nothing if not efficient. Not only did I dispatch a villainous bloodsucker—no offense—but I wrote a fully accurate report on the matter. You're lucky you have me as a lieutenant for *les DD*, you know, especially when I'm here working while you're out having glorious carnal fun with your dashing rake of a fiancé."

My words were meant to tease, but Daphne sensed the sadness behind them.

"Oh, Charlotte, I'm so sorry. I know this past year has been tough for you, what with Philippe's crimes, the devastation of the blood plague, and my engagement to Étienne. I know what it is to see another's happiness when you yourself are laid low by life's blows. But you know you are always welcome here. You will always have a home with Étienne and me. We both love you, darling," she said, putting a hand on mine.

"I know, Daphne," I said. "But I've been hiding out with you for far too long. You and Étienne have a life to start living. It's time I returned to Philippe's—to *my* estate. There are things there that I need to put to bed."

"Like François?" she teased, referring to the latest in my string of occasional lovers.

"*Non,* no longer. He was beautiful, certainly, but so self-absorbed. And you know, I think he was stealing my stockings. Every time he came around, I discovered I was missing one. He must have amassed quite a collection by now," I sighed. "Really, if he wants to wear them, fine, but at least he could buy them for himself and stop taking mine. Although, I suppose if the occasional errant stocking is the price I must pay for some thoroughly enjoyable bed sport, I should be grateful." I laughed, but it sounded hollow even to my own ears. Naturally, Daphne picked up on it right away.

"Someone will come along for you, Charlotte. I'm sure of it. Philippe was not your match, but you have one out there. You'll see. One day, true love will come right up to you and knock you senseless, and you'll be as much of a lost cause as I am," she smiled beatifically at me, and if I didn't love her immeasurably, I would have kicked her in the shin.

"If true love knocks you senseless, then *mon Dieu*, I am much happier with a string of wholly inadequate but temporarily sufficient lovers. After everything that happened last year, I'd much rather keep a firm hold of my senses."

Daphne grinned at me and stood. "Ah, well. You'll have to fall in and out of love on your own time. We'll be late for our meeting with The Order. Once they have this report in hand, they'll issue the formal execution order for Sade, then the real work begins. They'll most likely want you to see it through."

"Good," I replied. "I don't often feel compelled to carry out assassinations, but after all of this," I gestured to the file, "I've never wanted to deliver justice so much."

"Yes," she said, pulling on her cloak and picking up her domino mask. "It will be good to see it through and put this whole case behind us."

"Of course," I said. "I think after this assignment, I'm going to take a little rest. Perhaps spend some time in the country or go on a grand tour around the continent. I've earned a bit of fun."

"I completely agree. And who knows? Perhaps you'll find your match when this is all over," Daphne added hopefully.

I laughed. "I doubt that, Daphne. I very much doubt that."

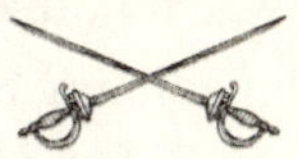

ANTOINE

That same evening
Island of Menorca, Mediterranean

"What have you done?" I whispered, gripped by horror. I stared down at the papers on his desk. *These cannot be right.*

King Louis would never stand for it. "*Général*, this is...*unthinkable*! You'll never get away with it."

He glared at me from across the room, face purpling with rage.

"Lieutenant, I don't recall giving you permission to enter my private study, let alone read my correspondence. Do you desire a thrashing, boy?"

The threat was not idle bluster, but I pressed on. "Why would you—why have you done such a thing? The war has ended. The treaty has been signed. We're stuck here on this godforsaken island to oversee the last of our withdrawal while the British drink their tea from the summit of our defeat. We have lost, Général."

"We haven't lost until *I* say we've lost, Lieutenant," he snapped, his eyes flashing with anger. He shook his head to regain control of his temper, then, eerily calm, he continued. "*Les armées du roi* are weak—inclined to *libertinage* and slothfulness. If we have been set back temporarily, so be it. I will regain control and force these useless, witless, spineless men in my command to embody the kind of strength and ferocity that we need in order to turn the tide and beat back the British."

He's gone mad. There was no other explanation for it. "The treaty has already been signed! King Louis—"

"King Louis doesn't care how I win, Lieutenant, only that I do. This is the way I will deliver a result. Something you know very little about," he hissed.

"You underestimate him," I argued. "He would not stand for such cruelty or treachery."

"Silence! You haven't the faintest notion of the king's true feelings. If we have faltered in this war, it is because the king is too distracted with domestic matters. The blood plague rages still, turning farmer, peasant, and *bourgeois* into filthy, soulless *sanguisuges*. He cannot control the vampires, so he must play at appeasing them until a cure can be discovered. That absurd emissary is as powerless as they come, and no one believes The Order is actually doing anything other than fueling rumors of revolution." He turned to face me, and I saw disconcerting wildness in his gaze. "I will save France at any cost—even if the threat is France herself."

"Sir, you cannot mean—"

"You are dismissed, Lieutenant," he snapped, pushing past me. He sat down at the desk and picked up the damning papers, then tossed them into the fire.

"No!" I reached for them, but strong arms hauled me back. Two other soldiers had entered the room and now pulled me toward the door. I stared at the burning evidence, quickly turning to ashes before my eyes. I hadn't thought far enough ahead—would I really have gone to the king with proof of such corruption? *It doesn't matter now.* Even if I did report it, no one would believe me without something substantial to back my claim. Général de Vaux had the reputation and influence to do as he pleased, like all powerful men.

Gritting my teeth and brushing the dirt from my uniform, I stormed back to my quarters. It wasn't long before the two soldiers showed up outside again. I frowned, already suspecting what was to come.

"A dozen lashings for insubordination and disorderly conduct," one of them said. "To be delivered at dawn."

A dozen. Those scars could join the others. "No dishonorable discharge for me then?"

The soldier narrowed his eyes at me. "Certainly not, *monsieur.*"

I went back inside and turned to my own correspondence. I knew I had a letter from my sister, Marie, waiting in the stack. My heart clenched at the thought. She'd been unwell since the murder of her son, Louis. My sister's family had been a bright spot in my otherwise gloomy existence, but with the loss of Louis, now everything seemed bleak. I prayed her grief would lessen with time, but it only seemed to consume her more, until I feared she would be swallowed by it. Young Louis had suffered brutal mistreatment at the hands of a corrupt aristocrat, the Marquis de Sade. As soon as I was able, I would confront the monster and have my revenge.

Her letter gave me no comfort—rather, it stoked my temper to a boiling point. Marie had questions about the circumstances of Louis's death. The things she suggested were horrifying, but something about them took root in my heart. *The général must see this.* Crumpling it in my shaking fist, I rushed from the room and back to the général's study. The two soldiers from earlier were standing guard out front.

"He is busy," one of them said. "Come back later."

"No," I said, trying to push past them. "He will see me now!"

The guards tried to restrain me, but I fought them both off, taking one down with a fist to the gut and knocking the other one out with a punch to the temple. I kicked the door open and faced the outraged général at his desk.

"We need to talk."

CHAPTER ONE
CHARLOTTE

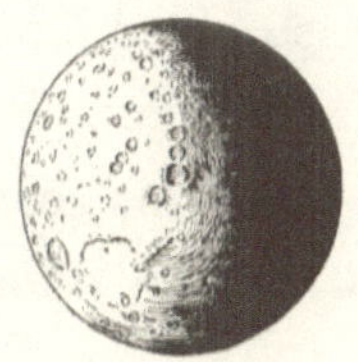

November 1, 1767
Somewhere outside Versailles

W HEN I CAME TO, SEVERAL SENSATIONS ASSAULTED ME. THE rhythmic gallop of dull pain inside my skull. The roiling of this evening's oysters swirling inside my guts. The earthy scents of sweaty horseflesh, leather, and mud tangling in my nose. Then, the slow and damnable realization that my hands and feet had been bound and I'd been thrown—rather indecorously, I might add—facedown across the ass of some idiot's cantering horse. *The nerve!*

I opened my mouth to protest, but the horse pulled up short, dangerously shifting the oysters. I choked out a groan as the bile started to rise.

"For the love of God, let me off of this animal, or I shall cast up my accounts all over you!"

My captor slid off the horse and lifted me easily. He—yes, certainly it was a *he*, and a rather splendid specimen of *he*, as I started to recall—set me on my feet, and I unsteadily hopped to the side of the road to be sick. I heaved and, tied as I was, began to pitch forward over the frost-covered leaf litter.

Calloused hands grasped my wrists and pulled me upright. I attempted to get a look at his face, but the low hood of his cloak and the darkness of the late evening—or was it early morning?—prevented me from doing so. The only part of him I could see was a strong, stubbled jawline and some very fine lips set in a tight line of annoyance.

"Easy, lad," he said softly, his voice as rough as his work-hewn hands. Chills danced up my spine.

Lad?

Ah, yes. A jumble of memories began to unravel. I frowned down at my Cupid costume. The once-pristine toga and breeches beneath were rumpled and stained with—*mon Dieu, please let that be dirt.* The small, feathered wings and golden circlet were gone, but I noted with relief that my wig was still secure.

What happened?

I'd been at Versailles for the king's All Hallow's Eve masquerade. My cousin Daphne and her fiancé Étienne had been with me. I was on assignment for les Dames Dangereuses —The Order's cadre of female agents. *But what had I been doing?*

I furrowed my brows to try and recall but immediately regretted it. The steady beat of pain in my head became a symphony of agony, and I vomited. I was dimly aware of a humiliating dribble down the front of my toga.

"Hell, lad, how much did you have to drink? Did Sade slip you something? Or are you just in your cups?" The soothing tone was gone, replaced by one of clipped irritation.

"I'm never eating another oyster again," I wheezed, feebly trying to wipe my mouth with my shoulder. *Wait...he said—*

Sade. The Marquis de Sade. My target. Yes. *Yes.* That was right —I was at the masquerade, dressed as a young man so I could lure Sade out into the garden and dispatch him there. Strangle him. *It should look like an accident*, The Order had said. A lover getting too carried away during a tryst, an incident too scandalous to be thoroughly investigated. *Not that anyone would press for an investigation.* Between Sade's crimes, the rumors, and victims from every social class, few—if any—would mourn his loss.

I remembered seeing Sade in the ballroom at Versailles. I'd successfully attracted his attention and plied him with a glass of drugged champagne, which had made him docile and willing. He'd followed me into that absurd hedge maze in the gardens and had been fumbling with the buttons on his breeches, when...*thwip!* An arrow—straight to the heart. *That doesn't seem right. An arrow? Sade is supposed to be strangled to death. I'm supposed to be the one to do it. Wait, that's it...*

I hadn't been able to complete my assignment. *Someone* had intervened, shot an arrow through Sade with, what, a crossbow? Yes, that was it. And there it was, hanging from the side of my captor's saddle. *My captor.* I tensed. This man had interrupted my assassination attempt and had murdered the Marquis de Sade. Who was he? Why did he want Sade dead? *Why has he kidnapped me and what does he want with me? And mon Dieu, why does that last thought send a perverse shiver of pleasure through me?*

Putain. Now is not the time, Charlotte. Focus!

Sade's death wouldn't look like an accident now. It would look like murder. Perhaps it would look like a political statement—a thought that truly worried me given the escalating tensions between the vampires and the aristocracy. *Merde.* Were Daphne and Étienne still back at Versailles? Had they tried to follow? They must be worried to death!

Despite myself, I chuckled. *Can the undead be worried to death?*

An owl hooted in the distance and the man shifted toward the sound. It was still dark out, but I could tell that night was waning. How much time had passed?

"How long was I out?" I rasped. The ache at the back of my head throbbed insistently, and I remembered a more pressing indignity. "You knocked me out! How dare you! What a horrible thing to do to someone you just met. I mean, we haven't even been introduced!" I tried to turn and face my captor with righteous pique, but I lost my balance and nearly toppled over. Again, he grabbed my bound wrists to steady me. "Oh, for the love of—could you at least spare me some humiliation and untie my ankles? I'm hardly in a position to run for it," I grumbled. "Being this unsteady on my feet is only adding to my nausea and increasing the likelihood that I will purge myself again."

The lines around his mouth tightened, but he kept silent. His bulky shoulders tensed beneath the cloak, and I fought to keep my lustful interest at bay. *Have I ever seen a man with such a build before?* I didn't think so. *He's kidnapped you, Charlotte, and likely not for some bed sport.*

I frowned. I did not enjoy being ignored, so I added, "You see, Monsieur, I'm afraid you're close enough to bespatter."

The threat seemed to have an effect on him. Carefully, he bent to untie the rope at my feet. Thighs like tree trunks tested the seam limits on his breeches as he loosened the knot. I gritted my teeth. He stood slowly but made no move to untie my hands. Of course, I considered running, but after taking measure of the man before me, the sorry state of my footwear, and the remaining oysters, I thought better of that notion. *He* obviously reached the same conclusion. I seethed and scowled up into his obscured face.

I saw little of him outside of his cloak, which was well-made but plain black wool, as if he had money but not the desire to spend it. *How...odd.* He was quite a bit taller than me—I faced his expansive chest directly—and broad-shouldered in a very *un*aristocratic sort of way, which clashed with the idea of him having any sort of wealth. *Curious!*

I shivered. Studying his cloak made me realize I was bitterly cold in the late October evening—*or is that early November morning?*—and I was still in my silly costume. It was fine for disguising my sex, but not ideal for the onset of winter temperatures. My breath condensed in frosty puffs in front of my face.

More memories solidified. He had been handsome. Rather, he *was* handsome. I remembered seeing him burst through the hedge maze back at Versailles and fall into the torchlight. A queue of chestnut hair, dark sweeps of lashes, vibrant green eyes, a once-broken nose that had been set well, and a thin, crescent moon scar that crossed from his brow to his cheek, and those lips... *Mon Dieu, such lips! A woman would sell all her jewels to hear sweet nothings drop from them.*

Though sweet nothings hadn't dropped from them. I recalled our altercation in the garden earlier in the evening. He'd been flippant, rude even, and had clearly misunderstood my intentions. However, I was fortunate he hadn't seen through my disguise.

Despite his enigmatic appeal, my temper surged.

"Kidnapping is a hanging offense, you know," I said archly. "I'd hate to see a neck as fine as yours stretched because of some silly mistake. Release me and I assure you that no harm will come to you from my quarter."

The man said nothing.

"You don't even need to return me to Versailles. I can make my own way. Simply untie me and let me go. You've done a great deal of damage, you see, and it needs to be put right. Perhaps if I can get back soon, I can figure out a way to spin your interference. A robbery? No, that would be absurd. A religious zealot, maybe. Sade's sexual deviancy was well-known, and I doubt the church approved. That could work, you know. I've a friend in the church with a debt to repay..."

I trailed off, thinking. If I could get back to Versailles, I could fix it. I would simply present Daphne with an alternate course of action, and she would convince The Order that this could still work for us. Either way, Sade was dead, which was the one silver lining. He wouldn't be able to abuse any more innocents, and the vampire peasants and bourgeoisie who clamored for his blood—literally and figuratively—would be temporarily assuaged. *A peace offering of death.*

My captor studied me silently, seemingly frozen to the ground. He obviously didn't grasp the immediacy of my needs. When he had crashed through the hedge maze at the palace, he had stared at me incomprehensibly when I chastised him for his haste. Perhaps he wasn't the intelligent sort—a shame, really, since he was so thoroughly enjoyable to look at.

I spoke with a slow, deliberate pace.

"Monsieur? *Parlez-vous français?* Can you understand me? First, I need to be untied. Second, I need to return to the palace. Well, no—second, I need some kind of cloak or coat. It's bloody freezing out here. *Then* I need to return to Versailles, which hopefully isn't more than an hour or two's ride from where we currently stand."

He continued to regard me mutely, but his shoulders shifted slightly. *Ah, so he does understand me.*

"Where exactly are we?" I demanded. I had no idea how long I'd been unconscious. The navy sky was lightening to a lovely periwinkle, which meant the sun was soon to rise. Dread pooled when I realized Daphne and Étienne would not be able to find me now. They'd be beholden to their vampire schedules and would be below ground for the next day. My trail would probably be cold by the time they could reach me. *I am on my own.*

"Are you well enough to carry on?" His voice was like the dregs from a chocolate pot—deep, dark, and luscious. In another world, at another time, perhaps I would have tried to seduce him.

"I should think so," I nodded. "You don't need to worry, Monsieur. Untie me and I'll be perfectly able to make my way back from here."

He grunted and leaned forward to grab my wrists.

"Thank you, Monsieur. I appreciate your attempts to remove me from a dangerous situation at the masquerade, but I assure you, all will be well when I can get back and sort everything out. I say, that doesn't feel like the knot is loosening there—"

He hoisted me up onto the horse and swung himself up behind me. It seemed to take very little effort for him to lift me, which was both disconcerting and tempting. *Dieu, Charlotte. Stop thinking such things!*

"Forgive me, Monsieur, but we seem to have an error in communication. You aren't releasing me, which doesn't make any sense. I've already told you that you won't be in any danger from me for what happened at the palace, but you must let me go so that I can deal with things, *d'accord?* I mean, I don't really know what else you could possibly want with me. I'll only slow you down, and I'm sure you have lots of other lives to inconvenience."

"Silence," he hissed.

If there was one word I did *not* appreciate—especially from a man—it was that one. I'd certainly heard it enough from my former husband whenever he felt I was being inappropriate, which was to say, quite often.

"I—WILL—NOT!" I shouted, punctuating my words with fierce jabs from my elbows into his sides. I whipped my head back as hard as I could and felt it connect with his nose. He grunted, but I yelled.

Charlotte, you idiot! That's where the brute knocked you senseless.

I didn't have time to regret my mistake and the sharp pain radiating through my head—I acted as fast as my reflexes would allow. With my captor temporarily distracted, I leapt from the horse and tucked myself into a ball to cushion my fall. Quick as a flash, I jumped up and took off through the forest, running in a zigzag pattern. I wasn't sure if the bulge I'd felt at my back was his masculine endowments or a pistol, but I wasn't going to take any more chances.

When I'd run far enough to reach the limit of my breathing capacity, I paused behind a large oak tree and listened. I heard the chorus of early morning birdsong and the distant burble of a stream. I smiled to myself. I didn't hear a twig-breaking, leaf-crunching, crossbow-wielding madman giving chase. Perhaps he'd reasoned I was too much trouble—a fact I could heartily agree with—and rode on with his smelly, vomit-inducing horse.

When my breath returned to normal, I started moving again but stopped just as quickly. Some distance away, I heard a knot of low male voices creeping down the road. I strained to hear them. Had my captor persuaded a passerby to help seek me out? Crouching down beneath a thicket of greenery, I peered through the branches.

I could just make them out where they gathered along the road—there were five of them, all in identical burgundy coats. I squinted. They looked like soldiers, but I didn't recognize their uniforms. Were they English? They wore that gaudy red, didn't they? What would English soldiers be doing here?

Leaning forward, I tried to get a better look. If I could get a bit closer, I might be able to hear what they were saying. I prepared to make my move.

"Don't."

The word was a whispered command coming from somewhere just above my head. I looked up and nearly shrieked. My captor was perched on a limb in the large oak directly atop me, staring murderously at the group of soldiers. *Merde.* How long had he been there?

Sullenly accepting that my *great* escape had been anything but, I narrowed my eyes.

"Don't *what?*" I hissed back.

"Move."

"Ha!" I retorted. "Forgive me if I'm a bit loath to take your advice. You did, after all, bludgeon and abscond with me. I'm beginning to doubt your intentions to ensure my safety."

He didn't acknowledge my response, but I knew he'd heard. I could see the muscles work in his jaw as if he were gritting his teeth. My former husband, Philippe, used to do the same thing when he would tire of my cheek. I considered it one of my greatest virtues, to be so infuriating to the simpler sex.

To prove my utter unwillingness to listen to the crossbow-wielding madman, I snaked forward through the undergrowth to hide behind yet another bush. I could practically feel the fury emanating from the oak tree behind me. From this better angle, I could hear the soldiers more clearly.

They were speaking French! Two of them had thick foreign accents—Prussian, I guessed. The other three were clearly Parisian. *But why the burgundy uniforms?*

"We must turn back. We won't be able to find him now. It's too late," one of the Prussians was saying.

"We can't just leave! We know he's in the area. Fan out," said another.

"We won't find him here," said the tallest Parisian. "These woods stretch for hundreds of acres, and he's had more training than all of us."

"But we have the advantage," grinned the first Prussian.

I probably would have heard more, but at that moment, I leaned a *bit* too far forward and a twig snapped beneath my palm. I froze, praying the soldiers hadn't heard.

They had.

Within seconds, the soldiers were upon me.

The tall Parisian hauled me up by the back of my toga, lifting me well off the ground. His anger at uncovering a possible spy dissolved into guffaws of mirth as the group took in my admittedly bizarre ensemble.

"Thank heavens!" I enthused, pitching my voice low and hoping my disguise was still intact enough to fool them. "Gentlemen, you have certainly saved my life. I was traveling with my master on our way home from the masquerade at Versailles when we were set upon by highwaymen! They tied me up, tossed me out of the carriage, and rode away with my master to ransom him. I must get back to Versailles to get help. Can you aid me?"

The outrageousness of the lie seemed to fit with my strange dress. I could see the wheels turning in the Parisian's head.

"Who's your master, boy?"

"The Comte de Brionne."

Oh, Charlotte, you ninny. The name—my name—had slipped out. Now, I had to work with it. Something like recognition flashed in the Parisian's eyes, and I tried to mask my panic.

"I thought the Comte de Brionne was dead," he said, but he didn't sound certain.

"Of course not!" I argued with mock affront. "I've been serving the Brionne family for several years now—I think I would have noticed such a thing, Monsieur."

The Parisian set me on my feet. His cold gaze assessed me.

"Have you seen anyone else come through here? Anyone else on the road?"

It was my chance to rid myself of the crossbow-wielding madman, but something unknowable prevented me from doing so. I shrugged.

"*Non, Monsieur.* I've been too terrified to come out from behind the bushes to see anyone else. You fine gentlemen are the only men that I've come across. Now, please, will you help me? Do you have horses? Or perhaps you can tell me where the nearest town is?"

"The nearest town is about three miles down the road," he said with an unnerving smile. "But I'm afraid you won't make it there."

CHAPTER TWO
ANTOINE

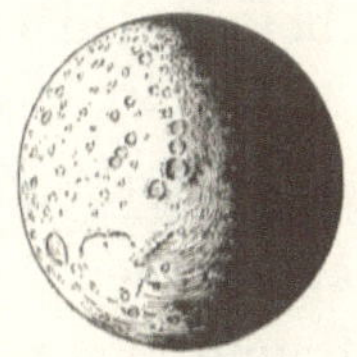

November 1, 1767
Somewhere outside Versailles

I watched in horrified fascination as the young man attempted to fight off all five of the soldiers at once, with his hands bound, no less. Granted, he didn't seem to be doing well, but that fact didn't appear to stop him or diminish his resolve. I had to hand it to the lad—he had spirit. What he didn't have, however, was the faintest idea who or what he was dealing with.

I cursed and leveled twin pistols at the two nearest soldiers. I knew it wouldn't stop them, but it could slow them down. I aimed and fired.

The two took bullets to their legs and went down. Jumping from the oak bough, I barreled toward the fray, tossing my pistols aside in favor of my short swords. In this chaos, I didn't want to risk hitting the young man—irritating though he was.

The other three turned in surprise when they heard the

shots, which gave the lad the opportunity to deliver a devastating knee to one's groin, then duck and roll behind the other two. I managed to slash one across his arm, causing him to drop his sword. The lad caught it, cut the ropes binding his hands, and picked up one of the soldiers' dropped pistols. Holding it aloft, he aimed steadily at the last soldier's head.

"Who are you?" The boy snarled. I could've sworn his voice rose an octave.

The soldier smiled. I knew he would tell the lad nothing.

"Leave it," I said. I approached the lad and tried to wrest the gun from him, but he aimed it at me instead.

"Don't," he warned, echoing my instruction from earlier.

The soldier sensed his opportunity and reached for his sword, but without batting an eye, the lad turned the gun back to him and fired, hitting him in the stomach. The soldier crumpled to the dirt, black blood spreading across the golden brown leaves. The lad pocketed the pistol—the lethal barrel sticking absurdly out of his toga—and turned back toward the road at a rapid clip.

I stayed to tie the wounded soldiers together. My stomach soured at the notion that I'd have to use my short swords to dispatch the lot of them. *Grim, bloody business, but it needs to be done.* As I began to reconcile myself to the task at hand, the wet slap of hoofbeats in mud gave me pause.

He didn't. Dieu, tell me he didn't.

I made it to the road just in time to see the lad race past me on *my* horse.

Putain!

I ground my teeth together and started after him—my horse, Tartuffe, was more important to me than anything. I ran behind him for a while, eventually losing sight of him on the road toward the town. I'd passed through it on my way into the city and knew there was only one inn, which was the most likely place the young man would go. The sun was rising, and I was certain he was as exhausted as I was, so I didn't think he would try and head back toward Versailles yet. It would mean chancing upon the soldiers again, and I didn't think he was that foolish.

When I get my hands on him, I'm going to—

I heaved an exhausted sigh. *You're going to what, Antoine?* I had no idea what I was going to do with him. I'd been so stupid, so rash. I should have waited for a better moment to kill Sade. I'd been biding my time for the last year, what difference would a few more hours have made? But I hadn't been able to stay my hand—I couldn't have—and now there was another young man involved. A young man who likely cared for the rotten marquis and was probably riding to the nearest town to summon the *gendarmerie* and have them cart me off to the Bastille for the killer that I was.

No longer just a killer.

A murderer.

The word seemed to hang about me like a slack noose. Would the lad turn me in? I quickened my pace. Either way, he was dangerous, *and* he was in danger. If this had all happened but a couple short years ago, I probably would have killed him and been done with the whole thing. Killing was what I'd been trained to do and had spent my life perfecting, all to impress a man I'd never accepted was impossible to impress.

Even now, I could hear his criticism in my ears. *Foolish boy! How could you be so stupid? All my influence, all that training, all your years of experience, and still you languish away as a mere lieutenant. Purchase your company command? Don't be an imbecile. You are an embarrassment to me and to our family name.*

I cringed, forcing my thoughts back to the present and the lad I should probably kill.

But I didn't want to kill him. I didn't even want to leave

him to the mercy of the soldiers who'd surely hunt him down. I'd had far too much death for one lifetime. Sade had deserved it—had deserved much more than the swift death I'd delivered —but the lad didn't. He'd been in the wrong place at the wrong time and was probably the victim of a deviant predator, just like Louis had been.

My stomach churned as I hurried on and tried to figure out what to do with the lad when I reached him. Killing him, certainly, was the last resort. Could he be reasoned with? If he knew what kind of a man Sade was, would he find himself lucky to have only just escaped his clutches? I frowned at that thought—likely not. I didn't think he'd be grateful to me for saving him from the marquis *or* the soldiers, especially since it was my fault he'd been endangered in the first place.

Merde.

Perhaps he could be bribed. I certainly didn't think he could be terrorized into silence. I'd seen the look in his eyes when he shot the soldier in the stomach. *Oh, yes.* I'd seen it many times, usually on the faces of men who'd left the battle-field bodily but who remained there in their minds. The lad had known suffering in his life, of that I was sure. I was also sure of the fact that he wasn't the effeminate, garrulous fop I'd originally believed he was. Something darker lurked inside him. *Like recognizes like.* I would not underestimate him.

By the time I finally, *blessedly*, reached the edge of the town, my lungs burned, my feet ached, and despite the chill, I dripped with sweat. The sight of the inn made my knees nearly buckle with relief. Exhaustion, cold, and hunger clawed at me, fighting for dominance over my senses.

I staggered through the door into the tavern and sat hard on a wooden bench. The innkeeper—a corpulent, red-faced fellow—approached me warily. Most men did. The scar across my face seemed to suggest I was the troublesome sort.

"I'm looking for a young man," I said. "Slip of a thing—dressed in a toga. He took off with my horse a bit ago. I'd very much like to see him returned."

The innkeeper grunted and shrugged. "The horse or the boy?"

I did not answer.

"Haven't seen him."

I narrowed my eyes. I knew he was lying, but I didn't want to cause more trouble than was necessary. Glaring, I tossed a handful of coins onto the table. The innkeeper's eyes widened greedily.

"The horse is in the stables," he said.

"And the lad?"

The innkeeper chewed on his lip, apparently waiting for something. My fingers itched to throttle him, but I reached for more coin. *You'll catch more flies with honey than vinegar,* Marie had always said. *Well, who wants to catch flies, ma sœur?* I'd always replied. The memory brought on a throb of heartache, but I set it aside.

The innkeeper jutted his chin toward a staircase behind the bar, leading up to the rooms.

"First door on the right."

I nodded and crossed the room in long, purposeful strides. Still debating what to do with the lad, I reconsidered my options. *Protect him. Plead with him. Bribe him. Kill him.* I swallowed my frustration and despair. I'd just have to play things by ear.

Figuring it would be better for me to have the element of surprise—he still had the soldier's pistol, after all—I crept up to the door and kicked it open. The heavy wood crashed into the wall, and I heard shouts from downstairs at the disturbance. I ducked into the room and froze, confusion clouding my brain like fog.

Standing in a small washtub in front of the fire was the young man—only, *he* wasn't a *young man*. I tore my gaze away from the rivulets of water sliding down an exquisite feminine form and stared into those same outraged brown eyes. It was only when I heard the unmistakable *click* of a pistol cocking that I realized she had the gun trained on me.

I gaped. "You—you're—*Mon Dieu...*"

"Get out!" she bellowed.

I scrambled back to the hallway and tried to close the door behind me, but only served to yank the damn thing off its hinges. The innkeeper stomped up the stairs, swearing roundly and demanding I pay for the damages. I awkwardly leaned the broken door against the opening to the room and took a step back. All the while, my mind struggled to process what I'd seen.

He was a *she. Mon Dieu, the sight of her naked. Those full breasts, the curves of those hips, that dark triangle of hair covering her sex. Not a man.* My body responded before my brain even registered the implication, making me uncomfortably hard. I fought to focus on something more productive than my arousal's clamoring need.

She had been in disguise—why? Why had she been with the Marquis de Sade? Who was she? Unease rustled through me. If she'd been at Versailles, chances were she was a member of the aristocracy. Was she in hiding? Perhaps avoiding some brutish or unsuitable marriage— I'd read things like that in romantic novels. But then, how did she know how to fight? She'd either learned from life's harsh experiences or by training. She didn't fight like a street urchin, though, so I reasoned it had to be some kind of formal training. She must be a spy then, but for whom? *Damn it!* Who *was* she? What the Hell was going on?

The innkeeper continued shouting at me. He made a move for the broken door, but I stepped in front of him.

"I'll pay for the damages," I growled. "It was an accident. We won't disturb you further."

The innkeeper spat on the floor at my feet and sneered. He opened his mouth to hurl another insult, but I'd had enough. I pulled my cloak aside and placed my hand on the hilt of my short sword.

"Go," I said. Eyes wide, the innkeeper stormed off, grumbling the whole time.

Turning back to the room, I knocked on the broken door.

"Leave me alone!"

Her guise now revealed, she stopped lowering her voice. The smooth, velvety timbre wasn't too dissimilar from a young man's voice, but it seemed so obvious now, I kicked myself for believing in the ruse.

"We need to talk," I said calmly.

I heard a derisive snort from the other side of the door, then a muttered, "Do we?"

"Please. Keep the pistol if you like. I just...need some information," I stammered. I knew the innkeeper and several tavern patrons were listening to our shouted exchange through the door, and my discomfort only grew.

"I have no information to give," she said petulantly.

"I do," I replied, lowering my voice. "And it might save your life."

I heard an exasperated groan and the sound of water swishing about. A vision flashed—soft, heat-pinked skin dripping with water and soap suds. Full breasts, long auburn hair, and a scorching gaze that promised a deep well of passion. My heart pounded in my chest. It had been too long since I'd been with a woman. Hell, I couldn't remember the last time I'd spoken with one for longer than a brief, curt exchange.

From inside the room, I heard prolonged muttering, then a damp stomping over to the door. She glared at me through the gap between the warped hinges and the wall, then angrily pulled me into the room. With a kick of disappointment, I saw she'd finished bathing and had wrapped herself in a shabby blanket stolen from the bed. She crossed the room with the haughty poise of a noblewoman and sat in a chair in the farthest corner of the room. The pistol lay on a table at her side.

The morning sunlight was just beginning to warm the room, and the golden light coming in through the window spilled across her alert form. I cursed myself for failing to recognize that she'd been a woman in disguise—seeing her now, I couldn't believe I'd mistaken her for anything other than a creature of devastating beauty.

She twisted her hair into a knot atop her head, showing off her elegant neck and shoulders. Her exposed skin looked softer than silk, except for the angry welts across her wrists where I'd bound her hands. *You wretched monster! Those wounds are your fault!*

I frowned, but she seemed to take no notice.

"Who are you?" we both demanded in unison. I reddened. She laughed.

"No, no. You go first," she said. "You are trying to save my life, after all. It's only fair that I have a name to direct my gratitude."

I ignored the sarcasm.

"I... Well, you may call me Antoine," I said.

Silence descended. She waited.

"Antoine," she finally echoed.

I nodded, trying to hide the irrational surge of pleasure I felt at hearing my name on her rose petal lips. When I didn't offer anything more, she rolled her eyes and carried on.

"Very well, Antoine. What information do you possess that you believe will save my life?"

I shifted uncomfortably, feeling as though I was being interrogated by an enemy. *You are, you fool.*

"Who are you?" I asked.

"I suppose you can call me Charlotte," she said.

"Charlotte...have you a surname?"

"Certainly."

"What is it?"

She rolled her eyes again, apparently tired of our exchange.

"Charlotte None-Of-Your-Concern. The information, Monsieur. I'm afraid I'm in a bit of a hurry."

"Why?" I asked, unable to help myself. She looked at me like I was a complete idiot.

"Those soldiers know exactly where I—we've—gone. This is the closest town for some distance, apparently, and I don't imagine they're particularly thrilled to be burying their comrade. I'd like to get out of here as quickly as possible. If you do, indeed, have life-saving information you wish to impart, I suggest you do it while our lives are still able to be saved."

At this, a knock sounded. Charlotte picked up the pistol and I went to see who disturbed us. A young girl stood in the hallway, arms full of clothing. I opened the door a bit wider, and she entered the room.

"You are most fortunate, Madame! I was able to find something suitable at my aunt's house. It's not as fine as you're used to, I'm sure, but it'll be warm enough to see you on your journey," she said.

Charlotte's frigid manner melted away and she smiled brightly at the other woman.

"*Merci,* Hélène, you absolute angel!" Charlotte went to the discarded Roman costume on the floor and pulled out a staggering amount of money for the girl.

"Oh, no, Madame! That's too much—I couldn't!"

"Nonsense, *chérie*. Keep it close to you. Don't let that bastard downstairs wheedle one coin from you, *d'accord?*"

The girl nodded fervently.

"Good. Now, be so kind as to bring up some breakfast for my companion and I, would you? *Merci beaucoup*," Charlotte said in a generous lilt. She ushered the girl back out and began to lay the garments out on the bed.

"Woolen stockings, good...good...quilted stays, very good. The skirt isn't a particularly flattering color for me, but it'll be warm enough to see me back to Versailles. Hopefully the soldiers who were after you won't pay too much attention to a woman..." she trailed off, muttering to herself again.

Distracted by the nearly sheer chemise spread across the blankets, I swallowed hard. Blood was rapidly leaving my head and venturing south again, making me feel slow-witted and uncomfortable. Distantly, I heard myself arguing.

"After me?"

"Well, I would assume so," she stated matter-of-factly. "They certainly weren't after me, and I imagine if you go around murdering marquises and kidnapping young gentle-men, it makes sense that you'd have a posse of Prussians and petulant Parisians pursuing you." She chuckled at herself. "Ha! Try saying that five times fast."

She lifted the edge of her blanket and began to slide on a woolen stocking, apparently unconcerned that I was in the room. She was still talking, but all I could hear was the rushing of blood in my ears. The blanket lifted again, affording me another tortuous glimpse of graceful, shapely legs, and my tattered composure snapped.

"You can't go back," I almost shouted. "I won't allow it."

She paused, tying a ribbon garter around her stocking, her eyes narrowing in warning.

"Please," I said. "You don't know what you're dealing with. If you leave without my protection, you won't make it back to Versailles."

CHAPTER THREE
CHARLOTTE

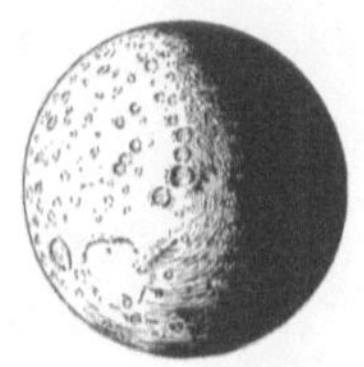

November 1, 1767
Somewhere outside Versailles

"Mon Dieu," I said, exasperated. "Will you please just tell me what you're on about?"

My patience was wearing thin. I was cold, tired, sore, and hungry to the point of ill-humor, which was not often a state I found myself in. If this brooding beau didn't stop gawking at my calves and carry on with his message, I'd have to resort to *unladylike* behavior.

Still, his eyes followed my movements, captivated. Deep down—very deep, of course—I preened with the thought that I'd pulled one over on him and that my unabashed manner had him unsettled. *Good.* He *should* feel bad for walloping my skull and tossing me across his horse's rear.

"*Monsieur,*" I prompted, hoisting the thick skirts in place and tying the last few ribbons. The garments were plain, but warm, and they would help me blend in with the common folk until I could get away. I sat back down to plait my hair to better hide it beneath a simple lace cap.

"You cannot leave," he said again. "They will find you."

"Your concern is noted," I said archly. "Was that your life-saving information? That those soldiers would be bent on revenge and scour the countryside hunting me to stretch my neck? *Please.* I expected that from the first. I doubt they'll bother a plain old maid, though."

"They'll find you anyway. They're not like normal men. They don't have to look for you. They'll be able to smell you from a mile away," he muttered darkly.

"I beg your pardon! How uncouth to comment upon my odor when you're the one who threw me across your foul beast and made me retch up last night's oysters. Besides, I've just had a bath."

That muscle in his jaw twitched—the one that indicated extreme displeasure. I smiled to myself.

"That's *not* what I meant," he growled.

"Then speak plainly, Antoine," I replied.

My use of his name seemed to unlock something inside him. Abruptly, he stood and started to pace the room.

"How do I know I can trust you?" He ran his hands through his hair, agitated. Loose waves escaped his tight queue, leaving him looking distressed and disheveled. It was adorable, really.

"You don't," I shrugged. "And honestly, I wouldn't advise it." I secured my cap and tilted my head toward the door. I could hear a slight creak outside—someone was eavesdropping. I motioned to Antoine to be silent, and he looked at me in confusion. I gestured to the door, grabbed the pistol, cocked it, and walked over as quietly as possible. I aimed forward while I threw the door open with my other hand.

The tavern girl, Hélène, shrieked and stumbled backward,

nearly dropping the tray she held in front of her. I lowered the weapon and grabbed her arm, steadying her.

"*Pardon, Madame!*" she gasped. "You startled me. I was just coming up with your breakfast tray and to see if you needed any help with your hair, but I see you have managed."

I smiled sheepishly. "My apologies. I'm afraid I read too many Gothic novels and have my mother's nervous disposition. I startle at the slightest sound."

She eyed the pistol warily but was eventually disarmed by my vivacity.

"Is that food for me? *Mon Dieu*, Hélène! Everything looks positively delicious. I've never seen pastries look so perfectly flaky and golden, have you, Antoine? Come, *chérie*, bring in the tray and have a cup of tea with us."

"Oh, I don't think I should—Monsieur Rocher would be furious if I was found out."

"Nonsense! You may tell your employer that you stayed to help me dress."

I tugged her into the room and secured the door behind us. She placed the tray down and began to set the table for two.

"No need, *chérie*. Antoine and I will not stand on ceremony. Please, have a seat. I'm sure your poor feet could do with a bit of a rest," I said with a wink. Hélène blushed prettily and sat in the chair across from Antoine, who tracked her with a hooded gaze. I felt irrationally annoyed with him—and with sweet, pretty Hélène.

Don't be absurd, Charlotte. You're trying to get information from the girl and dispense with this crossbow-wielding madman as soon as possible.

Nodding to myself, I pasted a bright smile on my face and sat on the bed. Neither Antoine nor Hélène reached for the tray of food. The smell of buttery pastries, warm bread, strawberry jam, and a simple, soft cheese made my stomach rumble. Not wanting to wait any longer, I poured everyone a cup of tea and began to butter a roll for myself.

"Monsieur Antoine," I began, realizing I didn't know his surname. "This is Hélène. She's been working here for—what was it you said to me, *chérie?*—four years now?"

Hélène nodded.

Antoine tore at a chunk of bread and spread some of the cheese on it. His expression was grave, but I paid no attention. I'd dealt with surly gentlemen like him before—in fact, I'd been married to one. I knew the best way past their grumpy defenses was usually in some mix of infuriating femininity and good-natured teasing. Good food and copious spirits didn't hurt, either.

I sipped my tea and bit into the warm roll. It was soft and sweet—almost melting on my tongue. I moaned in satisfaction.

"Hélène, do you bake these yourself? They are *divine.* Simply the best rolls I think I've ever had. Don't you agree, Antoine? Oh, you *must* try yours with the strawberry jam. It's positively sinful!"

Hélène smiled and blushed again at my praise. She lowered her lashes in a fetching sort of way, and Antoine's bread paused in its journey to his lips. I found myself dreaming of strangling them both. *That would be one way out of your predicament, Charlotte,* I thought sourly.

"I imagine you work long hours here, as this is the only tavern and inn nearby. You must receive such fascinating patrons!" I gushed with false enthusiasm, taking another drink of my tea.

Antoine's eyes flicked to me as he chewed his bread.

"Oh, yes, I suppose so," Hélène agreed.

"Do tell, *chérie,*" I urged. "Has anyone particularly interesting come through the inn recently? Any exceedingly handsome men? Or perhaps someone from abroad? I do so love to hear thrilling tales from people who've come from other parts of the world. Here, Hélène, allow me to refill your cup."

The bewildered girl automatically held out the chipped china.

"*Oui, Madame!* We had some soldiers in here not two days ago. But, how did you know?"

"Well, of course I didn't! It was only a guess—my curiosity is insatiable, you see. My father always said that I got it from my mother, bless them. Do indulge me, *chérie.* Tell me of these soldiers. What were they like? Did they bring news from some foreign front? What kind of uniforms did they wear? Oh, I do *love* a man in a uniform. I'd wager they were handsome."

Antoine's teacup shattered in his hand, spilling scalding tea all over him. Hélène leapt up to help clean up the mess, but he waved her away. He mumbled oaths that made her blush even redder—*Dieu, has the chit never heard such language working in a tavern?* —and she rushed to the door.

"I'll bring another cup, Monsieur, and I'll fetch some more rags." With that, she was gone, as was my opportunity to discreetly learn what she'd observed about the soldiers who'd attacked us. *Merde.*

Antoine's hand was an angry red, nearly matching the hue of his furious face. I huffed and yanked at his arm, pulling him toward the pitcher of cool water on the bedside table. I dunked his palm in and scowled up at him.

"You have got to be the most infuriating, thick-headed, blundering lout I've ever crossed paths with, and that's saying something considering my former husband was the true king of prize idiots," I hissed.

Antoine glared at me and pulled his hand out of the water, flinging droplets about the room.

"You're one to talk! Why are you badgering that poor girl?

Don't you realize how dangerous those soldiers are? If word gets round that some ridiculous woman was asking questions about them, she'll be in danger, too," he argued. "Besides, what do you mean by asking her if they were handsome? They're not handsome! They're horrible!"

I rolled my eyes at his petty male jealousy—if he had stirrings for Hélène, he could conquer her on his own time.

"I was trying to put her at ease so I could question her about them. I want to know when they came into town, what they said, why they're here—if she knew they were after you, in particular. I'm trying to find out more about them, since talking to *you* isn't getting me anywhere useful, and I need to know what I'm up against. I would have found out plenty from her if you hadn't behaved like a fool and sent her away when she was about to answer my questions."

"It doesn't matter. You don't need answers. All you need to know is that those soldiers are dangerous, they'll come for you, and I'm the only one who can protect you," he practically growled.

Reflexively, I made to protest but forced myself to pause and consider him. What did I know about this man? He'd snuck into Versailles, murdered Sade, abducted me for some unknown reason, and was trying to take me to—where, exactly?—when we were set upon by a group of soldiers he was obviously familiar with. That likely meant he was either a fugitive from justice even before his recent venture into aristocratic murder, or that he knew the soldiers personally and was possibly a soldier himself. He'd been armed to the teeth when he waded into the fray on the road and had handled himself well, so he was no stranger to violence, and he'd repeatedly professed his insistence at helping and protecting me. It could be a bluff, of course—he might be keeping a close eye on me merely because I was the only witness to his murder of Sade—

but I didn't think so. His barely restrained emotions made me think he was unused to deceit. It felt chivalrous to me. *A soldier, then.*

That rationale gave me little comfort. Even if he was a valiant sort, I still didn't know what his intentions were toward me. If I'd been caught in the same kind of compromising position, I would've been compelled to do away with any witnesses. Instead, he'd abducted me. Why? To try and convince me that Sade deserved to die so I wouldn't turn him in? Lock me in some dungeon and torture me into forgetting I'd seen him with his absurd crossbow?

I snorted. His actions didn't make sense. Either I was missing something crucial, or he was operating on panicked instinct without sufficient forethought. *He's a man, and probably a soldier, so I'd wager the latter.*

I took a deep breath and changed tactics. If I was going to get back to Versailles safely, I needed to understand Antoine and find out just how much trouble he was in.

I tore a strip of fabric from my discarded toga and dipped it in the cool water. Motioning for his burned hand, I held it out in a gesture of truce.

He regarded me suspiciously.

"The cool water will help lessen the pain," I offered. "And it will prevent the burn from blistering. Allow me to wrap it for you."

"I'm fine," he gritted out, but extended his hand anyway.

I dabbed at it gently with the cloth. Antoine flinched at first but started to relax after a moment. When his shoulders began to sag—either from exhaustion or reprieve—I seized the chance to question him.

"Why did you kidnap me?"

"I didn't kidnap you," he grunted.

I quirked a brow. "What, exactly, would you call it then?"

He clenched his jaw. "Protecting you," he said.

I laughed. He scowled. When I finally recovered, I shook my head.

"Protecting *me*," I chuckled. After so much training and so much blood on my hands, the thought seemed ridiculous.

"Would you rather have been found by the guards at Versailles? With your stupid costume arrows and a dead marquis at your feet?" he grumped, frowning.

"Who was he to you?" I asked.

"A loose end that needed tying," he said. His voice cracked roughly.

"And is that what I am?" I prodded, eyes darting to the pistol on the table. "A loose end that needs tying?"

He shook his head. "No. I don't know. Who was Sade to *you*?"

Two could play at that game. "As you say, he was a loose end to tie."

He didn't seem to be any more interested in offering information than I was. Having reached a conversational stalemate, we were silent for a time. Eventually, I spoke up again.

"Those men back there—they were hunting you." It was a statement, not a question, so he did not answer. "Was it something to do with your reasons for killing the marquis? Are you a soldier?"

"Are you a spy?" he countered. "Seems you know how to fight."

"Seems you have an arsenal of weapons tucked away in that cloak of yours. Was Sade your *only* target?"

He heaved a sigh. I could tell this verbal jousting was starting to grate on his nerves, but I hadn't gleaned anything helpful. I tore another strip of fabric from the discarded costume and wrapped it gently, but firmly, around the burn.

"There," I said. "That will do until you can find some salve, or a poultice."

He didn't pull his hand away—not immediately. I caressed it softly. His gaze followed the movements of my fingers across the makeshift bandage.

"Will you at least tell me where you intended to take me for protection?" I asked, quietly this time.

His eyes met mine—fathomless pools of mossy green. There was a flash of something helpless in his gaze, which quickly shuttered. He turned away and lifted a shoulder in forced nonchalance.

"You ask too many questions," he said roughly.

"Yes, and you haven't answered any of them. Don't you think I'm somewhat entitled to even the smallest scrap of information, given how ferociously you behaved with me? *S'il vous plaît, Antoine.* Tell me something. Anything!"

His cheeks reddened again, but I wasn't sure if it was from frustrated apoplexy, or from shame. My entreaty worked, however, because he relented.

"I don't know. I needed time to think. I thought I might bribe you to forget what you saw. Failing that, I...I don't know. I did not want to kill you."

"That's comforting," I chuckled.

He suddenly looked rather miserable, and my heart dropped.

"It's my fault you're in danger," he said. "I was careless back at Versailles, and because you were with me, the *bêtes de sang* will come for you, too."

"The Beasts of Blood? What are you talking about? Were those the soldiers?"

Antoine nodded.

Unease took root in my gut. "I've never heard of them. Are they King Louis's men? What do you know of them?"

He stood and paced, darting glances back toward the door. Clearly, he was worried about them. I crossed over to him and put a hand on his shoulder.

"Tell me what you know of them," I said again.

He frowned.

"You fear them," I observed.

He nodded. "As should you," he said.

"Why should I? I managed to kill one of them already."

"No," he said slowly. "Bullets do not kill vampires."

CHAPTER FOUR
ANTOINE

November 1, 1767
Somewhere outside Versailles

"Vampires," she exhaled.

Her breath stirred a lock of brown hair that had escaped her cap. I stared at it, transfixed.

"How is that possible?" she asked. "I know how the king feels about vampires. I can't believe he would allow his armies to be infiltrated. He does not trust them. Even with all the work the emissary has done, there's a difference between accepting the blood plague as an inevitability and throwing the full weight of his support behind the integration of vampires."

"Nevertheless," I hedged, dodging her questions. "It is so. Now do you understand why I cannot just allow you to traipse about the countryside alone?"

She narrowed her eyes. "I can take care of myself."

Before I could argue, she began tearing her discarded costume into large squares of fabric—fabric that probably cost more than the average Frenchman's annual wages—and packing up whatever she could find into little bundles. In went the rest of the bread and pastries from the breakfast tray, a candle and spare flint from the bedside table, the pistol and a small bag of powder and shot. When she'd finished scouring the room for anything else useful, she carefully tied the small bundles together and stashed them inside her skirts.

Clever girl.

"What are you doing?" I asked.

She looked at me with thinly veiled disdain. "Well, if your pursuers are vampires, that means we only have the rest of the day to make a head start. I must get back to Versailles."

She made for the door. I moved in front of her.

"Step aside, Antoine," she said forcefully.

I didn't move.

If she left now, it was possible she'd reach Versailles by nightfall. Then again, maybe not. The *bêtes de sang* would be fully recovered after going to ground today, and their speed would be increased—partly because they were supernaturally cursed, partly because of their penchant for cruelty and thirst for revenge. Besides, they knew I was here now. They'd be seeking vengeance upon this woman—Charlotte—but they'd certainly be coming for me. However I considered it, our chances of survival would be better if we stuck together.

I swore.

"I'm coming with you," I said.

Charlotte's eyes widened. "No, you're not!"

"I am. They'll be after us both now, and the least I can do is see you to safety. If that means taking you back to Versailles, so be it," I offered with grim determination.

"Don't be absurd. You murdered a marquis! I'll not have you risking your life unnecessarily because of some misplaced sense of obligation. I can look after myself. Now, I thank you for your assistance back on the road, and I assure you that your ruinous secrets are safe with me, but it's time for us to part company."

I stepped toward her, prepared to argue again, when the door exploded open behind us. I whirled around to see the innkeeper aiming a pistol straight at us. I groaned inwardly. This was the last thing we needed.

"Neither of you are going anywhere," the innkeeper smirked.

"What the devil do you think you're doing?" Charlotte exclaimed.

"Earning the reward," he said. "For him."

Damn. What a fool I'd been. Of course, he knew who I was.

Charlotte turned wide eyes on me. "There is a reward for your capture? *Mon Dieu*, Antoine, and that was before the events of last evening! Why is there a bounty on your head?"

I ignored her.

"Whatever they promised you—whatever the bounty—I'll double it," I said quietly.

The innkeeper's greedy eyes glittered with momentary interest, then wavered with doubt.

"I think not, Monsieur. Those men will return at night-fall, and I plan on handing you—both of you—over to them. I'd rather not find myself on their bad side," he said. He waved the pistol and gestured for us to precede him down the stairs.

"Just a minute, Monsieur," Charlotte said. "I'm not traveling with this man—might you be persuaded to let me go? I can assure you I'll make it worth your while."

The innkeeper and I exchanged a look. He seemed tempted but resolute.

"No, little bird, I'm afraid you both await the soldiers. Perhaps you can use your charms on them, no? They might let you go after all," he chuckled.

"You can't be serious," she said haughtily. "If it's money you want, I can *triple* what you're already getting."

The innkeeper's face twisted—he almost seemed to be regretting his decision—but eventually, he shook his head and pushed us out of the room.

Charlotte frowned but led the way down the stairs. She protested the entire way. The innkeeper guided us to the root cellar out back behind the inn. Hélène eyed us guiltily from behind the bar. *The traitorous wench.*

After flinging open the heavy wooden doors, the innkeeper shoved us both down a set of stone steps into the damp, earthen room. It was cramped and filthy. The walls were lined with shelves of dust-covered preserves and crates of junk. The room was barely high enough for me to stand up in.

"Make yourselves comfortable," he offered, his voice laced with sarcasm. "I'll be back for you with the soldiers when they return."

Then, he slammed the wooden doors shut and proceeded to lock us in. We both waited for the sounds of his footsteps to fade away before turning to each other. Shafts of sunlight streamed in through the weathered slats of the door, illuminating Charlotte's petulant scowl. She sat down on a wooden crate and sighed.

"This is all your fault," she grumbled. "If you hadn't shown up at Versailles in the first place, I'd be asleep in my delicious bed, awaiting a warm morning bath, a pot of chocolate, and a day of leisure pursuits."

"My apologies," I said gruffly. "But it was your fault for getting in my way and then not heeding my warnings back on the road. If you'd just come along willingly, we could have worked something out."

"Oh, yes, and then when you'd run into the *bêtes de sang* with me tied across your horse, they certainly would have let us both carry on our merry way unmolested! You'd probably be captured by now, and God only knows what they would've done with me. Probably drained me, or worse," she said bitterly. "And now we *are* in a bind, aren't we? That lousy innkeeper likely overheard our argument and—even as thick as he is—probably knows I was headed back to Versailles."

"Probably," I agreed.

She stood and went to the cellar door, testing the handle. The heavy iron padlock rattled on the outside. I joined her at the door and inspected the frame. Thick, solid oak blocked our way out.

Charlotte began to survey the room in much the same way that she'd surveyed the bedroom in the inn. It was deliberate, methodical, and thorough. It seemed at odds with the lifestyle that she'd described, unless my earlier supposition was indeed correct.

"Who do you work for?" I asked.

"What an absurd question!" she laughed. She'd uncovered a hammer beneath a length of canvas and hefted it in triumph. She continued to root around through the crates. "I don't *work* —I'm a member of the aristocracy."

She said it with such haughtiness that I believed her immediately, but her actions belied her protestations. What kind of a noblewoman knew how to fight and shoot and don disguises with practiced ease? I knew she was a spy—I just didn't know for whom.

She cried out in triumph when she found a small set of rusty tools, extracting a chisel. She moved for the door, and I realized quickly what she had in mind.

"Allow me," I offered, holding out my hands for the hammer and chisel. She raised a brow at me but handed them over.

"Why is there a bounty on your head?" she asked as I lined them up over the door handle.

"Tell me who you're working for," I countered. I brought them down hard, leaving a small dent just above the iron handle.

She *tsked*. "I told you, I don't work."

"Right. And the innkeeper was merely mistaken about me," I said, a smile tugging at my lips. I lifted the hammer again and brought it down with force. A greater chunk of wood dislodged and fell away. I needed to hurry, lest the innkeeper hear the racket and come to check on us.

"Fine," Charlotte huffed. "We both have secrets. But if we're going to get out of here, we need to trust each other at least a *little*."

A raspy chuckle escaped my throat. It had been a long time since I'd laughed.

"Certainly, Charlotte. Ladies first."

"Very well," she said arrogantly. "What's your plan for when we get out of here?"

My hammer paused mid-air. I hadn't considered that far ahead.

She smiled in mock sweetness. "How am I supposed to trust you if you don't know how you're going to keep us alive?"

I let the hammer fall on the chisel, and one of the boards in the door split. Not enough to break, but two or three more strikes ought to do it. All the while, my mind worked. We needed somewhere to hide out. A place the *bêtes de sang* wouldn't be able to follow. Somewhere we could stay until the likely uproar at the marquis's murder died down. Somewhere we could figure out what to do about each other and our precarious predicament. Away from Paris, away from Versailles, and far away from here.

Suddenly, I had it.

"Gévaudan," I said. "We'll go to Gévaudan."

Charlotte blinked in surprise. "Gévaudan? Down south? But it's so far away! It'll take us days—a week, probably—to reach it!"

I struck one final blow at the weakened wood, and it cracked along the split. I wiggled the iron lock and door handle and wrenched them away, then kicked the doors open.

"If we move quickly and rest only when necessary, we can make it in two and a half, three days," I said. I grabbed her arm and tugged her toward the stables.

She allowed me to pull her forward, then down behind the low bushes along the back of the inn. I knew we'd made a hell of a racket breaking out of the root cellar, and we needed to hurry. As soon as we ducked into the stables, Tartuffe's soft nickering drew my attention. He was in a back stall, perfectly content with a bucket of oats. Relief unknotted some of my muscles—if the innkeeper had mistreated my beloved black Andalusian, I would've had to break his arms, and I didn't think Charlotte and I had the time for that. Charlotte kept watch out the front while I saddled him, then led him around to the door.

"You're not going to toss me over your horse's ass again, are you?" she asked warily.

In answer, I swung myself up and held out my hand to her. She took it and pulled herself up like no aristocratic woman I'd ever known, sitting astride behind me.

"Ready?" I called back to her.

From outside, we heard a clatter followed by an enraged bellow. The innkeeper had discovered our absence. Charlotte started to respond, but I didn't wait for her words. I dug my heels into Tartuffe's sides and shouted him forward. He took off like a shot, weaving past the apoplectic innkeeper and making for the main road through town.

I heard Charlotte squeal in surprise at our abrupt departure, then felt her arms tighten around my waist as we galloped through the bustling street, attracting the angry shouts and incensed attentions of several villagers. We raced on, not daring to slow our breakneck speed until the town was well behind us and Tartuffe's sides heaved with exhaustion.

As we slowed to a trot, Charlotte's grip loosened, and she lifted her face from my back.

"What's in Gévaudan?"

"Shelter," I replied. I didn't want to go into details. If she wasn't going to trust me, I certainly wasn't going to trust her.

She made a noise of frustration I barely heard over the clop of Tartuffe's hooves.

She leaned closer, her breasts pressing into my back, and spoke in my ear. "But you think we'll be safe from the soldiers? The *bêtes de sang* won't find us or follow us? What's to stop them?"

"Nothing," I said, gritting my teeth to fight the rising tide of lust brought on by her excruciating closeness. The heat from her body sang through me like a siren's song. I swallowed hard. "I'm certain they will eventually catch up to us. This merely buys us some time."

She laughed. "How very soldier-like you think—or perhaps I should say *how very male you think.* You plan nothing out and wait for someone with more brains than you to provide guidance."

I stiffened.

"Now, I mean no offense. It's the fault of your sex to be creatures of action and, bless you all, sometimes you don't have enough blood in your brain because it finds its way to other extremities. Not that I'm complaining about male virility, of course," she carried on.

Irritation climbed up my spine. Not only had she insulted

my intelligence and that of my fellow man, but she acted like I was some thick-headed soldier incapable of thinking for myself—a nerve too often struck by my father's harsh criticisms. Even more irritating was the kernel of truth in her words—she was in this mess because I'd acted rashly back at Versailles. It didn't mean I was some incompetent fool, though.

"It's just that more often than not, men don't think things through, and women must enter in some capacity to assist—yet you call *us* the more emotional sex!"

A barely restrained growl climbed out of my throat. She either didn't hear it or carried on as if she hadn't. *Probably the latter.*

"Well, you needn't worry, Antoine, I am perfectly capable of being the brains in this temporary outfit. We will travel as far as we can until late afternoon, take a small respite, then get back on the road as soon as the sun sets. If these soldiers are vampires, they will travel at night, and we cannot afford to let them catch up to us. We must stay on the move."

"You don't say," I muttered darkly.

"Unless, of course, we are able to find some suitable accommodation in which to hide tonight. Then, as you say, we will arrive in Gévaudan and apparently pray the *bêtes* do not follow, since you have no other course of action in mind."

My temper flared and I pulled Tartuffe up short.

"If you'd rather take them on by yourself, by all means, Madame, take your chances with their mercies—only I can assure you, mercy is not something you are likely to receive from them. You would be lucky and *singular* to escape their clutches with your life," I warned.

She huffed her indignation.

"As for my *simpleminded plan*," I continued. "I take it you have not heard the news from Gévaudan all the way up in Versailles lately—or perhaps you're too busy insulting everyone, or maybe too wrapped up in your own selfish affairs to bother paying attention—but the entire town is locked down. Completely closed off to supernatural outsiders. The *bêtes* may follow us to the border, but they will not be able to enter. We will be safe—for a time."

I'd felt her bristle at my insults, but her curiosity superseded her ire.

"Closed off? Because of the blood plague?"

"No," I bit out, spurring Tartuffe forward. "Not because of the vampires. It is another threat they fear."

Her shock was evident in her slight gasp and the pressure of her arms around my waist. Reflexively, my mind went back to the sight of her in the bath, then dressing in that slow, torturous manner. I wondered if she acted so passionately in bed. Quickly, my senses returned, and I drew several deep breaths to calm my racing heart and stiff cock. It had been *much* too long since I'd bedded a woman, but I'd consider myself desperate indeed to try and bed this hellion.

"What other threat?" she prodded quietly.

"A werewolf."

CHAPTER FIVE
CHARLOTTE

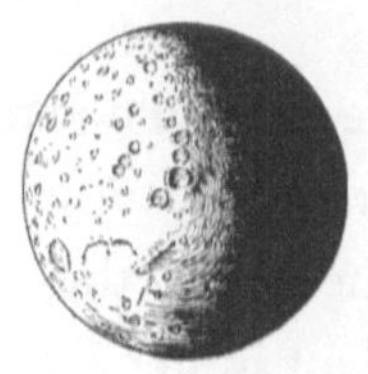

November 1, 1767
The road to Gévaudan

"WHAT AN INAPPROPRIATE TIME FOR YOU TO DEVELOP A SENSE OF humor, Antoine," I said with a laugh.

I could tell by the straight, hard line of his jaw he did not share my amusement.

"A werewolf," I repeated. "That would be preposterous."

"Is it? And yet, we so easily accepted that there is a strange disease turning normal men into immortal parasites. We execute witches for consorting with the devil. The church has us believe that demons may escape Hell and walk among us."

"Oh, demons *do* walk among us," I cut in. "Of that, you may be certain."

"But werewolves are beyond belief," he said sarcastically.

"Well, no," I answered. "But there must be some logical explanation."

He shrugged. "Perhaps there is. For our purposes, it does not matter whether the fear is based in fact. Their caution will allow us some sanctuary since no supernatural creature is allowed entry."

So, he does have a plan after all.

"How do they keep them out?" I wondered aloud.

"I've no idea. Walls. Armed guards. Prayers. Magical herbs and potions. Perhaps a battalion of forcefully opinionated aristocratic women who hurl unfounded insults all day. That would be enough to keep any man away," he grumbled.

I laughed again. "How unexpectedly amusing you are, Antoine! You must forgive me for offending you. My intent was to goad you into revealing your plans, and I'm afraid you fell rather well for my tactics. I would never believe you to be unintelligent. I hardly know anything about you."

I peered around him to see his face twist sourly and I stifled another giggle.

"Come now, we've quite a journey ahead of us. Surely, we can allow ourselves the small luxury of learning about each other. At least *something*. It will help us pass the time," I coaxed. "And, as an offering of peace, I'll start. Though I keep it closely guarded when I'm not at Versailles, my surname is Brionne. I am Comtesse Charlotte Nicole Louise de Brionne. There, now. Your turn."

Tartuffe's hooves thudded softly on the hard packed dirt, as steady as a metronome. Long moments of quiet passed before Antoine replied. So long, in fact, that I'd almost forgotten I'd asked him anything. I'd become lost in the world around us—the dull gray of the sky obscuring the November sun, the silvery bare trees and dead, fallen leaves lining the road, the distant fields of green and gold. It was beautiful, really. Like the scene of some salon landscape painting in a parlor of moderate good taste.

"De Valle," he said, somewhat suddenly. "Antoine François de Valle."

"Well done," I said warmly. "That's a lovely name. I'm sure I've heard it before, but I can't quite recall where."

He scoffed. "I'd appreciate it if you didn't bandy it about in public."

"Ah yes, because you're in hiding. The soldiers hunting you and all."

His posture had been rigid before, but now he turned to stone in front of me. It was impossible for me not to notice how he felt—the hard muscles beneath my arms. I'd wager he had a body like a Grecian marble of Zeus, or perhaps Ares. With that dashing scar, he would certainly be closer to the god of war. A pleasing shiver vibrated through me at the wicked imagery.

"Well, you needn't worry, Antoine. You've never met another who can keep a secret as well as I can."

"Because you're a spy?" he tested.

"A spy! What utter rot. I told you, I'm a comtesse. I live a life of leisure. Don't be so bourgeois, Antoine."

A lie. One of many.

"A lie," he echoed, his voice hinting at some dark humor beneath. "Don't bother lying to me, Comtesse. If you're going to pester me with your incessant prattling, at least have the courtesy to tell me the truth."

"I am a paragon of honesty! But if you're looking for other truths so you can better learn my impeccable character, I'll graciously oblige. My favorite food is asparagus."

"You're teasing me," he said. "Lying again. No one really enjoys asparagus."

"I do. I like it so much that sometimes I have my cook prepare it for me for breakfast. Gently steamed with a poached egg on top and toast points on the side."

My stomach rumbled at the thought. I reached into my pockets and pulled out one of the pilfered buns from breakfast, then offered one to Antoine. He took a bite and chewed slowly.

"*Civet de sanglier*," he said.

"I beg your pardon?"

"It's a kind of stew. Wild boar, chestnuts, vegetables, red wine. When I was a boy, my father was stationed in Corsica for a time. He developed a taste for the cuisine there and brought a cook with him when he returned home. Lucia always made it for me on my birthday. It's my favorite food."

"So, you followed in your father's footsteps to become a soldier," I observed. Immediately, Antoine tensed beneath me. *Wrong line of questioning—his father is apparently a sore spot.* I returned to the more acceptable subject.

"When was the last time you had it?" I asked.

"A long time ago."

"I envy your worldliness, Antoine. All I've ever known is society. Paris, Versailles. I should like to see the world someday." I could not keep the wistfulness from my voice.

"Have you never ventured abroad?"

"No. My husband—former husband—used to travel often. He would bring me presents and stories from all over the continent, perhaps to appease me, but it only whetted my appetite for adventure," I said with no small hint of bitterness.

"Where is he now?" Antoine asked.

Oh, what a question! When last I checked, he was locked away in the Château d'If for the rest of his miserable life for summoning a demon and murdering several people because he was desperately in love with my cousin. Who really knows, though? Perhaps he has had the good sense to die.

Not something I wanted to get into with my secretive travel companion.

"He is...gone. Are you married?" I asked.

"No."

"Why not? Didn't you ever want to?"

He shrugged. "I spent long years abroad, fighting in battles that no one really wins. It's cruel to start a family and spend all your time away from them."

"You speak from experience."

I didn't expect him to answer, but he nodded once. I grinned at his back.

"Well, now I know I was right about you, Antoine. You *are* a soldier. My first impressions are seldom wrong."

"It's lucky for you that mine often are," he chuckled. It was a deep, warm sound, so low that I felt it vibrate like the string of a harp plucked between our bodies. Heat sparked low in my stomach.

"I'll take it as a compliment that you don't still think I'm a young lad besotted with a depraved marquis. Will you tell me why you killed him?"

Instantly, a wall of icy silence fell between us. Try as I might, I couldn't get him to respond to any more questions. It appeared I'd crossed the line and our friendly tête-à-tête had ended.

We rode for several more hours through the countryside. Antoine picked up the pace in the late afternoon, perhaps hoping to find a suitable spot for us to rest for a while. The clouds above began to darken to an ominous pewter and thunder heralded the onset of a winter storm, but we still hadn't come upon the next town. The trees had thinned out, which would leave us dangerously exposed—especially if we camped somewhere and had a fire.

"Have you been this way before? Do you think we're far from the next town?" I asked. The road showed precious few signs of frequent use—scraggly, bare weeds crept in from the nearby fields and flat stretches of unblemished mud lay before us. Obviously, it had been days since anyone had come through.

Antoine frowned as fat droplets of rain started to fall. In the gathering storm clouds, it had been difficult to determine the point of sunset, and I realized it was too late. Surely the sun had gone down now, and the *bêtes* would be waking up to begin their hunt.

"There's no point in resting if we can't find some decent shelter," I said. "We should carry on as long as we're able. At least the rain will help disperse our scent."

Antoine nodded and spurred Tartuffe forward in a gallop. The rain came down in earnest, then, as if the forces of nature sensed our resolve to find somewhere out of the elements. Ten minutes later, we were both soaked to the skin and shivering, but at last we spotted a light down the road ahead of us.

The village was smaller than the previous one, boasting a dilapidated church, a couple boarded-up shops, and an ancient-looking tavern and inn. We trotted up to one of the empty horse stalls beside the tavern and dismounted. Antoine turned to enter, but I laid a hand on his arm.

"We'll need a cover story," I said. "If we're to escape notice in a small town like this. Especially if we're to hide here tonight from the *bêtes*."

"Shall I follow your lead then, Madame Spy?" Antoine smirked.

"I'm *not* a spy, it's just common sense. But yes, you may follow my lead. Keep your head low and your scar covered—it makes you rather rakishly noticeable, and I don't have the energy to deal with some overzealous tavern maids tonight," I said brusquely.

Antoine pulled the hood of his cloak down, but I saw his lips kick up in a lopsided grin, showing off his perfect white teeth and—good heavens—was that a dimple? *Mon Dieu.*

"Take my arm," I said somewhat breathlessly. "We're a young married couple on our way to Provence for our honeymoon and we got caught in the storm."

Antoine's eyes widened and his mouth dropped open, but he held out his arm and guided me inside the tavern.

Warmth enveloped us as we entered, along with the smell of baking bread and some savory stew. My stomach rumbled again in demand. I cast my eyes around and breathed a small sigh of relief—thankfully, it was nearly empty. A few soggy travelers sat in a far corner, and a robust woman with silvering hair bustled over to us.

"Smile," I hissed at Antoine through gritted teeth. "We're newlyweds, remember."

He smiled and pulled me closer to him, wrapping his arm around my waist. My breath caught involuntarily, and I let out a nervous giggle that was only half faked.

"*Bon soir, Madame,*" Antoine said. "My new bride and I were on our way to Provence but I'm afraid we cannot make it much further in this weather. Have you any rooms available?"

The woman tutted and handed me a cloth to dry my dripping face.

"You poor lambs! I've just the one room upstairs. It's no honeymoon suite, mind, but it's warm, clean, and dry."

"Bless you, Madame!" I said. "We'll take it. Would it be possible to get some of that delicious-smelling food sent up to us? We're nearly dead on our feet from exhaustion, and I don't know that I could sit in the tavern here without falling over. We journeyed all the way from Poitiers this morning and had our things sent on after us, but I expect they're half a day's ride behind us."

"What a journey you've had," the woman exclaimed. "So, you've no other clothes or supplies to see you through to Provence?"

"We planned on stocking up here, if that's possible," Antoine chimed in with a charming smile. "My wife and I will need some dry clothes and food for another two days. And my horse is out in the stall—he'll need to be tended to."

"Of course, of course. Georges! See to the horse outside!" she called to a disgruntled, rail-thin man. "You two, follow me! Dry off and get settled, and I'll send some food up right away."

We followed her up a back set of stairs into a tiny gable bedroom. She'd been right. It was cramped to a ridiculous degree—Antoine had to duck down to enter—but there was a fire in the small hearth, and it was clean. She handed us some candles and promised to be back swiftly with a hot meal and some dry clothes.

Antoine went to the window and looked out. The rain lashed against the glass and made it impossible to see very far down the road.

I dragged the moth-eaten armchair in front of the fireplace and collapsed into it.

"Why newlyweds?"

Antoine's voice sounded soft and distant.

"We're traveling together without a chaperone, and we don't look like siblings. Besides, would *you* want to disturb a couple of newlyweds in a cozy bedroom of a roadside inn?"

That low, warm chuckle rumbled from directly behind me, and I looked up to see him leaning against the back of the armchair.

"Fair point," he conceded. "Why Poitiers?"

I shrugged. "It was the first place that popped into my head that's about a day's ride away. I didn't want them to know we'd come from Versailles—or anywhere near Paris, for that matter."

Antoine dragged another chair toward the fire and sat in it

next to me. He stretched out long legs until his feet almost touched the hearth.

"But you say you are not a spy," he murmured.

I snorted.

"Perhaps you just haven't met that many quick-witted women in your lifetime. There are plenty of us out there, you know. It doesn't mean we are all spies."

"Perhaps," he said. The ghost of a smile played about his full lips.

They really are fine lips.

There was a loud knock at the door, and we both jumped.

"Only me!" The lady innkeeper said, bustling in with a bundle under her arm and a tray of food in front of her. Antoine jumped up to take the tray and set it on the small table by the window. The innkeeper nodded gratefully.

"I didn't have much luck finding clothing at this hour, but I found some clean nightclothes for you both. If you'll remove your own garments, I'll make sure they're cleaned and dried for you in the morning."

Antoine frowned but nodded. "We'll leave them out by the door, along with the dinner tray when we've finished. We're most grateful for your hospitality, but I'm afraid my wife is exhausted, so we'd like to be undisturbed for the rest of the evening."

"As you wish, Monsieur," the innkeeper winked at him, then bustled off with a giggle.

Despite the warmth of the room, I was still freezing. The rain had soaked the thick woolen dress and underclothes completely, making it waterlogged and heavy. I eyed the food hungrily but wished for the dry nightclothes with more immediacy.

"Turn around," I instructed Antoine. "I'd like to change."

"I thought we were meant to be newlyweds," he teased, that sly smile returning.

"Certainly not behind closed doors! Hurry up, I want to get changed and eat," I returned testily.

Antoine's eyes flashed in a curious way and suddenly my damp clothes and the winter chill were forgotten. My skin heated to a blush under his intent gaze.

"You didn't have an issue dressing in front of me before," he said, turning to face the opposite wall.

"Yes, well, I was in a hurry, and I didn't think we'd see each other again," I huffed, shucking the drenched skirts and petticoats as quickly as possible. My chilled fingers fumbled at the sodden knot securing my stays, but try as I might, I could not undo it.

"*Merde,*" I swore under my breath.

"Everything all right? Can I turn around now?"

"No, I can't get—oh, *putain*—it's really stuck. Well, there's nothing for it now. Antoine, I may require your assistance. The lace on my stays is knotted and—"

Quick as a flash, he was behind me, his hands working at the delicate ribbon. He took to his task with infinite care and patience, slowly pulling this way and that. His breath was warm against the nape of my neck, tickling several strands of hair that had escaped my cap. I shivered with pleasure for the second time that day.

I felt his hands still, but neither of us moved. A pulse of instinctive lust whispered through my body. Visions flashed—his full lips on my skin, his eyes squeezed tight in ecstasy, his hard, muscular body bared before me. My heart pounded. If I turned around now, I could kiss him—taste him. *What could it hurt?* Longing coursed through me. I shifted, but the air in the room changed. He'd stepped back and was returning to the other side of the room.

"There," he said in a gruff voice. "You are undone."

Mon Dieu, yes. In so many ways.

CHAPTER SIX
ANTOINE

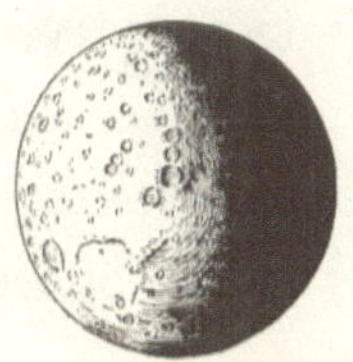

November 1, 1767
The road to Gévaudan

I'D ENDURED COUNTLESS MISERIES IN MY LIFE, BUT I WAS STRUGGLING to recall a more agonizing event than undressing a beautiful woman with no hope of bedding her. The softness of her skin, the rain-damp scent of her hair, the hitch in her breath at my nearness... I'd been moments away from ripping the blasted stays off her lithe body and sinking to my knees before her in a bid of sheer desperation. It had been so long since I'd enjoyed any kind of intimacy, I would've *begged*.

Fortunately, I'd recovered my senses in time. *Not now, Antoine. Not this woman. She is a spy, and she cannot be trusted. You do not want her.*

Don't I?

I listened to the soft rustle of fabric behind me, which invited torturous images of her naked again. My cock hardened uncomfortably in my breeches. *Dieu*, could she not hurry this along? It was maddening.

"Are you finished, Comtesse? Our food is probably cold by now," I grumbled.

"Yes, yes, *all right*. You may turn around. Only I shan't apologize for the indecency. If I'd stayed in those cold, wet clothes, I would have certainly gotten sick. Just...be a gentleman about it, would you?" she said, a touch of anxiety in her voice.

"I'm no blushing virgin nor slavering youth," I shot back. "I've seen plenty of women in various stages of undress. Yourself included, Comtesse. I'm perfectly capable of maintaining my composure. In fact, you are not even the type of woman to tempt me."

"What a relief," she said acidly. "Since you are not the type of man to tempt me. It makes our arrangement much simpler."

I turned around, but my sharp retort died on my lips. *You've already seen the woman naked,* I foolishly thought to myself. *How much worse can it be?*

Much worse.

She'd loosened her hair from beneath her cap, and it cascaded down her back in thick, glossy waves. The nightdress that the tavern lady had provided her was worn to threadbare softness, affording me glimpses of dusky nipples and that sinful dark triangle at the apex of her thighs. One sleeve slipped down her shoulder as she sat down before the table of food. She tore a chunk of bread from the loaf and set it into the steaming bowl of stew. Her easy movements and the tranquil domesticity of the scene filled me with a hunger far beyond food. How many times had I waded through the mud and blood of the battlefield, longing for something so simple—so *pastoral?*

She realized I was staring—she'd probably known all along, really—and raised a brow at me.

"Are you just going to stand there dripping on the floor while your food gets cold? If so, I'll eat your share. This stew is *delicious,* and the bread is warm from the oven. The ale is subpar and, frankly, I'd prefer wine, but it'll do."

She dipped the bread in the stew and raised it to her lips, licking the drips from her fingers. My mouth went bone dry. Frustration pulled my nerves taut, and I hastily started shucking my own clothes. Under different circumstances, I would've slept in them or gone nude, but they were filthy and wet from the rain, and I was damned tired of being cold. I turned around again and tugged my shirt off, tossing it into a pile with my coat, cloak, and hose. I reached for the innkeeper's proffered nightshirt when I heard a coughing, choking sound behind me.

Charlotte's wide eyes were watering, and her cheeks were pink, but she waved away my concern when I made to help her.

"No, no, I'm fine, Antoine. Really fine. Some ale went down the wrong way. Just give me a sex—*second*—and I'll be all right again," she spluttered. Her cheeks reddened even more, and I grinned. *Well, at least I'm not the only one overset.* That realization was quickly chased by another more damning one—if we both felt physical stirrings, it was a short road to ruin for us, and I couldn't allow that. Partly because I didn't trust her, partly because I needed to protect her, and honestly, partly because I needed to protect myself.

I pulled off my breeches and donned the nightshirt. It was just long enough to be decent but was far too tight across my chest. I stretched my arms out to the sides and felt the seams along the sides split a little. *Ah, well. The innkeeper will have to forgive me.*

I crossed the room and sat opposite Charlotte. She offered me the other half of the bread and a full bowl of stew. I raised my mug of ale to her and dove in.

Already, I felt worlds better. She'd been right—the stew

and bread were delicious, but the ale was inferior. Still, it swept through my veins and loosened my tight muscles. It had been some time since I'd been able to relax a little. I thought back to Charlotte's earlier questions and swallowed a mouthful of stew.

"Have you siblings?" I asked.

She smiled and swiped a hunk of bread in some butter. "No," she replied. "But my cousin Daphne is just like a sister to me."

"What of your parents?"

A look of melancholy passed over her face. "Mine died shortly after I married. A wave of illness took them both—not the blood plague, before you ask. Daphne's also passed on, as did her older brother. It was a difficult time for both of us. We clung together like wreckage in the storm. We'd been close as children, but grief has a way of hardening things—not just people, you understand, but relationships, too. With loss, love can become fiercer, just as hate can become more vitriolic. Our playful childhood bond cemented us together like drying mortar."

I was speechless for a moment, astonished by her ability to put into words something I'd so often felt myself. Marie and I had been cemented by my mother's passing and my father's cruelty, which was partly why her absence still felt so painful.

I swallowed hard. "Sisters are one of life's greatest joys— and miseries."

She laughed. "To be sure. I take it you have one?"

The bread turned to sand in my mouth. "I did, yes. Marie. She passed away a little less than a year ago. We were very close."

Charlotte reached forward and laid a hand on my arm. Heat bloomed beneath her touch.

"Antoine, I'm so sorry. How awful for you," she said, her face a study in sincerity. "It wasn't the blood plague, was it?"

"No," I said. I didn't want to go into details tonight. My mood turned black.

She sensed the change and withdrew her hand. She was quiet for a moment, searching for something to say, perhaps.

"My husband—Philippe—well, I don't actually know if he's alive or dead. The last time I saw him was as he boarded a boat for the Château d'If. He committed *terrible* crimes, Antoine, and was punished brutally for them. Rightly so, of course. But he was my husband, and I was devoted to him. He had been there when my parents died. Not in a supportive way, really, but he had been there. I've only recently learned to separate the truth of our marriage from my perception of what it was at the time. When I think back on it, I believe I grieved for him long before he went away, but that doesn't make it easier. It is a hard thing to lose someone. Their absences linger like nothing else in this life."

She drained the rest of her ale and popped the last chunk of bread in her mouth.

"What were his crimes?"

She sighed, a world weary, deeply sorrowful sound. "Antoine, you wouldn't believe me if I told you."

"Try me," I challenged.

She arched a brow. "I don't think that would be a good idea for either of us, do you?" She'd deliberately mistaken my meaning to avoid answering the question, a tactic I knew well enough, but for some reason, I found myself blushing beneath her heated gaze.

"Did you love him?" I asked, then immediately wished to take the words back. It wasn't my business whether she cared for him—he was her husband, after all. We were mere strangers. Still, I railed against the spark of jealousy that burned in my chest.

Charlotte tilted her head, thinking. "You know, I thought I did. But perhaps I just loved the idea of us. He was rich, titled, powerful, and not unattractive. He was a catch by the standards of the *tonne*. My parents were delighted at his offer. Alas, he fooled us all with his well-guarded villainy."

"Some people are masters of deception. They delight in hiding their true nature from the eyes of the world," I growled. My voice sounded rougher than I'd intended, but I was irritated by her memories of marriage and reminded again of my father's treachery. His betrayal felt as fresh now as it had been when I'd first discovered it.

Charlotte nodded. "I take it you have personal experience with that."

"Deception? Certainly. It's why I cannot abide dishonesty. The world would be a much better place if people didn't go around perpetuating falsehoods," I grumbled.

Charlotte covered a wince with a yawn—perhaps hoping I didn't notice. *As if I don't notice every damn thing about her.*

"Yes, of course. Well, Antoine, I'm exhausted. We should probably get some rest if we're to make an early start."

"You take the bed," I offered. "I'll sleep in the chair by the fire."

She snorted. "Don't be absurd. We can share the bed. You'll need to sleep if you're to be alert enough to get us to Gévaudan and keep an eye out for more soldiers."

I balked. "That's a horrible idea. I'll be fine."

"We're both adults, Antoine. I assure you that I have no interest in you carnally, and even if I did, I'm far too tired to attempt to seduce you. But if you're afraid that I'll attack you in the middle of the night..." She chuckled.

"I'm *not* afraid of you," I barked. "I was thinking of propriety and of *your* comfort."

She lifted her brows. "Well, I'm sure I've never been comfortable with propriety, but you may do as you wish."

She gathered up our damp clothes into a bundle and set them atop the empty dinner tray, then took it outside for the innkeeper. When she returned, she pulled one of the blankets off the bed and tossed it to me.

"I said I'll be fine," I protested.

"Yes, I'm sure you will. Do me a favor and take it anyway to spare me the guilt."

With that, she got into bed, pulled the remaining blankets up to her chin, and blew out the candle on the bedside table.

I sat down in the armchair in front of the fire, tucking the proffered cover around me. I was loath to admit that she'd been right about my level of comfort. Fortunately, the fatigue and ale had me dozing sooner than expected.

Some hours later, I woke with a start. The room was black as pitch, save for the dim glow of embers in the fireplace before me. Quietly, I listened, coming to full awareness. The storm had eased, and the rain had softened to a gentle tap upon the windows. What had woken me?

A distressed murmur rose from the bed where Charlotte lay. She mumbled something, then began thrashing violently in her sleep. *Nightmares.* I knew their sting all too well. Her cries grew louder, reaching a fevered pitch of sheer terror. I got up and went to the bed, trying to find her arm in the tangle of bed linens.

"Charlotte," I whispered. "Charlotte, wake up. You're having a nightmare."

I grabbed her shoulder and shook her gently. In an instant, she sat bolt upright, and her hand shot out to my throat.

Before my shock could register, she'd started to squeeze my windpipe, cutting off my breath. I pulled at her arm, surprised at her strength, until she seemed to come to her senses and let go.

I coughed and sucked in air.

"Antoine! Forgive me. I thought... I think I was dreaming. Are you all right?"

"I'm fine. You were having a nightmare. I worried that you'd wake the whole inn. Are you well?" It was partially true. Mostly, I'd been thinking of her, wanting to end her torment, but I hated to admit that, even to myself.

"Yes, of course," she said.

I sat on the edge of the bed, and she shifted over. Despite her insistence, I could tell she was shaking.

"What was your dream about?" I asked.

"Needlepoint."

"Very funny."

"You know, I don't even remember." Her faint reply was not convincing.

"You were shouting something about demons."

She didn't answer. In the quiet, raindrops tapped a soft staccato against the windowpanes, and I strained to listen for a change in her breath to see if she'd fallen asleep again.

"Antoine, will you stay with me?" she asked.

The uncertainty in her voice elicited some primal, instinctive response in me. I knew she was dangerous, but here—now —in this dark room, she seemed so...*vulnerable*. It didn't sit well with my image of her as a devious hellcat.

"If you wish," I replied, knowing on every level that this was a horrible idea. She scooted over in the bed, and I grabbed the coverlet from the armchair. For the preservation of my own sanity, I did *not* get under the sheets with her. We lay down together, separated by a few worn layers of fabric and all the chivalrous strength I could muster, though it was beginning to fail.

"Thank you," she whispered. "I apologize if it's silly."

"I find that nightmares visit those who have known more than their share of earthly horrors, not those who have some weakness of character. You needn't apologize for it."

"You have them, too," she observed.

"Mmm." Too often I saw the faces of men I'd killed, friends I'd lost in battle, and always the faces of Marie and little Louis. If I had mountains of soap and oceans of water, I'd never be able to wash all the blood from my hands.

"One day, I'll find a way to banish them," she said with a yawn. "Perhaps with a magic spell of some kind. God knows wine and prayers haven't helped."

The warmth of her curves next to my wretched body and the sound of her sleepy murmurings squeezed my heart. In the darkness, I could just make out the outline of her face. In another time, in another place, I could have imagined myself pressing kisses to her cheeks, her forehead, her lips. Tangling my fingers in her glossy chestnut waves, running my hands all over her velvety skin, reaching between her thighs to explore her intimate secrets... *Merde.* I was hard as a rock again. I hadn't been this overruled by lust since I'd been a lad. I turned on my side, hoping Charlotte wouldn't notice my uncomfortable condition.

Her slow, steady breathing gave me some comfort—she'd obviously fallen back asleep. My relief was short-lived, however. Blissfully unaware, she rolled onto her side and snuggled back against my warmth. Despite the blankets between us, I felt the firm press of her lush ass cradling my insistent erection. I bit my lip to keep from groaning. Surely, this was what awaited me in Hell.

I gritted my teeth and tried to count backwards from one

thousand, hoping for sleep. Given the softening of my feelings tonight, I could only pray that by light of day, my desire for the troublesome woman would wane.

One thousand. Nine hundred ninety-nine. Nine hundred ninety-eight.

CHAPTER SEVEN
CHARLOTTE

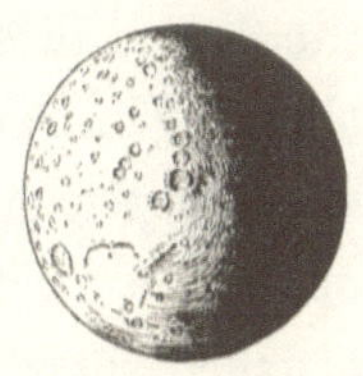

November 2, 1767
The road to Gévaudan

I woke slowly, blissfully warm beneath the comforting weight of a man's muscular arm. It was tossed over my ribs, gently cradled between my breasts. I smiled and reached behind me, snaking a hand down to playfully stroke my bedmate's morning erection. I couldn't remember the drunken dinner party that had brought this young stud from the halls of court to my bedchamber, but that wasn't going to stop me from getting one more good romp out of him before I sent him packing.

A low moan exhaled against my neck, and I felt soft lips kissing against my nape. I stroked him with more firmness, dimly trying to remember a name, a face, anything. I cracked my eyes open, taking in one of the shabbiest rooms I'd ever been in.

Horror gripped me as the realization dawned. I flung myself forward, falling to the floor as my feet tangled in the blankets. I followed the sound of my crash with a pained—*and furiously humiliated*—groan.

Antoine cried out and dove out of bed, reaching for his sword on the floor. He fumbled around wildly until, presumably, he also became aware of his surroundings. I heard him swear roughly and he leaned over the bed, taking in my indecorous state upon the floor. I disentangled my legs from the blankets and stood, shooting him an icy glare.

"Don't. Say. A. Word," I gritted out. "Nothing happened, but if anything *had* happened, it would have been a case of sleepy delirium and mistaken identity and nothing more. Understand?"

The expression on his face was stony, but I could have sworn a glint of laughter glittered in his eyes.

"I'm serious. If you bring it up, I'll kill you," I threatened.

He nodded. Then, from under his breath, I heard him mutter, "All due respect, Comtesse, but *you're* the one who brought it up."

My cheeks reddened at the innuendo, and I grimaced.

"Oh!" I shouted. "Well, I certainly wasn't the *only* one! You...you...*participated.*"

He shook his head and ran a hand through his loose brown locks. I was momentarily distracted by the flex of a bicep beneath the soft nightshirt.

"You said it yourself. It was a mistake. I was asleep and was merely reacting instinctively to a beautiful woman throwing herself at me." His face was set in its usual grave lines, but the humor hiding in his tone told me he found this whole thing *very* amusing.

"I didn't throw myself at you!" I stammered. I mustered as much indignation as I could, but it was difficult when my traitorous heart caught at the word *beautiful.* Antoine thought I was beautiful.

Oh, stop it, Charlotte! Don't be ridiculous.

"It doesn't matter. It *won't* happen again," I growled.

"Well, then you'll have to control yourself," he said smugly.

The bastard.

I was desperate to change the subject. "It's past dawn, and the rain has let up. We should hurry and be on our way."

My ploy, clumsy though it was, effectively distracted Antoine from my embarrassment. He went to the window and looked out.

As if on cue, we heard a knock on the door.

"No need to open the door, lovebirds, but I heard you stir and brought up your clothes and some breakfast! I'll leave the tray outside," the old woman called.

Dieu, if you're truly up there in Heaven, please heap blessings upon that creature, I thought as Antoine retrieved the food and clothes from the hall.

I refused to meet Antoine's eyes as he handed me the neatly folded pile of clean, dry garments, and sullenly retreated to the corner of the room to start dressing.

I forced myself to consider my predicament instead of my humiliation. I needed to try to get word to Daphne, but I didn't think Antoine would approve of me sending messages that might be intercepted by the *bêtes*. Never mind that as an agent of *les DD*, I'd been trained to send coded letters that were nearly impossible to decipher. He didn't need any more reason to convince himself of my secret profession.

After we finished dressing, I pinned my hair up beneath my lace cap and sat down to eat. The innkeeper had brought up a loaf of bread, a thick wedge of buttery cheese, and two apples. Without a word, Antoine and I polished off every crumb. Despite eating well last night and this morning, I still felt famished, as if my soul needed something other than simple bread and cheese. He stood to remove the tray, and I offered him a handful of coins.

"What's this?"

"Take it down to the innkeeper. It's my share of the food, laundry, and room cost," I said.

Antoine thrust the money back into my hands.

"Keep it. I've a purse of my own," he growled, strangely offended.

"I don't accept charity," I said, pushing the coins back toward him. "I can take care of myself, and I can pay my own way."

"If you think I'm going to let a woman—a *comtesse*, no less—pay our way out of a mess that I got us into, you're sorely mistaken. I always see to my own mistakes," he said sharply.

I could have continued to belabor the point, but my aim was more to get him to leave the room than to foot the bill. If he wanted to be a stubborn fool about finances, that was his pride-fueled prerogative.

I nodded. "Thank you. I'll be down in a moment—I have one or two things left to complete in my toilette."

He eyed me suspiciously but nodded and left. I went to the bedside table where I'd stashed my pilfered supplies the night before and withdrew a scrap of parchment, a small pot of ink, and a quill. After some thought, I decided against using our familiar code number cipher, since that would look even more suspicious than a silly letter to a family member.

D,

Hoping this missive finds you well. Sincerest apologies for dashing off early from the party—was called away unexpectedly. Hope the family isn't too cross with me. Promise to make it up to them as soon as I return home. Have decided to spend some time away to recover from this wretched rheumatism. I hear Gévaudan is nice this time of year. Will send you an update upon arrival. My love to E.

—C

It wasn't a lot of information, but I was being overly cautious. She'd at least understand that I was safe, the mission hadn't gone according to plan, that I was heading south and would write again soon.

I was preparing to seal the note when Antoine stomped in, startling me.

"What's that?"

"Nothing," I said, stuffing the letter in my pocket. He glared and strode forward, backing me up against the wall.

He *tsked*. "Hand it to me, or I shall forcibly retrieve it." His eyes glittered with the issued challenge.

Caged between his arms and the wall, my heart hammered in excitement. My gaze snagged on his mouth—those tempting lips stretched in a tight, frustrated line. Reflexively, my tongue darted out to wet my own lips. Antoine noticed.

The atmosphere between us changed, like the charged air in a thunderstorm right before the lightning strikes.

"Ha! You can certainly try," I challenged, but the bluster was gone from my tone. In its place was a throaty breathlessness I almost didn't recognize. *This man is rattling me, shaking my composure.* Heat blazed between our bodies.

One dark brow arched at my defiance, flexing the scar across his temple in a way I could only describe as *devastatingly handsome.* I tried to recover my senses—tried to stop staring at his strange, strong, handsome features long enough to ready myself for his *forcible retrieval* of my precious letter. I braced myself for the violence I suspected would come.

Instead, he kissed me.

His firm lips, so often set in that restrained frown, softened against mine. His tongue slid out, licking gently, tentatively, until I opened to meet him with the force of my unspent lust. *Dieu, he tastes delicious.* Like this morning's apples and mint tea, and the faintly salty taste of masculinity—nothing like the rank, perfumed sweets of my courtly lovers. His passion intensified and he pushed closer to me, crushing me against the wall. I felt his excitement press against my abdomen and it unleashed a new wave of desire in me.

I didn't hear choirs of angels singing. Rather, it sounded like legions of demons, moaning and writhing and goading me on, encouraging me to toss my skirts up and sink down to the floor on top of this glorious man.

I realized with a thrill that Antoine's hand was caressing me around the front of my skirt, reaching for the ties at the side and—

"*Ha!* You were saying?" he grinned, cheeks dimpling, holding my letter just out of reach.

He'd reached *right* into my skirt pockets and thieved it from me while I was lustfully compromised.

I gaped.

"You complete and utter cad! I cannot believe you did that!"

I was less embarrassed about the pursuit of my own carnal pleasure than I probably should have been. More than anything, I was angry at myself for letting him get the better of me, especially when I had to begrudgingly respect his unscrupulous tactics. I, myself, had often employed the same kinds of deception to extract information and influence. The rogue had beaten me at my own game.

There was also the possibility—as much as I didn't want to admit it—that I was disappointed he hadn't been as passionately moved as I'd been. My pride smarted.

He chuckled and stepped back, and I gritted my teeth at the sad loss of his warmth and the even sadder loss of the upper hand. I scowled at him and grabbed at the letter, which he held above my head as if I were a small, unruly child demanding sweets. Rather than embarrass myself further, I harrumphed and turned my back on him, hoping that even if he read the words I'd written to Daphne, he would merely think I was putting my cousin's worries at ease.

He frowned as he read, then handed the letter back to me.

"Why were you so protective of such drivel?"

I snatched the letter back from him. "Because a lady's personal correspondence is just that—personal. It's not for the eyes of every rapacious brute who doesn't respect a woman's privacy *or* personal boundaries."

"That's rich coming from the woman who crossed some very intimate boundaries early this morning," he snapped.

I put my hands on my hips and raised my chin haughtily. "It's really rather ungentlemanly of you to remind me."

"What does the letter *really* say?"

"You read it. It's familial drivel, as you say."

He snapped his fingers. "It must be some kind of coded message—*rheumatism?* You *are* a spy! Is she in on it, then? Your cousin? Of course, she must be. Who are you working for? The crown?"

"Don't be ridiculous. The idea of me—a comtesse!—working. You've clearly taken one battlefield blow to the head too many. I'm simply being cautious with what I reveal in the event the letter falls into the hands of the *bêtes de sang.* Really, it's common sense," I sniffed. I busied myself by packing my small parcels again, and once more looking for any supplies we might be able to use on our journey. Antoine stared at me, his characteristic frown tugging at his features once more.

"I told you last night, I can't abide deceit. Your actions may be putting us in further danger."

My temper was reaching volcanic proportions.

"How careless of me to put the both of us into great danger. If only *I* hadn't murdered a marquis in a palace, kidnapped an aristocrat, traipsed about the countryside with a bounty on my head, and run afoul of a murderous mercenary vampire death squad!" I snarled.

Antoine winced.

"But yes, you're right. A silly letter to my worried family with precious little traceable information is *surely* what will send us to our doom. Never mind the fact that we'd probably be in even more danger if Daphne *didn't* hear from me and sent a search party out after you. You think you have much to fear from the *bêtes de sang*? They'd be nothing compared to the wrath of my cousin if she knew you'd knocked me out and kidnapped me," I finished. I was breathless with anger and frustration.

Antoine folded his arms across his chest and stared hard at me.

"Fine," he conceded. "Keep your damn secrets."

I snorted. "As if I'm the only one keeping secrets! Why is there a bounty on your head? Why did you murder Sade? Why are there mercenaries after you? Why did you kiss me?"

I snapped my mouth shut. I hadn't meant to ask that last question. *Damn it, Charlotte!* No, damn this infuriating man. I'd never felt such a loss of control around anyone, and the fact that my life's work depended on my ability to maintain said control meant I needed to put as much distance as possible between us. The less I became untethered, the safer we would both be.

Antoine said nothing, his inscrutable gaze and hard frown hadn't even twitched when I'd fired my questions at him. *The horse's ass.*

I took a deep breath. "Forget it," I said. "Let's just get what supplies we can from this town and leave. We've already lingered longer than is wise."

He nodded once, picked up his things, and we headed downstairs. I smiled brightly at the innkeeper, jabbing Antoine with my elbow to remind him that we were undercover newly-weds. He flashed a grin at the elderly woman and inquired about the purchase of a second horse, some extra food, and additional warm clothes if possible. I handed her my sealed letter with a few coins, asking her to make sure it made its way to the next available mail coach.

We were successful with the extra food and warm clothes, but the innkeeper told us there weren't any spare horses to be had. I grumbled inwardly as I secured the thick woolen cloak around my shoulders. I was not looking forward to another day and a half of travel, pressed up against a thick wall of exas-perating masculinity. By Antoine's sour expression, I surmised he felt the same way. He paid the woman handsomely, filled the saddlebags, and mounted his horse, then pulled me up in front of him.

Thankfully, the rain had let up, but the sky threatened more bad weather and the temperature had dropped considerably. Even with the additional warm clothes, we both shivered and sniffled, suffering each other's company in vexed silence. Antoine kept Tartuffe moving at a steady pace, and it was some hours after our departure before we paused to stop for lunch and allow the horse to rest. We found a dry log to sit on and dug into the bread, cheese, and apples the innkeeper had packed for us.

"They aren't mercenaries, you know," Antoine said quietly, as if I'd just asked him a question and we hadn't been riding for hours with nary a word between us.

I shrugged, still put out by our earlier argument. Surpris-ingly, he continued.

"They're soldiers. An elite squad of young vampires, newly turned to provide a strategic edge to the army, to be exact. With increased strength, speed, and an unquenchable blood-lust, they're the perfect warriors," he said, biting into an apple.

"Soldiers. For France?" I couldn't help it. My astonishment and curiosity overruled my hauteur.

He nodded.

I struggled to process this information. "How? Were they infected before or after they joined? It must've been after, but I can't imagine them retaining their posts once they'd succumbed to the blood plague. No commander would allow for infected troops. The prejudice against vampires is too great, though it's a silly prejudice, in my opinion. In fact, I could see how they'd be a huge asset to the war effort—what with them being mostly immortal and all. Wait—no! It cannot be that they were ordered to infect themselves?"

A shadow passed across his face. "Not quite. They volunteered for the post."

"That's preposterous. I know for a fact the king is unaware of any vampire troops. He wouldn't trust them at all, given what's been brewing in Paris. On whose orders were vampire soldiers created? And to what purpose?"

"The reasons are...complicated. As to whose orders, I'm afraid those come from Général de Vaux, the Lieutenant Général of the king's armies and the current governor of Thionville."

The name was familiar to me, as was his title, but I couldn't recall having ever met him at Versailles.

"Is he your commanding officer? Do you take your orders from him, then?" I asked.

Antoine sighed. It was the kind of bone-deep sigh that seemed to rise from his feet all the way up through his body.

"I've taken orders from him my whole life, Comtesse. Général de Vaux is my father."

CHAPTER EIGHT
ANTOINE

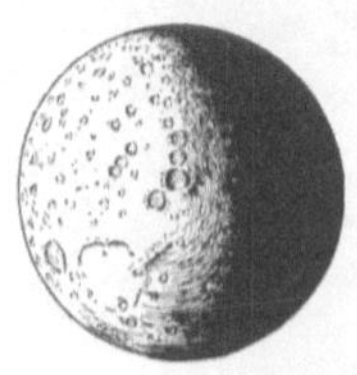

November 2, 1767
The road to Gévaudan

CHARLOTTE'S EYES WIDENED A FRACTION BEFORE SHE RECOVERED HER composure. Her brow furrowed as she studied the bread and cheese in her hands. She seemed to be puzzling things out, so I waited patiently for her to begin peppering me with the barrage of questions I knew would come.

"You told me your name was de Valle," she accused.

"De Valle comes from my mother's side. I have been traveling under that name since I left the front."

"I see. A half-truth, then," she sniffed. "The *bêtes* are your father's men?"

I nodded.

"Which means that he sent them after you. Is this because of some unresolved familial melodrama, or is this more to do with you being a deserter?"

My temper returned, quick as a flash. "I am *not* a deserter," I insisted.

"But there's a bounty on your head, and a group of your father's vampire soldiers after you," she mused. "It must be a particularly compelling family squabble for your father to seek you out with such industrious measures."

"It's complicated," I grumbled. I was already regretting my resolution to tell her some of my truths—an impulse that had struck when I'd seen the look of betrayal in her eyes after I'd kissed her and stolen her letter. *Trust a woman to twist the knife of guilt.*

"I'm sure it is," she replied, an edge of frustration creeping into her tone. "There's much I'd like to know about your relationship with your father, his motives in creating a superior soldier, his reasons for hiding those actions from the king, and why you feel the need to share this information with me now, but I suppose there are more pertinent questions first. Are there just the five of them? How skilled are these men? What will they do with you when they find you? Is the bounty for your capture or your death?"

The more she spoke, the more agitated she became, eventually abandoning her food and standing to pace in front of me. I tossed my apple core into the woods behind us.

"Yes, as far as I know, there are only five of them. They are a kind of...experiment, I suppose. They have been given more training than an average soldier, but they are newly turned and lack the experience of both seasoned vampires and seasoned soldiers. That makes them half as predictable and twice as dangerous as normal vampires and normal soldiers, which is why I cannot say for certain what they will do when they find us. My father would not have ordered my death, so I suspect he merely wants me to return to him, but whether the *bêtes* will obey that order is *questionable*, at best."

Charlotte paused her pacing and stared at me with those penetrating brown eyes. *Dieu*, she was beautiful. The early winter chill made her cheeks rosy in the same way that she blushed when she was flustered. I caught myself fantasizing about chasing that blush across her naked body but shook myself out of the vision. She was a spy. She probably used her beauty and charm to manipulate men with the detached precision of a clockmaker tending his cogs. *Do not fall for her, Antoine.*

She pursed her lips and nodded decisively, wrapping the food back up and putting it in her pocket.

"We shouldn't delay any further then," she said crisply. "You can tell me about the rest on our way to Gévaudan."

Her posture was stiff as she mounted Tartuffe, sliding forward on the saddle to allow me to heave myself up behind her.

"You're angry with me," I observed. "Is it because I got the better of you earlier or because of the danger I put you in?" I was unable to resist the temptation to tease her a little, though I kept my expression stoic as I guided us back to the southern road.

"You didn't get the better of me! And I'm not angry," she bit out.

I chuckled at the ironic denial.

"I'm *not* angry," she repeated. "I am *annoyed.* And it has nothing to do with the danger we are in. I can handle myself, thank you very much."

Of that, I had no doubt.

"Why are you annoyed with me then?" I prodded.

"It doesn't matter," she said curtly.

"It certainly seems to," I argued. "Whatever it is, I'm sorry. There, now. I've apologized. You can cease your petulance."

"Oh, for Heaven's sake! You are *such a man!*" she cried in exasperation. She turned halfway to glare at me from one eye, then opened her mouth to launch into what I could only assume would be a scathing, seething tirade, when she stopped and froze, as if she'd been struck. She craned her neck to squint behind us, coming up out of the saddle.

"What is it?" I asked.

"Hush!" she hissed. "Don't look now, but there is someone behind us on the road, traveling at quite a clip."

"On foot or horseback?"

"Horseback," she said warily. "It's a man on a lovely bay mare. He's dressed in dark green—looks bourgeois to me. I can't quite make out his face yet because his hat is pulled down rather low."

I made to turn but she stopped me with a firm hand on my arm.

"If you look now, it will be too obvious. Let's just continue on our way as the newlyweds we are and be prepared if it's trouble," she said, facing forward again.

I watched her slide her hand into one of her pockets and heard the sound of a pistol cocking. *So, she's kept the soldier's weapon this whole time!* I'd nearly forgotten about it. Reflexively, I felt for my own dual pistols and my short swords at my side. My crossbow hung from the saddle, though it would be useless in a roadside fray.

We were silent for the next several minutes, tensely waiting for the approaching man to either address us or ride on. As we listened to his horse trot up behind us, I felt the active tension gather in Charlotte's muscles, like a coiled snake ready to strike at a moment's notice. *Magnifique.*

"*Âllo!*" the man called. "*Bonjour, mes amis!* What fine weather we are having today! I only hope it doesn't rain later. Nothing worse than getting caught out in the rain, eh?"

I felt Charlotte relax a fraction, but I wasn't sure why. Looking up at the sky that almost certainly promised rain, I started to respond to the stranger, but Charlotte stopped me.

She didn't take her hand from her pocket. "It's worse to be caught out in the snow. Where are you headed, *mon ami?*"

"I go only where my masters send me," he said cryptically.

I stared down at her, perplexed. Her manner had me rattled. She almost spoke as if she knew this man, but that was impossible. She turned back to look at the stranger, darting a glance at me. She seemed more anxious about my presence than the man approaching.

She'd been right about him. He was dressed in dark green wool coat that was plain but well cut. He wasn't poor, but he wasn't an aristocrat, either. He'd obviously been traveling at some speed for some time, given how high the spattered mud reached on his clothes. I noted a few droplets of it on his cheek, as well—though with his dark eyes and placid expression, that was the only remarkable thing about his countenance. All in all, he was not unpleasant to look upon, but rather forgettable. He pulled up alongside us and I watched them greet each other with a guarded smile. *What the devil?*

"*Bonjour, Monsieur,*" I said.

The stranger inclined his head at me but spoke again to her.

"Your companion?"

"Yes," Charlotte said, a touch anxiously. "I, too, go only where my masters send me. It's all right. He travels with me. Do you have news?"

The man reached into his coat. I laid my hand on my pistol, but Charlotte shook her head.

"It's okay, Antoine. This man is an...acquaintance," she said, fumbling for the right word.

So, she does know him. Irritation and irrational jealousy sparked, and I clenched my jaw.

"An acquaintance?" I echoed, incredulous. "Out here? Impossible. What the Hell is going on? Who are you?"

I wasn't sure if I directed that last question at the stranger or at Charlotte, but it didn't seem to matter as they both ignored me.

The man's expression didn't change as he handed her a letter. It was almost as if he wore a mask of humanity and it made me uneasy. Charlotte took the letter and nodded.

"Some miles back, there's an inn with a lovely innkeeper—she has a message for my cousin. Please see that she gets it. And tell her that I'll send a full report as soon as possible. We go to Gévaudan," she said, now focused on the letter in her hand.

"Charlotte!" I hissed. I couldn't believe she'd just revealed our plan.

Still, she ignored me. The stranger seemed to take this as his cue to leave, however, and he raised a gloved hand to his tricorn hat.

"In the darkness..."

"And in the light," Charlotte returned without looking up. She was engrossed in her letter, her brow furrowed.

The stranger winked at me, turned his horse around, and galloped back in the direction he'd come. Lucky for him that he'd managed it before I could yank him from his saddle and demand a rational explanation for this bizarre exchange. I reasoned, however, there was only one explanation—rational or not—and I'd known it since the very beginning of my encounter with this woman.

"You *are* a spy! You lied to me," I practically shouted.

She sighed, folding the letter carefully and tucking it into her bodice. The small action distracted me momentarily from my anger.

"Yes, yes. All right. I'll explain some things to you, but we must keep moving. Things are dire and we need to reach Gévaudan before nightfall, if possible."

The worry in her voice was genuine, but I didn't spur Tartuffe on just yet. The tangle of my emotions grew tighter and more knotted as I tried to sort things out in my head. *Charlotte lied to me. You lied to her, too, Antoine.* Had I? Not really. *Lies of omission are still lies, you fool, and it's your fault you're in this mess with her to begin with.* Anger surfaced again, but it was unclear if it was at myself or at this deceptive woman. I chose to direct it at the latter.

"Start talking," I growled.

"I'm not a spy," she said slowly, choosing her words carefully. "I am an agent of The Order. Not just The Order—*les Dames Dangereuses*, to be more specific."

I barked out a laugh. "Come now, you don't expect me to believe *that*."

She tensed with affront. "And why not? You have been accusing me of as much since we met, you oaf."

"The Order is an absurd conspiracy—some portentous bedtime story to prevent people from rising up against the king. *Don't speak ill of His Majesty, lest The Order hear you! Stay away from the vampires, lest The Order come stake you! Don't forget to eat your vegetables, children, lest The Order find out!*"

Thunder rumbled in the distance, prompting me to kick Tartuffe into a trot.

I could feel Charlotte's frustration in her posture, but her tone was dismissive.

"Believe me or don't—you're the one who wanted an explanation."

"I want the truth, Comtesse," I countered.

"My explanation is no lie. Neither is The Order and my allegiance to it. Had I been able to find a way to speak with that messenger alone, I would have. Unfortunately, we're running short on time, and I'm forced to trust you with what you heard."

"Who was that man? And how the Hell did he find us?"

"I don't know him by name," she said. "But he is another agent of The Order, too. I assume he found me the way any agent would—asking the right people the right questions and drawing the right conclusions. The first innkeeper and that tavern girl, Hélène, were not far from our point of origin. We are on the main road south. We've only had a short head start and were forced off the road by bad weather. It was only a matter of time before a person with an ounce of sense and a fast horse found us."

I scoffed. I wanted to believe that none of this made sense, but I knew deep down everything fit. The disguise, the training, the fighting, the manipulation... I just didn't want to admit that this beautiful, charming woman had the ability to wreak so much havoc. *Who are you kidding, Antoine? She's been wreaking havoc on you since you laid eyes on her.*

She must have interpreted my silence as a challenge, because she continued in a low, steely voice.

"I'm telling you the truth, Antoine. I was at Versailles to assassinate the Marquis de Sade on behalf of The Order. His execution had been finalized weeks before, but we had to wait for the right moment. I was to be that moment, you see. A lovers' tryst gone awry—a too shameful but entirely accidental death. The king never would have signed the death warrant—I mean, Sade *was* a marquis, after all—but it was decided that he needed to be stopped. His depravity could no longer be ignored or covered up. He deserved to die."

At her mention of Sade, I turned to stone, fighting the nausea and rage that blighted me every time I heard his name.

"He should have been dealt with properly, but you interfered. And so, help me, Antoine, if you breathe a word of any of this, or tell anyone about what you just saw on the road back there, I will not hesitate to use your interference to protect myself," she said icily.

I couldn't believe the audacity of the woman.

"First you lie to me, then you threaten me. *Tsk, tsk.* Is that any way for a comtesse to behave?"

"It's not a threat. It's my one and only attempt at setting terms. If you make trouble for me, rest assured, trouble will find you, too."

Rain started to fall—corpulent, nearly frozen droplets that hinted at becoming snow. I spurred Tartuffe on, now almost as worried about the weather as the skirted enigma in front of me.

"Trouble has already found us, Charlotte, with or without your lies."

"I'm sorry if you feel betrayed, Antoine, but you must understand that I was doing everything in my power to simultaneously protect you and extract myself from this situation," she called back. With Tartuffe's increased pace and the worsening weather, I could barely hear her words as they whipped past me on the wind.

"I told you I cannot abide deceit," I shouted in her ear. "Why didn't you admit as much to me when I first asked you?"

"I wouldn't be a very good covert agent—"

"You mean *spy!*"

"—if I admitted the truth about every aspect of my life to every random gentleman who asked," she said loudly. "Besides, you certainly have a lot of secrets for someone who professes to be such a paragon of honesty."

"I've never lied to you," I shot back. "Everything I've said has been the truth."

"Lying by omission is still dishonesty, Antoine. You can hardly think it's fair to expect me to divulge everything about myself when you won't even tell me why you were hunting the Marquis de Sade down in the first place."

Her words struck true, but I was still too angry to agree with her outwardly.

"I don't want to talk about it," I growled.

"Well, *I* don't want to talk about being an agent for The Order!" she shouted back at me. "But that doesn't seem to matter to *you!*"

"The Order is a myth! Just tell me who you're really working for, and I'll let it drop!"

We barreled on, our speed matching the rise of our tempers. I leaned forward into Charlotte's back, trying to ensure that she could hear my words over the wind and driving rain.

Mistake.

My blood boiled with exasperation, but the further I pressed against her in our rain-soaked clothes, the better I could feel her luscious curves jostling against me. The rhythmic pace of Tartuffe's feet striking the mud bounced Charlotte's ass against my hard cock, making me damn near feral with need.

"Why won't you believe me?" she barked, oblivious to my overwhelming desires. "Hell, I'll show you the damn letter he gave me—it's a report about Sade's associates. Signed and stamped with The Order's seal. I couldn't make that up or lie about it! I only lied about being an agent. Everything else has been the truth. Unlike *you.*"

"I already told you. Just because I haven't told you everything about my past doesn't mean I've told you any falsehoods!" *Dieu, help me.* I could see her chest heaving before me, her nipples puckered in the cold, wet fabric of her bodice. It nearly made me weep.

"Actions speak louder than words, Antoine," she shouted bitterly.

"What are you talking about?" I demanded, confused.

Suddenly, she recovered her composure and bit her lip, then shook her head. "Nothing. Never mind," she replied.

I slowed Tartuffe down, allowing him time to catch his breath and trying desperately to collect myself. I guided us off the road into a small grove of trees that provided a modicum of shelter from the rain. Despite the cold, I could see steam rising from our bodies. I dismounted to stretch my legs and, without waiting for her agreement, lifted Charlotte from the saddle.

"What do you mean?" I asked again, calmly this time—my gaze boring into the warm chocolate of her eyes.

She blushed. "I said it's nothing! I was angry. It doesn't matter."

Slowly, I reached up to brush a wet lock of hair from her cheek.

"It *does* matter."

She snorted in derision.

"Charlotte, I will not let it drop."

"Fine," she capitulated. She crossed her arms in front of her chest and threw me a withering glare. "Fine. For someone so opposed to deceit, you certainly had no problem using it on me this morning at the inn."

"Ah. When I stole your letter?"

She nodded once.

"And you're upset because I got the better of you?"

"No! Well, yes, but..."

"But that's not all," I finished. "How else did I deceive you, Comtesse?"

Charlotte twisted her face in agony, clearly embarrassed. She paced our secluded grove, muttering to herself beneath her breath. When I put my hand on her shoulder to stop her, she whirled on me.

"You made me believe!" she yelled. "You made me believe that you wanted me!"

Chagrinned, she covered her face with her hands and groaned.

"I will never forgive you for making me say that out loud," she muttered. "Now, can we be on our way? Night is falling and the *bêtes* will soon catch up to us if we don't keep moving. I don't suppose you know how much further we have to go before we reach Gévaudan—"

Whatever her last words were, she didn't have time to speak. Unwilling to resist any longer and unable to help myself, I grabbed her by the back of her neck and pulled her lips to mine.

CHAPTER NINE
CHARLOTTE

November 2, 1767
The road to Gévaudan

I'D NEVER PARTICULARLY ENJOYED BEING MANHANDLED IN SUCH AN aggressive fashion when it came to men, though I knew plenty of women who did. Antoine, however, was different. His touch wasn't an entitled drive to satisfy his own wants—rather, it was an outpouring of emotions he didn't seem to be able to express verbally.

The force of his passion was volcanic in its intensity, prompting me to step back and grab hold of him simultaneously.

One hand behind my neck, the other snaking around my waist to bring our bodies as close together as physics and anatomy would allow, he devoured my lips like a man going off to duel at dawn. Gone was the calculating sweetness of our kiss this morning—in its place, raw need and desperation.

His tongue tangled with mine as his hand slipped down to give my ass a firm squeeze, provoking a satisfied whimper from me and a groan of desire from him. He guided me back against one of the trees and pushed his arousal against my stomach, sucking in a harsh breath at the friction.

Pulling back slightly, he cupped my face in his hands and leveled his darkening green gaze at me. It stripped me bare and terrified me with its honesty. *The honesty of a man you do not deserve.*

"That was *not* deceit," he whispered. I shut my eyes, thrown utterly off balance by the impact of what had just happened. "Charlotte, look at me."

I forced myself to meet his eyes, fully intending to laugh off the awkwardness I started to feel, but found myself unable. My sharp retorts and witticisms died in my throat. I didn't want an uncomfortable silence or an indifferent conclusion to this strange encounter. I just wanted more of him. I reached up and set my lips to his again, half-expecting to meet some kind of resistance, but he yielded to me immediately. I threaded my fingers through his hair and sucked at his tongue, dizzy with lust. He dragged his lips from mine and licked the droplets of rainwater on my neck, then nuzzled his way back up to my ear.

"Oh, Antoine," I breathed.

"*Dieu,* Comtesse," he growled, tugging at my earlobe with his teeth. "I want you so badly I cannot think straight, but we should not continue. We cannot if we don't trust each other."

"Who says we cannot? Trust has nothing to do with sex."

He narrowed his eyes at me, his desire warring with his frustration. "You truly want me to continue?"

In response, I wrapped one leg around his waist and reached down to slide my hand along the impressive, hard length of him. He choked out a sound halfway between a cry and a moan, then yanked my hands away from his delicious body and pinned them down at my sides.

For a moment, my heart sank, interpreting the gesture as

rejection. *He should reject you, Charlotte. He is everything that is honorable and straightforward, and you are more artifice than flesh.*

Afraid at what I might see reflected in his gaze, I tilted my face up to his, expecting to hear the censure I so often heard from my former husband. No such words came. Instead, he grinned wickedly, flashing a dimpled smile that made my knees wobble. Taking one hand and lifting my sodden skirts, he reached beneath the hem of my chemise and stroked cool fingers up my inner thighs.

"Your skin is like silk," he murmured. "Finer than anything a man like me should be allowed to touch."

He slid two fingers through the seam of my sex, pressing one fingertip against the bud of pleasure and prompting me to utter a stream of obscenities that made his breath quicken.

"From the first moment I saw you, Comtesse, I knew you would be this maddening. So passionate," he teased at my ear, rubbing firm circles with his fingertip and sliding his second finger inside me.

"*Putain de merde, oui, l'amour.* If you stop now, I will kill you!"

I grasped wildly for his breeches, but he stayed my hand and brought his lips to mine for a searing kiss.

"Not yet," he panted. "I've been wagering with myself that seeing you in ecstasy will be the most beautiful thing I've ever seen, and I plan to settle that bet first."

I whimpered something unintelligible—even to my own ears—and ground my hips against his hand.

"Now do you understand? My desire for you, Comtesse, is the most honest thing that has existed between us since we met days ago."

Faster and harder his skilled fingers worked until my bliss closed in around me and I began to see stars. His other hand came up to caress my breast through the drenched fabric of my dress. He sucked at my earlobe and pinched my nipple almost to the point of pain, sending me screaming over the edge. When my climax broke, Antoine held me through it, letting me ride the waves of pleasure in his arms. When I sighed in satisfaction, he dropped my skirts, swept another kiss across my lips and licked his fingertips.

"Perfection," he said with a smile.

I stared at him in wonder. Who *was* this man? He'd gone from gruff murderer to grumpy soldier to devastating rake in the time that I'd known him—a scant matter of days. *A man to keep you on your toes, Charlotte.* If I wasn't careful, I could fall for him, and that would most certainly complicate the life I'd worked very hard to craft for myself in the wake of Philippe's destruction. Suddenly self-conscious, I closed my eyes.

"Antoine, I'm sorry, I—"

A twig snapped behind our grove of trees and we both froze.

"Well, well, well, that *was* entertaining," came an accented voice from the darkness.

The darkness. What fools we'd been! In our sexual frustration, we'd completely abandoned good sense and had delayed too long. Night had fallen, and from the thick Prussian consonants emanating from the blackness beyond, the *bêtes* had found us.

Merde.

Antoine realized it, too, and stepped in front of me protectively. *The idiot.* Two of us could fight better than one.

From all around us, the five soldiers came forward slowly. They had our routes of escape blocked. Tartuffe whinnied as one of the *bêtes* seized his reins and grinned predatorily, showing off an impressive set of fangs.

"We have no quarrel with you, *petite*. It's the gentleman we're after," said one of the Parisians.

"Speak for yourself," grumbled the other Prussian. I recognized him as the one that I'd shot in the stomach. He kept his hand on the pistol at his side and narrowed his gaze at me.

My mind worked. On foot, we wouldn't stand a chance. If we could get to Tartuffe, we might be able to get away, but I wasn't certain how likely that would be. They had us surrounded and it was five on two. If I had more than the one pistol, I might be able to manage it, but between Antoine and I, a fight was doomed from the start. Perhaps I could negotiate.

"Why are you after him?" I asked the Parisian who'd addressed me.

Antoine's whole body tensed, as if he were preparing for the attack.

"That's none of your fucking business," snarled the angry Prussian.

"Well, at present, he's my escort, so I'd say that's entirely my business. I have a hard time believing that King Louis would approve of his men depriving a helpless woman of her travel companion and protection out in the middle of nowhere," I sniffed.

"Forgive me, lady, but your protection does not concern us at present. Perhaps when we've finished with Lieutenant de Vaux, we can come to some other arrangement with you," one of the other soldiers said with a smirk.

"Is it the bounty you're after?" I tried. "Whatever it is, I'll triple it." I didn't think the *bêtes* would go for it, but I was stalling—desperately trying to come up with a plan that didn't involve us getting drained and left to die in the woods outside Gévaudan.

"Charlotte," Antoine warned. "Please. I'll handle this."

I arched a brow at him. *Oh, really?* He didn't appear to be handling it at all. I pursed my lips.

"I'll come with you," Antoine told the *bêtes*. "But the lady leaves unharmed."

I rolled my eyes. Even if they did agree to that, I didn't trust them to uphold their end of that particular bargain. I'd known too many men in my life. Not everyone had Antoine's sense of honor.

The first Parisian smiled and inclined his head. "Of course, Lieutenant de Vaux. We can be civil, can't we, men?"

The group of men chuckled, sending the hairs on the back of my neck straight up.

"Please," I tried again, anxious at Antoine's misplaced chivalry. *Surely, he doesn't believe them, does he?* "Please. What is it you're after? Is it money? Influence? Say the words and I'll make sure you get whatever reward you desire. Eternity is such a long time, gentlemen—I can see to it that you have enough money to last you until the end of days."

That attracted the attention of the soldier to my left—the third Parisian.

"Oh, sure! You'll just run right up to the king and demand compensation for us, will you?" he snickered.

"Don't be ridiculous," I scoffed. "I would *never* run. A lady *glides.*"

The first Parisian barked a laugh. Antoine scowled at me.

"Who the Hell are you?" the Parisian asked, eyeing me up and down.

"No one," Antoine growled. "She's no one and none of your concern."

Bless him. I raised my chin haughtily and inclined my head at the vampire.

"Monsieur, you have the privilege of addressing the Marquise de Balay. You must forgive my state of dress and my earlier deception on the road. Monsieur de Vaux and I have had a very long and unbelievable journey. It's really quite a story," I said. I didn't want to give him my real name just yet, so the borrowed title would do for now. Antoine continued to glare at me, apparently finding refuge in playing the grumpy soldier again. *So much for my dashing rake.*

The Parisian considered me.

"I'm listening," he drawled.

"*Putain, Hugo,*" the grumpy Prussian swore. "We don't have time for this. Let's just take the lieutenant, drain the girl, and be on our way."

That familiar muscle in Antoine's jaw twitched—the one signaling extreme displeasure. The Parisian—Hugo, it seemed—frowned at the Prussian.

"I want to know who we're dealing with, Frederick. Don't you?" he said darkly. "Please, continue, *Madame la Marquise.*"

"Well, it started back at the All Hallow's Eve masquerade at Versailles," I said brightly. "I was there with my husband, the marquis, but he was *so* cross with me! You see, I thought it would be a riotous good time to come dressed as Cupid—which was how you gentlemen found me, remember?—and he certainly was less than pleased with my choice of costume, so he avoided me all evening, the cad!" Sighing heavily and willing blood to my cheeks, I looked down as if scandalized. "We had a rather public argument, I'm afraid. Oh, I cannot imagine what the gossips are saying right now! Anyway, I decided to leave the ball early and went out to meet my carriage, when Lieutenant de Vaux happened upon me. He's an old family friend, you see, and he valiantly agreed to escort me back to my château, but, oh, gentlemen, you know how a lady's temperament is, don't you?" I shot them beseeching looks and saw that I had their full attention. "I decided after the humiliating spectacle at Versailles, I wanted to spend some time alone, away from my fool of a husband, and I insisted on darling Antoine accompanying me to our country estate down south."

The lie became bigger and bigger as I prattled on, playing for time and hoping to come up with another plan of escape. *Think, Charlotte. We can't be that far from Gévaudan. Less than half a day's ride, if Antoine is right. Surely there are more people journeying this way, and it's only a matter of time before someone comes upon us and offers some kind of assistance, or, at the very least, a big enough distraction to allow us to escape.*

Eventually, however, I ran out of words. The long days and sleepless nights had caught up with me, and I fumbled over the end of my imaginary tale.

"And there you have it," I tried with false hope. "Now, will you gentlemen allow us to leave? What say you?"

"What say I? I say that was the most incredible work of fiction I think I've ever heard," Hugo chuckled.

Merde.

"Truly remarkable," laughed the less grumpy Prussian. "I haven't had entertainment like that since we left the front."

"You're quite the actress. I'm almost sorry that we'll probably kill you anyway," Hugo grinned, his fangs glinting in the moonlight.

"I'm not," hissed the grumpy Prussian.

Antoine tensed, prepared to leap forward at the soldier holding Tartuffe. Hugo caught the posture, naturally, and *tsked.*

"Please, Lieutenant. We've dallied enough. Just come with us and *maybe* we'll let your little tart live when we're done with her."

I heard a low growl then and turned bewildered eyes on Antoine. Was the noise coming from him? It seemed to emanate from every direction around us. Antoine reached for me protectively and I realized the noise was coming from just outside our grove—a realization that didn't *exactly* fill me with relief.

"What the Hell is that?" the grumpy Prussian hissed. "Hugo, do you smell that? What *is* that? Who's there?"

All five of the *bêtes* turned, sniffing the air, and listening with their supernatural senses. At once, they homed in on one direction—right behind me. Goosebumps rose along my skin as my dull human senses picked up on the thing they all stared at.

Once more, a low, feral growl vibrated through the frigid blackness of night.

Antoine twisted slowly, peering at something behind my left shoulder.

"Charlotte," he whispered. "Get ready to *run*."

The fear in his eyes chilled my blood to ice, and it barely registered when he calmly slid his hands from my waist to the dual pistols at his sides.

Tartuffe whinnied in fear and bucked, yanking the reins from the vampire's grasp. He hissed and grabbed for them, which became the spark that our powder keg of a situation needed. The thing at my back snarled. I turned in time to see a dark shape leap forward, knocking me to the ground with a pair of savage claws. I felt the sting of them raking my shoulder —*merde, I hope those scratches are not too deep*—and braced for a second blow, but none came. The thing had fixed its attention on the vampires. Antoine dove down and rolled atop me protectively, then all Hell broke loose.

CHAPTER TEN

ANTOINE

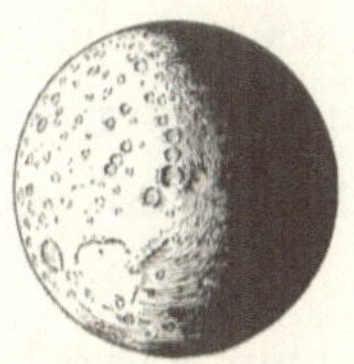

November 3, 1767
The road to Gévaudan

CHARLOTTE AND I WATCHED, STUNNED, AS THE LARGE CREATURE WENT after Frederick. In the darkness, it was almost impossible to see what it was, but it had the penetrating yellow eyes, ominous growl, and wild ferocity of an exceptionally large wolf. Moonlight glinted off fangs and claws and sketched an outline that was something *more* than canine—but I couldn't wrap my head around the idea that we were being attacked or saved by yet another supernatural creature. If, however, it *was* merely a wolf, I didn't want to stick around to find out where the rest of its pack lurked—now was the perfect time for Charlotte and me to escape the *bêtes de sang*.

Hugo aimed his pistol at the creature and fired, but the shot went wide, and the beast turned on him. Frederick hissed and pulled out his short sword, slashing wildly at the creature's back. The other soldiers rushed to Hugo's aid. He seemed to be having some trouble keeping the beast from closing its massive jaws around his neck.

"Now, Charlotte!" I urged. I grabbed her arm and hauled her up, running for Tartuffe.

I heard a snarl from behind us—whether it was the beast or the soldiers, I couldn't tell. Steps away from my horse, a great force yanked me back and I fell to the ground. I stared up into the vicious, grinning countenance of Hugo. Long, bloody gashes marred his face. He leveled his pistol at me.

"We're not done here, Lieutenant!" he shouted.

The vampires behind him had subdued the beast and were piling on top of it to hold it down, ready to shoot it at Hugo's word. The creature growled again and snapped at one of the soldiers, then pitched its head back and let out a guttural, unearthly howl. It sounded halfway between a wolf and a man in absolute agony. I shivered in fear.

Hugo turned toward the horrifying sound, and I reached for my sword but didn't move fast enough. From the darkness behind me, I heard Charlotte run forward. She kicked out at Hugo's knee with the full weight of her body, snapping his leg in two. Hugo screamed in pain as she fell on top of me, then rolled to the side in a predatory crouch. She snatched my short sword from my side and held it at Hugo's throat. He snarled at her and scraped his fangs across her arm, but she was too enraged to notice. She held him fast, aided by his sickeningly twisted broken leg.

"Let the beast go!" she yelled at the soldiers. "Or I will cut off your friend's head. I doubt that's a wound he will be able to recover from."

"Charlotte," I warned. "I don't think that's a good idea."

"I don't think it's after us," she said. "And I can't just leave it to the mercy of these monsters."

The soldiers eyed each other, frozen in fury. Charlotte

pressed the blade into Hugo's neck, drawing forth a line of thick, black blood. Hugo choked and screeched at his men. "Do as she says!"

The soldiers flinched and loosened their hold on the beast, whose large yellow eyes fixed on the blood dripping from Hugo's throat.

"Antoine," she said steadily. "On the count of three, we're going to make for your horse and get the Hell out of here. One... two...three!"

The last vampire let go of the beast and Charlotte shoved Hugo forward, precipitating a sickening collision of bone, blood, and fangs. Instantly, Charlotte and I jumped on Tartuffe's back and kicked him into a furious gallop. Behind us, I heard the ferocious sounds of a grim battle being waged—the creature's teeth, claws, and massive size against the vampires' fangs, speed, and superior numbers. My gut twisted, but the only thing that mattered now was the fact that neither enemy gave chase.

I looked down at the torn sleeve and oozing gash in Charlotte's shoulder—a shoulder that had been perfect and unmarred before I'd let my desires carry us into disaster and *very nearly* death. How could I have been so foolish? I wasn't a brainless adolescent! I was a man—a man who'd long ago learned how to control his baser urges and set aside fanciful romantic notions in the face of duty. Then, suddenly, this woman—this *dangerous* woman—showed up, and in the space of a few days, turned my entire world upside down. *Damn it, Antoine. What has gotten into you?*

Charlotte was making me lose sight of things—my vengeful action against Sade and the very real repercussions of that action, my father's betrayal and the *bêtes de sang*, my future beyond the military...not to mention the fact that I barely knew Charlotte and trusted her even less. Especially now that I'd seen her in action more than once. What kind of a spy took on five supernatural soldiers at once, didn't bat an eye at shooting a man in the gut, and knew exactly how to snap a man's leg in two with a well-placed jump kick? No kind of intelligence agent I knew—to say nothing of the fact she was a *woman* and a damned comtesse.

That certainly didn't stop you from pushing her up against a tree and taking advantage of her, I thought darkly. But the way she'd responded to my touch had unleashed something inside me—something I now recognized as nothing less than utter damnation. Given that we'd only just escaped the clutches of the *bêtes* and some unknown creature with God-knew-what motives, it was distressing that I was still fixated on Charlotte and her effect on me. I should be trying to understand our predicament, but... Well, I'd thought myself a fool for less.

My bitter oaths died on the wind as we galloped on, Charlotte clutching Tartuffe's mane in a pained grip. I knew we were some distance away from Gévaudan, but I didn't dare stop until we reached either the city gates or sunrise. I only hoped we could hold on until then.

"How's your shoulder?" I said at Charlotte's ear.

"I'll be all right," she called back to me. "I can dress the wound when we get to Gévaudan, but I don't want to stop if I can help it."

Her face was pale, and her brow was damp, but I hoped that was from the earlier rain and not the onset of shock and fever. The tattered fabric at her shoulder was dark with her spreading blood, much more than had been there moments before. If we didn't find shelter soon... I didn't want to consider the alternatives.

We raced on, eventually slowing to a trot. Tartuffe's sides heaved and Charlotte's eyes occasionally fluttered closed. Right about the time I was considering a rest, the sky began to lighten, and I saw Gévaudan appear in the shallow valley before us. Encircled by a lazy, aquamarine river, the medieval town of stonework buildings was at once charming and ominous. Surrounding the township was a wall of thick timbers that looked like they'd been built in a hurry—as did the pikes along the road that were topped with fly-infested wolf heads in various states of decay.

I nudged Charlotte awake as we approached two guards flanking an iron-spiked gate. Her face was distressingly pale and there were dark purple shadows beneath her eyes, but she snapped to attention like a solder at inspection.

"Charlotte, we've arrived. Hold on just a bit longer," I murmured.

She nodded and adjusted her cloak to cover her wounded shoulder. In a flash, her weariness and discomfort evaporated, and she pasted a dazzling smile on her face. Her ability to transform her entire countenance in an instant both impressed and disquieted me. *Could she turn so easily on me?*

The guards nodded at us. *"Bonjour.* What's your business in Gévaudan?"

"Just passing through," I said in what I hoped was a charming manner. "My new wife and I are on our way south, but we've run into some troubles along the road. We're stopping in for supplies and a couple nights of lodging while our carriage catches up to us. Broke a wheel some miles back and didn't want to wait it out in the poor weather."

"Any supernatural incidents on your journey here? Or particular allegiances to vampires?" The guard queried.

"Mon Dieu, non!" Charlotte gasped. "Certainly not. That's why we went out of our way to come through your fine commune in the first place—we knew we'd be safe from *paranormal* influences."

The guard eyed her and flicked his gaze to the sunrise over

his shoulder, apparently verifying our adherence to a daylight schedule.

"Very well. There's a curfew in effect. The gates are locked at sundown and unlocked at sunrise. Any wolf sightings or *unusual* behavior is to be reported."

"Goodness," Charlotte blinked. "That seems quite serious."

"Werewolf attacks, Madame. We've lost too many innocents not to take it seriously. But the beast only attacks at night and hasn't breached the wall yet. You'll be safe inside. There are three inns off the main street. You should be able to find lodging in one of them," he said. He stood to the side and pulled a massive lever, raising the iron-spiked gate. I dismounted and led Tartuffe and Charlotte through.

Once inside, with the *bêtes* and the creature behind us, I felt a flutter of relief, but it was fleeting. The early sun disappeared behind a blanket of clouds, casting a dim gray pall over everything. The hustle and bustle that I expected from an early market day was subdued and hurried, as if the town's residents were in a state of collective mourning—anxious to return to their homes as quickly as possible.

Off the main street, I noted a bakery and a couple of stalls of produce, as well as a modest-looking tailor and draper. As soon as we could find a room and I'd tended to Charlotte's shoulder, I'd head back out for supplies. I kept one eye on Charlotte, worried that she'd drop from Tartuffe, but though her face was strained and pale, she stared resolutely forward. It was hard not to admire her mettle, especially considering I'd seen soldiers in battle suffer lesser wounds and pass out in a dead faint.

There you go again, Antoine—mooning over this damn, dangerous woman that you swore to leave alone. Merde. I just needed some food, some rest, and some distance from her; that was all. *And the truth,* said a small voice in my head. *It bothers you that she's keeping secrets from you, even as you keep secrets from her, too.*

"What's the matter with you?" Charlotte asked, startling me. "We've made it to safety, and you look like you swallowed a lemon."

"I do not," I grumbled.

"Do so," she argued. "Besides, you weren't even injured. You don't see me scowling at a town full of grief-stricken countryfolk."

I exhaled wearily. "I'm just tired. It's been a long journey and I'm eager to find an inn."

Charlotte snorted.

"Well, we've already passed the one back there. Are you looking for a particular establishment or are you merely the persnickety sort?"

I swore under my breath. I'd been so distracted I'd completely missed the first of the three inns. Attempting to save face, I scanned the street ahead and saw a sign for one of the others, The Wild Rose.

"This one looks more comfortable. We'll stop in here," I said. Charlotte flashed a grin, but it quickly turned into a wince. I picked up our pace.

When we reached the inn, I helped Charlotte dismount, led Tartuffe around to the stables, and headed inside. Fortunately, it was empty, so we didn't attract too much attention. I repeated our now-familiar newlywed story, paid the dour innkeeper handsomely for the best room, a large meal, and a bath to be sent up, and practically collapsed with exhaustion and relief when I finally shut our door behind us.

Charlotte sank onto the bed and sighed. "Should we discuss what happened last night?"

I didn't know if she referred to our lustful entanglement, the *bêtes*, the horrifying creature, her saving me, or our lucky escape. I grimaced, knowing she likely meant all of it, but I didn't think either one of us had the energy to broach such overwhelming subjects just yet. I shucked off my damp coat and hung it next to the fire.

"We should, but I think it's best to wait until we've recovered a bit. Let's look at your shoulder, get some food and rest, and then figure things out."

Charlotte nodded, likely too tired to argue. "Antoine, might I prevail upon you to collect some supplies for my wound? I daresay I've had worse than this, and I know what's required to set it right."

I bristled at the idea that she'd had a worse wound than a lacerated shoulder, as well as at the idea that I couldn't—or wouldn't—tend to her.

"Will you let me look at it first, or does part of your treatment plan involve ordering capable men about?" I grumbled.

Her eyes widened in shock, then narrowed.

"You think you can care for me better than I can care for myself?"

"I didn't say that," I snapped. Fatigue was making me sharper than I wished to be.

"You certainly implied it! Are you a doctor as well as a soldier *as well as* an assassin? For all I know about you, Antoine, you may be since you've refused to tell me practically anything about yourself. Why should I trust you?" Her temper flared, catching me off guard. I had no desire to argue, but I was unable to stop myself from getting riled.

"Well, you obviously didn't have a problem trusting me to toss your skirts up and ravish you," I uttered darkly.

She gaped at me then and surprised me by tipping her head back and laughing.

"*'Ravish'* me! Oh, Antoine, the things you say sometimes. Positively delightful."

I scowled, reddening in embarrassment. "It shouldn't have happened. I…I apologize. I took liberties that I shouldn't have. I'm sorry."

"I'm not. Don't be ridiculous, Antoine. I'm hardly some blushing virgin. We both wanted it to happen, and we both participated, and I don't regret it. Of course, it makes things, what, complicated? Awkward? But we're adults, and as I told you, I've never been one for propriety." She flexed her arm and cringed again.

"We can discuss it later," I said quietly. "For now, please. You're obviously in pain. Allow me to assist you."

She sighed. "You are right, of course. I'm sure you've seen your fair share of battlefield trauma. It's not that I think you're incapable, it's just that I am rather used to looking after myself these days. The last time I allowed myself to be looked after, I'm afraid I was rather blindsided by a man who told me once too often not to worry—he'd take care of everything. And *Dieu,* he did take care of everything! Just not in a way that would have benefitted me at all." As she spoke, she began to disrobe, and I fought to keep my thoughts respectable.

"Was that your husband?" I asked, coming over to assist when she beckoned.

She fumbled with the ties on her bodice, a sign that her strength was wavering. The mark on her lower arm where Hugo had scratched her with his fangs seemed more superficial than serious, but it still infuriated me to think of him harming her. If he came after her again, I'd drive a stake through his heart and cut off his head, for good measure.

"Yes," she huffed. I peeled the blood-soaked fabric from her shoulder as gently as I could. She hissed in pain, and I frowned. Marring her perfect skin were three jagged cuts, just shallow enough to not need stitching. She kept perfectly still as I inspected them, flinching when I stood from the bed and accidentally jostled her.

"Well?" She gritted her teeth. She shivered slightly in her rain-damp chemise and stays. *Heaven help me.*

"You don't need stitches," I said. "But you'll probably have a scar."

"Lucky for me, exposed shoulders are out of fashion right now," she huffed with a forced laugh. "If you're going to treat me, please hurry. I'd rather not let it fester. I certainly hope you aren't a proponent of leeches and purgatives."

I shook my head. "I've seen too many men die from such ministrations. I'll wash and bandage it and see if the cook has any garlic and thyme oil for a poultice."

"Garlic and thyme oil? Do you plan on fashioning me into a stew?" she chuckled. The color had faded even more from her cheeks and lips, worrying me further. I stood and made for the door.

"I don't know why it works, but it does," I replied. "You'll just have to trust me."

"Trust is no small thing," she murmured.

I agreed. I offered her an encouraging smile, which she returned with an unfocused gaze.

She wavered slightly, then her eyes rolled white, and she passed out, falling backward onto the bed.

CHAPTER ELEVEN
CHARLOTTE

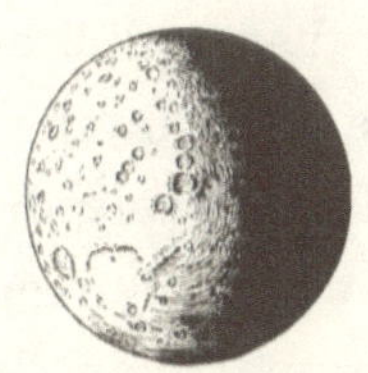

November 18, 1767
The Wild Rose
Gévaudan

I felt sunlight streaming in above me. Even though I kept my eyes tightly closed, its warmth was a comforting caress across my face. I was bombarded by a confusing array of scents—blood, herbs, flowers, freshly washed linen, leather, baking bread, burning wood.

I groaned. My throat burned from dehydration and disuse. *That can't be good. I wonder how long I've been in bed.*

Memories began to return to me, slowly, as if I could only see them from behind distorted glass—Sade's death, Antoine, vampire soldiers. The cold, rainy road to Gévaudan. A passionate embrace and brain-searing climax in a wooded glade, followed by a violent attack and a strange creature. Excruciating pain in my shoulder. Then the town and this inn.

But the sun was out now, and I sensed more than just Antoine nearby. How long had I been unconscious?

I cracked one eye open and looked around. Another cloak hung by the fire, but the room was otherwise empty. On the small table, I saw a tidy pile of bandages, small jars of medicines, and a set of severe-looking surgical instruments. Immediately, my hand went to my shoulder. It was wrapped in fresh bandages—as was the scrape on my arm from Hugo's teeth—but I didn't feel more than a dull ache from either injury. Whether it was Antoine or the mystery cloak owner, whoever had tended my arm had done a splendid job.

I rose, frowning down at my ragged chemise. I couldn't wait for a proper bath and some clean clothes. *Soon. Find Antoine first.* I went over to the cloak and felt around the pockets for any clue as to its wearer but came up empty. The garment was a lovely royal blue and was small and delicately cut, I suspected for a woman. I sniffed at the collar and sleeves and smelled faint odors of herbs, rain-damp wool, and something exotic, yet vaguely familiar—*lime blossom.*

"Van Helsing!" I exclaimed.

As if summoned, the curvy, dark-haired doctor bustled into the room carrying a cloth-covered tray. Lunch, perhaps. She regarded me with mild surprise, her deep blue eyes widening a fraction behind her spectacles.

"Ah, excellent! I had a feeling you'd be awake today," she said in her lilting Dutch accent.

"Where is Antoine?" I demanded. I flinched at the harshness of my tone. I hadn't meant to ask that, but the question had tumbled out of my mouth before any of the others. *What are you doing here? How long have I been in bed? What day is it? What of the vampires and that creature? Is there food on that tray? I'm ravenous.*

She cocked a brow at me and grinned. "After days at your bedside, the lieutenant was finally persuaded to get some much-needed food and rest. He's sound asleep next-door, in my bedroom."

At this, an unexpected flash of overheated anger and fierce possessiveness surged in my blood, screeching *"mine! He's mine,"* prompting me to practically growl at her.

"In *your* room?"

Van Helsing studied me intently over the rim of her spectacles, her eyes sparkling with curiosity.

"Very interesting," she murmured to herself. "Yes, Comtesse, he is resting in my chambers. It is nothing untoward, I assure you. In your comatose state, you thrashed about quite wildly, and he would not have been able to sleep in this room, let alone in that bed with you."

The explanation made sense, but I felt a tug of unease.

"Comatose state? What are you talking about? How long have I been here? How long have *you* been here? How did you even know to come here—and how did you get here in the first place?" The questions came on a rising tide of panic. *Something is certainly amiss.*

"Relax, please, before you overexert yourself. Here, sit on the bed and let me check your wounds. Yes, yes. Very good," she soothed as she led me back to the bed and started to unwrap my shoulder. "First, today is the 18th. You've been mostly unconscious for about two weeks now—"

"Two weeks!" I shrieked. "Tell me you're joking. It cannot have been so long."

"I'm afraid it has, Comtesse. You succumbed to a strange type of infection and a blood fever. Your friend, Lieutenant de Valle, did his best for you—and a fine job he did, I might add—but when you didn't recover after the first two days, he had the good sense to send an urgent message to your cousin. She, of course, had the *better* sense to send me to your aid, a wise move considering she and the duke would not be allowed to enter the city due to their supernatural condition."

Two years ago, Daphne introduced Doctor Van Helsing to me as the woman who'd saved her current husband's undead life. When Étienne, the vampire emissary to King Louis, had suffered an assassination attempt via quicksilver poisoning, Daphne had used her considerable influence and wealth to find the best vampire doctor in France—well, all of Europe, probably. Not only did Van Helsing heal Étienne, but she'd been instrumental in encouraging them to realize their love for one another.

After that, *les Dames Dangereuses* and even the men of The Order seldom used any other physician, and it became nearly impossible to secure her services due to the high demand for them. Fortunately for me, she and I had become friends of a sort, and she'd patched me up more times and in more ways than I cared to think about.

Her words whirled around in my head, giving rise to a new barrage of questions. *Strange type of infection?* I blanched. If the most eminent supernatural physician in Europe believed your illness *strange,* that certainly didn't bode well for you. And a blood fever? From a mere scratch? I reached for the shoulder she was still unwrapping, but she swatted my hand away.

"No, no," she tutted. "You're healing well now, but I won't have you corrupting the process. For once, Comtesse—*Charlotte*—do as I recommend and allow your body the proper time to recover. You are safe enough here for now. Lieutenant de Valle is helping to look after your needs, and Daphne and Étienne are in the next town over, waiting for you to be fit enough to meet with them. All is well. Simply rest. *Please.*"

Despite her making perfect sense, I scowled. "I've been *resting.* Now I feel rest*less.* At least give me leave to go check on Antoine. There are...things...we need to discuss."

Van Helsing regarded me for a moment, then went back to her examination of my shoulder. She pressed firmly into the tender flesh, and I expected to draw back in pain, but felt no more than a fleeting discomfort. *Strange, indeed.*

"Remarkable," the doctor muttered to herself.

"What's remarkable?" I replied, unable to see what she was marveling at beneath the mound of linen piled up on my shoulder.

Before she could answer, the door exploded open and Antoine barreled in, twin pistols drawn. Van Helsing and I jumped.

"You're awake!" Antoine said in a tone of stunned confusion. He lowered the pistols. "I'm sorry. I heard voices and I thought perhaps someone else had..." He trailed off and blushed. Taking a tentative step into the room, he cast accusing eyes upon Van Helsing. "Doctor, you promised to tell me the moment she awakened."

Van Helsing rolled her eyes. "Lieutenant, you needed sleep just as much as she did. Incidentally, she woke only a few minutes before you burst in here with your inappropriate weapons drawn." She shook her head. "You French, with all your hotblooded violence and passions. It's a wonder the entire country hasn't come down with apoplexy."

Antoine's jaw worked, clenching and unclenching as if he had a great deal to say to the doctor but was trying very hard to restrain himself.

"Comtesse," he coughed out awkwardly. "Are you well? I mean, how are you feeling?"

"I'm fine, Antoine, really. Remarkably well, even," I said with a smile. "With Doctor Van Helsing's care—and with your care, she tells me—and the rest of several days, I feel almost as good as new."

He nodded. "Excellent. Outstanding." He cleared his throat

and fiddled with his loose cuff. Van Helsing watched his discomfort with growing amusement.

"Well, I've been up for some time. I do believe it is my turn to get some sleep now. Lieutenant, do keep an eye on our patient. Please try not to overexcite her or let her engage in any *vigorous* activity. I'll check in again later this evening," the doctor said, trying unsuccessfully to hide a smile.

Antoine looked murderous but nodded. "Thank you, Doctor."

Van Helsing winked at me, packed up her small valise of supplies, and headed for her room, leaving Antoine and I in what had become an uncomfortable silence. I took in his disheveled appearance and wondered how much of it was the result of prolonged stress at my illness and how much of it was because he'd obviously woken from sleep in a panicked state.

"We must talk," he said abruptly.

"Of course," I replied. I scooted over to make room for him, but he eyed the bed uneasily and dragged a chair over to sit directly in front of me.

"You were ill. Feverish. For days!" His manner was oddly accusatory.

I balked. "My apologies. Next time, I'll be sure to align my social calendar with yours before taking sick."

Antoine's green eyes sparked with irritation and barely restrained emotion. "I didn't know what to do when you wouldn't wake."

I was struggling to follow his line of overset inquiry.

"I can understand that," I said slowly, treading carefully. "But contacting my cousin was clearly the right choice."

"For *you*, perhaps!" he countered.

My brows rose in surprise. Suddenly very tired, I laid back against the pillows on the bed and waited. It was obvious he needed to get something off his chest, but what it was, I couldn't tell. After a few moments, he ran his fingers through his hair, tugging the dark waves from his queue. His scar flexed white, contrasting sharply against the tan of his skin and the dark stubble of beard on his cheeks.

"I put myself at great risk," he said finally. "Your cousin and her husband are more than just nobility. They're *dangerous*, Charlotte, and they know I'm involved with Sade's murder and your...your...disappearance."

"Is that what worries you? Honestly, Antoine, it will be fine. I'll explain everything to them. They're not like other aristocrats."

"That's not the point," he said in exasperation. He stood and paced the room.

"What is the point, then? You seem to be driving toward something, and I'll be damned if I can figure out what it is. If you're angry, then speak plainly and let us have it out."

"I cannot be around you, Charlotte!" he shouted. "Your very presence is a distraction and a danger to me. When you are recovered, we must part ways."

Shocked and stung by his outburst, I tried to quickly cover my hurt. "Fine. But you kidnapped *me,* remember. I've been trying to part ways with you since I regained consciousness."

"I've been trying to protect you," he grumbled.

"Well, I don't need your protection," I shot back.

He eyed my wounded shoulder and scoffed. "Yes, I forgot. You're some secret agent for a mysterious, mythical order of powerful zealots charged with protecting the people of France from supernatural threats."

"That's not entirely correct, but you're on the right track," I replied tartly.

"Ha!"

"At least I explained my reasons for attempting to kill Sade," I said. "You've been perfectly content to keep your own secrets and not offer me anything. You could be some escaped lunatic who hunts down noblemen with crossbows just to pass the time. Or maybe you're a social radical, trying to steadily eliminate the aristocracy...perhaps even a jealous, scorned lover of the torturous madman and you came out to settle a score."

Anger bloomed in his expression, turning his whole face red and his jade eyes wild. I sensed I'd touched a nerve, but I wasn't sure which one.

"Silence!" he bellowed. "For the love of God, can't you be anything other than aggravating?"

I glared at him. "Can't *you* be anything other than infuriating? If you're so aggravated and I'm such an inconvenient distraction and a danger to you, then *leave!* I didn't ask you to remain!" To emphasize my point, I threw one of the pillows at him. Despite the action startling him, he caught it mid-air. *The battle-hardened reflexes of a soldier.*

"I will," he fired back, but his tone had lost some of its edge. "As soon as you're well again."

"I'm fine," I sniffed. "How many times do I have to tell you? I don't need your protection."

"Maybe you don't," he said wearily. "But you have it anyway. I am honor-bound."

"Oh, *hang* your honor," I tossed back. I almost winced at how petulant I sounded.

"I won't," he said sullenly. "My honor is all I have left."

I snorted in derision. "This from a man who kills without reason."

His eyes snapped to mine. "Never. There is *always* a reason."

"What, your own perverse pleasure?"

He looked at me then, anger waning, and came to sit at the foot of the bed. He stared at his boots, or perhaps it was the floor, but either way, he could not meet my eyes. He was quiet for a time, thinking, and when he spoke, his voice was thick with emotion again. Not anger, this time, but a haunted sadness. My heart clenched and I suspected I would regret my words.

"I killed Sade for revenge," he said quietly. "Not for my own perverse pleasure, though I'd be lying if I said I didn't feel some satisfaction from watching him die."

"Who was he to you?" I asked.

He blew out a breath. "To me? A stranger, in fact."

I made a noise of frustration, and he finally looked up at me.

"He was not a stranger to my sister, Marie, or to her son, Louis. Marie's husband died some years ago, leaving them in dire circumstances. My nephew was still a boy then. Marie was utterly shattered. It had been a love match, you see. He'd been a tailor, exceptionally skilled but barely able to put bread on the table. My father never approved of the match and withheld his wealth and connections only until Marie was desperate. He only stepped in to offer assistance on the condition that he would be in charge of Louis's education and upbringing. Marie had no choice but to agree. She thought my father would send Louis to the elite military academy that he'd attended, but instead, my father wanted more for the boy. He wanted Louis to have better for himself—connections, a chance for a wealthy match, exposure to a world that was now beyond Marie's reach. To do this, my father reached out to an old friend from school—from the military academy."

"Sade," I breathed. "Your father and he were friends?"

Antoine's jaw tightened and he nodded once.

"My father is a brilliant general, Charlotte. He never loses in battle because he will sacrifice *anything* to get what he wants. The lives of others mean nothing to him. I can only imagine what he offered Sade in exchange for Louis's tutelage and introduction to court. I shudder to think."

I chewed on my lip. "You think your father offered Sade Louis's innocence in order to gain his aristocratic influence?"

He nodded. "Four and a half months after Louis was sent to Sade, we received word that he'd taken ill and died. Marie was inconsolable with grief, so I retrieved Louis's body myself to make the funeral preparations. If it was illness that took Louis's life, I'll throw myself into the Seine," he said bitterly.

"What do you mean? How did he die?"

"I recognize signs of torture when I see them, Charlotte. The marks on his body—it was unspeakable. He was only fourteen years old." A muscle below his eye ticked, and it struck me that perhaps he wanted to shed tears for his nephew and sister but simply refused. He clenched his fist. "Of course, most people didn't know about Sade's reputation for depravity at that point, but the rumors would soon follow. Louis became just one of a number of the marquis's victims."

"Do you really think your father knew? That he willingly sent his own grandson into the clutches of a vile predator?" I asked, astonished.

"At first, I didn't think so. But the more I grieved, the angrier I got. How could my father not have known about his friend's inclinations? Eventually, I confronted him. We were stationed on the island of Menorca in the Mediterranean then, after the treaty had been signed and the fighting had ended. I'd had a letter from Marie. She was...unwell. Alone and grief-stricken, I think her mind wandered to the same place that mine did. *Did Father know?*"

He paused, swallowing several times. I could see that he wanted to go on, that he needed to, but it was too hard for him. Compelled by the look of pain on his face, I grasped one of his hands. This seemed to steel him. Finally, he continued. "I cornered him one evening in his study. *'Of course, I knew, you fool!'* He told me I was naive and weak for allowing my grief to get the better of me, that Louis should have been stronger, and that it was Marie's fault for birthing a whelp from such a disappointing match. *'Sade is a brute and a scoundrel, but the world is full of them, Antoine. You're just too stupid to learn how to use them to your advantage!'* I couldn't believe it. I lunged at him. I managed to get two good punches in before his guards dragged me away and beat me senseless."

"The *bêtes*, you mean?"

He nodded. "They hadn't been turned yet, but soon after. I wrote to Marie that night, but I didn't tell her the truth. I couldn't. I told her that Father hadn't known, but that I would set things right anyway. I thought I was sparing her emotions from any more blows, but I needn't have worried. She took her own life before we made it back home. I told my father it was all his fault—both her death and Louis's death were on his hands. He didn't care. *'I'm on my way to becoming the most formidable general in France, Antoine. There's more blood on my hands than you could possibly imagine.'* When we arrived home, I packed up and left, unable to think about anything other than making Sade pay for what he'd done."

"And your father?" I asked.

Antoine turned intense, emotion-filled eyes on me.

"He's next."

CHAPTER TWELVE
ANTOINE

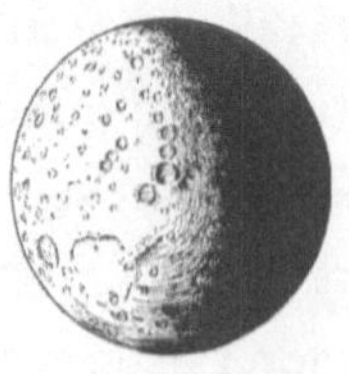

November 18, 1767
The Wild Rose
Gévaudan

Charlotte sucked in a breath. "You're going after your father?"

I nodded.

"To kill him?"

"After taking out the *bêtes de sang,* that is my intent," I replied coolly.

Charlotte huffed out a breath. "Oh, certainly. Of course. Once you dispense with an elite vampire death squad—all *five* of them—it'll be no trouble at all to find and defeat one of the most formidable generals in France. I'm sure he *hasn't* connected you to Sade's death and surely *isn't* expecting you to do something so foolish in your anger and grief." Her voice dripped with sarcasm.

"He is too proud and too entitled to think of me as a serious threat," I argued.

"He is your *father*, Antoine! Even if you do manage to exact your revenge on him, have you thought nothing of the consequences? The danger you're already in for Sade's murder will be that much harder to escape when your own flesh and blood perishes by the same *mysterious* crossbow ailment. Those who know your family will make the connection. As glad as I am that the world is rid of a man like Sade, there will be repercussions for his death, which is why *I* was sent to take care of him. Things were meant to go according to plan and now they are decidedly more...*sticky*."

"It's not just my personal vengeance, Charlotte. There are other things he has done that he must answer for. Of course, I've considered the consequences to my actions, but if hanging is the price to pay for justice and for the safety of all the innocents spared by Sade's depravity and my father's ambition, then so be it. Besides, as I told you before, I have every intention of parting ways with you as soon as you're out of danger," I said firmly.

"*Dieu* spare me from the misguided pride of men!"

Charlotte's stomach rumbled and she rubbed at her temples. She'd said she felt better when I first came into her room, but I could tell she was tiring, and I had no desire to argue with her, especially after I'd revealed so much about myself. Not only had I told her about my family's private trauma and my plans for killing my own father—dangerous enough, given that I was still trying to work out how much to trust her—but I'd practically admitted my desire for her was driving me to distraction. *You may as well just tell her she holds all the cards, you fool.*

The longer I stayed, the harder it was for me to maintain my distance. I'd been so devastated by her poor health, I thought I'd go mad. Every night, I watched her violent thrashing in bed, I prayed for her, calling out to a God that I'd long abandoned who had no reason to come to my aid. I watched her weaken in her fevered dreams and had curled myself around her protectively, deludedly hoping to impart some of my own strength through the merest touch of skin. I could only hope she had no memory of my weakness, my soft kisses on her damp brow and velvet caresses on her back, trying to hold her nightmares at bay. It certainly wasn't the behavior fitting the toughened, emotionally calloused man I'd fought to become.

I convinced myself that my desperate need to save her was because I'd failed so long ago to save Marie, but at this point, I had to admit that I'd grown...*fond* of her. It infuriated me beyond words. When I'd come into the room to see her conversing easily with the pretty Dutch doctor, I'd almost sunk to my knees in sheer gratitude that she'd made it through the worst of the illness and would soon return to her vivacious, exasperating self. Of course, it had been much easier for me to reach for my near constant anger than to throw myself at her, strip her bare, and kiss every inch of her skin.

I stood to go.

"Wait—where are you going? I still need to know what's happened these last two weeks. Have you seen or heard anything of the *bêtes* or that creature? Are we going to discuss what, exactly, we think we encountered that night?"

"Rest, Charlotte," I said. "I can tell your strength is waning. We'll discuss everything later."

"I feel fine! I've had just about enough of people telling me to rest. I've been resting for two weeks, and I want to know what the Hell is going on," she growled in frustration. She slammed her fist down on the bedside table.

It shattered into a jumble of splintered wood.

We both stared in shock at her fist, which looked none the worse for wear.

"How did you do that?" I demanded, coming over to inspect her hand.

"I...don't know," she replied in bewilderment. "Perhaps it was an exceptionally weak table, the cheaply made kind, you know? I didn't think I struck it that hard, but... I don't know, Antoine."

Her astonishment turned to concern.

"I'll fetch Doctor Van Helsing," I offered.

Charlotte nodded, dumbstruck.

"Don't bother," came a bleary voice at the door. "You two make so much noise, a person cannot sleep anyway." Van Helsing entered and rubbed at her eyes, then caught sight of the destroyed table. If she was surprised, it did not show. She regarded Charlotte carefully. "I take it you did this?"

Charlotte nodded again.

Van Helsing pulled Charlotte's hand from mine and turned it over. There wasn't a mark to be seen.

"Hmm," the doctor mused. She unwound the bandage from the smaller cut on Charlotte's forearm, where Hugo's teeth had found purchase. Beneath the linen wrappings, the skin appeared unblemished.

"That is interesting," Van Helsing murmured, more to herself than anyone else. Finally, she unwrapped Charlotte's shoulder and tossed the bandages aside, revealing unmarred, perfect skin.

"It appears you have healed," Van Helsing said simply.

"Healed?!" I exclaimed. "Doctor, no wound could have healed so fast. It looks like she was never in that attack to begin with. What the Hell is going on?"

"Van Helsing," Charlotte murmured, her voice barely a whisper. "I have only seen people recover from injuries this quickly because of one reason. Tell me, please. Have I succumbed to the blood plague? Am I a vampire?"

I could have sworn I saw a shadow of concern cross Van Helsing's face, but it faded so quickly, I might have imagined it.

"Vampire? No," Van Helsing said quietly. "Look, Charlotte. You're sitting quite peacefully in pure sunlight."

Charlotte tilted her face up toward the window and held her arms out before her, letting the late afternoon rays spill across her skin.

"Vampires cannot do so," Van Helsing continued. "Do you feel any ill effects?"

"No," Charlotte replied. "No, I feel rather good, actually. Quite hungry, though." Punctuating this statement was a rumble from her stomach. She chuckled. "Apologies."

"I'll get you something to eat," I offered. "There's a bakery just down the way."

"Are there any butcher shops in town?" Charlotte asked. "I'm ravenous for something more fortifying than bread. A joint of mutton, perhaps, or some beef? I've plenty of coin in my purse. In fact, that would be a delightful errand for me to get out and stretch my legs. Don't bother fetching me anything, Antoine. I shall go myself." She made to stand, but Van Helsing held her back.

"Relax, Charlotte," the doctor said. Her tone turned cryptic. "I have something here for you."

She went to a small wooden table with a cloth-covered tray and came forward. Charlotte sighed.

"Again, you attempt to imprison me here against my will. You're lucky I'm too famished to care and that whatever gastronomical delights you have on that tray smell too delicious for me to belabor the point. Is it stew? Bring it here, Van Helsing."

The destroyed table all but forgotten in the wake of Charlotte's hunger, the doctor brought the tray forward, a line of worry creasing her brow. She set it on the foot of Charlotte's bed and removed the cloth.

It was a thick slice of beef, so rare that I couldn't be certain it wasn't actually raw. Charlotte stared at the meat, then lifted her eyes to Van Helsing.

"I...I don't understand," she said, the fear and worry from earlier creeping back into her tone. She wrinkled her nose at the plate when Van Helsing pushed it toward her. "I can't eat that! It's practically mooing! Send it back, please, and have them cook it properly."

Van Helsing sighed. "Charlotte, listen to me. I have only seen something like this once before. I'm not even entirely sure that I'm right about it, but all your symptoms... Well, assuming this is the same thing, I fear you may have contracted a variation of the blood plague."

My jaw dropped. Charlotte paled.

"But you said I'm not a vampire! The sunlight—look!" Charlotte cried, flinging back the sheets and standing. "I don't have fangs!"

"No, you're not a vampire. To become a vampire means an exchange of blood has taken place—you must feed and have been fed on. But this...this is something different. There is some other fluid exchange or combination that has taken place in your bodily humors. You were scratched by the *bête* and scratched by this mysterious creature out in the woods. Antoine said it was like a wolf, yes?"

Charlotte nodded in horror.

"This is preposterous," I exclaimed. "You can't be serious, Doctor. Two illnesses changing into something completely different in a person's body? Outrageous. There must be some other explanation."

"I'm not entirely certain myself, Lieutenant. It's just that all these symptoms fit. The rapid recovery and extraordinary healing, the inexplicable strength, the enhanced sense of smell, the desire for meat..." the doctor ticked these off on her fingers.

"I most certainly do *not* desire that bloody meat," Charlotte began, her voice rising in hysteria. Her eyes glittered as she looked at the plate of raw beef, and I doubted the validity of her refusal. "What are you suggesting, exactly? That I've become some vampire-like wolf creature?" The realization struck her like a blow. "I'm...I'm a damned werewolf?!"

Van Helsing's mouth twisted in a frown, and she shrugged helplessly. "As I said, I don't know for certain."

"There are several problems with your reasoning," I argued, finding this all utterly unbelievable. "Charlotte isn't sprouting fur all over her body and howling at the moon."

"Well, it *is* the afternoon. We don't know what will happen when the moon rises," Van Helsing reasoned. Then, upon seeing the frightened expression on Charlotte's face, tried to backtrack. "Allow me to run some small experiments. I could be wrong about all of this. I've only seen something like it once before, and that was a long time ago. It wasn't even the *same thing* exactly, but...*merde*. Charlotte, I'm sorry. We just don't know enough about this particular disease—the blood plague, I mean—to rule anything out. We've only just started to understand how it works, and even then, more by luck than any scientific triumph. I cannot tell you not to worry, but I can tell you that I will do everything in my power to help you. We will do our best to figure this out, all right?"

A tear spilled from Charlotte's eye, but she nodded. "Of course. Thank you, Van Helsing."

I couldn't believe she was accepting this ridiculous diagnosis. *What a notion!* It was only days ago that I was having to convince her of the possibility of werewolves existing, and here she was, suddenly accepting that she herself had become one.

It's absurd! The doctor had to be wrong. There had to be another explanation.

I opened my mouth to speak, but Charlotte held up her hand in warning.

"Please," she said in a small voice. "I need some time to think. Doctor. Antoine. I'd like to be left alone for a little while."

Van Helsing nodded and gestured at the plate of meat. "Try to eat something. You're still recovering, and you'll need your strength to get through this."

I watched the doctor leave and turned back to Charlotte.

"Don't believe a word of it," I urged. "What she's suggesting...it's impossible."

"Please, Antoine. Leave me alone right now. I need to think."

"Fine. I'll go get you some *real* food. From the bakery! Bread, tarts, pastries, whatever you wish. Asparagus and poached eggs, if I can manage it. Don't worry, Charlotte. All is not lost." I stepped close to her, unable to resist running my fingers along her cheek. She turned away from me, and I frowned.

"I'm sorry, I—"

"Just go," she insisted.

Feeling hopeless, angry, confused, and a thousand kinds of foolish, I did as she asked. As I closed the door behind me, I caught a final glimpse of her burying her head in her hands. Suddenly, my earlier words came back to haunt me. *When you are recovered, we must part ways.* Oh, Antoine, you utter ass.

How can I leave her now?

CHAPTER THIRTEEN
CHARLOTTE

November 18, 1767
The Wild Rose
Gévaudan

I STARED IN DEFEATED DISGUST AT THE SLAB OF MEAT ON THE PLATE. My stomach rumbled shamefully. *It is like a steak,* I thought to myself. *Only it is quite rare. Just eat it, Charlotte. You have had worse before.* I picked up the silverware on the tray and cut into it, my vision blurring behind a veil of hot tears that gathered in my eyes.

How could this be? *A werewolf!* A kind of mutation of the insidious blood plague that had so challenged and changed our country. It didn't feel real. I glanced at the pile of splintered wood on the floor next to my bed and frowned. *I didn't hit it that hard, did I?*

Closing my eyes, I took a bite of the meat. The moment it touched my tongue, I gave up an involuntary sigh of relief. It tasted heavenly—like the best meal I'd ever had, multiplied by a thousand. I opened my eyes to look at the plate in a warped hope that it had somehow transformed into something else, but it hadn't. A tear slipped down my cheek as I took another bite. *No doubt about it now, Charlotte. You're eating raw meat and it's the best damn thing you've ever had.*

Grateful to be alone, I allowed the tears to fall as I devoured every scrap before me. Immediately, I felt strength return to my muscles and my senses sharpen to a previously unknown degree. Sounds became clearer, smells became more complex—even my eyesight intensified. I looked out the window at a tree some miles away and was able to count the leaves on one autumnal branch. *Seventy-two.* The distortion of the glass windowpane didn't hinder me a bit.

I took a deep breath and focused on the new feelings in my body. Physically, I felt the same as before, but with an added intensity and acuity. I simply felt *more.*

Was this what vampires felt when they turned?

Or werewolves? Or was this unique to me and my deviation?

I certainly didn't feel like a *wolf.* I still felt like a woman—like me, Charlotte. Did I look different? Would I behave differently? Was everything about me bound to change in the same way as my appetite? I grew melancholy at the thought. It had taken me a long time to recover from the disaster of a few years ago and my marriage to Philippe. I'd only just accepted myself in this new role as an agent of The Order and *les DD,* and because of one disastrous assignment, I now found myself having to accept a whole new identity. *Again.*

I didn't know how long I sat in bed staring out the window, but by the time I came to my senses, the warmth of the afternoon had cooled, and the sky had melted into a lovely sherbet sunset. I couldn't just sit here any longer. If I was what Van Helsing suggested—*a werewolf*—I needed to be certain. I needed to understand more about myself...more about this condition. Feeling stronger and having enhanced senses was a far cry from growing fur and running amok on all fours, baying for blood. *Or would that be howling for meat?* Who was to say that was how this blood plague variant would manifest?

Van Helsing said she wanted to run some tests on me.

Well, *I* wanted to run a few of my own.

Resolved, I threw back the covers and went to the corner wardrobe. *Finally, a spot of luck!* My borrowed wool gown and underclothes were clean and folded inside. I donned them quickly and tiptoed quietly from the room and down the stairs. I hoped Van Helsing and Antoine were resting and wouldn't hear me sneak out. I needed some time alone to figure things out before they showed up at my bedside fretting over something that none of us really understood. *Yet.*

I pulled the hood of my cloak over my bound hair and lace cap, hoping there wouldn't be any boisterous men around to trouble me. It was early enough in the evening that I didn't think there would be too many drunken louts about, especially in a somber town bracing for the next disaster, but one never knew. Trouble could find a lady anywhere.

Heading out the door, I turned in the opposite direction from the town's front gate. This way appeared less populated than the main streets. I pulled my cloak around me and tried to keep to the lengthening shadows. It would be dark soon, and then it'd be easier for me to stay hidden from prying eyes in a town of only humans. *A town of only humans!* I wrinkled my nose in distaste at the thought—as if I was already thinking myself better than human.

I furrowed my brows. *No, it is more than that.* Aside from the fact that Daphne and Étienne—my friends, nay, family—were vampires, I felt a sense of unsettling tension in a town that considered all supernatural beings evil. In Paris, all but the aristocracy had overwhelmingly accepted the inevitability of the blood plague. Certainly, that was out of necessity rather than widespread ill intent—it was better to drink blood than starve to death. Being in Gévaudan, a town that shut out the rest of the world because of fear, made me worry over the other parts of France. Étienne often said a revolution was coming—a war between vampires and humans. If he was right, I was sure the vampires would take Paris, but what would happen in all the small towns like Gévaudan? I dreaded to think.

I picked up my pace and found what I'd been hoping for—an unmanned back gate set into the town wall. Through the bars, I saw a rickety bridge set over the river and a dusty road disappearing into the dark forest beyond. The gate looked easy enough to scale, but because night hadn't fully descended, I reasoned it would be less noticeable to simply pick the large, iron padlock than to hoist my skirts and risk someone seeing me climb the wall.

I pulled out a hairpin and deftly picked the lock, being sure to close the gate behind me on my way out of town. I hoped I wasn't putting the people of Gévaudan at some great, unknown risk by defying their lockdown orders, but if I was to understand all that had happened to me, I needed a secluded space to do so.

Besides, if I *did* manage to transform into some kind of wolf creature, I didn't think a town as anti-supernatural as Gévaudan would approve of my doing so within one of their inns.

Once I crossed the bridge and reached the line of trees marking the edge of the forest, I allowed myself a sigh of relief. I'd managed a tidy little escape from the confines of the town. I walked along the road winding through the woods for what felt like hours, but as the dusky sunset faded and night gathered in around me, I marveled at the lack of exhaustion that would have normally overtaken me. Rather, I felt energized. I considered that was because I'd been cooped up in an inn for two weeks, but a small voice in my head suggested it was linked to the rise of the large, luminous moon.

Merde.

I stared up at it, wondering what one had to do to transform. If I were a werewolf—*you probably are a werewolf, Charlotte*—how would I change? Did it just happen? Did I have to do something? Did I need to be naked? Did it start with a growl or a howl?

Feeling a bit foolish, even though I was alone in a dark forest, I took a deep breath, tipped my head back, and let out a howl.

Nothing happened. It sounded nothing like a wolf, though... Perhaps I needed to practice? Should I be louder?

Maybe I needed to be deeper in the woods to really *feel* my "inner wolf." I shrugged and stepped off the road, weaving through the trees and bushes. At last, I came upon a small grassy hill that looked rather romantic in the moonlight. If I were a werewolf—*again, Charlotte, you probably are a werewolf*—this was where I would promenade.

I sat down on the grass, spread my skirts around me, and tried howling once more. Again, nothing happened. *Charlotte, you really have lost your mind.* I blew out a breath of frustration. The moon was high now, but I felt as normal as I ever had.

Perhaps Van Helsing was wrong. Maybe the infection had healed, and the table had been shoddy, and everything I'd been sensing had been the bodily culmination of an inordinate amount of stress. One could only hope.

Right, Charlotte, give this one more attempt, then if nothing happens, we'll return to the inn, tell Van Helsing she is wrong, and continue on our merry way, with or without Antoine.

Satisfied, resolute, I stripped my clothes off until I was completely bare. I folded them neatly, set them aside, and strolled to the top of the hill. It was remarkably freeing, being utterly naked out in a forest, and felt exceptionally sinful. I breathed deeply, inhaling the scents of frost-glittered grass, ancient trees, moss, and dirt. I closed my eyes and stilled my mind as much as possible, focusing on the sensations of the world around me. My stomach churned—*probably the raw meat disagreeing with me*—and I started to feel lightheaded. Oddly, it only now occurred to me that I didn't feel the cold at all.

Something inside me seemed to be gathering, drawing up, tightening. There was nothing for it now. I was going to try this one more time and then put the whole thing behind me.

Ignoring any remaining whispers of self-consciousness and shame, I dropped to all fours on top of the hill, tilted my head back, and howled with everything that vibrated through me. Blood rushed through my ears as distantly, the answering howl of another wolf pierced the night.

Merde.

Pain exploded in my body. I screamed and fell to the earth, writhing in agony. Every nerve was on fire, every bone breaking, every inch of skin scraping away from my flesh. I howled again, this time involuntarily, and only briefly registered the alien timbre of my voice. *What is happening to me?*

But I knew. Deep down, through the haze of torment, I knew what was happening. I sobbed my acceptance of it, and as I feared, the sound reverberated as a distinctly canine whimper.

Abruptly, the pain ceased. Dread like I'd never felt before pooled in my mind, and I was loath to open my eyes. Everything felt different. Everything *was* different. I didn't want this to be real. It needed to be a nightmare that I would wake up from soon, cuddled in bed with some courtly fop. *Or Antoine.*

I cracked one eye open and looked down. What I saw made my heart sink.

A mutant paw in place of a hand, tipped with long, sharp claws. An arm covered in glossy dark fur. Something brushed me from behind, and I whipped around to catch it—*mon Dieu, a tail!*

"I have a bloody tail!" I tried to scream, but of course it came out as a warped growl.

Mon Dieu. Yes, Charlotte, it's true. You're a werewolf.

Panic seized me. I needed to see just what I looked like. Was I an actual wolf? Or some kind of twisted monster? *If only I had my looking glass.* Then I remembered the river around the town. I could certainly see my reflection in that.

I attempted to stand, rather stupidly, and fell forward onto all fours. I took a few hesitant steps in this shortened creature form, gradually learning the muscle movements, and stumbled down the hill. It took a little bit of time, but eventually, I accustomed myself to walking with these strange, new limbs. One foot—*er, paw*—in front of the other. I traced my steps back toward the town, avoiding the road as much as possible. I didn't want to stumble upon any late-night travelers, and I certainly didn't want to be seen by the *bêtes* or found by Antoine.

Soon I came upon the river, black and glittering in the light of the moon. I padded down to the water and braced myself. I peered in.

What looked back at me wasn't simply a wolf. From a distance, perhaps, I might look like one, but I had a shorter muzzle, longer teeth, and loping gangly limbs. *I am a monster!* I tried to contain the cry of anguish but could not. I unleashed another chilling howl that—had I still been human—would have terrified me to hear in the distance.

I sat at the edge of the river, my awkward haunches folded beneath me. I stared into the water at my red-brown eyes for what felt like ages, contemplating my new aberrant existence, wondering how and why I'd been cursed, if there was a way back to a normal life, what it would mean for my future—if, indeed, I had a future. Were there others with this condition? Van Helsing had mentioned one other, but surely there were more. I couldn't be the only one with this horrifying variation of the blood plague, could I?

Gradually, the sky began to pale to a blueish purple, and I realized with a wave of anxiety that sunrise was coming, and I'd left my clothes at the top of the hill. More importantly, I needed to figure out how to change back into, well, *me*.

I started to run, digging my claws into the damp earth and pushing myself forward. I'd never moved so fast before. Trees became a blur of brown and silver as I raced past. I leaped over fallen logs and brambles, feeling like I was truly flying. For a moment, my cares were all but forgotten.

I reached the hill in no time and trotted up to my neatly folded pile of garments. I laid down on the ground and took a deep breath, reaching for that place inside that I'd found earlier this evening. I quieted my mind, thought of my human body, tilted my head back and howled.

Again, the answering howl of another far-off wolf, only this time, he seemed closer than before. Then came the fluttering in my stomach, the strange lightheadedness, and the gathering of something from within.

Then, the explosive pain. *Putain de merde!* It felt less intense than before, though still excruciating, and I wasn't sure if that was because I was going from monster to human, or perhaps because I was mentally prepared for the utter agony of changing shape.

I was momentarily dazed when it stopped, but was immediately overset with exhaustion and hunger. I donned my clothes quickly, certain I looked horribly disheveled. *Almost as if you spent the night romping about through the woods like a wild* woman—*or a werewolf,* I thought with a frown. *Dieu. How am I going to explain this to Antoine?*

My heart pounded as I made my way down the hill toward the road again. I couldn't tell him. He thought Van Helsing was mad to even consider this. Besides, he'd already told me he had every intention of going off on his own, on his stupid revenge mission to kill his father. *Imbecile.* He didn't want to carry on with me, anyway, so why *would* I have to tell him? Let him think the doctor was crazy, that I was healed and healthy from the accident thanks to my impeccable constitution, and that I was going back to my normal, happy life back in Paris. He could believe all the lies I was giving up on telling myself.

And that is that, I thought with a vague sense of loss.

"Excuse me, Madame, but are you in need of some assistance?"

Lost in my own misery, I hadn't noticed the approach of a figure from behind. Somewhat odd, considering my new supernatural senses took in everything all at once. I turned around to see a man on the road behind me, dressed in clothes so black they seemed to absorb every ray of light from the growing dawn.

The man removed his tricorne in a graceful sweep and bowed. His long black hair was pulled into a loose queue, and black eyes glittered beneath thick, dark brows. He was handsome, in an eerie sort of way.

"I heard you muttering to yourself," he said with a slight accent. "You seem distressed."

I felt my hackles rise—*wait, do I still have hackles?*

I surreptitiously rubbed a hand on the back of my neck. Nope. No fur. *Dieu, Charlotte, pull yourself together! Remember who you are! You are an agent of les Dames Dangereuses and a comtesse, for goodness sake!*

And...a werewolf?

I straightened.

"I wasn't muttering," I said firmly. "And it is improper for you to address me, as we haven't been introduced, but I'll forgive you this time, since you seem the chivalrous sort. Although...perhaps I shouldn't make that assumption, given you're suspiciously traipsing about through the countryside with no horse, carriage, or apparent aim."

The dark man chuckled. "Forgive any impropriety. Your French customs are unknown to me. I'm here to visit a friend in the area and figured I'd make an early start."

I arched a brow. Something about him was familiar, but I didn't think we'd met. He couldn't be with the *bêtes*, could he?

"Are you?" he took a careful step toward me. "In distress, I mean."

"No," I snapped, suddenly uneasy.

He nodded once and a small smile slowly tugged at the corners of his lips.

"I don't mean to frighten you," he said silkily. "I only wish to see you safely to your destination. Where I come from, it's dangerous for young ladies to be out on the roads alone."

"I'm fine," I said. "The town is not far, and I'd prefer my own company than that of a stranger."

"Ah," he said, taking another step to close the distance between us. "So, you are in distress."

"Whether or not I am in distress is *really* none of your concern," I replied. "I appreciate your noble intention, sir, but wish to continue on my way."

The haughtiness in my tone would have offended most men. The man in black, however, was unmoved. He continued to smile at me in a bland sort of way, but it was a strange mask on his intense face. I quickened my steps.

He followed.

"If you are distressed, Madame, perhaps I could help," he offered.

"Why are you so intent on helping me?" I shot back over my shoulder. I was hurrying now, practically running. "I told you, I'm fine!"

"I can sense that you are not," came a thrum at my ear. I whirled to see him next to me, when moments before he'd been a good distance behind me. I stood frozen in terrified fascination as he reached forward and plucked a leaf from my hair. He twirled it between long, pale fingers and his small smile became a grin.

A grin full of sharp, pointed teeth.

"In fact, I can sense that you are more than distressed, *petite louve*. You are almost wild with fear. It's a heady scent, you know. If you're a quick study, I can teach you to recognize it."

Who is this man? How does he know about me? Where has he come from?

Panic built in my muscles, urging me to flee. Before I turned to run, I caught a glimpse of his black eyes again—only they weren't black. They were yellow, rimmed with red.

The eyes of the beast.

CHAPTER FOURTEEN

ANTOINE

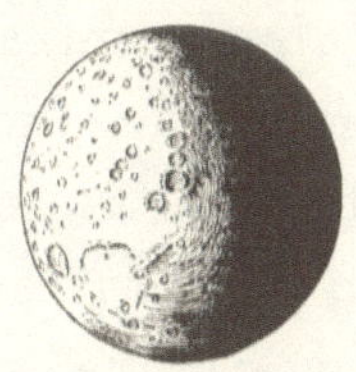

November 19, 1767
The Wild Rose
Gévaudan

Of course, she was gone. I expected her to be gone. What I didn't expect, though, was to see her out for a pre-dawn promenade with some unknown gentleman. *The absolute nerve of the woman!* Mere weeks ago, she was writhing in pleasure in my arms, and here she was having intense flirtations with some male passerby.

Antoine, you utter fool. You know she is not for you. Why do you care? She's a spy and a liar, and...quite possibly some kind of werewolf.

No. I wouldn't even think it. Doctor Van Helsing had to be wrong. There would be a logical explanation.

A logical explanation. Like Charlotte insisted when you mentioned the werewolf of Gévaudan.

I didn't know if I believed it then, and now I was determined to disbelieve it. Charlotte had simply been angry, and the table had been weak.

From my perch on the rooftop, I couldn't quite hear what the man in black was saying to Charlotte, but she suddenly stiffened. She looked frightened. Before I could make my way down from the roof, she bolted for the town gate, running faster than I'd ever seen a human run.

I jumped from the roof and ran toward the town gate as well, praying I would be able to reach her before any harm could come to her. Who was that man? What had he said or done that had frightened Charlotte? If he so much as *breathed* ill upon her, I would hunt him down and eviscerate him.

Not that Charlotte is yours to protect, said the annoying voice in my head. Still, I could be chivalrous, ensure that she was safe before we parted ways.

I dodged townsfolk as I wound through the alleys and streets. The sky was turning a lovely pink hue with the rising sun, which felt like a hopeful respite from the cold, melancholy gray that hung above Gévaudan.

Finally, I spied Charlotte on the road ahead. She saw me almost immediately—quickly enough for her to shuck her pallor of fear and school her features in an expression of haughty indifference. She slowed her pace and smiled at me when I reached her.

"Antoine! Good morning. It looks like it's going to be a fine day today, don't you think?"

Had this been a few weeks ago, I would have thought she was mad. Now, I'd come to recognize her expert deflections.

"Who the Hell was that?" I growled.

"Who?"

"That man! The one you were *flirting* with just outside the gate," I accused. I was in no mood for her outrageous denials.

"I have no idea what you're talking about," she shrugged.

"Perhaps you're overtired, and your eyes are playing tricks on you. I'd recommend a nap and a light meal. I saw a bakery just down the street if you're feeling peckish. I certainly am! Ooh, do you think they'll have any meat pies?"

"Charlotte." I grabbed her arm and stared hard into her eyes.

She stared back at me, the very portrait of innocence. If I didn't know her better, I'd have thought she was right, and I'd been mistaken. The only thing that stopped me was a strange glint in her eyes—a flash of red I almost missed. Something was off and I felt a rising sense of panic.

"Where have you been? Who was that man? What were you doing outside the gate at this hour? It's barely sunrise! Do you realize you could have met the *bêtes* out there on your own?"

The forced innocence on her face twisted into irritation. Rather than answer my questions, she pushed past me and stormed down the street, muttering darkly.

"Honestly, Antoine, I don't have to answer a single one of your damn questions! Leave me in peace, for pity's sake!"

I stood in the middle of the street for a moment, staring at the bedraggled hem of her dress as it whipped around her feet.

That went well, I thought to myself. My anger spent, I felt a wash of acute embarrassment at my frustrated tirade. I contemplated my next move. *Should I go after her? Should I chase down the man outside the gate? Should I return to the inn, pack my things, jump on Tartuffe, and ride away, never to see the infuriating woman again?*

Probably.

Only I knew I wouldn't. Whatever complicated feelings I now harbored for Charlotte, I could at least acknowledge that my honor compelled me to ensure her safety—even if it was at the expense of my own. *But how can I if she won't let me? She won't even tell me the truth.* I frowned. I was no good with women—especially aristocratic women. In their company, I often found myself perplexed by their behavior and tongue-tied around their flirtations.

I groaned in exasperation and stomped after her, splattering mud everywhere in my ire.

"Watch what you're doing, you oaf!"

I turned to see a thick lout of a man wiping mud from his face and shirt. *Merde.* The last thing I wanted was trouble. We were meant to be laying low.

"Apologies," I grumbled. "I did not see you there."

"Like Hell," the man said. "You ruined my clothes!"

I gave him a once over. His clothes were so filthy, it was impossible to distinguish one patch of mud from another.

I gritted my teeth. "As I said," I repeated. "My apologies." I reached into my coat pocket and extracted a few coins, then tossed them at the man. He didn't reach for them, simply let them fall into a puddle at his feet.

"You don't seem very sorry," he said, pushing his sleeves up. He obviously wanted a fight. The stress of the last few weeks surged, and my temper flared.

"I've apologized and offered you fair compensation for my mistake. What more do you want?" I snapped.

"Retribution," he said with a wicked grin. Before I could answer, he let his fist fly, clipping my jaw as I dodged clumsily. I'd known the blow was coming but had underestimated his reflexes. I rubbed the spot he'd hit and nodded to him.

"So be it," I said. I shucked my coat and rolled up my own sleeves. *A fight might do me some good. Possibly release some of the tension I've been carrying around since I met Charlotte.* I feinted right and planted a fist into his stomach, but he came up swinging. I managed to duck the blow and threw my shoulder into him, knocking him to the ground. He grunted with the impact, and I got a few good punches in his sides, but he hooked his leg around mine and used the opportunity to flip me face-first into a sizable mud puddle. When I surfaced, I looked up and realized we'd attracted a crowd of eager onlookers.

"Five on the man with the scar," someone shouted.

"I'll take that bet," said another.

"Come on, lads! Ten on Jacques and his iron fists!"

Iron fists? Oh, Hell.

The man called Jacques landed a painful knee to my groin and an impressive uppercut sent me reeling. I tried to stand, but he kicked me as I rose, leaving me with a ringing in my ears and a bloodied lip.

As my thoughts began to cloud, a shabby hem swirled into view.

"I beg your pardon," came a fierce feminine voice. "But what do you think you are doing to my husband?"

Charlotte.

I lifted my face from the mud and saw her standing in front of me, facing "Iron Fist" Jacques.

"None of your concern, little miss. Just a private disagreement between gentlemen," he replied.

"Go back to the inn, Charlotte," I spit through the blood and filth streaming down my face.

"I certainly will not," she replied, never taking her eyes off Jacques. "Monsieur, my husband can be a complete and utter horse's ass, but he is *my* horse's ass. I must beg your pardon on his behalf. Might we not settle this dispute with a degree of civility? I wager you could use a warm meal and some fortifying spirits to start your day off on a better note. If you'll escort me to the best establishment, we can all breakfast at my husband's pleasure."

Dieu, she could charm the fleas off a stray. How I hated her in that moment. Embarrassment and anger welled up inside me at the thought that she'd intervened—probably thinking she'd rescued me from a sound thrashing. *One you likely deserve, you fool.*

"I don't need your help," I growled at her. She ignored me, spiking my temper again.

Jacques frowned, flexing his meaty fists. The crowd, disappointed with the interruption, booed and jeered, goading Jacques and me back into violence. I was definitely ready. Jacques seemed less sure.

I finally stood, wiping my dirty, bloodied face on my sleeve. I clenched my fists, moments away from venting all of my anger, frustration, and irritation on Jacques's ruddy face, but he raised his hands to the crowd and called for quiet. He nodded at Charlotte.

"Madame, I would be honored to breakfast with you. I reckon this town has seen enough bloodshed to last us a while anyway," he rumbled, extending his arm to her. She beamed at him in a way that made me want to rip his limbs off and beat him with them.

"So, I gather," she tutted sympathetically. "You must tell me all about it!" She took his arm, surreptitiously slipping her other hand in her skirts, where I heard a soft *click*. So, she'd had her pistol cocked and ready in her pockets.

Ready to defend me.

I stared after them in stupefied silence as they meandered down the road. The crowd dispersed, hurling a few insults at me as they did.

What the Hell had just happened? I tried to take stock of the situation, but my head throbbed, and my mouth tasted of blood, and I found it hard to focus. Surely, the comtesse-agent I'd accidentally kidnapped, dragged to the south of France, endangered countless times from natural and supernatural threats, and might harbor some flame of begrudging affection for, hadn't just saved me *again*?

I'd never felt so useless—so much a fool. My father's words rung true in my ears, as did Charlotte's early criticisms. *Always acting so rashly, too stupid to think things through, making a mess of everything and everyone. Antoine, the blundering imbecile languishing away as a mere lieutenant. Antoine, who could not save his nephew or his sister. Antoine, who could not save Charlotte, his...*

His what? What was she to me?

Before I could think too much on it, I heard her calling my name. She and Jacques were standing in the middle of the street some distance away, waving me over. As black as my mood was, I could not resist her bidding. I grabbed my coat—the only garment I possessed not covered in mud—and stalked over.

Charlotte cocked a brow at my brooding expression but tried gamely to make introductions. Jacques stuck his hand out and I eyed it suspiciously.

"Your good lady wife has explained some of your troubles," he said. His deep voice was like a wagon wheel over a rutted gravel road.

"Has she?" I was unable to keep the censure from my voice.

"It's nothing to be ashamed of, darling," Charlotte interjected. "The vampires who robbed us on the road were supernaturally strong and numerous. We were lucky to escape with our lives, despite your bravery."

"Indeed," I said, too exhausted to argue or keep up with her myriad stories—*or should I say,* lies.

"Jacques has forgiven your slights," she continued. "And wishes to make amends, and then we can all put this whole *memorable* experience behind us."

She eyed me pointedly. Her meaning was clear—we'd attracted too much attention and she wanted me to shake hands with the man and then disappear, just another typical brawl with some ill-behaved traveler. I wasn't *at all* an outlaw on the run from his father, a band of vampire soldiers, a possible werewolf, and the legal repercussions of murdering a marquis.

"I'm sorry for the, um…" Jacques gestured to my bleeding lip.

"Don't trouble yourself over it," I replied.

We were quiet for a moment, sizing each other up, until Charlotte rolled her eyes and cleared her throat.

"Well! That's settled. Jacques, you were telling me there was a lovely spot up ahead where we could get some meat pies and perhaps a pot of coffee or tea. Not to worry, *mon ami*, I always carry a little nip of brandy with me—the perfect way to warm up a morning in November! Now, you also mentioned some of the recent troubles you've all been having with some kind of local beast—pray, tell me over our meal," she trilled. "Your little town is *so* lovely, I hate to think of something so ominous marring its serenity."

Jacques smiled down at Charlotte. It seemed innocent enough, but it piqued my temper again and it took all I had to follow behind them without strangling them both. We stopped a short distance from the Wild Rose and went into a neighboring tavern.

"It's only a tavern at night, madame," Jacques said apologetically. "In the daytime, they serve tea when they can get it, and sometimes lemonade—perfectly respectable for ladies. I promise you the meat pies are the best you've ever had. My wife, Annette, is the best baker in Gévaudan. She runs the restaurant in the daytime, and I take over as publican in the evening. I'll introduce you, Madame."

"Why, Jacques! This is your establishment? *Mon Dieu*, you are clever, aren't you? My husband and I are absolutely overjoyed to sample the best that Gévaudan has to offer. Come along, Antoine, don't sulk back there. A nice hot meal and some good company is just what the doctor ordered. Go on, then, Jacques—Antoine and I will be right behind you. Choose for us the best table, *d'accord?*"

Charlotte pulled me aside and fixed me with a steely glare.

"You and I are going to have a *serious* discussion when we finish here. I cannot believe you would be so pig-headed as to start a fight at seven o'clock in the morning with the burliest man in town. We're trying to escape notice, Antoine!"

"He started it," I grumbled. "I tried to apologize but the fellow wanted a fight. If you think about it, I was actually being very obliging by offering him one. Would've been rude of me to refuse."

She raised her eyes heavenward. "*Dieu* save me from the hopelessness of men."

Needled by her lack of faith in my abilities—and me, in general—I tried to turn the tables.

"I'm willing to have this serious discussion," I began. "But you have a lot of explaining to do about your whereabouts last night and that man on the road."

"Don't be ridiculous," she sniffed, turning to join Jacques at the far end of the tavern. "I don't have to explain myself to you."

"Perhaps you don't," I admitted with a shrug. "But if you expect *me* to explain *myself*, it's tit for tat."

She threw a saucy glance over her shoulder.

"I'll bear that in mind if I'm in the mood for tat."

Blood rushed to my face in a furious blush, then surged south to my cock as her insinuation—obviously meant to unsettle me—landed with its intended effect. *Merde.* This woman would be the death of me.

Or you'll be the death of her, I thought miserably.

Every decision in the last few weeks had not only made me the fool, but they'd also put her in grave danger. Granted, she'd been more than capable of handling everything that had come her way, but the fact remained she would have been much better off if we'd never met. With a grave reluctance, I realized my honor and sense of obligation—all that I felt I had left—were causing more problems than they were solving. What was more, she'd protested so much that she hadn't needed my protection, and she was right. She *didn't* need my protection, but she certainly needed me to stop putting her in harm's way. Every moment we remained together was one more moment I was endangering her and clearly *not* protecting her.

I looked at her across the room, laughing easily with Jacques. Her warm brown eyes glinted with mirth and several curls escaped her cap with the movement. In that moment, she didn't look like a spy, or an agent, or a *comtesse*, for that matter. It was as if every part of her body felt every feeling, and she overflowed with joy like she overflowed with passion, or with frustration. As much artifice as there was to Charlotte, Comtesse de Brionne, there was even more that was genuine. The kind of genuine that men became hopeless around.

That I have become hopeless around.

With a knife-sharp sense of despair in my heart, I knew what I had to do. As much as I wanted Charlotte, I had to leave her.

CHAPTER FIFTEEN
CHARLOTTE

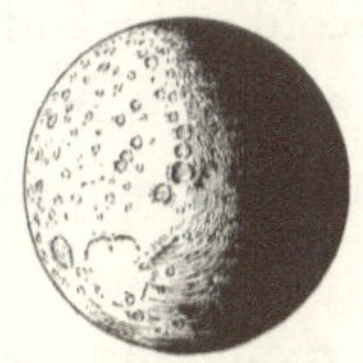

November 19, 1767
The Wild Rose
Gévaudan

As we made our way back to the inn, we were pursued by a black cloud that had nothing to do with the weather and everything to do with Antoine's surly countenance. Whether it was due to my exhaustion, our current circumstances, or the strange interaction I'd had with the "beast" this morning, I had no patience for his melancholy.

"That Jacques turned out to be a fine fellow," I said. "It's unfortunate you two got off on the wrong foot—or should I say, *fist.*"

Antoine frowned but said nothing.

"Lucky for you, I was there to help handle the situation," I continued. "If I hadn't, I daresay you would've ended up with more than a black eye and a bloody lip."

Still, Antoine remained quiet. He simply refused to rise to

my bait. The telltale muscle in his jaw flexed, though, proving that at the very least, he was listening.

"A simple *thank you* would suffice," I sniffed, playing my last card. He *had* to respond to that. We'd reached the Wild Rose and trudged our way up the stairs, plagued by fatigue. "Monsieur, would you send up a bath, please?" I called down to the innkeeper. I was cold, sore, and filthy from last night. I wanted to rest, but above that, I wanted to bathe.

"Thank you?" he practically choked on the words.

At last, he speaks.

We'd reached our room and he pushed me inside. I expected him to slam the door, but he closed it very slowly and quietly, which unnerved me more than his anger would have.

"Yes," I said, trying to recover my bluster. "If it hadn't been for me, you would've been beaten to a pulp by the Iron Fists of Gévaudan. Not only did I stop the assault, but I managed to sweet talk us into a lovely breakfast, as well."

Antoine's green eyes darkened. He opened his mouth to says something but thought better of it. He shook his head and began removing his mud-caked clothes, not caring that I was in the room and we were mid-conversation. Well, I was mid-conversation. He was silent, grumpy, and taciturn.

And suddenly shirtless.

Mon Dieu. I couldn't help but stare. I'd caught glimpses of him our first night in the inn but hadn't had the opportunity to give him a proper look. His unfashionably bronzed skin was crisscrossed with a roadmap of scars that pointed to a life of violence and pain. It made the scar on his face look like the least of his troubles. Soft, dark hair dusted his chest and narrowed to a thin line leading below his belly button—a different kind of road, and one that I found myself wanting to travel the most. He reached up to tug his hair from its customary queue, shaking the loose waves out and running his fingers through it. Muscles that I'd only seen in anatomy books bunched and flexed beneath his skin, unlike any man I'd ever been with. He moved to unbutton the falls of his breeches and paused, catching my eye.

"Perhaps it is ungentlemanly, but I hope you'll permit me to have the first bath. I'm certain you don't want our room to reek of blood and filth," he ground out. I'd almost forgotten that he was still annoyed with me. That fact didn't have any impact on the inferno of my desire.

"*Dieu*, Antoine," I breathed. "You're beautiful." *Did I mean to say that out loud?*

He blushed and turned away from me. "Comtesse, I'm sore and weary of your incessant teasing. If you've no wish to tell me about your night last night, so be it, but if you have any humanity in you, you'll grant me some peace."

I probably deserved that.

"As you wish," I replied quietly. "Though you must know that I am not teasing you."

He said nothing, but some of the stiffness in his back eased. I opened my mouth to speak again, but the innkeeper knocked then, bringing forth a wooden tub and two maids with steaming pitchers of hot water. After several trips back and forth to fill the tub, the bath was ready. I gestured to Antoine to go ahead.

"By all means, your needs are greater than mine," I said, though I doubted if anyone could presently surpass the strength of my need to touch him.

I went to the window to draw the curtains and offer him some privacy, listening to the sounds of him shucking his breeches and slipping into the water. His exhale of satisfaction made my heart race. My awareness of him in all his sullen, magnificent nudity was quickly becoming more than an inconvenience—it was becoming a torment.

Driven by lust, I turned to face him again. The sight was like a kick to my stomach. Water dripped from his wet locks and soap bubbles glided down his chest. I bit my lip but refused to hold back any longer.

"Of course, you'll need someone to help you wash your back," I said.

He quirked a brow at me. "What happened to giving me some peace?"

Embarrassed and angry at his rebuttal, I whirled around and snatched my cloak off the bed.

"Well, go on and wash it yourself then, but don't come crying to me about doing so with those bruised ribs," I snapped. My hand was on the doorknob when he called my name.

"Charlotte."

I stopped but didn't face him.

"*Charlotte*," he said again, softer this time.

I peeked at him from the corner of my eye. He held out the bar of soap and I considered it. *Thank God I don't give a fig about my pride.*

"I will be the very personification of peace," I said. "As quiet as the second half of a sermon, when everyone has dozed off in church."

I grabbed the soap before he could object and threw my cloak back on the bed. Kneeling behind him, I dipped my hands into the warm water and started to lather the soap across his shoulders. They were warm and smooth, except for the scars, but the muscles beneath felt as hard as iron. I couldn't resist giving his biceps a little squeeze. He sighed again and smiled, then leaned back against the tub and looked up at me. This close to him, I could see flecks of brown and gold in his green eyes—the colors of sunlight filtering through a lush forest canopy. Under my intense scrutiny, he became self-conscious again and closed them.

I gently threaded my soapy fingers through his hair, though he'd already gotten the worst of the mud out. My nails scraped lightly along his scalp, and his full lips parted on a moan that made my nipples tighten and my skin prickle with heat. Tiny soap bubbles slipped down the path of his scar, tracing the moon-shaped curve from his brow to his cheek. I gently wiped them away with my fingertip, which drifted to his lips of its own accord. His rough, stubbled cheeks hadn't seen a razor in some days, but it didn't make him look unkempt as it often did on other men. It was almost as if his face needed the roughness of his cheeks and the long scar as armor against being *too* beautiful.

Too beautiful? Really, Charlotte? You've already committed to keeping Antoine in the dark about the truth of your new supernatural state, and here you are practically swooning over him just because he's ruggedly handsome and brooding. And infuriating. And certainly honorable but misguided in his feckless attempts at chivalry. Could he ever understand the life you lead? Poisoned by a failed marriage, accustomed to wealth and the entitlement of the aristocracy, surviving and thriving in a web of so many untruths and half-truths you've almost forgotten what it is to be honest—and that was before you transformed into some previously unknown supernatural abomination. No... I bet if you slice a bit off Antoine de Vaux, he will bleed honor all over you.

My thoughts heralded an onset of melancholy that stilled my hands. Antoine's eyes opened again.

"Have you finished your explorations, Comtesse?" he asked softly.

The hushed words were like a lover's caress. He was so unlike any of the men I'd been with, and I finally realized how dangerous my own feelings had become. I wanted him. Not just for the night, but for weeks. Months. Years, even. *Merde.* There was nothing for it now. I'd simply have to say goodbye to him and leave Gévaudan. As a newly turned werewolf, every minute I stayed in this anti-supernatural town was another minute I was putting everyone in jeopardy, not to mention the danger I found myself in with my feelings for Antoine.

I'll pack up tonight and leave while Antoine sleeps. Daphne and Étienne are in the next town over. With my new abilities, I fear crossing paths with the bêtes *considerably less. Perhaps they'll come for me, and I can dispatch them to protect Antoine.*

I pulled away and stood, determined to ignore his suddenly troubled expression.

"Charlotte, what's the matter? Are you unwell?"

"No, I...I'm fine, Antoine. Perhaps a little tired, that's all," I said, attempting to find my lighthearted tone again. "I'll leave you to your peace."

"Wait, Charlotte," he said. "Please. Don't go."

He rose from the bath and water sluiced down his body, dragging away the last of the dirt and soap suds. He stood before me completely naked, visibly aroused, with an entreaty on his face that I found myself precariously close to accepting.

"What of your peace?" I asked, taking a step toward the bed to retrieve my cloak. He wrapped a towel around his waist, and I failed to hide my disappointment. He got out of the bath and came toward me.

Staring deep into my eyes, he blew out a resigned sigh. "Because of you, I don't think I'll ever know peace again."

He brought his hand up to my cheek and caressed it with his thumb, then pulled me to him for a passionate kiss that felt like pleading, longing, and goodbye at the same time. His other hand let go of the towel and found my waist, expertly locating the ties of my skirt.

Just this once, my body cried. *Just this once before never again. But what of the blood plague? Am I putting him at risk of infection if we make love?* I hesitated.

"Antoine, the blood plague…the variant…I don't want to corrupt you. I won't take your choice from you," I whispered.

He pulled at the ribbon tying my skirts in place and brushed his lips across the skin of my neck.

"You were scratched by a werewolf *and* a vampire. Do you plan on scratching me that hard? Or biting me?"

I couldn't keep the teasing from my tone as I ran my hands over his hard body. "Perhaps. I make no promises."

He tilted my head up and dropped kisses along my jaw. "I accept the risks. Nothing you do will corrupt me beyond what my own sins have wrought."

Resolved, I wrapped my arms around him and my skirt tumbled to the floor in a heap. Without taking his lips from mine, he began to unpin my bodice and loosen my stays. Layer after layer fell away, until I was down to my stockings and chemise. He knelt to grasp the hem of the garment, looking up at me with heated intensity.

"Are you sure?" he whispered, his hands starting to tremble. "Do you wish me to continue?"

Emboldened by his uncertainty, I pulled the chemise over my head and sat on the edge of the bed, spreading my legs before him.

"Do continue," I managed, adoring the blush that spread from his face to his chest.

Smiling with relief, he leaned forward, pressing a kiss to the inside of my thigh. He slowly slid his hands up my calves to my knees, tugging them further apart, then ran them lightly over the tops of my thighs, around my waist and behind my ass. Pulling me forward on the bed, he found better access to all the places I longed for him to go. As his stubble scored the insides of my legs, I twitched in anticipation and heard his rough chuckle.

"Are you always so sure you'll get what you want?" he murmured, tracing the outer folds of my sex with his tongue. The effect was immediate and explosive, prompting me to throw my head back and swear. He repeated the move on the other side, then dragged a feather-light lick along the seam, ending it just below the apex of my pleasure.

"I asked you a question," he whispered, dropping kisses back down my thighs, moving away from where I needed him.

I wiggled forward, trying to make my preference known, but he only smiled up at me deviously.

"Yes," I blurted in frustration. "Yes, I am accustomed to getting what I want, but only because I have the guts to fight for it."

"We should all be so lucky," he said.

He set his tongue to me again, this time in the exact place of my torment. Moving in circles, he sucked at the bud of my pleasure and slipped his fingers inside me, working me to the peak of bliss. Before the orgasm could take form, he pulled away and pushed me back down onto the bed. I whimpered in disappointment. He grinned wolfishly, obviously quite pleased with himself and the torture he was wreaking upon my needy body.

"Perhaps I should be better about demanding what I want, secure in the knowledge that I would get it."

He crawled up my body, marking my skin with gentle, little bites on his way to my lips again.

"What is it that you want, Antoine?" I panted, nearly feral with lust. "It might be within my power to give it to you."

He nudged my legs apart with his knees and rubbed his

hard cock against my sex, teasing a moan out of me that sounded alarmingly like a growl. *Dieu*, I needed him. *Now.* Libidinous to the point of madness, I grasped his cock and slid the tip inside me, cooing with satisfaction at his grunt of pleasure. He pulled back with what looked like great effort, gritting his teeth. Mischief sparkled in his eyes.

"I want your pleasure, as well as mine," he said.

"You have it," I moaned, arching up to meet him.

Again, he pulled back.

"I want to give you pleasure, Charlotte, without you having to take it for yourself. Just this once, let me take care of you."

The sincerity in his eyes nearly made me weep. For the second time, I didn't want to ruin our intimacy with sarcasm or wit. *This is goodbye, after all.* Embarrassed by the emotions caught in my throat, I merely nodded. He smiled down at me and leaned forward for a searing kiss.

"Tell me," he said, kissing my neck and trailing his fingers across my nipple. "No games, no lies, no deflections. What do you like, Charlotte? How do you like to be touched? What shall I do to you?"

"I..." Through the fog of passion, my brain stuttered to a halt. *What do I like?* I tried to consider the question. Each time I'd been with a man, or a woman, I'd found myself becoming what they wanted me to be. Submissive, dominant, silent, loud, loving to be punished or needing to exert some discipline... Even my husband had needed me to be someone else in bed. I'd found pleasure and passion with partners, but no one had ever asked me before.

What do I like?

The question overwhelmed me, and humiliating tears pooled in my eyes, blurring my vision. I squeezed them shut and tried to get ahold of myself, but Antoine noticed. He seemed to read my thoughts, because he kissed my forehead, then my cheek, then my neck again.

"Don't be embarrassed," he whispered. "We shall find out together."

He placed his hands on my breasts and lightly massaged them, then began rolling my nipples with his fingertips. My embarrassment now forgotten, I arched up again, seeking more of the exhilarating contact.

"Your breasts are flawless. Like beautiful vanilla cakes topped with rose petal nipples. They taste sweeter than any dessert I've ever had," he said, almost to himself. "I've dreamed of you so much, Charlotte. Of dining on the banquet of your body and sipping at the wine of your lips." His hand moved down to my sex again, which ached from unspent lust. "But here," he growled, dipping his fingers inside me again. "Here you taste like the nectar of the gods. I think I could die from the perfection of it."

All conscious thoughts fled. My entire body vibrated with need. He moved his fingers slowly at first, pressing his thumb to the pearl of my sex. It felt like hairline cracks were breaking all over me as my excitement mounted, until I was certain I was going to fracture and explode into millions of pieces.

Antoine withdrew his fingers before I could and I almost sobbed at the loss, but then he lifted himself above me and positioned his cock at my entrance.

"Have I given you pleasure, Charlotte?" The hopefulness in his face was cherubic, but as he slowly slid inside me, he swore enough to make Lucifer himself blush.

"Yes," I panted. "Yes, Antoine. You have given me pleasure."

He rocked forward, and we both moaned in a chorus of satisfaction.

"What more shall I do to you?" he asked, punctuating each

word with a thrust of his hips. His hand was between us again, his thumb on my pearl once more.

Dieu, I am so close...so close...

"What more do you want of me?" he demanded, thrusting harder, faster. Stars began to twinkle in front of my eyes as I began the crescendo. Heat built to a fever pitch, and I came apart as he did, crying out into the passion-thick air.

"*Love* me."

CHAPTER SIXTEEN
ANTOINE

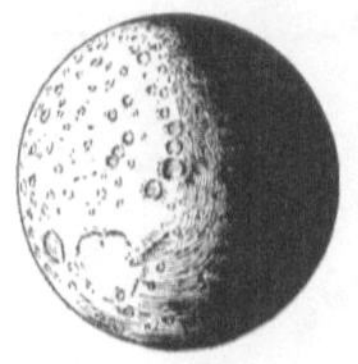

November 19, 1767
The Wild Rose
Gévaudan

Love me, she had said. Surely, she hadn't meant it. *Surely* it had just been the heat of the moment and the carnal excitability. We'd both been taut with sexual tension, and the release was what we'd both needed. I'd needed to have her before I said goodbye—to plunge myself into her wet heat and taste every part of her. I'd needed to hold her, so that I could let her go. *Hadn't I?*

Love me. She'd probably meant it in a sexual way. Perhaps she'd meant *fuck me.* Or *make love to me.* She couldn't have meant it the way I heard it. I could not—would not—allow my heart to trip over words carelessly shouted as a sexual climax.

She doesn't mean it, Antoine.

It didn't matter. I was leaving tonight. Firmly resolved to put distance between us for her safety, I would wait until she was asleep, pack my meager belongings, and leave. Tartuffe and I would be long gone by the time she awoke—hopefully drawing the *bêtes* away from her while avoiding the fallout from murdering Sade. Heading south was the best option. I could only hope she would find safety with her cousin and the emissary.

"Antoine," she said softly, placing her hand against my cheek. "That was wonderful."

Forcing myself to return to the present, I pulled her close and tucked the covers around us. I dropped a kiss on her forehead. Guilt whispered through me.

"I'm sorry about this morning," I said.

She leaned her head against my chest, and the intimacy of the gesture threatened to break my heart. *In another time, in another place, this would be enough for me. Here is the family you longed for—the family you lost.*

"Well, I'd say you more than made up for it," she said with a coy smile.

I swallowed. "Charlotte, why did you leave last night? Where did you go?"

She sighed and nuzzled into me, but I felt her muscles tense.

"I went for a walk, Antoine. I needed to clear my head and get out of this room. I've been stuck in here recovering and it was driving me mad."

I didn't think she was lying, but that wasn't the whole truth, either. I stroked her arm lazily.

"And the man in black?"

She smirked. "Jealous, Antoine?"

I frowned. That was part of it, to be sure, but I didn't want to admit it out loud to her. She looked up at me and laughed.

"Be at ease. I promise I'd never met him. He saw me on the road back to Gévaudan and asked if I needed any assistance, since it is odd for a woman to be out walking at night by herself," she said with a little shrug.

Again, not entirely a lie, but also not the full story. I decided not to press her any further, since I didn't think it would do me any good.

"It is odd," I admitted. "And dangerous. You could've come upon the beast, or the *bêtes*. I hate to think of you in danger, especially when I can't be there to help protect you."

"That is very sweet," she said, kissing my jawline. "But I can protect myself."

"I know you can. I just...wish you didn't have to. It is your choice to live a dangerous life—I would never take that choice from you. But I can't imagine it's easy for the people who care about you, seeing you so reckless with your safety."

I could tell by the hard set of her mouth that I'd overstepped. She pulled away and fixed me with a steely glare.

"Reckless? Antoine, look around you. The world is dangerous. I have worked hard to acquire the skills I need to survive. If I am in danger on occasion because of my work with The Order, it is for a good cause. As to my loved ones and their opinions on how I choose to live my life... Perhaps they have more faith in me than you do."

At that, she rose from the bed and collected her chemise from the floor. The loss of her warm body next to mine was worse than the pain of starvation.

"Skills to survive?" I scoffed. "You're a comtesse, Charlotte, not a peasant. Is it really about survival? Or is it about something more? Something that you have to prove to everyone, or prove to yourself?"

"You know nothing about my circumstances," she shot back at me. "What I've had to overcome! Why I chose to learn what I did and why I do what I do—why I won't rely on anyone else to protect me. Why I have fought to learn how to protect myself. *You do not know.*"

"Why don't you tell me then?"

"That's not something I'm keen to go into with you right now, Antoine. Suffice it to say that you shouldn't be passing judgment on someone whose life you know nothing about," she snapped.

"I'm sorry. And it's not that I don't have faith in you," I said, rising to go after her. "It's just that I don't understand why you would willingly become a spy when you could be at home living a life of leisure. You shouldn't be worrying about the fate of France."

"Ah, and so, because I'm a woman and an aristocrat, I should just stick my head in the sand, keep my hem and my hands clean, and leave all the important work to the men in power? Because they're doing such a spectacular job of it," she snarled.

"Well, yes—I mean, no! What I mean is that you should be living a life of comfort, not having to worry about such political entanglements," I argued, already regretting my words. I reached for my breeches, watching her dress and grow increasingly frustrated with each subsequent layer she put on.

"Clearly, you've never been to court if you think the life of an aristocratic woman is anything but political entanglements," she scoffed.

"Charlotte, you can do anything you want. I know you are capable. I'm sorry that your circumstances have forced you to be so. I just wish you could live an easier life—a safer life." *Let me protect you. Be mine to protect.*

"That's rich coming from the soldier son of a decorated, wealthy, war-mongering general. Why is it men are the only ones who should be allowed to choose their futures and their fates? Why can't I?"

"You can," I argued. "Who said you couldn't?"

"You did! You just can't accept that this life *is* my choice. Certainly, I should be allowed to control my life as long as it aligns with what you see for me—what society sees for me," she said bitterly.

"I just don't understand why you would choose such a hard path," I said, shaking my head.

"Oh?" she rounded on me. "Why did you follow in your father's footsteps, Antoine? Why aren't you at home managing the family estate? How many men did you kill on the battlefield in an attempt to secure your father's absent approval? Was that why you needed to murder Sade? Was it really about revenge, or was it to prove something to your father—maybe you need him to know that you're a man to be reckoned with," she sneered.

Her words sliced me to ribbons. I didn't know what was worse—her perception of shameful truths that whispered through me, or the fact that she'd fired them at me like bullets. I gaped at her, unsure of what my next words should be. I was angry and hurt and confused by how quickly things between us had escalated from bliss to battle. *At least it will be easier for me to leave.*

I finished dressing and strode to the door.

"You are right," I admitted quietly. "My troubled relationship with my father has caused me to make many decisions I'm not proud of. But after the deaths of my sister and my nephew, I realized I needed to set things right. I knew it would be ruinous for me—that, once I'd begun, I'd find myself hurtling toward my own judgment day." The words had poured out of me so fast I'd said them all in one breath. I had to pause to draw in another. "I used to have much to prove...to my father, to the world, to myself, but not anymore. Not to you, either, Charlotte. I've done too many things—killed too many men, made too many mistakes—to be a good man, but I've accepted that I don't need to be a good man to right my wrongs. I'm only sorry that you were another wrong along the way."

I opened the door, glancing back only once to see her staring at me with a mixture of anger and hurt on her face. Tears welled in her eyes, and she opened her mouth to speak, but I did not wish to hear the words. I closed the door behind me and descended into the tavern. In a sort of numb resignation, I paid the innkeeper the remainder of our bill, bought a bottle of cheap wine along with some additional food and supplies, and went out to the barn to saddle Tartuffe.

"You're going then, Lieutenant?"

Hand on my sword, I whirled to see Doctor Van Helsing brushing out her dapple-gray mare. I'd been so distracted when I came in, I hadn't noticed her in the shadowy back corner of the barn.

"I am," I replied. "Thank you for your services, Doctor. I appreciate you traveling all this way to help care for Charlotte."

Bright white teeth almost glowing in the gloom, she smiled. "I do not think you need my help to care for her."

I felt my face grow hot and I scowled. I repacked the saddle bags, trying to hurry away from the too perceptive woman. Tugging at Tartuffe's reins, I nodded to her by way of farewell.

"A moment, Lieutenant," she said, leading her horse out.

Merde. Is she leaving, too? Please don't be heading in my direction.

"I'm heading south to meet up with the duchesse and the emissary. They have some medical supplies for me but are not permitted to enter Gévaudan. Would you be so kind as to see me on my way?"

Oh, Hell.

"Forgive me, but I'd rather not, Doctor. I'm afraid I've

delayed much too long here and I'm eager to get back on the road," I muttered. "Is there anyone else who can see you safely to your party?"

She shook her head. "I'm afraid not. It is far too treacherous on the roads around here for me to travel by myself. I must insist. It will be good for you, I think—I can tell you all about my experiments with the blood plague and my research. I'm sure you will find it all fascinating. Come along, Lieutenant!"

Unable to think of a way to extricate myself from the company of the commanding doctor, I frowned. The last thing I wanted was to ride for hours listening to some scientist prattle on about the plague, but she was right—the area around Gévaudan was exceedingly dangerous. I suspected the *bêtes* were still lurking around, and who knew what had happened to the beast.

"Very well," I grumbled. "I don't think I'll be good company, but I'll make sure you arrive at your destination safely. You're ready to leave now?"

"I am," she said, mounting her horse. "I packed while you were...otherwise occupied."

I reddened again and tried to hide my embarrassment by saddling Tartuffe.

"Do try to keep up," she called back to me as she turned down the main road toward the town gate. "I'm in something of a hurry."

"I'll do my best," I grumbled, spurring Tartuffe to match her horse's pace.

As the town gate came into view, I glanced back over my shoulder. I didn't know what I expected—or hoped—to see. Perhaps Charlotte running into the street, tearfully waving me down, shouting apologies out over the crowd. I'd jump down from my horse, run back to her, wrap her in my arms and kiss her, swearing that I'd never leave her again, and she'd tell me she was giving up The Order and any other dangerous pursuits so we could retire to her country estate and raise four precocious children. She would say we should go ahead and make plans for a spring wedding. She would insist on inviting my father, who would have given up his power-mad, bloodthirsty ways in the hope of repairing our relationship, then a messenger would arrive to say he's been tracking me down all this time to tell me Marie and Louis were, in fact, alive, and waiting for me back in Thionville. The *bêtes* would stop hunting us, the beast of Gévaudan would leave the town in peace, and all the sufferers of the blood plague would wake up human again, washed of their sins, and with tables groaning under the weight of food.

Despite my melancholy, I smiled at the absurdity of my imaginings. If only happy endings were as prevalent in real life as they were in novels.

"What is it that delights you so, Lieutenant? I am certain it is not my company," Van Helsing said, slowing to ride beside me.

"Nothing," I replied, chiding myself for losing focus. "It's nothing, Doctor. You mentioned that you had some new findings about the plague. Why don't you share them with me?"

Apparently, that was the right question. Her face lit up with excitement.

"It's really quite fascinating, Lieutenant..."

"Please, Doctor, just call me Antoine."

"Very well, Antoine. As I was saying, it's a fascinating disease. You see, the body *appears* to die when infected, but I don't believe that is actually the case. I would say it's more like the human part of the body goes into a kind of hibernation and the blood plague takes over the faculties of the infected," she began, growing more animated by the minute.

"How is that possible?"

"I have no idea!" she said excitedly. "But think of it like this: your body is a coach and four. When the plague comes upon you, it is as if the driver falls asleep at the reins. The horses continue to pull the carriage along without the driver steering, with often disastrous results."

I nodded grimly. "But the need for blood as sustenance?"

"I believe it is a property of the plague. Somehow, in order to reproduce itself, which must surely be the drive of everything on earth, a regular human diet is insufficient. It requires more blood to keep the body going. Isn't that amazing?"

I turned a skeptical face on her. "I wouldn't call it amazing. Apocalyptic, perhaps. Sinister, definitely. Hopeless, as well."

"Oh, but you're so wrong, Lieutenant—er, I mean, Antoine. I find it is anything but hopeless," she said earnestly.

"Are you suggesting that the vampires of the world may recover and become human again?"

She considered my question. "Truthfully, I do not know. Perhaps not. But after all, is it so bad for the infected to remain vampires?"

"Doctor, that's blasphemous! You really think it's permissible for people to live by feeding solely from another? Such a parasitic existence is frankly damnable."

She tipped her head back and laughed. "My friend," she chuckled. "I wonder if you only feel that way because it is the poor feeding off of each other, as opposed to the aristocracy feeding off of them?"

I opened my mouth to argue but reconsidered. She was right, of course, and the irony of it made me feel sick.

"I never thought of it that way," I said. "But still, think of what it means for humans overall. What happens when there is no blood left?"

"Ah, that *is* the question I hoped you would arrive at. What, indeed? What would happen if a vampire fed on another vampire? Or on another species, for example? These are all questions that must be answered. How can we understand the true nature of a malady if we do not understand all the variables?"

"You're speaking of Charlotte," I observed. "What do you know of her condition?"

She was quiet for a moment, peering down the road ahead of us. The afternoon had waned into a beautiful rose-colored dusk. As lovely as it was, I could not ignore the premonition of unease I felt at seeing the gathering night.

"As I said earlier, I have seen something similar before, but it was many years ago. It wasn't exactly the same circumstances, but the symptoms were very much alike."

I leaned forward in my saddle, trained on her every word. Her eyes flicked to me, as though she was nervous of how I would respond.

"You care for her, do you not?"

"It doesn't matter," I replied. "We lead different lives. It would be best if we stayed away from each other."

The words sounded false even to my own ears. Van Helsing quirked a smile at me and nodded knowingly.

"So you say. Well, then you should know of her fate. I believe Charlotte has become something entirely different. Perhaps she is unique—I cannot say for certain. She has a form of the plague, but it is not vampirism. She does not thirst for blood. I believe that when she was infected with the beast's claws and vampire's bite that night in the woods, somehow, the plague took on a new form. The supernatural essences in her body merged and shifted. We might call her a werewolf because that's a familiar mythology to us, but the reality is much different. She has mutated. She has become something altogether different from what we know. If we continue with my runaway coach metaphor, it would be like saying her coachman fell asleep and her carriage careened out of control, but then was suddenly hijacked by bloodthirsty highwaymen."

"That's a horrible prognosis," I said grimly, suddenly reconsidering my decision to leave her. Guilt and regret warred with my resolve. *I should turn around and get back to her—help her figure this out.* "What can be done for her? How do we regain control of her carriage?"

"I'm afraid that is up to her. She must learn. I do not think anyone else can do much for her, except to help and support her." She eyed me meaningfully. "And to love her."

"What you say sounds absurd," I argued, ignoring the tail of her comment. "And blasphemous—against God and science. Surely someone can help her—surely *you* can help her. There must be a treatment, or a ritual, or...or...something, dammit! How can you be so sure about these things? How do you know all this?"

The news settled on me with the heavy weight of despair and Tartuffe tensed. He nickered softly, and Van Helsing's mare responded, nudging closer.

"Shh, easy, Lucy," the doctor crooned. "Antoine, you're worrying the horses. Calm yourself."

The hairs on the back of my neck suddenly rose, and without thinking, I reached for my pistols.

"Tartuffe is a warhorse, Doctor," I said softly. "He does not care a whit about my anxiety. We are being watched. Do you have any weapons on you?"

Van Helsing's eyes widened in alarm. "Watched? Weapons? Certainly not! I'm a doctor; my entire purpose is to *save* lives, not to end them. Weapons, pah! Although, I suppose if you consider the surgical instruments that I keep in my medical bag, but they are..."

Before she could finish her sentence, we heard movement

in the woods to the left of us. As if on cue, four of the *bêtes* materialized from the bushes and closed in on us. I did not see their leader, Hugo, and I wondered if the beast had made short work of him after Charlotte and I had made our escape. As they'd caught up with me again and Charlotte had been gravely wounded in the process, I ruminated that our escape had been for naught.

Van Helsing eyed the vampires apprehensively.

"I don't suppose you gentlemen are stopping us because one of you is in need of a doctor?"

Frederick grinned, showing a great deal of fang, and cast his gaze over me.

"All in good time."

CHAPTER SEVENTEEN
CHARLOTTE

November 19, 1767
The Wild Rose
Gévaudan

AFTER ANTOINE LEFT, I STARED AT THE DOOR FOR A GOOD LONG WHILE and let the tears fall. I cried for the cutting things Antoine had said to me. I cried for the guilt about the horrible things I had said to him. I cried for the loss of my normal, human life. I cried about the shame of my former husband. I cried because I felt like I was mourning the loss of something new and beautiful with Antoine, despite all the reasons why we shouldn't be anywhere near each other. I cried because for those precious moments in bed with him, I finally felt like I'd found what I'd been searching for with all the lovers I'd taken since my husband.

I'm only sorry that you were another wrong along the way. Was that what I was? Was that what we were? Would he only look back on our time together with regret? To my knowledge, I'd never been someone's mistake before. The revelation smarted.

In the midst of my glorious wallow, I felt acute pangs of hunger accompanied by an unladylike rumble from my stomach. Darkness had fallen, and I found myself ravenous with an appetite I didn't think would be easily sated. Deciding food was more important than my misery at present, I sniffed and wiped my eyes, straightened my shabby travel-worn dress, and made my way downstairs to the tavern.

The Wild Rose was busy, which suited me just fine. The din of drinkers and diners would help distract me from my ill humor. I approached the front and asked for whatever meat they had on offer, roasted if necessary but preferably rare, plus bread and vegetables. I also bought myself an entire bottle of wine, ignoring the disdainful look of the innkeeper. In times like these, I truly missed Daphne and her impressive wine cellar.

Daphne!

Dieu, I'd almost forgotten. She was just in the next town over! I needed to get to her and explain the situation. Perhaps she would know what to do about, well, *everything*.

When my food arrived, I ate as quickly as I could without attracting attention. I took a swig of the wine, then thought better of it and corked the bottle. I needed to figure out how to get out of town unnoticed and getting belligerently drunk— while amusing—would make that a degree more difficult. I paid the innkeeper, who continued to glare at me, and returned to my room to pack.

I didn't have much, but I was able to stash my meager belongings and remaining supplies in my pockets and bundle up in my cloak. Only then did I fully realize that my things were the only things that remained. I knew Antoine had left, but it struck me too late that Dr. Van Helsing had, as well.

I was disappointed that she had departed without at least saying goodbye, but knew it came with the territory of being the most formidable doctor for supernatural sufferers—she was constantly in demand.

As I left the inn, I debated my options for travel. Antoine had taken Tartuffe, and I didn't see any other horses available. The mail coach wouldn't arrive for another few days, and I could take my chances trying to hitch a ride along the road, but because of the infamous reputation for the beast and the dangers in the surrounding woods, other riders and travelers were scarce. Unless I wanted to walk the fifteen miles to the next town where Daphne and Étienne were lodging, it appeared I was stuck in Gévaudan.

Or was I?

Last night, I'd been able to run through the woods at breakneck speed and barely feel fatigue. Did I dare try again? Could I make the journey without being seen by anyone? If I could bundle and tie my clothes to my back, I could find a secluded spot to transform and dress before anyone would be the wiser. A thrill went through me at the thought—almost like I felt when I was a child sneaking sips of father's cognac. *Positively wicked!*

I reasoned I didn't have much of a choice. If I wanted to get to Daphne and Étienne, this would be it. I hurried down the main street to the gate, nodding at the two guards posted out front.

"My husband sent word that our carriage has been repaired," I said with a smile. "Do open the gate for me, gentlemen, so that I may depart."

One of them grumbled something about it not being safe for me to wander through the woods at night, but they raised the gate at my request. I warily eyed the rotting wolf heads on pikes outside the town wall. I didn't think it would be wise to tempt fate and come back to Gévaudan.

I walked quickly, pulling my cloak tightly around me, not

because I felt particularly cold, but because it would seem odd to the guards out front if I didn't. The moon was high and full, casting a beautiful silvery light on the trees and road ahead. It hadn't rained in a couple of days, and with the winter chill setting in, I suspected the first snow of the season would soon fall. When I'd gone about a mile, I drifted away from the road and into a thicket of bushes. I undressed, bundled my clothes tightly and slung them over my shoulder, hoping my plan would work.

Taking a deep breath, I stilled my mind and reached for that place inside me—finding it at once peaceful and wild. Then came the explosion of pain. I screamed, but it came out as a howl, and despite the transformation being just as unbearable as before, it felt quicker this time.

I looked down at my claws and my chest, bundle of clothing still firmly tied, and took off at a gallop. The dark forest blurred past in streaks of green, silver, blue, and black. *Dieu, but it feels so good to run!* There was a freedom to it that I'd never experienced, and it was so satisfying, it felt absolutely sinful. Faster and faster I raced, reaching out with my enhanced senses to see and hear and smell everything around me. It was impossible to take it all in, and yet impossible for me not to.

All at once, I caught the scent of several familiar things that made me stop short. I guessed I'd gone about eight or nine miles south from Gévaudan, and through the undergrowth, it arose—death, rot, black powder. *The bêtes.* Also, herbs, wool, lime blossom. *Van Helsing.* More came at me— horse, leather, apples. *Antoine.* Then, just at the edge of my awareness—earth. Blood. Musk. *The beast—or rather, the man in black.*

My hackles raised of their own accord, and a low, angry growl emanated from my throat. Apparently, I'd just come upon a rather interesting little get-together. The animal part of me raged with a fierce need to protect my friend and my lover.

I listened closely and heard the distinct sounds of voices a little way off, deeper into the woods. Creeping silently toward them, I came upon a low hill, into which was set a cave. A fire crackled at the entrance and two of the *bêtes* stood guard out front. Further in, I could see two soldiers standing over Van Helsing, who was bound and gagged, seated up against the wall of the cave. After a moment, I spotted Antoine—unconscious, covered in blood, crumpled upon the floor. I sensed his slowing heartbeat; he was weakening. Panic and despair unleashed something primal in me, and I fought to maintain control of my senses.

"Easy now, *petite louve*. If you charge in there alone, they will surely kill you."

The words were a whisper at my ear, startling a yelp from me. I whirled to see the man in black standing next to me, glaring at the soldiers with his unnatural eyes. In this light, they looked more red than yellow, and despite my own frightening state, I shuddered in fear. My lips pulled back in an involuntary snarl, but he raised his hand to stay me.

"You have nothing to fear from me, Comtesse. On the contrary, I am here to protect you." His voice was deep and hypnotic, lulling me into a strange sense of comfort.

I would have scoffed had I been in human form, but it came out as a sniff. He chuckled.

"I have much to explain to you—not at this moment, but soon. For now, I think it's time we finished off these so-called *beasts of blood*. Don't you?"

I didn't trust him, but the soft *thump* of Antoine's heart sounded dangerously thready. What was the saying? *The enemy of my enemy is my friend.* I glared at the soldiers, then back at the man. He appeared to sense my resignation. He grinned, displaying two sets of fangs—teeth unlike any vampire I'd ever seen.

"Excellent. I'll take the two at the front. While I have them occupied, you sneak in and take out the two in the back," he directed, his tone suffused with ennui. He began to disrobe, and I looked away, embarrassed. Again, that dry chuckle. "Ah, and one more thing, *petite louve*. If you decide to eat them, I daresay you'll have a terrible stomachache afterward. Take it from me."

With that, he shifted into the wolf-like beast I'd seen before. It was a gruesome sight, watching the immediate restructuring of bone and skin and sinew. In wolf form, he nodded once to me, and we took off in opposite directions. The closer we got to the cave, the stronger the scent of blood.

Dieu, please let Antoine be okay.

"Frederick, do you smell that? I think it has returned —*ulp!*" Before the vampire could finish his sentence, the beast leaped atop him, clamping its jaws tightly around his throat.

The other soldier out front dove into the fray, hissing and screaming. I turned away to avoid witnessing the gory spectacle, praying that the wet crunching and yelping sounds meant things were going in our favor. The two soldiers inside saw the fight taking place out front and turned to help rescue their comrades, but they weren't expecting a second monster, which gave me the advantage. I jumped in before they could draw their weapons and knocked them both to the ground. I attempted to bite one around the neck but was clumsy and instead ripped open his shoulder. He screamed and pushed me off with impressive strength while the other soldier lunged at me with his sword. I dodged the attack, praising my balance on four legs instead of two, and clamped down on his arm, ripping his hand off. His sword clattered to the ground, and he screamed, clutching the bleeding stump where his hand had been. Before I could attack again, the first soldier slammed into me, knocking the wind from my lungs and pushing me back against the cave wall. He leaned forward, fangs bared in an attempt to bite my throat, but I twisted away in time, and he reeled back with a mouth full of brown-black fur.

"Arrrgh!" he spat. "What the Hell are you?"

His comrade moaned on the floor, attempting to staunch the flow of vital blood from his arm. I snapped at the vampire holding me, trying to force him off balance, until he stumbled backward and tripped over his prone companion. He rolled mere inches away from my unconscious Antoine, which elicited an automatic snarl from me. He raised a brow, apparently realizing my loyalty, and held his sword at Antoine's throat.

"One more step and I'll kill him," he threatened. I growled but backed off. He raised his other sword at me, preparing to strike. *"Stupid creature!"*

Before the lunge came, Antoine's eyes flew open, and he thrust his own sword upward, impaling the vampire from below. He crumpled to the floor on top of the other soldier, who was dangerously close to passing out.

Antoine looked at me, dazed and bleeding. To my utter dismay, his eyes filled with horror, and he gripped his sword until his knuckles turned white. He struggled to get to his feet and hobbled in front of Van Helsing protectively. She tried to speak around the gag in her mouth and her muffled cries echoed off the walls of the cave. Antoine's eyes darted to her before waving his sword threateningly at me.

"Antoine, calm yourself! It's me!" I tried to say, but it came out as a canine whimper.

I need to change back and let him know that he's safe—that I'm safe.

I closed my eyes and tried to find my humanity deep

within, but the pain from my injuries was too distracting. Antoine picked up a stone from the cave floor and threw it at me, hissing and shooing.

"Be gone, foul beast!" he shouted. "Get back! We've no quarrel with you—leave us be!"

Van Helsing struggled some more, trying to attract Antoine's attention. I cowered against the wall of the cave, worried that, in his fear, Antoine would run me through with his sword. He took a step toward me, but in bounded the other creature, letting out a warning growl as he paced in front of me.

The shock at seeing two werewolves stopped Antoine in his tracks. He paled and stumbled to his knees, clutching at a bloody gash in his side. Again, I whined.

Thankfully, Van Helsing is here—she can patch him up.

I cut my eyes to her, but she was staring at my comrade with a mix of...*what?* It looked like disbelief, sadness, and... longing? *How odd.*

I heard the soft click of a pistol cocking and looked to see Antoine leveling his twin flintlocks at us.

How rude! I barked at him, but he gestured toward the mouth of the cave, indicating we needed to leave.

Again, the other beast growled, but I was not about to test Antoine's charity when he was gravely injured and near death at the hands of the *bêtes.* Tail tucked humiliatingly between my legs, I trotted outside. I would fetch my clothes, find a quiet place to shift, and come back to help Antoine and Van Helsing.

I thought I heard the other beast following me, but when I turned around, he was gone. *Merde.* I was unsettled by his sudden appearance and disappearance, and needed to ask him about a million questions that were racing through my mind, namely, *who are you, what are you, why are you here, how do you know me, what the devil did you do to me?*

The visceral remains of the two soldiers out front littered the grass and bushes. I wrinkled my nose, glad for the darkness. I didn't want to see any more blood tonight. The tally so far was at least three of the *bêtes* were dead—or, dispatched, as it were. That left the one called Frederick gravely injured and handless, and the one called Hugo... Well, I wasn't certain what had become of him.

I walked slowly back to the small glade where I'd stashed my bundle of clothes. My ribs hurt from smashing into the cave walls, and the bitter taste of plague blood lingered in my mouth. *Dieu*, I was tired. Had I really rested for two weeks during my transformation? It felt like I hadn't slept in a month. My stomach rumbled with hunger, despite having eaten a large meal just this evening. I suspected I needed to eat more often if I spent more time in this form, given that I'd just run several miles and fought a gruesome battle.

Enough, Charlotte. Relax. Take a deep breath. Find your center and shift.

I relaxed. I took a deep breath. I focused on my center.

Finally, I shifted. The pain of the transformation didn't ebb as quickly as it had previously, and I looked down at my naked body to see dark bruises and scrapes all over me. *Merde*. It appeared the fight had damaged me more than I'd thought. I dressed quickly and hurried back to the cave, calling for Antoine and Van Helsing. I was met with silence.

The cave was deserted, save for the bodies of the three *bêtes* who had met their respective ends. There was no trace of Antoine or Van Helsing, and only a thin trail of blood led away, which I knew to be from the remaining injured vampire. The sun would rise in a few hours—I suspected he would be going to ground.

Try as I might, I could not catch the scent of Antoine or Van Helsing. The area stank of blood and battle and of the other creature, and with the pain of my wounds, it was difficult for me to focus. Perhaps they'd rode on to meet with Daphne and Étienne, and I would come upon them in the next town.

I trudged slowly back up to the road and walked for a while, debating what I would say to Daphne and Étienne when I met them. I was certain they would immediately detect my transformation, so prevaricating was out of the question. Besides, I would need their help cleaning up after Sade's murder and exonerating Antoine.

Antoine. My heart stuttered and worry churned in my gut. He hadn't looked well when I'd seen him in the cave. I hoped he and Van Helsing had made it safely away, and that I'd soon reunite with them. I wasn't going betray my earlier resolution to part from Antoine. And while I didn't think I necessarily *had* to explain myself to him, I wouldn't soon forget the look of abject horror on his face when he saw me in my supernatural form. Perhaps it would be better if there was a little more honesty between us. He deserved that much.

The night lingered, but finally, I spotted a small town in the distance. Grandrieu! That must be where Daphne and Étienne were—and possibly Antoine and Van Helsing. I tugged the hood of my cloak over my head and hurried on, hoping against hope that we'd be able to sort everything out.

CHAPTER EIGHTEEN
ANTOINE

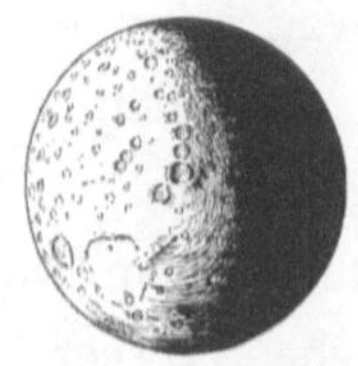

November 22, 1767
Grandrieu

I REMEMBERED VERY LITTLE ABOUT THE DAYS FOLLOWING OUR AMBUSH and the battle in the cave. I'd flitted in and out of consciousness, plagued by the horrors of what we'd just endured. I was dimly aware that Dr. Van Helsing had tied me to Tartuffe's saddle and led both of us, plus our horses, to the town of Grandrieu. It was smaller than Gévaudan but a bit more cheerful—though I'd been to funerals that had more cheer than Gévaudan, so that wasn't saying much.

We'd checked into another inn and Van Helsing, bruised and bedraggled as she was, insisted on tending to my wounds before seeing to her own comfort. After the painful poking and prodding, she informed me of three broken ribs, a stab wound to the side, numerous lacerations, a concussion, a dislocated shoulder, and two sprained fingers, but no vampire bites that she felt would cause infection of the blood plague. She stitched and bandaged what she could with her meager supplies and helped to set my fingers and shoulder, which brought on enough pain that I slipped back into unconsciousness for three entire days.

Dreams of Charlotte haunted my delirium. The sweetness of her lips, the angles of her face, the sparkle in her brown eyes when she teased me into—and out of—an ill humor. Damn, but I wanted her. I wanted to feel her again, wanted to taste her again. I wanted to make love to her endlessly and protect her from everything that would harm her or make her frown. I wanted to wake up with her every morning and share meals with her—even if it meant eating asparagus for breakfast. I envisioned a world where we could marry and have children— each one with wavy auburn hair and the glint of mischief in their gazes. My cracked lips formed a smile at the thought, until the fevered vision warped, and our children sprouted the fur, claws, and fanged teeth of the beasts we'd encountered in the cave.

Beasts. More than one. Was one of them the creature that had attacked Charlotte? What were they? Where had they come from? How many of them were there? Why hadn't they attacked Van Helsing and me? Did they have some particular distaste for vampires? Was Charlotte going to become like them? Then, a more frightening thought emerged—what if one of them *was* Charlotte?

I nearly vomited at the thought, just in time for Van Helsing to hobble into the room with a tray of food and her medical bag.

"Excellent timing," she said. "I'm glad you're awake. I would have hated to pull you from the rest you badly need. How are we feeling this evening, Lieutenant?"

"Restless. Injuries or not, I need to be on my way. Have you any news of Charlotte? Did you meet with your acquaintances here? Ouch! Would you stop poking at my ribs?" I twisted away from her, trying to ignore the pain from her ministrations.

"You are lucky," she muttered. "Even without supernatural assistance, you are healing quickly." She glared at me over the rim of her spectacles. "You heal because you have been unconscious, and you are here resting. If you leave now, all my good work will be for naught. Stay a few more days, eh?"

"A few days! Absolutely not. Out of the question," I barked.

"Yes, I did find my friends here," she continued, breezing past my retort. "They are most anxious to make your acquaintance. I told them I would be happy to introduce you once you were well enough."

I blanched at the thought. Charlotte's cousin was here and probably wanted to see me hanged. I'd heard rumors of the duchesse before, of course. Once a cherished jewel of the court of Versailles, then stuck in that awful marriage to the Depraved Duke, and then widowed in mysterious circumstances. All of this was followed by her engagement and turning at the hands of the most famous blood-drinker in France, the king's own vampire emissary. My stomach churned with anxiety.

"What news of Charlotte, Van Helsing?" I couldn't keep the pleading from my tone, and it annoyed me.

"You have nothing to fear," the doctor replied. "I'll not have you reopening that wound on your side when it is healing so well, so please do be still. Here. Eat something."

She pushed a tray of food into my lap, and before I could take a bite of some rather dubious-looking soup, the door crashed inward, and an impassioned vampire duchesse whirled in. She was dressed in a sapphire-colored silk gown and fur-trimmed cloak that probably cost more than several years of my lieutenant's salary.

"I know he is here and awake, Van Helsing, so stop trying to put me off!"

I made to stand and bow before her, but Van Helsing put her hand on my chest.

"Don't even think about trying to get up," she warned. "Duchesse de Duras understands that you are recuperating, doesn't she?" The doctor flashed an admonishing look at our intruder.

"You!" Her strange violet eyes pinned me back to my pillow. "You are the man who kidnapped my cousin after murdering the Marquis de Sade? The man who has apparently run afoul of Général de Vaux, the most formidable officer of His Majesty's army, who has demanded an absurd bounty for his capture?"

Merde. Well, I can't outrun the consequences of my actions forever. I may as well submit to the justice of The Order. It won't be any different from the justice of the crown. Both see me dangling at the end of a rope.

I swallowed and nodded.

"Yes, Your Grace."

I waited, ready for her to unleash a tirade that ended in an order for my execution. Instead, her lips parted in a grin.

"You can't imagine how pleased I am to finally meet you."

My mouth fell open in shock, but before I could reply, a man entered the room. He was fashionably dressed and unnervingly handsome, and I reasoned it must be the vampire emissary, Étienne de Noailles.

"*Mon amour,* I know you want to have a chat with the lieutenant, but don't you think it's prudent for us to wait until he is at least up and *not* eating?" He eyed me uneasily. "And when he is more appropriately dressed?"

I looked down and realized that Van Helsing must have removed my shirt to dress my wounds and had not bothered to offer me anything else to clothe myself. I reddened in embar-

rassment and tugged the blankets further up my body in a
futile attempt at modesty.

The duchesse blinked at me, then back at her husband.
"*Non.*"

Van Helsing let out an amused giggle and the duchesse
winked at her. The emissary scowled at both of them.
Inwardly, I prayed the floor below me would open up and
swallow me whole.

"Your Grace, Monsieur l'Emissaire, may I present Lieutenant Antoine de Valle. Do be gentle with him. I've only just
put him back together," Van Helsing said with amusement.

I inclined my head in as deep a bow as I could manage
without tearing the bandages from my shoulder and chest.

"Is it de Valle?" the duchesse asked, tilting her head. "Or de
Vaux, I wonder."

I blanched.

"Lieutenant," the emissary said, nodding.

I cleared my throat. "Monsieur. Your Grace. Forgive me for
not getting up. And, if you don't mind, I'd appreciate you
calling me Antoine. I'd rather not use my family name in public
when things are...the way they are."

"Certainly, only you must call me Daphne. Titles are for
ballrooms and court, and my fiancé and I avoid those as much
as we can," she said, taking the chair the emissary offered and
sitting opposite me. "Antoine, it seems you have my cousin's
knack for finding trouble. You must tell me everything that has
happened."

I could no longer keep my curiosity at bay. "Please, Your
Grace—Daphne. Where is Charlotte? Is she here? What has
happened?"

Van Helsing cleared her throat and gave the duchesse a
warning look.

"Has something happened to her? *Mon Dieu*, please tell me.

Is she all right?" I leaned forward, felt a twinge of pain in my ribs, and fell back on the bed with an exhale of frustration.

"Rest easy, Antoine," Daphne said. "Charlotte is well. She arrived half a day before you and Van Helsing."

"Where is she? I must see her. We have things we need to discuss." I looked around frantically, trying to locate my clothes. I needed to get to Charlotte.

Daphne turned an apologetic face to me. "I'm sorry, Antoine, but she's gone."

"Gone? What do you mean? Where?" I looked at her, then at Van Helsing, who frowned sheepishly at me.

"She didn't want us to tell you she'd been here, Antoine. She wanted to make sure you were safe and well on your way to recovery, but she said she could not linger." Van Helsing pushed her spectacles up the bridge of her nose.

"She was here? And she just...left?" The disappointment I felt hurt more than my wounds.

Why did she leave without speaking to me?

I remembered our last words to each other had been in anger, but surely, she'd known it was the heat of the moment. She must have known my feelings for her were...different. *More.*

"She told us much of what happened over the last few weeks," Daphne said. "But I'd like to hear your side of things, as well."

"What did she tell you?" Panic edged into my voice.

The emissary smiled, his eyes glittering in the candlelight. "Some version of the truth, I expect. If you've spent much time in her presence, I'd wager you take my meaning."

I licked my parched lips and reached for the cup of watered-down wine on my tray.

"Why did you kidnap Charlotte from Versailles?" Daphne pressed. "Let's start there."

"I didn't kidnap her," I insisted. "I was protecting her. I thought she was a young man and that the marquis was going to take advantage of her. She was in the wrong place at the wrong time. We were about to be discovered, and at her feet was a dead marquis, shot through the chest, and her with a quiver of stupid costume arrows. I did not want her to be accused of the murder that I knowingly committed."

"Most honorable," Daphne said. "Why did you murder the marquis?"

"Didn't Charlotte tell you?"

She answered with a noncommittal shrug, which could have meant anything. I sighed, angry with the coy machinations of these women.

"My reasons are my own," I ground out.

"Your reasons must also be ours, if we are to protect Charlotte," Daphne replied. "And you."

"I do not need or want your protection," I snapped. "I just want to be left alone."

"*Mon Dieu,* man, you murdered a damned marquis! You cannot just be left alone," the emissary laughed. "We are beholden to the king and The Order, but we will do what is necessary to protect Charlotte and respond appropriately."

He had a point.

"Monsieur, we are very good at keeping secrets," Daphne said.

My mood darkened. "Sade abused, tortured, and murdered my nephew," I said, bile rising in my throat. "My beloved sister, Marie, killed herself from the grief and shame of it. My father knowingly placed young Louis in Sade's charge, likely offering the lad's innocence in exchange for Sade's tutelage and influence. Because of my father's need for power and control, my family is destroyed. I will not hide from the consequences of my actions, but if you are here to elicit some sort of apology and request for absolution, you will not get it. Sade deserved far worse than the quick death I gave him, and I regret nothing."

Daphne was quiet, but I recognized something like anguish flashing in her eyes. Her gaze shuttered before I could be certain. The emissary appeared to sense her feelings, though, and placed a gentle hand on her shoulder.

"We understand," he said. "More than you know."

"Sade's fate had already been decided by The Order," Daphne said, rising. "He was marked for death by Charlotte's hand, but it was to appear as an accident. Now that it looks like murder, there may be an investigation. Étienne and I will do what we can to settle things, but there are grave consequences to your actions, Antoine. The danger we are all in is very real. Sade certainly deserved death, but you should not have intervened."

"My vengeance is not your concern, nor is it The Order's or the king's. Sade was a deviant and a predator, and I've just saved everyone the trouble of figuring out what to do about a murderous aristocratic problem. You should be thanking me for doing your dirty work," I grumbled.

Daphne smiled, but there was something dangerous in it. "I do not shy from dirty work, Antoine. Neither does Charlotte. She is not simply a comtesse. She is not simply my cousin. She is not simply an agent of *les Dames Dangereuses* and The Order. Hell, Charlotte is not *simply* anything."

"I know that!" I shouted, angry that the duchesse was deigning to tell *me* about Charlotte.

She placed a hand on my arm. "Charlotte is not even *simply human* anymore."

My gaze flew to hers. "You know?"

Étienne chucked darkly. "Of course, we know. We're

fucking vampires, Antoine, don't you think we'd recognize a werewolf in our midst?"

The sickness I felt had nothing to do with the pain of my injuries or the dread at spilling my secrets to these powerful and dangerous individuals. I looked at Van Helsing.

"The beasts in the cave," I said. "One of them was her."

She nodded.

Horror and despair washed over me. Even though Charlotte was still alive and was not mine to mourn, I felt a keen sense of loss. I had not protected her, and because of me, she'd become a monster. The forgotten self-loathing returned, and I attempted to quell my rising nausea.

"What now?" I whispered.

"Now, you rest," Van Helsing insisted. "If you don't allow yourself time to heal properly, it won't matter what happens with The Order or Charlotte. You will die from festering wounds and not be alive to plead your case to either."

"You know what I meant," I growled at her. "I care not for my own future. Where is Charlotte? What happens to her? Can she be saved?"

"Saved?" Daphne inquired. "Why, Antoine, what *can* you mean?" She grinned, and the firelight glinted on her vampire fangs.

"*Pardon,* I meant no offense. I understand you may have chosen your fate, but Charlotte did not choose hers. She will have to live this cursed life for eternity."

The emissary lifted a shoulder in nonchalance but regarded me pointedly. "Eternity is not so bad as long as you have someone to share it with."

"My point is that she did not have the choice."

"Neither did I," Étienne replied. "*My* point is that even though I had no choice, I adjusted to life with the plague. Charlotte will do so, too. She is nothing if not resilient."

"You didn't see how devastated she was back in Gévaudan when she learned that she had contracted this new condition," I argued.

"Perhaps she is more accepting of it now," Étienne shot back. "I know where you're coming from, Antoine, but it is hardly the sentence you think it is."

I opened my mouth to argue further, but Daphne stepped between us. "Étienne, would you give us a moment, please? You, too, Doctor."

Looking rather murderous, Étienne bowed curtly and ushered Van Helsing from the room. Daphne sat back down and leaned forward to study me.

"What will you do if she cannot be, as you put it, *saved*?"

"What do you mean?"

"There is no cure for the blood plague," she said. "It is unlikely that there will be a cure for her. Her condition may not be unique, but it is rare. We know even less about it than we know about the blood plague. What then, Lieutenant? What will you do?"

Outraged that she was trying to draw so much out of me, I pursed my lips. I wanted nothing to do with this duchesse and her strangely accusatory questions.

"Nothing," I barked. "I only want to see that she is safe. It is my fault that she was endangered in the first place, and it is a mistake I mean to rectify. Once that is done, I will be on my way. I have things to settle with my father and I aim to ensure that the remaining *bêtes* are dispatched properly."

She tilted her head, eyeing me like a naturalist viewing a specimen under glass. "And then what?"

"Pardon?"

"After that, I mean. Where will you go? Assuming you go after your father—a wholly stupid idea, I might add—and dispatch the remaining *bêtes*, you will not be welcome back in the army. You would be on the run, I would think—trying to avoid the justice for Sade's murder, your father's, and potentially five French soldiers. Is that the life you're prepared to lead?"

"And what if it is?" I nearly shouted. "It isn't your concern!"

She raised a brow and stood again, making her way to the door. "It might not be mine, but it certainly seems to be Charlotte's."

CHAPTER NINETEEN
CHARLOTTE

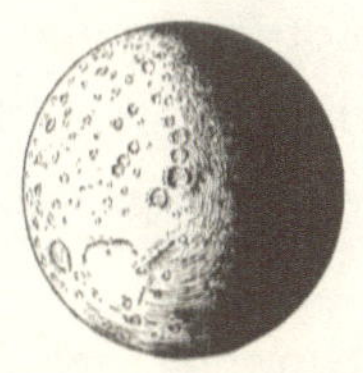

December 13, 1767
Château de Ruisseau Magdelaine

Snow fell in soft, sleepy clumps outside, blanketing the manicured grounds below. Since I'd arrived back home, autumn had ceased to hold back winter, and Paris had been frozen in an unending cycle of snowfall and freezing rain. It made everything in the city look as if it were plated in silver and dusted with powder.

My breath fogged the glass of the window and though I knew it was cold, I didn't feel it. I'd come to accept that part of my condition with some appreciation—no more freezing hands and feet during the winter, no more perspiring during thick, stagnant summers. My wardrobe could be more about fashion and less about function, which was one of the few things I truly wanted in life.

It had been weeks since I'd left Antoine at Grandrieu. Guilt gnawed at me, but I knew he was in the capable hands of Van

Helsing, Daphne, and Étienne. Still, every day I wondered if I'd done the right thing. There was so much unresolved…so much unsaid between us. I'd started numerous letters trying to explain things—to admit that I was the grotesque beast in the cave, to tell him the truth about my former husband and divulge my secrets, to remind him that we were better off staying away from each other. To apologize for our last words and tell him I wished things were different—could be different. To confess my feelings for him had become something…*more*.

Every draft ended up in the fireplace. It was futile for me to say such things to him when several facts remained: Antoine was on a doomed revenge quest with his own demons to battle, and battling demons was something I'd already had my fill of. I had a duty to *les DD* and The Order, to Daphne, and to king and country. I was doing important work for the fate of France and wouldn't abandon my purpose to—what? Give up everything to marry again, have a litter of children, and set up residence in the countryside? While admittedly tempting, I rolled my eyes at the thought.

There was also—quite possibly—the fact that I might now be immortal. Daphne had given up sunlight for her love because she couldn't bear to spend a mortal life without him. I would never ask that of any man, let alone one I wasn't even sure could bear to be in the same room with me without argument. Plus, I'd seen the horror on his face in the cave. It was forever burned into my memory. There was no way on heaven or earth that Antoine would willingly offer himself up for the bite, be it vampire or a werewolf. And who was to say that was how the infection would be transmitted anyway? Van Helsing had been most evasive about the specifics of my supernatural state. Everything I'd learned about my condition had been through trial and error over the past weeks, and I suspected I had a long lifetime—if not eternity—to learn the rest. If only that man in black, the beast, hadn't run off after our battle in the cave. I hadn't seen hide nor hair of him anywhere, and I'd run the midnight miles in creature form to find him.

The Order had been thrilled, of course. When they learned of my new condition, they politely requested a demonstration of my lupine abilities, and so here I was tonight, dressed in a formal gown of dark purple-black silk and a domino mask, ready to go before them and perform like some kind of pet. My stomach twisted in disgust. I believed in The Order and wanted to ensure they were on the right side of things in France, but any time I had to appear for them, it soured my insides with distaste. *The dusty old prats.*

I'd considered declining, of course, but it would make things go a tad more smoothly when I explained what had allegedly gone wrong with the Marquis de Sade's death. Daphne and I had worked out a plan back in Grandrieu, and I hoped it would prove satisfactory for them. The cover story about Sade's death was already circulating by the gossip in court, which was the only opinion any aristocrat truly cared about. *Killed by one of his unwilling lovers in a fit of passion! Sade died as he lived—wretchedly.*

If The Order took us at our word, Antoine would be safe from one threat, at least. As to the remaining threats—his father and the *bêtes* who'd gone to ground since the attack outside Grandrieu—well, I feared he was on his own with them. Knowing he was a capable soldier did little to soothe the waves of dread plaguing me about it.

A knock at my bedchamber door startled me from my musings. My butler, Charles, inclined his head and informed me my carriage was ready to depart.

"*Merci,* Charles. I'll be down shortly."

I stashed a small dagger in my skirts and fastened my favorite bracelet, a ring of black pearls on an expanding cord that I had often employed as a garrote. I was as ready as I ever was. I picked my way carefully over the snow-covered stairs and stepped up into the carriage, but not before catching a whiff of orange blossoms.

"I didn't think you were coming tonight, as well," I said to the dark interior of my carriage.

"What, and miss the show? *Please,*" Daphne said, the grin in her voice evident.

"The whole thing is absurd!" I complained. "Frankly, I'm annoyed I have to spend my entire evening with a bunch of obnoxious old men when I could be spending it drinking brandy in the tub with a roaring fire and a stack of erotic novels."

I signaled to the coachman to drive on, and we rumbled down the tree-lined drive of my estate.

"Charlotte, *chérie,* we both know that's not how you really want to spend your evening," Daphne said gently. Her supernatural eyes glowed in the dark like a predator. Did mine do the same?

"You're right," I sighed. "Drinking brandy in the tub is dangerous. Much too heady. Champagne, though—perfectly safe."

She laughed. "So, I see we're not discussing the tall, dark, brooding reason that *you* have gone all broody."

"I have not! How dare you suggest such a thing. I'm as silly and flippant as I ever was," I insisted, pulling a flask from my garter and taking a swig. I needed a little liquid courage to get through this evening. I offered it to Daphne, and she took a drink, as well.

"Charlotte," she said in a low voice. "It's *me.*"

I frowned. "I know. I'm sorry. It's just...later, *d'accord?* We will talk later. I need to focus to get through this tonight."

She nodded and we sat in companionable silence for the remainder of the ride. The carriage wheels crunched wetly through the snowy ruts in the road. I peered out the window, saddened by what my enhanced vision could now see. Worsening poverty unfolded throughout the city—more poor souls lost to the blood plague than ever before. I wondered if there were any humans remaining outside of court. It had been a choice for Daphne, brought about by the luxury of love, but most of the other vampires had infected themselves as the only alternative to death by starvation. If this was partly due to the grain blight and the catastrophic absence of food, what would happen when France ran out of blood? Had The Order considered that?

Before long, we slowed to a stop in front of an abandoned cemetery on the outskirts of the city. The thick blanket of snow obscured many of the graves and I said a silent prayer for the forgotten inhabitants of this desolate place. Daphne and I descended from the carriage and walked to a shabby mausoleum at the back. She unlocked the heavy metal door and pulled it open, revealing an empty tomb lit by tall braziers and an ominous stairwell descending underground.

We both paused a moment, steeling ourselves for what we knew would be a trial, picked up our skirts, and went down the stairs. At the bottom stretched a long corridor lined with candles that flickered in the cold, damp air. Shadows danced along the black stone walls and, from a distance, my supernatural hearing picked up the hushed voices of men murmuring in secret conversations. Daphne adjusted her domino mask— mere formalities since we would be the only two women in attendance and our identities within The Order were well known—and we approached the large oak door at the end of the corridor.

I knocked three times and a liveried servant opened the door, bowing low before us. I'd been inside only twice before, mainly because I was used to conducting business through coded messages sent via other agents. The room was impressive, if a bit creepy. Lining the walls were massive bookshelves filled with years of filed intelligence reports. Large annotated maps of France hung like tapestries in between. Daphne adored the atmospheric chamber, but I felt like a bug in a bell jar surrounded by the twenty or so men who made up The Order's inner circle. Tonight, especially, they studied me with an intensity that put my previous discomfort to shame.

No sooner had we set foot inside the room than a masked gentleman approached me and smiled obsequiously.

"*Mes agents,*" he purred. "Thank you for coming this evening. I think we have quite a bit to discuss, so let's take our seats and begin, shall we?"

Each person made their way to the large oval table in the center of the room. Two servants offered everyone glasses of wine or cognac, but they paused upon reaching Daphne and me. We were offered tea or sherry. I snorted in derision.

"Don't be ridiculous. We'll take cognac, as well. Lord knows I'm going to need it tonight," I grumbled.

The man to my left chuckled and winked at me from beneath his mask. *Is that the Duke of Nevers?* The servant filled our glasses and melted into the background.

"Before we begin with the more *physical* aspect of tonight's meeting," the first man said, "we wanted to hear your version of the events leading up to the...ehm...infection."

"You've no doubt read my statement, as well as those from the duchesse and the emissary," I replied.

"Yes," said another man. "But we'd prefer to hear it from you, if you don't mind. Refresh our collective memories."

I narrowed my eyes in annoyance but smiled as sweetly as I could.

"Of course, gentlemen. I trust I don't need to remind you *why* we issued the death order for the Marquis de Sade, and since the beginning of the evening passed exactly as planned, I won't bore you with those details. I'll start, shall we say, with the moment when I led him into the garden for the fatal faux tryst. Perhaps the drugs were not as strong as we thought, or perhaps he had a much stronger constitution than I expected," I lied. "He came quietly enough, but he became rather overzealous in his attentions. He certainly would have discovered my identity in his feeble attempt to ravish me, had not a passing solder spied us through the garden gates at the back of Versailles. Thank God for Lieutenant Antoine de Vaux! I was knocked unconscious in the fray and the gentleman in question picked me up and took me to a nearby coaching inn to recover. It was there that I learned of the bounty on his head and that he was pursued by the *bêtes de sang*—a heretofore unheard of and thoroughly illegal group of private vampire soldiers under the command of Général de Vaux."

"Preposterous," came a disbelieving voice from the back. I glared but continued.

"The *bêtes* caught up with us on the road to Gévaudan—the town we headed for to try and escape their vigilante justice. During our confrontation outside the town, we were attacked by, presumably, the beast that had terrorized Gévaudan, and I was injured in the process. Dr. Van Helsing was summoned to see to my care, and I made my way home after that."

Daphne and I had discussed our version of events in detail, and we agreed to omit certain parts of the story unless absolutely necessary. *Stay as close to the truth as possible,* she'd said. *That will make the lies much more convincing.* As I looked around at the masked men seated around the table, most of them were nodding, thoughtful. In agreement that my story—while bizarre and fantastic—was at least plausible.

"And what of Lieutenant de Vaux?" came a voice at the other end of the table. It was one I didn't recognize.

"I haven't heard of him since I left and returned home. As his capture was not part of my assignment, I left him to his own fate," I replied, attempting an air of nonchalance. Outside of clearing his name with The Order, I wanted him to be beneath their notice. It was a gamble, to be sure, but one I needed to make to secure his safety.

"You didn't think to turn him in? Or inform any other authorities of his whereabouts?" That same voice at the end of the table. *Who is that man? Why don't I recognize him?* With my new powerful supernatural senses, I was just getting used to the scent of each man at the table. Hopefully it would help me to identify them later.

"Of course not. Doing so would have jeopardized everything," I snapped.

"How so?"

"He'd seen me with the Marquis de Sade. He saw me with another agent on the road to Gévaudan. He knows of my condition. If he's not a complete imbecile—and I daresay he isn't—he will put things together if he's properly motivated. I did not wish to give him that motivation. Our meeting was inconvenient at best and I was eager to part ways." I shrugged.

"Do you suspect treachery? Will he try to blackmail you, do you think? Perhaps we should do better to ensure he does not allow the puzzle pieces to fall into place..."

"Don't be absurd," Daphne spoke up. "Such rash action will only draw more attention and put him in a defensive position. He has his own troubles to worry about. Best to leave him be. Charlotte and I will task a detail of DD agents to keep an eye on him." She placed a surreptitious hand on mine beneath the table and gave it a little squeeze. She'd sensed that I would rise to Antoine's defense and stepped in to diffuse the situation.

"That's not good enough," said the man at the end of the table. "I say we bring him in."

I slowly began to remove my glove, attracting the attention of each man in the room. "I don't think that's a wise course of action," I stated. Continuing with my other glove, I started to shuck layers of my dress, boldly staring into the masked faces of each agent.

"Wh—why not?"

I was down to my chemise, stays, petticoat and stockings now. Confusion was thick in the room, but gazes were riveted.

"Lieutenant de Vaux saved my life," I said, affecting a bored tone. "As such, he is under my protection."

With the last word, I found my inner beast, called her forth, and shifted form. I'd been practicing every day, and while it still caused me great pain, I was getting better at tucking it away. Through the rush of blood in my ears and the involuntary howls and growls that spilled from my muzzle, I heard the gasps and astonished murmurings of the men. When my transformation was complete, I sat back on my haunches and waited. A scent of fear hung in the room, which I found very satisfying.

"Remarkable!"

"Do you think she can understand us in this state? Is it capable of reason?"

"*Mon Dieu,* what a horrifying creature! It's as if Lucifer himself created a wolf. It certainly must be evil for how ugly it is."

I growled and bared my teeth at the prat who'd spoken the last comment. *The nerve of some men!*

"I daresay she can understand us, even in her current form," chuckled another. "I'd watch my tongue, if I were you."

"Very well then. She is a beast—that much of her story is true. But what can she *do*? We all know vampires possess supernatural strength and enhanced senses. Does she, as well?"

I nodded. The men were suitably impressed.

"Gentlemen," Daphne said, clearing her throat. "Charlotte has requested I answer your questions about her abilities to the best of mine. Allow me to elucidate more on her condition, based on what we know so far, which is—regrettably—very little. Van Helsing may shed more light on this new variation of the blood plague, but we do know it is rare indeed. Charlotte has the enhanced senses of a vampire, albeit with a more accurate and wider ranging sense of smell. She has the same speed and strength that we vampires do, and so far, we have been evenly matched in each contest. She does not hunger for blood but seems to prefer raw meat instead. She can transform at will and generally appears to be of a similar likeness to a wolf, with the notable exceptions of a human brain and consciousness."

"And what of her soul?" came the voice of the man in the back. "Is it lost to the fires of Hell, as yours is?"

Daphne narrowed her eyes at the insult. "I would not presume to judge her soul, nor its fate. As one of the supposedly soulless brethren, however, I might offer in defense that, in our line of work, we have met far more humans with no guiding religious light nor moral compass. Men, you would say, who are more certainly destined for Hell than many of the sufferers of the blood plague."

At this, the man in the back stepped forward and removed his mask. I was certain I'd never seen him before, but there was something about him that rang vaguely familiar. Unconsciously, my hackles rose, and a low rumble of warning sounded from my chest.

"Forgive me for not making introductions earlier, *mes agents*," one of the older gentlemen said. "This evening we have a guest in our midst. Duchesse, Comtesse, may I present Général de Vaux."

CHAPTER TWENTY
ANTOINE

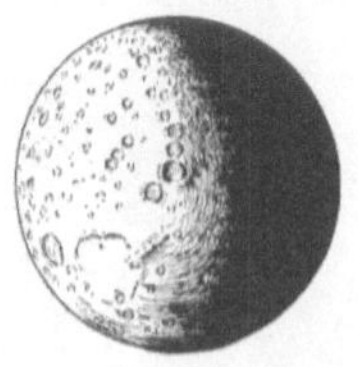

December 13, 1767
Cimetière des Âmes Oubliées

IF I'D KNOWN HE WAS GOING TO BE TRAIPSING AROUND A GRAVEYARD, sneaking into tombs at night, I might have reconsidered my decision to follow my father. Yet here I was, crouched in a bush, soaked with melting snow and misery, still sore from my healing injuries, waiting in the worst place for the worst confrontation with the worst man. Things felt as hopeless and bleak as the weather.

I'd lost count of the nights since I'd left Grandrieu. They all seemed to blur together into one long stretch of frigid darkness. Sleep eluded me, and when I could shut my eyes for longer than a few hours, my mind conjured dreams of Charlotte. *Charlotte.* I still ached with her absence and the sadness I felt knowing she'd been in Grandrieu and had left without seeing me. When I decided to return to Paris to hunt down my father, I'd considered calling on her, but had thought better of it.

What would I have said? Would she even receive me? I could see it now—a shabby, damaged outlaw showing up on the steps of some grand estate, inquiring after a comtesse. Her servants would probably summon the authorities and I'd be carted off to the Bastille just for being a suspicious character—even without the murder charge and bounty on my head. I hated how much I needed her, as if every day since we'd parted had me living a sort of half-life. For the sake of my own sanity, I was determined to leave her alone. She had a life of passion and danger and...*werewolfishness* to return to and I had my vengeance. Neither of us wanted to watch the other go down in flames, so perhaps it was best if we simply turned our gazes away.

Another carriage arrived and the door opened. As soon as the woman descended from the interior, I knew her—masked or not. *Charlotte.* She appeared as if summoned from my very thoughts, not that she was ever far from them these days. As she stepped down onto the snowy ground, she was followed by the duchesse, who led her to the mausoleum where my father had disappeared. Fear pulled my nerves taut, and my stomach dropped. *No!* It couldn't be. *What the Hell was going on?*

I debated storming in after her, but every time I'd acted without thinking, it had ended badly for both of us. I needed to get her alone—to talk to her. *Nothing more.* What business would she have in this forlorn cemetery? Did it include my villain of a father?

The familiar dread and memories of trauma spurred me into action, and as soon as they were out of sight and her coachman was distracted, I crept through the bushes and discreetly climbed into her carriage. I wouldn't charge in after her, but I would wait for her here to ensure we had a chance to speak with one another.

Dieu, please let her be okay. Please protect her from my father. What could they be doing in there? It had to be the business of The Order, but I was certain that my father wasn't a member. *Why has he come?* My anxiety became almost too much to bear.

After an interminable amount of waiting, men started to file out of the dilapidated tomb, two or three at a time. I did not see my father, but after an eternity, Charlotte appeared with the duchesse following behind. They were having a somewhat frenzied conversation with each other until they both arrived a short distance away from the carriage. They stopped and turned to each other, bodies tense.

Damn! Of course, they can sense me. How stupid could I be?

"Charlotte, *chérie*, I do believe you have a visitor," Daphne said.

Charlotte's face tightened with emotion and—*is that longing?*—before she schooled her features in a mask of vexation. Her eyes narrowed on her carriage. "What is it about my carriage that seems to invite unannounced visitors? I must have the most unobservant coachman and footman in all of France."

"You know, it's such a beautiful winter night. I think I'll walk home," the duchesse said. I barely caught her wink. Charlotte's expression was drawn, and once again, I regretted the decisions that brought me here.

She stepped up into the carriage and sat on the seat opposite me. I waited with bated breath.

"So," she said. "Here we are."

"Charlotte," I said. I hated the way it sounded—like a whisper of hope.

"You look like you haven't eaten or slept in a week," she said.

I frowned and grunted, not wishing to lie to her or admit that I couldn't rest with thoughts of her haunting me.

She continued. "I'm only slightly surprised to see you, but I'm afraid to inform you that you're only the second person to ambush me in my own conveyance this evening. Daphne beat you to the punch earlier."

"It wasn't planned," I admitted.

"Of course, it wasn't! I assume you're here because of your father," she continued. "And not because you've just been out there paying your respects or going for a moonlit stroll through an abandoned cemetery."

I didn't trust myself to say much, so I grunted in assent. "What was he doing down there? He's not a member of The Order."

She leaned forward, and a shaft of moonlight spilled across her lovely face. "Perhaps you could tell me," she said. "After all, I'm sure you've been following him around. You know him better than most. What's his end game?"

"What did he tell you?"

She snorted. "He was a distinguished guest of The Order. He came under the guise of questioning me as to your whereabouts and to hear my testimony about Sade's botched assassination and my subsequent turning."

Panic crept into my voice. "He knows you're a werewolf. And that you were a match for the *bêtes*?"

"Well, he saw me change with his own eyes. But I'm uncertain how much he knows about our altercations with the *bêtes*. I didn't tell him anything that happened outside Grandrieu. I didn't think it would be prudent to tell The Order I was involved in the deaths of several vampire soldiers, which, by the way, you *never* thanked me for," she added with an air of petulance.

"Wait. He saw you change? What did you tell The Order? What did you tell *my father*?" I couldn't help the betrayal in my tone.

She signaled to her driver and the carriage pitched forward. "Oh, Antoine, don't get your hackles up. I didn't tell him or anyone else in The Order anything damning. I told them you killed Sade to protect me—not entirely a lie—and that we went to Gévaudan to escape the *bêtes* sent on your father's behalf. He denies it, of course. Says he sent human soldiers after you, and they must have been turned after they left his command. He says he only hopes for your safe return, so he can reunite with his beloved hero of a son."

I scoffed. "I'll bet."

"What's he really after, Antoine?"

"Truthfully, I do not know. But we can be sure it'll be about money, power, or any other self-serving greedy aim. I promise that's closer to the truth than any of that rot he's spouting to The Order."

She sat back against the cushions away from the moonlight, and I temporarily mourned the loss of her beauty.

"And what are you after?"

I shifted uncomfortably. The ache of how much I missed her hit me full force. *Dieu, why must this be so difficult?* "I told you before. I'm after him."

She was quiet, studying me. "Is that really all you want?"

"Yes. No! Damn it, it's all I can have, Charlotte. All I deserve," I said forcefully. *Seeing her is a mistake. Being this close to her is a mistake.*

"You're the only one who believes that, Antoine."

"What do you want me to say?"

"For pity's sake, Antoine, I want you to think about your life. Where it's going, what you want, what happens after you see your revenge mission completed—*if* it is completed. What would satisfy you? How would you find happiness?" She waved her hand in the air, exasperated. "What lies beyond the death of your father?"

"I...I don't know," I admitted. "I never felt I had the right to a future beyond his death. My life—my purpose—ends with him. I guess I always thought I'd hang for it, so I never allowed myself the luxury of dreaming about more."

"That can't be everything," she pressed. "You can't have *always* hoped for a suicide mission in your thirties. I know that's not what young Antoine dreamed of as a child."

I felt a blush creep up my cheeks. *Certainly not. Young Antoine dreamed of a pretty wife to embrace, children to spoil, winters throwing snowballs and summers eating strawberries beneath shady trees. A home overflowing with love and laughter, where death and disappointment dare not tread, with a partner like sunshine. Young Antoine dreamed of a woman like Charlotte, werewolf or not. Hell, Young Antoine probably would have loved the idea of a supernatural wife.*

"It doesn't matter now," I snapped. "My path is marked out, and my fate is sealed. Events have been set in motion."

"What utter horse shit," she laughed. "Why is it privileged men seem to have everything in the world laid at their feet and they still aren't satisfied? You may not be able to control the cards you're dealt in life, but you can certainly choose how to play them."

"So says the aristocrat born into a life of privilege."

"You're right," she admitted. "But at least I'm doing something with it that goes beyond my own selfish desires. And it doesn't mean I haven't had to adjust to less-than-ideal circumstances from time to time."

She had a point. "So, you transformed in front of all those men." Irrational jealousy bristled in me.

She stiffened. "They were far more receptive to my altered state than you were."

I could've choked on my shame and regret in that moment. "I didn't know that was you in the cave! I was half conscious at the time. And anyway, they were only receptive to it because they want to use your abilities to their advantage," I grumbled.

She crossed her arms in front of her chest. "You know, I've never pushed a man out of a moving carriage, but I think I might enjoy the experience."

I gritted my teeth. "Thank you for saving my wretched life. *Again.*" The words were hot and bitter in my mouth, but it was worth it to hear the slight smile in her voice when she answered.

"It's becoming a habit," she said. "Whatever will you do without me here to protect you?"

She'd meant the words in jest, but emotion seized my reply and tied it into a knot in my throat. The air between us became charged; the unsaid words hanging in the atmosphere like fog. I didn't know if or when I would get another chance to speak to her, so I said the one thing that had been weighing on my mind every day since we'd parted.

"Charlotte," I breathed. "I'm sorry."

"For what?"

"Christ, for everything. For the last words we spoke to each other in anger. For what happened in the cave. For being an insufferable ass in Gévaudan. For endangering you time and time again and getting you mixed up with the *bêtes* and now my father. For setting off the cascade of events that turned you into a fucking werewolf. For kidnapping you in the first place."

"You didn't kidnap me, you were protecting me," she said wryly.

Despite my misery, I chuckled. "If only I was. If only I could. Perhaps if I was better at protecting things, everything would be different."

She blew out a breath. "Antoine, if there's one thing I've learned in this life, it's that there are more than enough torments to go around. You needn't add to them yourself.

Would my life be any better if I hadn't become infected? I don't know. Would it be any better if I wasn't an agent for The Order? Perhaps, but it would certainly be duller. Would it be any better if my husband hadn't summoned a demon to try and force Daphne to love him? Actually, yes, probably, but I would still be married to a man I did not truly love."

Horror gripped me. *Surely I'd misheard her.* "He did *what?*" White hot rage surged through me, quicker than lightning. "I'll kill him. Is he still alive? It doesn't matter. I'll drag him back from Hell and kill him again."

She smiled sadly. "My point is that we can speculate all we want. It doesn't change the way things are. Most of the time, it makes everything more painful because of failed expectations. We are where we are, we are *who* we are, and all we can do is make the best of it," she said.

I nodded. "It does not stop me from wishing things were different." *It does not stop me from wanting you. It does not stop me from needing you. It does not silence the part of me that wants to have a family and a safe haven with you; the part that dreams of walking away from everything to be yours forever.*

She seemed to take my meaning because her voice had lost its teasing edge when she replied. "Nor I."

We were silent for a beat, listening to the muted, snow-covered sounds of the street under the carriage wheels. I opened my mouth to say something—any one of the unspoken things that had been circling my head for the last few weeks—but words seemed to fail me. Desperation won out and I reached forward, pulling her to me and covering her lips with mine.

CHAPTER TWENTY-ONE
CHARLOTTE

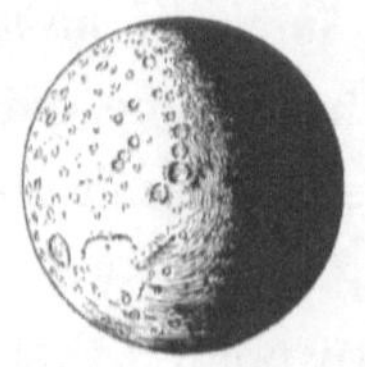

December 14, 1767
Château de Ruisseau Magdelaine

HE CAME BACK. NOT FOR ME, EXACTLY, BUT HE CAME BACK, nonetheless. Was that enough for me? In this moment, I didn't care. The scent of him in my carriage elicited a primal response in my body—*my mate has returned.*

Ridiculous, Charlotte.

His kiss was fire and ice at once, and I met him with the full force of my desire, which only seemed to have grown in our time apart. I slid my hands up his neck and threaded my fingers through his hair. For a moment, everything between us other than this was forgotten. I tilted his head back and scraped my teeth along his jaw, drawing forth a deep growl that sent vibrations of need along every one of my nerves. A low moan escaped my throat, spurring his ardor. I nibbled at his ears while I hastily tugged at his coat, sliding cool palms beneath his shirt to his warm, bare chest. Every part of me was aflame. *Dieu*, I wanted him—this surly, complicated man. Now and forever.

"Charlotte." His voice came out in a rough tremor.

"Antoine?" *Why have you come for your father and not for me? What are your feelings for me? What are your feelings for my being a werewolf? What will happen to us?* I ignored the trepidation and the dark thoughts that circled my mind.

"I feel I must tell you..." he began, caressing my breasts through the bodice of my gown.

"If your words are anything but filthy ones right now, Antoine, keep them to yourself," I chuckled, until his hands slid to my thighs and he bunched my skirts in his fists. Straddling him on the seat of the carriage, I reached for the falls of his breeches, almost losing myself at the feel of his straining erection pressing against my sex. My composure, already frayed and failing, snapped. I gripped his hips and rocked against him, pulling forth from him a moan that was sweeter than any sound I'd ever heard on earth. *Fate be damned—I'm going to have this man.*

"Charlotte," he panted. His fingers fumbled with the bodice of my expensive gown. The silk was like water in his calloused fingers, making it difficult for him to untie, unlace, and unpin me. I struggled with the buttons on his breeches, eager as I was to bare him to me.

With a little growl of frustration—one that sounded alarmingly lupine—I ripped the front of his breeches, scattering the damned buttons across the carriage floor. I let out a triumphant laugh and saw the glaze of lust in his eyes sparkle. With a wolfish grin, he did the same to my dress, ripping it clear down the front. I squealed with laughter.

"This dress cost me a fortune," I huffed, ending with a whimper when he took my nipple into his mouth.

"Send me the bill," he murmured, sucking gently. I gasped

and writhed on his lap, reaching down to wrap my hands around his hard cock. He swore, lewder and more guttural than I'd heard from him before. I slid my hands up and down, mimicking the movement of the carriage as the wheels jostled us back and forth. Already, I was close. *So close.*

"Charlotte, *putain de merde!* You must stop. I want you, my love—I need you." He slid a finger through the warm, wet folds of my sex and growled his desire. "You're so wet, *l'amour*...all for me. How I've dreamed of this perfect pussy since you left me. It's all I can think about. Late at night, alone, I fantasize about the pleasure that lives here." He pushed me back off his lap and against the wall of the carriage. Dropping to his knees, he licked at the insides of my thighs, working his way up to the pearl of my pleasure. I squirmed beneath his touch.

"This teasing will be the death of me, Antoine," I whimpered. "Kiss me like you mean it."

He grinned up at me and dove forward, sucking and licking at the apex of my sex until I was ready to come apart. He would have continued, but I pulled his face up to mine for a fervent kiss, then wrapped my legs around his waist.

"I need it all, Antoine," I demanded. "Give me everything." *What does that mean, Charlotte? What am I asking of him?*

"Everything," he agreed.

I grasped his cock and guided him inside my ready heat on a satisfied moan from us both. It was exquisite—magnificent. He moved slowly at first, seemingly unaware of the words as they fell from his lips. "I'll give you everything, Charlotte. Anything. *Putain, oui, chérie, juste comme ça.* My life, my heart, my soul—they are yours. *Yours.*" My cries cut through the night, and I pushed him back against the opposite wall of the carriage, grinding on top of him with boiling, out-of-control lust. He reached up to twine his fingers through my hair, sending a jolt of lightning from my scalp down to my sex.

"Harder, Antoine, *mon amour!*" I cried. He needed no more encouragement. He lifted me and turned me around, bending me over the seat in front of us. He stroked my breasts and pinched my nipples, and my knees buckled.

"How hard, *petite?*" He slapped my ass, and the sweet sting elicited a thrill and a curse from me. *I need him. I need him. I am his. He is mine. Mine.* I tried desperately to regain my sanity, then abandoned it entirely.

"My body mourns the loss of you, *chéri,*" I pouted, wiggling back against him. "It would be cruel indeed to leave me so unsatisfied."

He slid into me again—*Dieu, I would never know another man like this*—and I moaned a litany of filth that made him groan. *It will never be this way again. There will never be another Antoine. Eventually, you will be parted by time itself.* Whispers of fear and regret echoed through me, but I chased them away with the explosive pleasure of each thrust. I would worry about everything when I wasn't joined with the man I loved.

The man I loved.

"I will never let anyone hurt you, *mon amour.* I will never let another man have you. You are mine. Your body is mine. Your heart is mine. All of it," he grunted, driving into me. He reached forward to find the peak of my pleasure and I almost screamed. "You are mine, Charlotte. *Mine.*"

"Yes," I panted. I felt my body draw up, as an archer draws a bow.

"Say it," he begged. His clever fingers had worked me to the point of combustion.

"I am *yours,*" I shouted, coming apart beneath him, around him.

With a final thrust that nearly toppled the carriage and a roar that fractured the night, he joined me in *la petite mort.*

We stayed braced against each other for several minutes,

trying to catch our breath and hopefully avoid the awkward words that often followed. Antoine kissed the back of my neck and slid out from me, and my body immediately protested. He'd given me pleasure unlike any I'd ever known, but my need for him was unmatched. As frightening as that thought was, I didn't want to face the consequences of our actions. I was not ready to return to the shaded reality of our world just yet.

The carriage slowed to a stop at my estate just as we were sheepishly attempting to right our clothes, and I stared at his grim, furrowed brow as he eyed his ripped breeches. I couldn't help but laugh.

"These were my favorite breeches," he said forlornly.

I wrapped my ripped dress around myself and took his hand. "I'll buy you a new pair. Now, come inside. I'm certain I have something appropriate you can wear—or not."

His green eyes flashed with hope and despair and lust like a promise, and he opened his mouth to say something rational. I stopped him with a finger to his lips.

"Tomorrow, Antoine. Just this tonight," I whispered. I dropped a kiss on his lips, and he nodded.

We exited the carriage and I winked at my driver's knowing smirk as we descended. I led Antoine upstairs to my bedchamber. He was quiet, as he always was, but I sensed a change in him. As soon as I shut the door, I was on him again, pressing my lips to his and meeting his eager tongue stroke for stroke.

Dieu, is this part of my supernatural state? Or is this something else entirely?

I pulled his shredded clothes off, casting them to the side. He really was beautiful—a study of hard muscles beneath golden skin and dark hair, staring at me with that mix of lust and possession that made my head spin.

"You realize at some point, we are going to have a conversation about Gévaudan, your turning, Grandrieu, and my father," he said, slowly tugging my skirts back down my hips. They fell to the floor in with a soft swish.

"Of course," I nodded, running my fingertips over his sculpted abdomen. "We obviously desire each other to the point of madness. We're just doing this to get it out of the way. When we're done, we'll be able to focus. Honestly, it would be irresponsible of us to try to settle things before we were satiated."

He grinned at the lie but made no argument. My hands trailed down the dusting of dark hair at his belly button and he sucked in a breath. He raised a hand to caress my cheek and tilted my face up to his.

"There are other things I want to discuss with you, Charlotte," he said in a low, deep voice. My belly flipped, and before I could remember every logical reason that separated us, I allowed myself a moment to entertain the idea of what he might say. A brief wave of warmth and happiness washed over me. I stepped backward to the bed and beckoned to him.

"Certainly," I smiled seductively as he devoured me with a heated gaze. "But if there are things you wish to say to me, you'll have to come whisper them in my ear."

He smiled that heart-achingly handsome smile, dimples and all, and crawled forward to me. His touch was tender, languid, not the frenzied need from earlier. The sweetness of it was at once too much and not enough.

My anger and frustration hadn't evaporated, but they waited in the corner of my mind. *Charlotte, you damned fool. You know you cannot have him. You cannot be with him. He is an outlaw and will probably go to prison if he murders his father. He will insist you leave les DD and The Order. Even if these things are surmountable, there is one thing remaining that is not: you are a werewolf, and he is human.*

Antoine noticed my distracted mind and pulled away instantly, worry etched on his handsome, scarred face. "Charlotte, are you well? Do you wish me to stop?"

I shook my head, squeezing my eyes shut against the tears that threatened to fall. "No, *chéri*. Not tonight. Do not stop for anything tonight."

He gave me a relieved smile and muttered a rough, "Thank *God*," and bent to kiss me. It was soft and sweet and promised a night of dark pleasures ahead.

If only that could be enough.

CHAPTER TWENTY-TWO
ANTOINE

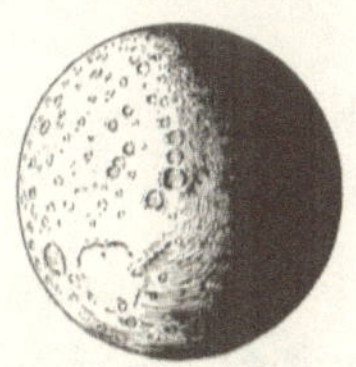

December 14, 1767
Château de Ruisseau Magdelaine

I woke from what surely had been a dream. Cracking one eye open, I stared into Charlotte's slack, sleeping face and smiled. *Not a dream.* Tucked up in her massive bed, tangled in the softest sheets I'd ever felt, entwined with the only woman who alleviated as much suffering as she caused. She snored lightly and I swallowed a laugh. Her eyes fluttered open, and she gave me a slow smile.

"Any regrets?" she asked.

"Only that I didn't come round sooner," I said, pulling her into my arms.

"Mmm," she said through a yawn. "Why didn't you?"

Because I am an outlaw, you are a monster, and I am in love with you. Before I could answer, there was a soft knock at her door. I made to get up out of bed, but Charlotte put her hand on my chest.

"Stay," she instructed. "My servants are used to an *unusual* household. You need the rest and they'll have brought us breakfast."

I was embarrassed and uncomfortable, but I did as she asked. She bade her butler enter, and sure enough, he came in with a large tray covered with food.

"Good morning, my lady," he said. "I have your messages from yesterday."

"*Merci*, Charles," she said, reaching for the tray. "Ooh, poached eggs and asparagus!"

"And I'm afraid there is a gentleman here to see you," he continued, obviously anxious. "He has refused to come back at another time and prefers to wait."

I was instantly on edge. "Who?" I demanded.

To his credit, Charles didn't miss a beat.

"There is a Général de Vaux here to see you, my lady."

Blood drained from my face and my stomach twisted. I launched myself out of bed, scrambling for my breeches.

"I'm going to kill him!" I growled. "Why is he here, Charlotte?"

"I've no idea," she said with a shrug.

"He must be after you for the deaths of the *bêtes*. Or perhaps he suspects you'll lead him to me. Christ, once again, I've put you in grave danger!" I shoved one leg into my ripped breeches and frowned down at them. "I knew things would only get worse. I'm like an ill omen for you, Charlotte. I just didn't think he'd bring you into this... How dare he show up at your doorstep!"

Charlotte cocked a brow at my tirade and nodded to the butler. "Charles, would you mind finding some clothes for the lieutenant? And please inform Général de Vaux that I'll be down shortly. He may wait in the yellow drawing room." She swiped a piece of toast through egg yolk and popped it into her mouth in an unconcerned manner.

"You can't be serious," I said. "You can't receive him, Charlotte. He's incredibly dangerous and I'm certain he's not here for a social call."

She dabbed at her mouth with a napkin and uncovered a second dish on the breakfast tray—a plate heaped with raw meat. She began to tuck in unapologetically, as if she hadn't heard me in the first place.

"Charlotte," I warned.

"Antoine, do have some breakfast. You're clearly in need of rest and nourishment. The hollows in your cheeks and under your eyes look positively cadaverous." She pushed a plate across the bed toward me. "And please sit down. Charles will find you some clothes, but I'm afraid the rest of my staff may be somewhat alarmed by a naked man running through my household, despite my more liberal leanings."

My temper flared. "I don't feel like you truly appreciate the severity of the situation, Charlotte."

"Why do you say that?"

"You're calmly eating breakfast! And you're about to go meet with my father as if he isn't a traitor and the reason my family has been destroyed! I'm serious, Charlotte, I'm going to kill him." *Where are my short swords? And my pistols?*

She finished eating and stood, and it took me a moment to refocus after watching the sheets fall from her beautiful body. She pulled on a long silk robe and crossed to her dressing table, where she sat and started to comb through her glossy brown locks. Her eyes met mine in the mirror, and for a moment, the ever-present humor faded from her face.

"I'm going to meet him, Antoine, and I'm going to find out what he wants. My guess is he's here to try and get information from me about you—assuming he doesn't already know you're here. Have you considered the possibility that as long as you've been watching him, he's also had someone watching you?"

"I have." *I haven't.*

"Please, Antoine. Trust me this once. When he leaves, I'll come back and we'll talk, *d'accord?*"

"Absolutely not. You *cannot* meet with him. He's dangerous, Charlotte, and cunning, and—quite frankly—evil. I don't want you to have anything to do with him."

She sighed and turned around. "Do you trust me?"

I blinked.

She winced slightly. "I know I haven't given you a very good reason to, and I understand your hesitation, given your past and my present *hobby*, but if you could set those things aside and look into your heart."

I pursed my lips. "What are you asking of me?"

"Simply this: let me talk to him. Let me do what I'm best at and draw out his purpose."

"As charming as you are, he'll see right through you. He already knows you're a spy," I argued.

"An agent," she corrected. "Perhaps. But will you at least trust me to try? I want to protect you, Antoine, but I can't do that if I don't understand his aims," she stood in front of me, imploring. "Please. This is what I'm good at. This is why I became an agent. Stay here and wait for me."

I saw her now without any artifice, as bold and genuine as I'd ever seen. I had no choice but to agree. "But if he threatens you..."

"Yes, yes. If he threatens me, you may cut off his head, though I'd fancy doing it myself." She smiled and reached up to kiss me.

Before I could rethink my decision, another knock sounded at the door and her lady's maid entered to help her dress. Charles followed, handed me a robe, and escorted me to the next chamber down the hall, where a roaring fire and full, steaming bathtub awaited me.

Charles seemed to sense my distress. When the other servants had left, he leaned in close. "When you're finished, sir, you may wish to entertain yourself with a book. If you take the back stairs and turn left, you'll find the library at the end of the hallway. It's just next to the yellow drawing room. It may be a bit chilly in the winter, though. Such regrettably thin walls," he said.

Startled by his candor, I couldn't help but ask. "Does your mistress know you listen at keyholes?"

He smiled. "Lady Charlotte is a spy, sir. She pays us to listen at keyholes."

Well, then.

He laid out a jacket, waistcoat, breeches, hose, and shirt—fine enough to see me to court—and left me to my bath.

As I sank into the warm, perfumed water, my muscles clamored for the chance to relax and unknit their knots, but my mind raced with the knowledge that my father was downstairs and was here for Charlotte. I hurried to wash, shave, and dress, hoping Charlotte would take her time in going down to see him.

As Charles suggested, I crept down the back stairs and found the library just where he'd said it would be. My heart pounded. My father was in the next room. Did he know I was here? Was he here to threaten Charlotte? I'd kill him if he did.

Perhaps I should go next door and confront him.

It felt as if Charlotte was going off to fight my battles—again. *Dieu,* how many times had she done that? That was all she'd been doing since we first met, and I couldn't keep letting her fight for me just because I was too depleted to fight for myself.

I should be the one protecting her—even if I've done a poor job of it thus far.

Just as I was resolved to go next door and end things the way they should have ended ages ago, I heard the soft rustle of fabric down the hallway and the door to the drawing room opened. I scooted a chair close to the wall, but found it was unnecessary to press my ear directly against it—Charles had been right about the thinness of the walls. I could hear every word.

CHAPTER TWENTY-THREE
CHARLOTTE

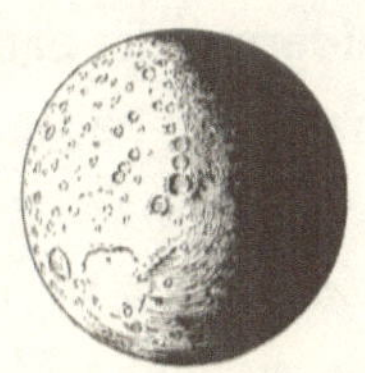

December 14, 1767
Château de Ruisseau Magdelaine

"Général de Vaux! What an unexpected visit," I said, whirling into the room. Light filtered in through the front windows and illuminated the général's morose visage—quite different from my impression of him in the dark tunnels of the previous evening.

Mon Dieu, but he looks so much like Antoine! He was shorter and slimmer than Antoine, and was of course without the visible scars and marks, but they shared the same aquiline nose, full lips, and piercing green eyes. Antoine's had warmth to them, like a lovely green field on a hot summer's day. The général's were hard and cold, putting me in mind of oily seaweed washed up on a winter's shore.

He bowed smartly, dressed in his military uniform with his formal powdered wig. I inclined my head and gestured for him to sit.

"You've been kept waiting," I said. *Not an apology.*

"Forgive me," he said. "I called unannounced. I don't wish to take up much of your time. I simply had some questions for you following your testimony last night that may have been...*inappropriate* for the ears of The Order." He smiled like a predator.

"Well, Général, you know of my allegiance, so it seems like a fruitless journey considering the ears of The Order are right alongside my head. That *must* be disappointing. Would you care for some refreshment? Some tea, perhaps? You do look a bit bilious, and tea is *wonderful* for the digestion. Those English may yet have something right, *non*?" I tittered, waving for a footman.

He narrowed his eyes and frowned but carried on. "No tea, thank you. Comtesse de Brionne, I'm certain you don't share everything with your masters."

"My masters? My goodness, Général, who can you mean? My father and my husband are no longer with us, so I wouldn't—"

He cut me off, jawline flexing in that similar air of annoyance that he shared with Antoine. "Are you being purposely coy, my lady? It's just that it rings of obtuseness, and I cannot abide stupidity in any form."

"I certainly wouldn't take credit for being *accidentally* coy, Monsieur, but it is unfortunate that your patience seems so tested. Are you sure you wouldn't like some tea?" I smiled politely, pouring my own cup.

"I don't want any damn tea!" he spit out, then exhaled and composed himself. "I just need some answers."

"I daresay we *all* need answers, Général, but you haven't even asked me a single question yet. Imagine that! How can I be of help to you if you don't elucidate what you need in the first place? And to be sure, I am *most* eager to be of service to you. You do seem frightfully important." I nodded as earnestly as I could.

In addition to the tightening muscles in his jaw, a sizable vein on the side of his head began to throb. With my supernatural senses, I could hear the blood pumping through it. *He must have a splitting headache.*

"I came to ask where my son is," he said through gritted teeth.

"*Mon Dieu!* Have you truly lost him? You know, when I lose things, they're often in the last place that I look for them. When did you see him last? Oh, I offered you tea, but perhaps you'd like something to nibble on instead? My chef makes the most delicious pastries, but I think probably plain bread for you, *non*? You seem like a plain bread sort of man."

His face began to turn a mottled sort of red. The vein throbbed.

"Now, don't take offense, Général! I just meant that you seem the type to deny yourself certain pleasures in order to live a more ascetic lifestyle. Truly honorable. I imagine a life waging various wars would lead one to such simplistic tastes. Provincial, if you will. Forced to enjoy things that you could get on the frontlines of wherever the king sent you. If I were in such situations, of course I would develop a healthy resentment for the king, but as such, I haven't. He's such a dear, you know. I don't think I could stay mad at him for long." I prattled on, reaching for the tray of pastries in front of me. I looked up, expecting to see steam piping out of his ears, but instead, he was eerily quiet. He smiled coldly at me.

"Is he here?" he murmured quietly.

"His Majesty? Of course not. I imagine he's at Versailles. Why on earth would he be here?" I bent forward to pick up a tart, and his fingers clamped onto my wrist in a vice-like grip. He squeezed, which perhaps would have hurt without my supernatural strength. "Goodness, if you wanted a tart, you simply had to ask. Lemon or cream?"

His eyes flashed with rage and his voice was deadly calm when he spoke. Each word dripped with venom. "Listen to me, you damned, spoiled, ridiculous little slut. I know you lied to The Order. I know you were somehow responsible for what happened to my men. Antoine is too stupid and weak to have dispatched them. I'm certain you know what happened to him and quite possibly where he's hiding. It would be easier if you told me now," he said, twisting my wrist as if he would break it.

"Général," I sighed. While I could have easily pulled free of his grasp, I let him retain his grip, and his illusion of control, for a moment longer. "You must not be thinking clearly. You came into my home to threaten me for information? You're sitting before a comtesse, who you know to be connected with the most powerful people in all of France, who you *actually* witnessed transform into a werewolf—and you're going to break my wrist if I don't tell you what happened to the adult son who left your command? Forget the tea, do have yourself a brandy and a lie down."

I considered changing then and there, biting his arm off and then delivering it to Antoine as an early Christmas gift, but I restrained my more feral impulses. Obviously, the général was suffering from some kind of brain fever. One thing was clear, however—he knew far less than I suspected. I wondered how much information his remaining men had been able to impart to him before their demise.

Apoplectic, he released my arm and stood abruptly. "I know Antoine is responsible for the death of the Marquis de Sade. I know why, as I suspect you do. If he returns to me, we will work things out in our familial sort of way. If he doesn't return to me, I'll see him hanged for being a deserter. Perhaps when you see him, you will tell him that."

"As I told you before, after Gévaudan, we parted ways. If you wish to send your son to the gallows, I'm afraid that's your business. It would make for an awkward family reunion, since I'm sure you'll be joining him for treason."

"Treason? My only aim was to protect my country. I will do so at any cost and the king knows that. If you think he wouldn't sanction a few vampire soldiers to further his foreign ambitions, then I daresay you don't know him as well as you think." He straightened and brushed off his coat.

I smiled frostily. "We'll see about that. Charles will show you out. I would say that it's been a pleasure, but it hasn't, and I'm sure you wouldn't know pleasure if it slapped you across the face, so I'll just say *au revoir*."

His face twisted with anger, and he strode to the door, pausing with his hand on the knob.

"I know my son. Whatever happened between you, I'm certain he'll come here. I'll be waiting. You think you can protect him from me? You have no idea who you're dealing with," he threatened.

"Oh? Wait—you aren't a washed up, double dealing, traitorous blackguard who sacrifices his own family to further his warped political ambitions? Hm. I must've thought you were a wholly different Général de Vaux." I laughed.

His hand flew to the sword at his side and a low, wolflike growl vibrated from my chest.

"You could try it, you know, only I wouldn't. I'm still picking your pet vampires from between my teeth. Do you think you stand a better chance?"

His hand fisted but left the vicinity of his weapon. "I'll be watching you," he hissed.

"Of course, you will, Général!" I shot back. "But if I ever

catch your scent around my home again, I will rip out your throat and eat every part of you but your black heart. *That* I will send to Antoine in a little box for him to bury with his sister. A life for a life—a heart for a heart."

He did not reply, but his posture tensed, and I knew my message had landed. He turned to go without another word, disappearing down the hall. I heard the front door close behind him.

I sat back down and reached for my abandoned tart. "Antoine," I called to the other room. "You may come out now. He is gone."

I waited, knowing full well he had been listening in the library next door.

"Antoine?"

I went across the hall to the library and peered in. It was empty. His scent lingered, so I knew he had been there for at least part of my conversation with the général, but at some point, he'd left. Looking around, I saw the wide-open French doors that faced the side of the estate, directly opposite the stables.

A small square of parchment fluttered from the top of a table to the ground. I stooped to pick it up.

Charlotte,

I know what I must do to lay my ghosts to rest. Do not follow me —I'll only endanger you further.

Yours,

Antoine

"Oh, Hell."

CHAPTER TWENTY-FOUR
ANTOINE

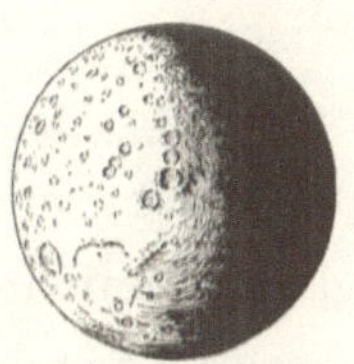

December 17, 1767
Château de Sade
Condé-en-Brie

I'd heard all I needed to hear. The longer I listened to them talk, the more things took shape in my own mind. Puzzle pieces fell into place, connecting Louis's death to the Marquis de Sade and the *bêtes de sang*. I may not have the evidence to support my suspicions, but hearing my father threaten Charlotte had brought about the clarity I needed to see the bigger picture.

He is here for me. Not because he wanted to see my safe return, but because I am one of the few people who could work out the truth of his crimes. I was the one in danger, after all. I knew exactly what my father intended—he would go through Charlotte to get to me. She might not fear him, but she didn't know how diabolical and cruel he could be. I couldn't let anything happen to her. *I wouldn't.*

He obviously suspected our connection, otherwise, he

wouldn't have shown up at her doorstep to threaten her. The move was bold, but odd—it was reckless to ostracize a known member of The Order, especially when he knew her connections and her supernatural state. I'd seen her in wolf form. The vision still terrified me.

My father's actions were that of a desperate man: unpredictable, treacherous, selfish. He was like an animal caught in a trap, fearing the repercussions of the king discovering what he'd done. He would attempt to bury the evidence.

I pulled my cloak tighter around my body, leaning over the horse I'd stolen from Charlotte's stables. *She'll have to forgive me.* The frozen wind lashed against me. I had spared no time in setting off for the Marquis de Sade's estate outside Paris. Before confronting my father, I wanted to be certain my suspicions were correct.

I need proof! And I know just where to get it.

I couldn't believe I hadn't thought of it sooner, but my need for revenge had obscured more of my logic than I cared to admit. My father had burned the damning letters that would have seen him hanged, but that had only been *half* of the correspondence. Sade would have my father's letters, and I'd wager they were locked away in his study—assuming my father hadn't already sent his vampire guard dogs to destroy the evidence of his treachery.

It took me a day to reach the grand estate. Twice I'd gotten turned around on the snow-covered backroads, delaying me a frustrating amount. Despite Sade being dead only a short time, his grand residence appeared almost empty. There were fresh horse tracks marring the snow on the drive and one window glowing with muted gold light, but there was no domestic bustle around the building. *Perhaps it's one lowly housekeeper caring for the estate and the rest of the staff have already been dismissed.*

I guided my horse into a thicket of trees alongside the road and waited. My hands felt frostbitten and my cheeks were raw from the cold, but it was worth the discomfort to take the time to ensure I'd be alone. Finally satisfied, I circled the back of the manor and stabled the horse, taking great care to not be seen. The gardens were winter barren but looked a touch overgrown, making me wonder how long it had been since the marquis had been here. I peered in window after window but found no one.

The glow of firelight was visible from the windows lining the back balcony. If I could find some purchase, I could pull myself up and enter through the doors.

When I swung myself up over the balcony railing, shock stole my breath.

There, sitting at the large desk in the study, sat my father.

The lights hadn't been from a housekeeper or a servant. It had been him—*my father*. He must've passed me on the road when I'd gotten lost earlier. The sharp claws of anxiety seized my lungs and it took massive effort to will myself calm.

It was as if no time had passed. His face looked a bit more gaunt, but his eyes still glinted with the arrogance I remembered from childhood. I took advantage of his unawareness and kicked the doors in, which crashed open in an eruption of broken glass and fractured wood. He startled but recovered quickly, hands falling upon the pistol at his side. When recognition dawned, his face twisted in a grimace of disgust.

"Antoine! What in God's name do you think you're doing?" His hand did not leave his weapon.

"Général. I could ask you the same question."

"Don't be impertinent," he snarled. "Where have you been? Why have you come here?"

"I suspect you and I are here for the same reason—your letters to Sade," I growled.

"What the Hell are you talking about?" he shot back. His bluster didn't hide his twitching hand, however, and my gaze snagged on a thick stack of letters.

I chuckled humorlessly. "Well, for once, my timing has been fortunate. Hand them over, Father, or I shall shoot you and take them."

A sinister smile tugged at his lips. "It's a pity this is what it took for you to find the steel in your spine, boy. Yet you dare presume to threaten me after everything I've done for you. You must be stark raving mad," he shot back.

"Mad? Quite the contrary. For the first time in years, I feel an alien sense of clarity. It was a kind of madness that drove me forward after Marie and Louis's deaths, and truth be told, I've thought of little else but paying you back tenfold for what you did to them. I dreamed of Sade's death, and yours, for too many nights. *But no more, Father.* I have a new dream now, and your blood doesn't play a part in it."

His hand twitched on his pistol, and I pulled mine immediately, training the sights on his heart.

"I don't *wish* to kill you any longer, but I will if necessary. You made your bed with Fate, and now you'll lie in it. I'm going to take those letters and report your actions to the king. It will be his decision if you dangle at the end of a rope, or spend your life in prison."

He scoffed and rolled his eyes. "What are these *actions* you speak of?"

"Your *bêtes de sang*, for a start. That you had intentions of creating an entire army of vampire soldiers who would answer to you and only you. That I had the evidence, but that you destroyed it," I said.

"No one will believe you," he smirked. He picked up the stack of letters and I eyed him guardedly. "Least of all the king."

"They will believe me when I tell them you planned as much with the Marquis de Sade."

His smirk faltered and suspicion passed through his gaze. "What an absurd notion."

"Is it?" I accused. "Why else would you have sent Louis to him? What could you possibly have to gain by offering your only grandson to a known monster? It couldn't just be for influence. As power mad as you are, you have enough influence on your own. No, it had to be something else. The way the blood plague has alienated the human aristocracy—you saw the writing on the wall. What better way to protect yourself from vampires than to have your own militant force of the undead? It was never about protecting France. It was about saving yourself."

"Madness, indeed," he growled. "Perhaps you should be in an asylum."

"How did it first come about? Did you approach Sade with your plan? Or was he in on it from the very beginning? Let me guess—you knew in order to convince perfectly respectable Catholic soldiers to abandon their promise of Heaven in a blood-drinking bargain, you'd need the funds to secure their loyalty and their souls. You approached Sade then, didn't you? He could help finance your private army of the damned, and you would give him your own flesh and blood as payment." The words were ash in my mouth, and bile rose in my stomach. I felt sick as I laid the accusations before him, as if the truth was poison itself.

He stilled, wary. "That's ridiculous. And even if it were true, you don't have a scrap of proof. Everyone will think you're just the dimwitted, bitter son of a well-appointed and honorable général."

"I'm not leaving here without that proof," I threatened, cocking my pistol. My father's grip on the letters tightened and his eyes cut to the fireplace. "Even if you burn them," I continued. "I have the testimony from The Order and the word of two very powerful aristocrats. That's enough circumstantial evidence to rip your whole world away from you. In the court of public opinion, you'll be as good as gone," I said.

He frowned. "You know, Antoine, I am sorry to hear you say that. You always had such potential—not that I ever truly expected you to fulfill it, of course, but I did what I could to give you a promising start."

"You gave me nothing but cruelty and disdain," I hissed. "The only good thing you ever gave to me was Marie, and you took her away from me as certainly as you sent Louis to his death."

He narrowed his eyes and stomped twice on the floor. In an instant, there was someone else standing in the doorway.

Hugo.

"I believe you have some unfinished business with Lieutenant de Vaux," the général said. He turned to me; hatred written across his face. "He no longer has my protection. He is no longer my son."

Hugo's eyes darkened and he grinned viciously, showing off his fangs. He rushed toward me, grabbing me by the throat and pinning me back against the wall. He lifted me easily off the ground and I lost my grip on my weapons. As I struggled for air, I saw Hugo's fangs extend and he leaned forward, preparing to bite.

The général strode to the fireplace, casting a triumphant glare as he raised the letters in his hand. "You fool," he snarled. "You should have shot me when you had the chance. You'll never win against me. You never had it in you. You'll always be—"

An explosion of wood and glass sounded from below. I used the distraction to grab for my short sword, slashing wildly at Hugo's stomach. A gash appeared and he hissed in pain, but his grip on my throat only tightened. Distantly, I heard the général shouting. Darkness began to creep into my vision from the loss of precious air, just as I felt Hugo's fangs sink into my throat.

The pain was intense but fleeting. *Am I dead?* Hugo suddenly released me, dropping me to the floor. The pain that resounded throughout my body informed me I was still alive. *For now.* Shaking my head to clear it, I looked up to see why Hugo had dropped me. Across the room, he was entangled with the most terrifying, beautiful monster I'd ever seen.

Charlotte.

Gasping for breath, I watched them battle each other, almost evenly matched in strength and speed. Hugo grappled with Charlotte's massive form, twisting around to avoid her snarling jaws closing around his throat. The général shouted at Hugo as he skirted the fight, inching closer to the door to make his escape, the forgotten letters still clenched in his fist. Hugo shrieked as Charlotte's claws raked gashes along his chest, and he sank his teeth into her shoulder. She yelped in pain. The général shouted in triumph.

Desperate to be useful, I struggled helplessly on the floor. I tried to call to her, but only gasps came out. I reached up and felt blood gushing from the wound in my neck. *Merde.* I crawled across the floor to the fight, intent on reaching her. If this was to be my fate...my end...so be it. *Let me die close to the woman I love.*

I looked up to see the général shouting, screaming at Hugo to kill her. He had his pistol raised, taking aim at her enormous shoulders.

No!

A shot rang out. Time slowed to a crawl.

The général staggered backward, surprise written on his

face. He stared at the smoking pistol in my hand, then down at the bullet wound in his chest—his bright blood staining the crisp blue and white of his uniform. With a solitary tear and a huff of astonishment, he fell to the ground.

Dead.

My pistol slipped from my blood-slick hand, and I fell back to the floor.

Charlotte froze, gripping Hugo's throat with her claws. She turned to me, red-brown eyes wide and howled an unearthly, terrifying howl. My strength began to wane. I closed my eyes, prepared to accept the end.

"Charlotte," I whispered to the gathering cold. "If only you would have loved me, I would have been yours for eternity."

CHAPTER TWENTY-FIVE
CHARLOTTE

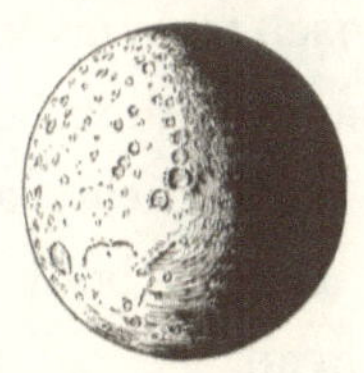

December 17, 1767
Château de Sade
Condé-en-Brie

No. No!

I'd spent too long searching for Antoine. It wasn't hard for me to pick up his trail at first, but I'd been thrown off by the snowstorm and it had been nearly impossible for me to track his scent. I'd lost precious time in finding Sade's estate, and by the time I came in, I'd only caught the tail end of his confrontation with the général. Then, Hugo had materialized, damaged and scarred from his encounter with the beast, but very much alive. *So, he hasn't been dead all this time.*

But I'd been too late. I broke down the door and raced upstairs just in time to see Hugo sink his teeth into Antoine's neck. Red-tinged fury descended as I launched myself at the vampire. He'd met me blow for blow, until I saw Antoine slump to the floor. No. *No! He is mine. Mine.*

I'd grabbed Hugo and lifted him from the ground. I would

tear him limb from limb and spread his insides across the snow.

Antoine wheezed and I turned. *No!* I couldn't be too late! Blood leeched from his throat, spilling across the floor. I felt a rising wave of hysteria.

Hugo's brittle laugh choked out from between my claws as he attempted to free himself from my grasp.

"So much for your happy ending," he snarled.

Bastard. I squeezed until I heard a crack and black blood oozed down my arm. Hugo's body slumped to the floor, followed by his severed head.

How's that for a happy ending, you vile bloodsucker.

As quickly as possible, I shifted back to my human form and crawled over to Antoine.

"Antoine," I whispered fervently, trying to staunch the flow of blood from his neck. "Antoine, darling, you must hold on, do you hear me? It isn't your time yet."

He smiled weakly at me, his heartbeat slow and thready.

"Charlotte," he murmured. "You were magnificent. You saved me again. You're always doing that. I don't deserve it."

"Hush, Antoine. You must maintain your strength. I'm going to take you to Van Helsing—she'll put you right. Just hold on a little longer, *d'accord?*" Tears began to stream down my face, falling onto Antoine's forehead as I pulled him into my lap.

"I'm sorry for everything," he said. "Except for kidnapping you. If I hadn't, I would've never met you, my beautiful, infuriating spy."

I sobbed a laugh, trying desperately to figure out what to do. "You cannot leave me, Antoine. You've only just come into my life. We have so much more ahead of us."

His beautiful emerald eyes began to lose their luster. "Tell me," he whispered. "Tell me what we would have ahead of us."

I sniffed and wiped at the tears. "A spring wedding," I said. "We would have asparagus and poached eggs at the wedding breakfast, and *civet de sanglier* for lunch. You and I would sneak away to make love in a wooded glade, then we would jump on Tartuffe and ride for the first roadside inn we could find. It would be clean and comfortable, with a lovely old innkeeper who would keep the fire stoked and bring us wine and pastries."

He smiled and gazed up at me. "Perfect. I wish I could stay with you. I love you, Charlotte. More than anything. I love you more than any man has ever loved any werewolf."

A cry of anguish escaped my throat.

Wait. Any werewolf. A werewolf. I froze.

"Antoine," I said. "Werewolf!"

He was fading, slipping into unconsciousness, and I shook him awake.

"Antoine, let me scratch you. My werewolf claws—don't you see? That's how I was infected! You've already been bitten. *Please.* Please. Let me try. Will you let me try?"

His eyes were unfocused, and his smile was placid, resigned. He was ready to accept the death that I would not. "Anything for you."

Instantaneously, I transformed. *Pain be damned.* As soon as my claws formed, I dug them into Antoine's arm, silently praying and begging his forgiveness. He winced and whimpered, and I changed back to human form just as quickly.

"Do you feel any different?" I asked, shaking him. "Does it feel like you're changing?"

He looked up at me with a sad smile, closed his eyes, and slipped into unconsciousness.

CHAPTER TWENTY-SIX
CHARLOTTE

December 31, 1767
Château de Ruisseau Magdelaine

"No, Comtesse, there is still no change in his state. Please stop asking me. As soon as something happens, I will come inform you!" Van Helsing waved me off, exasperated.

"Charlotte, *chérie*, come and have a bite to eat. You're wasting away," Daphne ordered, pulling me toward the dinner table.

"I already told you—I'm not hungry. I want to go upstairs and sit with Antoine," I muttered petulantly, sounding very much like a spoiled child.

"Absolutely not," Van Helsing said. "You will disrupt his rest and the healing process."

"This is a fine domestic mutiny on New Year's Eve," I grumbled. "And in my own home, too!"

"It's for your own good," Van Helsing chastised. "And yes, do as the duchesse says—have a bite to eat. There's meat on the table for you."

I sat, scowling, but pulled the plate in front of me. It had been two weeks since the night in the manor house, and every hour had felt like a lifetime.

When Antoine had fallen into unconsciousness, I'd transformed back into my wolf form and carried him to my home. I tended his wounds as best as I could, then took off to bring Van Helsing here. She had no doubt been considerably perplexed by an aggressive werewolf trying to explain a somewhat complicated situation to her through barks and growls, but she eventually got my meaning well enough to get on my back and ride with me back to my château. Once there, she gave him the same tender care she had me, shooing me from the room while Antoine teetered on the precipice of mortality.

I paced the halls, driving her to the brink of madness before she finally convinced me to bring Daphne and Étienne here to keep me company. I'd done so and was immensely grateful for the comfort of family and the distraction, but truthfully, all I wanted was to crawl into bed with Antoine and hold him while his blood fever raged.

In the last few days, the fever had broken, but he had yet to wake. Van Helsing continued to minister to him most carefully, and she had proclaimed him to be in recovery but would give me no more information than that.

Blessedly, Daphne had helped me tidy things up for The Order. The damning letters Antoine had gone to retrieve were smeared with the général's blood, but fortunately, still legible. They outlined his corruption in detail and were more than enough evidence to put this grim matter to rest and prove Antoine the hero I already knew him to be. We presented the evidence to both The Order and the king, along with our account of the events that had led to the deaths of the *bêtes de sang* and Général de Vaux. Naturally, the truth was hidden from the rest of the court and the people of France—what an embarrassment for the king—and an official rumor was whispered in the right circles at court. *The général had taken ill in Menorca and died during the evacuation of French forces from the island. Such a tragedy!*

The Order had suggested a posthumous award for Antoine's bravery and loyalty, but I wouldn't hear of it. *Posthumous, my foot.* He still clung to life—perhaps by the tips of his fingers, but he would make a full recovery. I would see to it. If the Devil came to claim him, he would have to go through me first.

I finished the meat in front of me, and Charles came in to set down a plate of asparagus. I smiled, remembering my promise to Antoine.

Étienne saw the dish and wrinkled his nose. "Honestly, Charlotte, why do you bother with other food? If meat is enough to sustain you, isn't that rather superfluous?"

"Oh, I don't know, *mon amour*," Daphne smiled, eyeing him from beneath her lashes. "Food can be about more than sustenance. It can be about pleasure, too."

Étienne turned a heated gaze on her, and I half expected them to make love right there at the dinner table. He turned back to me, however, and grinned.

"Apologies, dear Charlotte. Sometimes I forget there are worldly pleasures other than my soon-to-be wife."

I stuck my tongue out at him and drenched the vegetable in a lovely lemon cream sauce. I was halfway through the plate when my supernatural hearing picked up movement from upstairs. *Antoine!* Quicker than quick, I rushed upstairs and into his chambers.

He sat up in bed, blinking blearily at me. A slow smile spread across his face. My heart stuttered and, rather embarrassingly, I choked out a sob. Immediately, his smile faltered.

"Charlotte," he said softly. "Please, don't cry. It's all right. I'm all right."

I ran to the bed and launched myself at him, burying my face in his chest. He stroked my back and whispered soothing things to me until I was finally able to compose myself. I tilted my tear-streaked face up at him and kissed him, then slapped him on the shoulder.

"Don't—you—*ever*—scare me like that again," I wailed. "You are not permitted to die unless *I* say so! Do you understand me?"

He chuckled and nuzzled my throat. "I'm sorry. Next time, I'll make sure I've cleared it with you."

"There won't be a next time," I grumbled. "How do you feel?"

"Hungry," he said. "Restless."

"Do you feel like a werewolf?"

"I don't know. What do werewolves feel like?"

I grinned. "Hungry and restless."

"Then yes."

Van Helsing entered the room carrying a plate of meat and her doctor's valise. She moved me to the side and unwrapped Antoine's bandages, gently palpating the places where his injuries had been. As I hoped, his skin was unblemished, and he looked as if he'd never been at death's door. The doctor performed a thorough examination and handed him the plate of meat, which he devoured and declared to be the best thing he'd ever eaten. Van Helsing nodded to me, confirming my suspicions.

He is alive. He is a werewolf. And he is mine.

"I'll leave you two to...ehm. *Discuss* things," she said, pushing her spectacles up and smiling at me. "Try to take it easy, Lieutenant. Or should I say *Capitaine.*"

Antoine stared at me in confusion as Van Helsing closed

the door behind her. I was already disrobing, eager to feel him alive and warm beneath me.

"*Capitaine?*" he asked.

"*Oui,*" I said, tugging my skirts down over my hips. He smiled, his emerald eyes sparkling again and tracking me with green fire. "After the night at Sade's, Daphne and I made a full report to The Order and the king. They believed you would soon leave this mortal realm and offered a posthumous commendation. I refused on your behalf since, of course, I knew you would recover, and I told them when you were healed, you would return for your official promotion in rank. Congratulations, Capitaine de Vaux."

"De Valle," he corrected. "I've heard enough of *de Vaux* for this lifetime, I think."

"As you wish," I replied. He tugged his nightshirt over his head and tossed it to the floor. I stared at him hungrily, admiring the muscles moving beneath his bronzed skin.

"What else has happened since then?" he asked, rising from the bed to approach me.

I bit my lip and pretended to think. "Oh, not much. Your father is dead, and his estate has passed to you, Sade's crimes have become public knowledge, the *bêtes* are well and truly gone, Daphne and Étienne have finally set a wedding date, and Gévaudan has seen nothing of the beast since we left. There are rumors that it has made its way to Paris, but no one truly knows." I pulled my chemise over my head and threw it atop Antoine's. "Christmas was rather dull, but I did get you some wonderful gifts, and Van Helsing, Daphne, and Étienne are here to celebrate the new year with me—with *us*—and..."

Before I could finish, Antoine swooped me up and carried me over to the bed. He dropped me onto the soft blankets and smiled, his dimples flashing. I pulled his face to mine for a heart-stopping kiss.

"And?" he pressed, while I wrapped my legs around his waist and sat astride him.

"And I'm going to make love to you until you need another two weeks to recover," I said huskily, caressing his chest.

He sat up to kiss my breast and my breath caught in my throat.

"Marry me, Charlotte," he murmured, dropping kisses along my collarbone.

"I thought that was a given," I gasped, squirming with desire.

"It is for me, but I wanted to make sure. I love you. I don't want to spend eternity without you by my side. Stay with The Order if you must, but be mine. *Please*," he said.

Tears threatened again and I reasoned I'd cried enough lately, so I covered his lips with mine and slid him inside me. He moaned and gazed up at me, eyes bright with passion.

"So," I gasped, pleasure dancing along my whole body. "A spring wedding?"

EPILOGUE

VAN HELSING

April 13, 1768
Van Helsing's Clinic, Rue Ordener

"Take care of that scraped knee, little one! You must keep it clean. We don't want it to fester, now do we?" I handed the child, probably no more than five, an apple to soothe her tears. Her mother smiled gratefully, and I slipped a small loaf of bread in a bag and handed it to her. "No charge today, Madame. Just keep an eye on these children of yours and come see me if her knee doesn't look improved in a few days."

The woman ushered her three children out the door of my clinic and I sat down with a sigh. It had been a long day. Between my research into the blood plague, the house calls to newly turned vampires worrying over their bodily changes, and maintaining hours in the clinic for the less-fortunate families of Paris, I was exhausted. My days seemed to get longer and longer, and I felt stretched and threadbare. The lingering winter hadn't helped, either. I longed for the warmth and freshness of spring. *When was the last time I saw a field of wildflowers?*

The bell chimed on my door again, and I put down my cup of tea without taking a sip. Weariness settled over me, and I tried to shuck it like a coat. When I looked up, though, I smiled.

"Charlotte!" I grinned. "My friend, what a delight to see you. It's been a while, but I know you are busy with wedding preparations. You look well, Comtesse."

She smiled, and some of the fatigue dissipated. Charlotte had a smile like sunshine, and as a shy, austere foreigner, I gravitated to her friendship like a bee to a flower.

"Thank you, Mina! My goodness, you do look exhausted. You simply must stop overextending yourself. I worry for your health," she fussed, coming over to wrap me in a fierce hug.

I waved her concerns away. "You care for the people of France in your way, and I care for them in mine. Only, I think I got the better bargain. I don't have to kill anyone." I gestured for her to sit down and locked the front door for a moment of peace.

Comfortable in my clinic, she poured herself some tea, pulled a packet of pastries from her pockets, and placed them on the tea tray. *Trust her to come bearing food.*

"Little cakes for us, and I've a large basket of bread in the carriage for you to give your patients," she said.

I grinned and bit into a cake. "Almond! My favorite," I said, eyeing her suspiciously. "What do you want, Charlotte?"

"Whatever can you mean?" she asked sweetly.

"You only bring me almond cakes when you need something from me," I said. "Otherwise, it's lemon, raspberry, cream, chocolate..."

"What an exceptional agent you would make, Doctor. If

only you would come and work with us at *les DD!*" She laughed.

I sighed. This wasn't the first time she'd come around to recruit me. "Charlotte, I told you before. I am happy in my role. I will help The Order as I can, but I like not having to answer to anyone but myself."

She pouted but winked at me. "Ah, well. They cannot say that I didn't try! Now tell me, my friend, what do you know of the beast of Gévaudan?"

The cake turned to sand in my mouth, and I coughed.

"Wh—what? Why?"

She eyed me perceptively. "Well, you see, there have been some sightings here in Paris and because of my state, I've been tasked with hunting him down. It's just that he doesn't seem to want to be found, and I've exhausted almost all my leads."

I paled but tried to keep my face a mask of indifference. "Oh?"

"Yes," she nodded, picking up another cake. "And I suddenly remembered that night in the cave outside Grandrieu...the way you looked at him. As if you'd seen him before—as if you knew him."

I took a sip of my tea, alarmed to see my hands shaking.

"Me? That...that's absurd!"

Charlotte cocked a brow, staring pointedly at my hands. "Darling, do me a favor and don't *ever* play cards. You do not possess the capacity to bluff."

I swallowed, not trusting myself to reply.

She sighed and placed her hands over mine. "Wilhelmina, I won't force it out of you. If you don't want to tell me now, that's all right. I'll keep your secret. But I know there is a connection between you, and if I know about it, someone else is sure to discover it. The Order is on his heels, and that means they'll soon be on yours, too."

My heart pounded. I'd run so far and so long from my past...I knew that it would catch up with me at some point. I just didn't think it would be today. *Here. Now.*

Charlotte seemed to take pity on me and leaned forward to give me another hug. When she pulled away, her effervescent manner had returned.

"Now, of course, I'll need your opinion on several *crucial* details about the wedding. Antoine tries so hard to be indulgent, you know, but every time I ask him about opinions on ivory silk versus cream silk versus eggshell silk, his eyes glaze over and he grunts something unintelligible. Do come over this evening, won't you? I'll have cook prepare your favorite foods if you'll help me decide on decor," she gushed.

Still reeling from her devastating news, I could only nod.

"*Parfait! Au revoir, chérie, et à bientôt!*" She hugged me a third time, kissed my cheeks, and whirled out the door of the clinic before I could find my tongue.

I blew out a breath. Lord, I needed something more fortifying than tea after that. I donned my cloak and closed up the clinic, fully intending on heading down the street to the nearby public house, *Le Raisin Perdu. A full dinner and several glasses of wine, I think.*

The sun had set, bathing the street in a soft seashell pink. This was my favorite time of day—when I gave myself permission to rest, relax, and try to prepare for the work that lay ahead. I closed and locked the door, and when my back was turned to the street, I froze. Something instinctive whispered through my body: *run.*

I whirled around, tripping clumsily over the hem of my skirts. I put my hands out, bracing for the fall, but it did not come. Strong arms saved me. When I opened my eyes, I found myself staring into the past I'd fought to forget.

Dark, pitch-black eyes bored into mine, and his frighteningly beautiful face softened into a devastating grin, displaying two full sets of fangs. He opened his lips to say something, and in that moment, I was certain my heart stopped.

"Good evening, Mina."

To be continued in book three of the *Vampires in Versailles* series, *The Doctor and the Devil*.

LONG LOST
A VAMPIRES IN VERSAILLES STORY

AUTHOR'S NOTE

This short story was originally published in a holiday-themed charity anthology some years ago. The events take place after the end of the first book, but before the epilogue that leads to Van Helsing's book.

CHAPTER ONE
CHARLOTTE

January 20, 1768
Versailles

"IT'S YOUR TURN, MINA, DARLING."

"I hate this game. I don't want to play," Doctor Van Helsing grumbled. She shifted from foot to foot, tugging at the front of her bodice and anxiously running her hands over the tops of her wide *panniers*.

"You look absolutely gorgeous, *chérie*," Daphne assured. "That powder blue silk brings out your eyes so well."

"I feel like an over-iced pastry," she huffed. "I should never have let you talk me into coming to this dreadful ball. What are we even celebrating? Christmas was a month ago and we had our New Year's *réveillon* already."

I looked around at the luxurious decorations—boughs of blue spruce wove around a pale blue silk-covered table, which practically groaned beneath the elaborate spread of decadent dishes. Spiced wine-drenched roast meats, delicate seafood bisques, beef and pork pies, an embarrassment of fine cheeses, tropical fruits from distant lands—*think of the expense!*—and pastries topped with edible sugar snowflakes glistened beneath glittering silver candelabras. Blue and silver draperies hung at the windows, putting me in mind of a snowy bluebird morning.

"The winter solstice?" I asked.

"That's in December, *chérie*," Daphne replied absently. "Perhaps His Majesty is simply feeling festive and wishes to celebrate the beauty of winter."

I shrugged. "What does it matter? As long as we have an opportunity for the work at hand…"

"I'd much rather be back in my clinic," Van Helsing complained. "I have so much work to do."

I handed the petulant Dutch physician a glass of champagne.

"Take your medicine," I said with a wry smile. "You'll feel much better."

She wrinkled her nose at the glass. "Champagne gives me a sour stomach and a sore head."

"It's a requirement for socializing with the aristocracy," Daphne chuckled, candlelight glinting off her needle-sharp fangs. Despite being a wealthy and powerful duchesse, her engagement to the king's vampire emissary and her turning had left her on the outskirts of the *tonne*—though it was a consequence she heartily embraced. With the blood plague sweeping through France and the hungry peasants and *bourgeois* deliberately infecting themselves to avoid miserable starving deaths, the few humans of the aristocracy were becoming increasingly anxious. As recently turned supernatural beings, Daphne and I were working hard to try and force the king and court to see reason—to make peace and lend aid to those in need—but we were starting to lose hope. It seemed the more dire the need, the more ferociously the aristocrats clung to their power and wealth.

"The odious Vicomte de Malin has been eyeing you all evening," I teased. "That's fortuitous. If he asks you for a dance, you'll want the fortification. Besides, perhaps the effervescence will improve your mood."

Van Helsing cut her eyes to the vulgar aristocrat, who winked at her. She blanched and downed the glass of golden courage in one abundant swig.

"Don't worry, we'll protect you. If he's foolish enough to try anything untoward, I will take him out into the gardens and eat him," I giggled. My stomach growled, proving my willingness to shift into my werewolf form and dispatch anyone who laid a finger on my dear friend.

Daphne stifled a groan. "You'd have to save some for me, Charlotte. I haven't fed in two days. If I don't get some blood soon, it may affect my cheerful disposition."

Van Helsing and I looked at Daphne incredulously, then let out an unladylike eruption of laughter. Daphne was kind and loyal but known for her at-times *tenacious* character. She pretended to scowl, but her violet eyes glittered with mirth.

"Go on, then, Mina," I wheedled. "It's your turn."

"Pass. Daphne may go in my stead." Van Helsing plucked another glass of champagne from a passing tray. She hiccoughed and frowned at the leering vicomte.

Daphne sighed. "Very well. If I were not engaged to my handsome, charming Étienne—"

I rolled my eyes. "Yes, yes. We know. This is just a game, Daphne!"

"I would seduce Comtesse de Renarde, stab Monsieur Honoré, and sup on Malin," she finished.

"You wouldn't!" I cried, scandalized. "How could you stomach him?"

Her pupils dilated and her nostrils flared—I could sense her hunger. "Very fat. Lots of blood," she murmured, almost trance-like. I cleared my throat and she collected herself, opening her fan to disguise her embarrassment.

"That man is *awash* with garlic," I pointed out. "His blood would reek of it."

"That is a silly superstition, Charlotte. I quite enjoy garlic. The Italians are onto something, you know."

"Still, don't you think you'd want to bite someone else? He still believes bathing is ill for his health."

"Surely, but you dictated the rules of this game and you said they had to be in this ballroom. I challenge you to find a courtier who *does* bathe regularly."

"Fair point," I replied. "Honestly, I don't think I could sleep with *or* eat someone who believed such nonsense." I wrinkled my nose in disgust.

"Well, it's your turn, anyway, if you're so high and mighty about it," Daphne sniffed.

"Right. If I were not engaged to my precious, perfect pastry, Antoine—"

"*Urp.*" Van Helsing covered a burp, mortified. "Sincerest apologies, *mes amies.*"

"I would seduce that lovely lady-in-waiting—what's her name, Danielle? I would certainly stab Malin—though I don't think I'd stab him; I'd probably throttle him because I wouldn't want his poisonous blood all over my lovely gown. And I would sup on Monsieur Honoré."

"He beats his servants, you know," Van Helsing said quietly.

"Yes, we know," I replied, narrowing my eyes at the wealthy landowner. "It would be slow and rather painful for him, I'm afraid."

Daphne nodded sagely. Van Helsing began to look a tad green about the gills.

"Are you well, Mina? You do realize champagne is meant for sipping, not gulping, don't you?"

The doctor nodded, opening her fan with an unsteady hand. "Might we play a different game?"

I arched a brow. "It's not like you to be ill at the discussion of viscera. Do you need some air, *chérie*?"

She nodded vigorously. "It must be the champagne."

I reached for the jewel-studded *chatelaine* at my waist—an heirloom handed down from my mother. The delicate silver chains used to bear all the keys to the rooms of my family estate, but since my mother died, I'd taken to wearing the elaborate pin as a piece of sentimental, yet functional jewelry. Now, instead of the keys, at the end of each chain hung a tiny compartment disguised as a gemstone. The compartments held a set of small lock picks, a tightly coiled *pianoforte* wire I used as a garrote, and I still had enough space for secret messages, occasional poisons, and in this instance, smelling salts. I tugged at the ruby-covered box and offered it up to Van Helsing, who looked at me with the same disgust she would have displayed if I'd tried to hand her a beheaded snake—or an English pastry.

"Don't be ridiculous," she hissed, but her lips were pale and her complexion took on a waxy sheen.

Daphne and I led her through the sparkling gilt room, stuffed with over-important people all trying to catch the eye of His Majesty, King Louis XV. As soon as we made our way to the snow-covered courtyard, I breathed a sigh of relief. Van Helsing gripped the edge of the icy balcony and stared out into the torch-lit gardens.

"It was rather stifling in there," Daphne said, unsuccessfully hiding her concern. "Mina?"

"I'm fine," she said, closing her eyes. "I just detest these things."

"I've seen you face down supernatural terrors, amputate limbs, and stitch your own flesh wounds," I said. "Don't tell me you're overcome by a silly little party with a bunch of pompous wastrels?"

"Give me broken bones and septic wounds over an *allemande* any day," she mumbled. "Though...I don't attend to as many of those wounds as I once did. Lately, it all seems to be about helping new vampires through their transitions. I worry France will run out of blood before we see the end of the grain blight, and then who knows what will happen. We already know the blood plague has the power to mutate—" She looked at me pointedly. "—and I don't want to know what happens when vampires start to feed on each other. My research hasn't been as promising as I'd hoped." She wiped her damp brow with the back of her hand and frowned. "If only the king would do more to help feed his people. I truly fear what comes next."

"He will not," came a velvet voice through the snow-soft silence of the garden. Daphne's fiancé, Étienne, Duc de Noailles and vampire emissary to the king, materialized from the darkness and strode forward, sliding a possessive arm around his soon-to-be duchesse's waist and pulling her in for a ravishing kiss. Snowflakes dusted his raven-dark hair but wouldn't melt without the body heat of humanity. A small, unruly lock had escaped his queue, which—aside from his devilish beauty and rakish charm—was yet another thing that made him stand out at court. He never wore the powdered wigs or pastel colors that were fashionable, but was usually clad in rich, jewel-toned velvets and dark-as-sin silk brocades. His lean, muscular form and sharply angled face did nothing to discourage the notion that he was anything other than what he was—a predator, a *former* libertine, and ever hungry for the love of his eternal life, Daphne.

"Forgive me, *ma cher*, for taking so long. Antoine and I were trying to convince him to import more grain, but he won't hear of it. The prices of food will continue to rise, and so will the numbers of blood plague sufferers," his golden eyes flashed, matching the bite of his bitter tone. "He believes those that choose to turn are abandoning God and deserve to be punished. Not that he would say such things to us, of course. We only hear the rumors of what he says when he is alone with the other nobles."

"Choosing to survive on blood to avoid death by starvation isn't any kind of choice," came a second voice from the darkness. The low rumble of my beloved's tone raised goosebumps along my skin and sent my heart fluttering. Unlike Étienne, Antoine didn't appear to materialize from the gathered night —softly, he stepped forward like a cautious wild creature approaching from some dangerous, otherworldly woodland. Even dressed in his sharp captain's uniform, there was a touch of the primal about his tall, muscular form, his broad shoulders, and the moon-shaped scar that ran along his cheek. His chestnut hair was pulled back tightly, and his strong jaw sported a whisper of stubble that never seemed to leave his cheeks, no matter how often he shaved.

"Antoine!" I breathed, flinging myself at him and burying my face in his chest. He smelled as he always did—even before I turned him and saved his now-immortal life. Earth, leather, mint, apples, and horseflesh—he'd been out riding his favorite black Andalusian, Tartuffe, before coming here tonight. I stood on my toes to nip at his neck, a strange sort of *bon soir* between mates and a promise of lustful adventures ahead.

He blushed and dropped a soft kiss on my cheek. Unlike Daphne and Étienne, Antoine was still shy about public displays of intimacy and affection, which naturally propelled my ardor to white-hot intensity.

"Are you particularly fond of those breeches?" I said brazenly, sliding my hands over his firm ass. "Or will you give me leave to rip them to shreds when we get to the carriage?"

His blush spread from his cheeks to his ears and throat—my reward for being so bold. His moss green eyes darkened like night falling in a forest, and he leaned forward, brushing his stubble across my cheek.

"If you keep teasing me in public," he murmured in my ear. "I will be forced to punish you when we return home."

A satisfied growl emanated from my chest. "Tell me how," I breathed.

"Oh, do save it for the ride home," Daphne begged. "Those of us with supernatural senses can still hear you."

"Spoilsport," I pouted. Antoine winked at me, making me seriously consider leaving the ball early.

"Please," Van Helsing interjected. "Give me leave to return to my clinic. Or to go home. I'm too weary to be polite to the men whose servants I treat for various forms of abuse."

"But we only just arrived!" I complained. "And it's incredibly lucky that the Vicomte de Malin has been lusting after you —we're so close to finalizing a course of action for him and we could use your help in learning his whereabouts over the next few weeks."

"I do not work for The Order," Van Helsing replied. "I do not want to be involved in your organization's brand of punishing justice. I only care to heal people and to find a cure for the blood plague."

"Of course, *chérie*. We know how you feel about The Order, and we'd never ask you to betray your conscience. We only wish to know when he'll be leaving for his country estate. We just want to have a little...*exploratory adventure* in his private study. There are questions about some rather indelicate and potentially treasonous activities. We've asked his servants but they're too afraid to tell us anything," I explained, approaching to link arms with her.

"What will The Order do with the information?" she asked hesitantly.

The Order—a long-shadowed organization of the powerful and elite—often performed their own investigations into potential threats to king and country. They delivered justice that was, at times, beyond His Majesty's reach. Daphne and I had been working from within to curb their penchant for violence against impoverished vampire-kind, but it was getting harder to convince them to do what was necessary to support the middle and lower classes. Under the guise of establishing a group of women agents to serve The Order, we'd formed *les Dames Dangereuses* and were keeping a close eye on our male contemporaries. I didn't fault Van Helsing for being distrustful of them—I often felt that way myself. Still, I did what I could to help provide balance and ensure that the people being *punished* truly deserved what came their way. The Vicomte de Malin deserved more than most.

"Truly, *chérie*, I cannot say. But if we find the proof that we're looking for—that we are almost certain is there—I suspect he will meet an untimely end." I shrugged. "Given the number of servants from his household alone that you've patched up, I would think you'd consider that a fitting end."

"I can't have another man's death on my conscience," she said quietly. The phrasing struck me as odd, but I didn't press. It was likely she had seen death come too often in her line of work. I understood and respected her decision, but I couldn't hide my disappointment.

I nodded. "As you wish, *chérie*. I'll not press you again. Daphne, it looks like we're on with our original plan."

Suddenly Antoine, who stood furthest back from our little cabal and closest to the ballroom, hissed at us.

"Hush!" he whispered. He tipped his nose up to catch the scent of something on the wind. "He's coming, *mes amies*."

He and Étienne melted back into the darkness, leaving Daphne, Van Helsing, and I alone on the terrace. As predicted, Malin strode toward us with the equally distasteful Monsieur Honoré in tow.

Van Helsing flashed a pleading look at Daphne, undoubtedly hoping she would not address the men. As the highest ranking among us, Daphne could control the entire situation. If she did not acknowledge either man, they wouldn't speak to us. Unfortunately for Van Helsing, our plan dictated otherwise.

"*Bon soir,* Monsieur le Vicomte. Monsieur Honoré," she nodded briefly, her predatory smile looking polite and frightening all at once.

Both men bowed low. "Your Grace," they said in unison. Malin eyed Van Helsing with the same hunger as Daphne eyeing his pulsing neck vein. I didn't bother to hide my grin.

"Are you enjoying the wintry festivities, Monsieur Honoré?" I offered, reaching deep for my aristocratic charm.

"Indeed, Comtesse de Brionne, though I could enjoy it a bit more if you'd save a dance for me. Something vigorous, perhaps, to match your fertile temper." He smiled lasciviously at me, eyeing my breasts pressing against the low neckline of my bodice. *Disgusting. Perhaps I would simply eat him, after all.*

"Of course, Monsieur," I tittered. "I'd be delighted."

A disembodied growl punctuated the night air. The sound sent a thrill through me. *Ah, sweet Antoine seems a tad jealous. Poor thing. I'd much rather dance with him, but I must suffer through this to distract Honoré enough to let Daphne extract the information we need from Malin.*

Malin extended his hand to Van Helsing. Daphne

attempted to redirect his gesture by ushering us back toward the ballroom again, but he remained unmoved.

"And you, Mademoiselle? I don't believe I've had the pleasure." The way he said *pleasure* made all three of us try not to grimace. Still—this was *the plan.*

"I'm afraid Doctor Van Helsing was just leaving, Malin," Daphne replied. "Perhaps you'd favor me with a turn about the room instead."

Something like shock lit in the vicomte's piggy eyes. "A physician! But she is a woman! How utterly absurd."

"I say, *Doctor,* I fear some of my humors may be out of balance. Perhaps we may find a quiet room where you might *examine* me," Honoré oozed, earning a mule-like guffaw from Malin.

"What a ridiculous liberal notion," Malin continued. "A *woman* in the sciences. If your spinsterhood has forced you into a profession, pet, perhaps we could come to some sort of arrangement? I've only just cut ties with my former mistress— an opera singer of some note. There's a ready vacancy to be filled. Or perhaps you'll allow me to fill *your* vacancy."

Fury rolled off Van Helsing like waves heralding a storm at sea. Another uproarious bout of drunken laughter came from the pair. My lip curled in disgust before I could school my expression in aristocratic blandness, and unfortunately Honoré noticed. His hand was on my wrist in a movement much quicker than I would have expected.

"Have you something to add, Comtesse de Brionne?" He glared at me, cruel eyes assessing my response through the sour fog of spirits. I felt my canine teeth lengthening.

Daphne kicked me from beneath her skirts—a clear direction to *stay the course. Remember the plan.*

I swallowed my rage and hunger, turning an absurd pout on the man.

"But Monsieur Honoré, you promised *me* a dance. Surely you haven't forgotten already?"

His grip relaxed—I almost mourned the opportunity to break his hand and rip his arm from its socket—and his oily grin returned.

"Certainly, Madame," he replied, tugging me forward. Though I was much stronger than he, I allowed him the luxury of believing he held the upper hand. Precious few aristocrats knew of Antoine and my supernatural state, and we aimed to keep it that way.

Daphne stepped forward as well, poised to offer Malin her hand for the dance no one wanted. Van Helsing cut her off, offering the vicomte a frosty smile to match the cold blue of her eyes. Even I shivered, and I'd long since stopped feeling the cold. Had the man an ounce of sense in him, he would have recognized the danger in her expression.

"Monsieur," she said, glacial eyes glittering. "I do have a vacancy on my dance card." She extended her arm to him and the delighted, disgusting ass led her inside. She glanced at Daphne and I with a look that said, *Leave him to me.*

I only hoped there would be enough of him left over when she was through with him.

CHAPTER TWO
CHARLOTTE

January 20, 1768
Versailles

FAT, WET GLOBS OF SNOW DRIPPED THROUGH THE TREES AND splattered on top of the frozen mud that crunched beneath the carriage wheels. If I were human, I would have been extremely put out by the frosty conditions, but they barely registered. The only temperature I felt anymore was usually in relation to Antoine, and it was only ever feverish.

Irritatingly, he sulked in the carriage as we ventured home, making it exceedingly difficult for me to peel his clothing from his brooding form. I made a noise of frustration as I attempted to yank the coat of his lovely blue and white formal uniform down over his impressively broad shoulders and expansive chest. He did not lift his arms to aid me, but held me firmly in his lap, jade eyes boring into mine.

"You are not listening to me, *mon amour*," he said in a low voice as I fiddled with the buttons on his breeches.

"Of course, I am! It's simply that I can hear you better when you are naked."

He didn't smile outright, but I could tell he wanted to by the way the edges of his lips twitched. He stayed my fervent touch with one hand and brought his other up to my cheek.

"I know your work is important, Charlotte, but you must understand how much I hate seeing other men paw at you."

"Jealous, Antoine? Or worried?" I teased.

"Neither. I trust you and I know you are more than capable of taking care of yourself. I just dislike how these titled men think they can press their advantage simply because you are a woman," he said softly, running his thumb across my lips. "Like you are a mere *plaything* to the likes of them. You're a comtesse, for fuck's sake, and my fiancée."

I leaned forward to press a gentle kiss to his forehead. "It's charades, *chéri*. That's all. When I flirt with them, it's never for pleasure. It's to give them the illusion of control. It's enough to be taken for granted, so that when I strike, they don't see it coming."

He harrumphed and frowned, flexing the moon-shaped scar across his brow.

"Besides, you are the only man for whom I would ever consent to be a *plaything*. I love you, Antoine—enough to spend eternity with you. But my work with *les DD* is for all the women in France who are at the mercy of powerful men. Not all of them are as lucky as I am."

My words unlocked him and he finally smiled, flashing dazzling white teeth in the darkness of the carriage. Hastily, he shucked his coat and slid one hand beneath the gold silk of my skirts.

"How much longer until we arrive home?" he murmured. "I want to hear more about your willingness to be my plaything."

I kissed him then, long and lush, sucking on his full bottom lip. Twining my fingers in his dark, wavy hair, I chuckled. "Darling, if you so wish it, I'll be your *anything*."

Supernatural eyes glowing, his hot gaze shot to mine. "You are my *everything*."

The carriage slowed, indicating that we'd approached the tree-lined drive of my family estate, where Antoine now resided with me. It was improper and scandalous, but we were engaged and since I was already a widow, I was allowed some latitude from the censure of the *tonne*.

"*Merde*," I swore. "Shall we send the carriage around again? We can be quick!"

His low laughter filled the space just as his clever fingers found the slick seam of my sex, already aching for him. Gently circling one fingertip at the apex of my pleasure, he growled in my ear. I bit back a moan.

"I do not *want* to be quick."

With that, he picked me up, kicked open the carriage door, and carried me up the icy steps to our home, still decorated for Christmas and New Year's *Réveillon* celebrations. Evergreen branches and holly boughs made the whole *château* smell like a wintry forest. Candles guttered in the chill wind, their light flickering on shining gold and red decorations. The scents of spices lingered in the air—ginger, cinnamon, and cloves—making my mouth water almost as much as Antoine did. When we reached the main bedroom on the second floor, he tossed me on the bed and dove down after me.

"I must make an early start tomorrow, *mon amour*," he huffed, tugging at the ties on my skirts. "I'm off to oversee the training of my new regiment." Before the heavy silk fell to the floor, he was already unpinning my bodice and nearly ripping the ribbon from my stays.

"I thought you said you didn't want to be quick," I teased. "I think this is the fastest you've ever undressed me."

He grinned and tugged his shirt over his head. I sucked in a breath. Even though we had eternity together, I didn't think I would ever get used to the raw beauty of him. Muscles like iron flexed beneath golden skin and dark hair sprayed across his chest and trailed below his belly button. The scars from a lifetime of battles decorated his too-perfect body, sharply contrasting his peaceful nature. He acknowledged my appraisal with a saucy wink, and I giggled and slipped out of my chemise.

"I can't help it," he retorted. "I've been thinking about you all evening." He pulled his breeches off and crawled up my body on the bed, dropping feather-light kisses up my legs and hips. "But I promise to take my time with your pleasure."

He nipped at my hipbone and spread my sex with his thumbs, baring my intimate secrets to him. He sighed in satisfaction, then drew one long, slow lick up my center, making me squirm and swear on an out breath. Pulling one of my legs over his shoulder, he nibbled at the inside of my thigh before returning his attentions to my desperate sex. Heat flared inside me like a bonfire of old tinder, and I knew it wouldn't take long for me to find my bliss. Again and again he licked, driving me toward some distant utopian galaxy that lay just beyond reach.

"Slow down, my love—I want you too badly," I pleaded. Chuckling at my torment, he found the peak of my need and sucked at it, then slid one long finger—then two—inside me. *Perfection.* "Please, Antoine, share with me *la petite mort.* I do not want it without you."

"As you wish, *chérie,*" he growled, lowering my leg from his shoulder and moving up my body. Impatiently, I wrapped my legs around his waist and reached down to find him—glorious, hot, and hard. Gritting his teeth, he hissed a breath.

"I was going to take my time," he muttered, somewhat forlorn. "But I fear this will be quicker than I wish."

I slid him inside me on a gratifying moan from us both. He struggled valiantly to move slowly, trying to be noble and prolong my pleasure, but my love for Antoine would put Aphrodite to shame, and I could bear his slow romance no longer.

"Antoine," I huffed, slick with sweat and desire. "This is only the first bout. Fuck me like you mean it, damn it."

That heart-stopping, lop-sided grin again and he drove into me with enough force to crack the heavy oak bed. *Yes. Yes!* Harder and faster he moved, reaching the place inside me that I believed would let me see the face of God—or perhaps Lucifer. My back arched and he took my nipple into his mouth, but soon abandoned it with an uttered string of delicious obscenities. Stars danced around the edges of my vision, and that distant world spun into view, dancing closer and closer until we crashed into it together, orbiting as one perfect heavenly body. Waves of pleasure rocked through me, and Antoine held me as we came down, vibrating with exhausted joy.

"*Je t'aime, Charlotte,*" he whispered. "Now and forever."

"I love you, too, Antoine," I replied, nuzzling into his neck. "I'm going to miss you while you're away. What am I to do without you?"

His large hand swept over my stomach to rest gently on the swell of my hip, and I could hear the smile in his voice when he answered.

"You'll just have to think of all the things we can do upon my return."

"Oh, I have a few things in mind already," I sighed, tilting my head up to nip at his earlobe. "But it would be best if we tested a few of them out—just in case. What if you don't enjoy them?"

"Well, then," he conceded, pulling me on top of him. "I suppose we should try them out. *Just in case.*"

I was delighted to learn that Antoine enjoyed every single one.

THE FOLLOWING EVENING, I AWOKE IN A DISAPPOINTINGLY EMPTY BED, save for the rose on the pillow next to me. From any other man, I would have scoffed at the saccharine gesture, but from Antoine, it was wonderful.

I'd hardly had time to throw on my dressing gown and call for some supper when Daphne whirled in, determined to yank me from my rest and relaxation.

"The sun has barely set, Daphne," I groaned. "What has you so vexed?"

"Have you spoken with her?"

"With whom, dearest?" I replied, stifling a yawn.

"Van Helsing!" she cried in exasperation.

"Not after last night, and not in detail. I lost track of her and Malin on the dance floor, and then after the dance ended, she handed me a note with some dates on it—presumably dates that he would be at his country estate—and left for the night. I assumed she simply danced with him, found out when he would be gone, and then went home for the evening," I shrugged. "Why? Has something happened?"

Daphne closed her eyes and pinched the bridge of her nose. "Malin never returned home last night."

Shock froze me in place. "You don't think..."

Daphne looked at me helplessly. "I don't know! I don't think she would do anything, but I certainly do not doubt her capacity to do so. She'd had a great deal of champagne and was absolutely furious about his advances."

"No," I stated firmly. "Certainly not. Van Helsing wouldn't have done anything to him. She has been so adamant about staying away from The Order and anything violent or nefarious. The bastard is probably with a mistress or sleeping off his drunkenness back at Versailles. I'm sure he'll turn up."

Daphne frowned. "Show me the note."

Unnerved by her manner, I went to my hastily discarded gown to get the note from its hiding place in my *chatelaine*. Antoine and I had been so distracted in our intimate attentions, I hadn't bothered to unpin the jewelry from its place on my bodice.

It was gone.

Panic edged into my chest, but I refused to let it take root. *It must be here!* Discarded in our hasty attempt to divest each other of our clothes—or perhaps it fell off in the carriage. I rang for my housekeeper, Madame Toussaint.

"Madame, have you seen my *chatelaine*? It is not here," I said, rifling through the mess of garments on the floor.

"*Non,* my lady," she replied, brows furrowing. "I have not seen it since you left for the ball last night. I'll assemble the staff and ask if it's been found."

"Check the carriage, as well, please," I said.

Daphne's eyes went wide as I hurried to dress.

"Do you think it is truly lost? Could it have fallen off your gown?" she whispered. "Or is it possible that someone stole it?"

"No—I don't know how they would have! Antoine and I came straight home after the ball. I had it when we went outside onto the terrace because I thought Van Helsing was going to faint, and then..."

No. Oh no. The fear I'd been holding at bay finally overwhelmed me as I considered the damning possibility.

"You don't think Monsieur Honoré took it, do you?" I choked out, incredulous. "Could he have? He was drunk! I don't understand why he would steal from me...it's only a mere bauble to him. He wouldn't know its true purpose or of my affiliation with The Order."

Daphne's brows knitted together and she blew out a breath. "It's possible that he's smarter than he looks. I don't know. What else did you have in the compartments? And what else was on the note from Van Helsing?"

I tried to remember. "I had smelling salts, my lock picks, my garrote, and a few other blank scraps of paper. And I only remember some dates on the note from Van Helsing, but we should probably check with her. Wait...did you go to her clinic already? What brought you here this evening?"

She sighed and came over to help me cinch my stays and pin my hair up. "I went by first thing this evening, but she did not answer. There were no lamps or candles lit and the door was locked."

Worry gathered in my stomach. "She is probably sleeping off the champagne," I said, but didn't feel entirely confident.

"With Van Helsing *and* Malin missing, plus your *chatelaine*, I fear there might be something more dangerous afoot," Daphne said.

"Well, first things first," I declared, putting on my favorite pair of gloves. "We must find Van Helsing and ensure that she is well. Let's go back to her clinic."

Daphne nodded. "Agreed. Let's take my carriage—it should still be out front and your footmen might be searching yours for your *chatelaine*."

We stepped out into the silvery night and I inhaled deeply. I'd loved the damp smell of freshly fallen snow before I was turned, but now with my supernatural abilities, I could sense a great deal more in the air. Woodsmoke from distant fireplaces, the domestic aromas of dinners being cooked, beeswax candles dripping, the earthy smell of horses and dogs, and skeletal winter trees—their bare branches bowing beneath the weight of the snow. I could even close my eyes and my nose would paint me a picture of all that lay before me—it was a wonderful boon to temper the excruciating pain that came with shifting form. I imagined Daphne and Étienne felt the same way about being vampires. The price of blood-drinking was a high one to pay for similar supernatural gifts.

Her footman ushered us into her well-appointed carriage and she settled back against the plush seats. She opened a small side panel next to her and pulled out a small champagne coupe and a crystal decanter filled with blood.

"Have you eaten, *chérie?*" she asked, filling her glass.

In answer, my stomach rumbled. Smiling, she pulled out a small basket covered with linen and handed it to me. Inside was a sizable cut of raw venison—one of my new favorites.

"Oh, thank you, darling! You're an absolute angel." I was *ravenous*. I pulled my gloves off and concentrated on extending one long claw from my fingertip. The dagger-sharp nail grew long enough for me to slice portions of the steak and I delicately dropped them into my watering mouth.

Heaven!

"So," I began after swallowing. "What do *you* truly think happened?"

She lifted one pale shoulder in a small shrug. "I have my suspicions, but I cannot be sure. To answer your next question, *no*, I do not think Van Helsing murdered Malin. I'm sure you're right and the blackguard will turn up—eventually. As to our other problem...I do not think it is past Monsieur Honoré to steal your *chatelaine*. Whether it was because he suspected you of hiding secrets, or because he is simply a greedy thief, I cannot say."

The venison churned in my stomach. The idea that I could have been thwarted by the evil man was disturbing at best and life-altering at worst. I'd only been bested by one man before, and I'd just spent the night in his arms. *Antoine.* I wondered where he was at this moment.

Sometime later, we arrived at Van Helsing's clinic on the *Rue Ordener.* She lived in a small apartment above the clinic and despite her success as a physician and notable scientist, she preferred to live a somewhat spartan lifestyle. I'd long ago offered to find her a larger estate, to help expand her clinic, to secure more funding for her research from the aristocracy, and *at the very least* gift her with a sizable wardrobe so that she might accompany Daphne and I to more parties. She'd laughed at several of the offers and scoffed at the rest, thanking me for my generosity but stalwartly refusing to live a life that didn't suit her. Daphne and I loved her for that.

I was heartened to see lamps lit upstairs and scent her familiar fragrance—wool, soap, herbs, almonds, lime blossom. I saw the relief in Daphne's face, as well.

Rather than enter through the clinic door, which was locked and bolted, we approached through a back stairwell off the side alley. When we knocked, she answered immediately, looking none the worse for wear.

"Bon soir!" she said, wiping her hands on an apron and ushering us inside a small study. "How are you, *mes amies?* You both look well."

"Where have you been? I was here only an hour ago," Daphne sighed in exasperation.

"I was out visiting patients," she replied, obviously perplexed by Daphne's manner. "Is everything all right?"

"Yes."

"No!"

Daphne and I spoke at the same time. Van Helsing's eyebrows shot up.

"Shall I make us some tea? I've got a lovely new herbal blend that will help settle your nerves," she said, busying herself around a shelf of small porcelain jars.

"Mina," I began, cutting Daphne off. "What exactly happened last night?"

"What do you mean? We were all there together the whole evening. What's going on?" she regarded the two of us suspiciously.

"No, *chérie,* I mean during that last dance and then afterward. I lost track of you while I was dancing with the vile Monsieur Honoré. Did something happen with Vicomte de Malin?" Daphne queried.

Her blue eyes turned frosty. "Such as?"

"We aren't accusing you of anything, Mina, but Malin happens to be missing. We simply want to know what you remember of him after the dance ended."

"Missing? When? How? *Mon Dieu...*" she sat down on a wooden stool and took a moment to compose herself.

"The gossip today was that he hasn't been seen since the end of the ball last night, and no one has come forward with any information. Not even Honoré has offered an explanation, and those two are thick as thieves," Daphne replied. "It's as if the man vanished into thin air after...after..."

"After we danced," Van Helsing finished. Her gaze snapped to ours. "I didn't kill him! We danced—that was all. I flattered him enough to merit an *unwelcome* invitation to his country estate, which he said he'd be leaving for in a fortnight. I scribbled the dates down and passed them to you as I left. I came home immediately after—I'm afraid I didn't see where he went after our dance. He was vile and certainly drunk, but I swear nothing else happened after that. Despite my distaste for the man, I would never have harmed him. I prefer he face justice in a lawful way."

I nodded. "Of course we believe you, darling. Did he say anything else to you that might indicate his current whereabouts?"

Van Helsing's face scrunched charmingly as she thought back. "I don't know. I don't think so, but I'm not a spy, so I wouldn't know what to listen for. He droned on about his former mistress—the opera singer—as if to convince me that he was fully done with her and that I would be a welcome addition to his nauseating, adulterous club."

Curiosity seized me. "What was her name?"

"She's Italian, I believe. Nadia something."

"Russo," Daphne and I replied in unison. We knew of the soprano—as famous for her violent temper as her vibrato. I couldn't believe that she'd let the awful vicomte even touch the hem of her skirts, let alone her person, but to each their own. It was a thin lead, but certainly a starting place.

"Well," I said with a smile. "You know what they say about a woman scorned."

Daphne grinned. "*Mes dames,* I believe we're headed to the opera."

CHAPTER THREE
CHARLOTTE

January 21, 1768
Versailles

THE *THÉÂTRE DES TUILERIES* WAS A SHORT DISTANCE FROM VAN Helsing's clinic, so we piled back into Daphne's carriage and made haste. Despite the hour and the bitter weather, the streets bustled with sounds of vampire peasants adjusting to their new supernatural life. Raucous laughter poured out of a handful of vampire-friendly taverns and the wind carried scents of sizzling *boudin noir* and spiced wine fortified with blood.

The winter chill had started to seep in despite the carriage's plush interior, and since Daphne and I were no longer bothered by the cold, we bundled Van Helsing in every available blanket.

"By the way, Mina, I don't suppose you recall seeing my *chatelaine* after the last dance at the ball, do you? It seems to have disappeared," I asked, now that her teeth had stopped chattering.

"*Non,* I'm sorry," she replied. "I only remember seeing it when you offered me your smelling salts. Truthfully, I was still too put out by the vicomte to pay much mind to anything other than returning home. Is it important?"

It had been a long shot, but I was still disappointed.

"It was my mother's," I replied. "My father had it made for her when they married. She gave it to me when she—" I trailed off, emotion catching in my throat. Reaching for a light tone, I continued. "I would very much like to have it."

She frowned. "I wish I could be more help. Perhaps it will turn up."

I opened my mouth to reply again, but the carriage slowed, signaling our arrival at the opera house.

"Are you certain you don't want to wait in the carriage?" Daphne asked. "Charlotte and I can handle this. We just want to talk to Signora Russo and...you know. *Sniff around.*"

I chuckled at the jest, but Van Helsing's expression was grave. "It was my choice to get involved last night, and it will be on my conscience if something has happened to the man. If he's hurt or injured, I may be able to help." Her eyes darkened and she muttered, *"Not that he deserves it."*

"Very well," Daphne replied, then looked at me. "Do we have a plan?"

I lifted a shoulder in a shrug. "Not really. Go in, gain access to her dressing room, ask her enough questions to ascertain if she murdered her former lover, and take it from there."

Daphne sighed. "Normally, I have more time to plan these things, but I don't think we can afford to wait."

"I'm sure it will be fine," I said, though I felt a little less confident without my *chatelaine* at my side.

There didn't appear to be a performance tonight but there was a lot of activity at the theater as the company cleaned, dressed the set, and rehearsed for *Orfeo ed Euridice.* Van

Helsing was somewhat anxious as we entered the grand hall, but I whispered to her to keep to the shadowy edges of the room and act as if we belonged there. I was prepared for someone to stop us, but as everyone seemed rather busy, no one paid much attention to us.

When we found the candlelit corridor behind the main stage, I breathed a small sigh of relief. We could hear the impressive trill of a high *c* coming from a room toward the end of the hall, which had to be Signora Russo.

Daphne knocked on the door and we heard a litany of profane Italian, followed by frantic shuffling.

"I said I didn't want to be disturbed until we're ready to rehearse!" she bellowed, pulling the door open with great force. Her beautiful brown eyes widened when she saw the three of us standing in the hallway, and before she had the chance to recover, I pushed forward into her dressing room.

"Madame Russo!" I cried, embracing her. "It is such an honor—truly! Please forgive my companions and I, but we are such great admirers of you that we were desperate to come meet you. We knew that you would be engaged on the night of a performance and decided to venture forth on an off night to make your acquaintance."

"Ah, *grazie*," she replied, still quite stunned and confused. Not wanting to give her the chance to recover and shunt us to the door, I continued.

"Duchesse de Duras, may I present the esteemed Signora Nadia Russo. I am Comtesse de Brionne, and our companion is Doctor Van Helsing—another ardent lover of the opera."

The singer curtsied deeply to us and opened her mouth to speak, but I cut her off again.

"You are playing the lead in *Orfeo ed Euridice,* are you not? That is *so* thrilling. I simply adore a tragic love story. Actually, I adore *any* love story, but the tragic ones always have the better music, don't you find?" I whirled around her room, inhaling deeply, trying to scent the vicomte or anything else suspicious, but the dressing room was a riot of overpowering fragrances. Perfume, stage makeup, dust, wine, stale sweat from old costumes, and the heady aroma of a rose bouquet on top of her dressing table.

"Such lovely flowers," Daphne commented, seeing where my attention fell. "And so hard to find exceptional roses in the middle of winter. You *must* tell me who your florist is."

Signora Russo's eyes widened a fraction and I could hear the hitch in her pulse. Seizing the opportunity, I went to the table and plucked the card from the center of the bouquet before she could stop me.

Forgive me, mon petit chou, the card read. I brought it up to my nose and sniffed—it reeked of the vicomte.

"My, my," I drawled. "It seems you have quite the devotee."

Anger colored the singer's face, darkening her chocolate eyes and turning her cheeks as red as the roses on her table. She crossed her arms in front of her ample bosom and nodded at the door.

"I think perhaps you ladies have overstayed your welcome," she said haughtily. "It's rather uncouth of you to pry into my personal affairs—admirers or no."

At that moment, a soft thump sounded from somewhere in the room. No one moved. Daphne, Van Helsing, and I looked at each other.

"Go!" Signora Russo shouted. "Get out!"

Again, the dull sounds arose, a muted shuffling and light scraping. This time, I pinpointed it to a large armoire in the back of the room, which I'd assumed was filled with elaborate opera costumery and the singer's personal clothing.

Daphne must have heard it at the same time, for she crossed the room in swift strides and threw open the door. Out tumbled the villainous vicomte—blindfolded, bound, gagged, and apparently beginning to regain consciousness.

We all turned to stare at Signora Russo, whose fury remained frozen on her visage. After several moments of stunned silence, she arched a supercilious eyebrow and shrugged.

"I'll have you know, *he* started it," she snapped.

We continued to stare in astonishment. Finally, Daphne recovered enough to entreat, "Do explain."

"He came to my room late last night—or perhaps it was early in the morning, I don't know. It was dark out, and he was stinking drunk. He brought me flowers and told me that he'd made a mistake ending our arrangement. I refused him. *No one* humiliates la Signora Russo! He did not take kindly to my rejection," she said, venom in her voice.

Van Helsing went over to the man and removed the blindfold and gag, but kept him bound. She looked him over and nodded to me.

"He's had a terrible knock on the head and has been given opium, I'd wager, but he's otherwise unharmed," she said.

"Laudanum," Signora Russo offered, matter-of-factly. "When he made certain advances, I hit him over the head with a candlestick, which dazed him enough for me to drug him. I planned to have the doorman take him back to his home after our rehearsal ended and leave him in the care of his good lady wife."

"You...you mean, you weren't bitter about being scorned and sought to end your torment by kidnapping him? Or killing him?" I asked, somewhat disappointed.

Signora Russo tipped her head back and laughed until tears gathered in the corners of her eyes.

"Goodness no," she replied. "When our arrangement

ended, I was able to find a much more agreeable patron. I was perfectly happy until he showed up again."

The vicomte moaned and slumped back down on the floor. No one approached him to help.

"She knocked out the vicomte and drugged him," Daphne whispered to me. "I'm a bit unsure about how we should proceed. What are we going to do with her?"

I grinned. "Recruit her."

TWO HOURS LATER, WE'D RETURNED THE INSENSATE VICOMTE TO HIS townhouse with a hasty explanation, but the Vicomtesse de Malin didn't seem overly concerned. She didn't even bother to inquire about the name of the woman he'd been with, leaving me to wonder if anyone actually cared for the bastard. His wife had simply wrinkled her nose at the bedraggled man and instructed the footmen to bathe him and lock him in his room.

As the carriage trundled back toward *Rue Ordener,* Daphne and I bickered about Signora Russo, who we agreed should be well compensated for her silence about the incident with the vicomte. I wanted to recruit her into *les Dames Dangereuses* immediately, but Daphne insisted we spend more time looking into her background and her politics before inviting her to join our covert agency. It made sense, I supposed.

As was her custom, Van Helsing grumbled the whole way back to her clinic, declaring that she never should have consented to help us in the first place. She swore roundly that she was done befriending vampires and werewolves, as we constantly made trouble for her. Naturally, I agreed, but reminded her that her life would likely be deadly dull without us, which she grudgingly acknowledged. Momentarily assuaged, she kissed us goodbye, and I promised to bring her a peace offering of her favorite almond cakes the following evening.

Daphne and I rested in companionable silence on our way back to my *château*.

"What are you going to tell The Order?" I asked.

"Most of the truth, I think," she replied. "Malin had a lover's quarrel and is now at home with his wife, safe and mostly sound...though I don't envy the recovery from a head wound and an ill-advised amount of laudanum. We'll still go ahead with the rest of our plans, assuming tonight's events don't impact his scheduled departure to the country."

"Of course," I agreed. "But running investigations into Malin and Monsieur Honoré's affairs will need to wait. I'm exhausted and starving. I long for justice, certainly, but first I wish to have a hot bath, a large meal, and a long sleep."

Daphne covered a yawn, which I took as tacit agreement. I noticed through the carriage's blacked out windows that the sun was rising and the dark sky was fading to a lovely periwinkle. When the carriage trundled up my drive, I gave her a brief embrace and dragged myself out and up the stairs to my front door.

I still found it difficult at times to keep to the nighttime schedule that the country increasingly favored, but I knew it would get easier with time.

"Madame Toussaint, please send up a hot bath and some dinner. Beef, if we have it, and some roasted carrots, bread and butter, cheese, and wine, please."

"Of course, my lady," she said. "Regretfully, no one was able to find your *chatelaine*. We checked the house, your wardrobe, the carriage—one of the footmen even went so far as to retrace the coachman's route to Versailles. It appears to be lost."

My heart sank, but I forced a smile. "Thank you, Madame. I appreciate everyone's efforts, nonetheless. I shall just have to have a new one, I suppose."

The disappointing news weighed me down with melancholy. I felt so careless, losing the one heirloom I truly cherished. A tear slipped down my cheek as I undressed, and with the fatigue, stress of the day, and hunger gnawing at me, I embraced the sadness and melancholy. By the time the large copper tub was filled with piping hot water, I was sobbing like a baby. I poured myself a large glass of wine, intent on drinking through my despair.

I was so wrapped up in my glorious wallow that I barely noticed Antoine until he rushed in, worry etched on his handsome face.

"Charlotte! What is it? Are you injured? What's happened?" He leaned forward to cradle my face between his hands.

"Darling!" I sniffed, surprised. "I thought you were away for training."

"I was—I am. But I missed you... I wanted to be with you. When the troops turned in after drills today, I shifted and ran here as fast as I could. Much faster than a carriage ride," he said, wiping my tears with his thumbs. "What has happened? Why are you crying?"

"It's nothing, *chéri*. I'm so glad you're home! How long do you have before you must return? How was it?"

Antoine pushed a damp lock of my hair from my face, the concern still heavy in his gaze.

"Charlotte," he murmured. "Tell me what troubles you."

Tears threatened to spill again and I swallowed.

"It will seem silly," I said quietly, swirling my hand through the water.

"If you truly do not wish to tell me, you don't need to," he said.

He pulled a chair over to the side of the tub, methodically removed his jacket and draped it over the back. He rolled the cuffs of his shirtsleeves up, slowly exposing his tanned fore-arms to the golden light of the candles and the crackling fire in the bedroom hearth. The corded muscles bunched and flexed, which was at once mesmerizing, soothing, and erotic. When he was through, he plucked my wine glass from my hand, refilled it, and handed it back to me.

"I promise I shall not laugh," he said.

He dropped to his knees behind me and tilted my head back, then started to pull pin after pin from my coiffure. I felt the soft weight of my hair fall around my shoulders as he worked, gently threading his fingers through my curls when he'd removed all the pins. The sensation was heavenly. I closed my eyes and relaxed into the pampering, exhaling much of my stress. He lightly massaged my scalp, then poured a bowl of the warm water over my head, careful to keep it off my face.

"I don't talk about them much," I heard myself saying. "My parents."

He picked up the lavender-scented soap and quietly worked up a lather, then spread it through my wet locks.

"They were wonderful, you know," I continued. "My father was kind and thoughtful, and my mother was warm and affec-tionate. They were lucky enough to have a love match—they wanted scores of children, but my mother couldn't have any more after I was born. Rather than resent me, like many aristo-cratic parents do without a son, my parents treasured me. I had a charmed childhood."

Antoine's large hands slowed, and he picked up the bowl to rinse the soap. He wrung out much of the water, then sprinkled a few drops of almond oil through my tresses and began to untangle the waves with my ivory comb. Comfortable in silence, he carried on his ministrations without interrupting.

"When my father first took ill, my mother would sit at his bedside for hours, reading to him, singing to him, helping him manage the estate—they were partners in love and in life. His death shook her deeply, and it wasn't long after that she..." Tears began to flow again, but I was compelled to continue. "Before she died, she gave me her *chatelaine* with all the keys to the house. Normally, the housekeeper would have it, but my mother was every inch the lady of the house. She worked to keep our servants comfortable and happy, and managed our family like a true queen. I've worn her *chatelaine* every day since she passed and now it is...gone. Lost, or stolen, I do not know. I know it's a mere bauble, but losing it feels like losing her all over again."

I breathed slowly, squeezing my eyes shut to keep the rest of my tears at bay.

"It isn't lost or stolen," Antoine said quietly.

My eyes snapped open and I whirled around to look at him, sloshing a good deal of water out of the tub.

"What?" I exclaimed.

He sighed. "Because I was ill—going through my turning over Christmas—I never got you a present. I knew the *chatelaine* was an heirloom from your mother, so I took it to a jeweler yesterday to have it cleaned, add a few more small compartments, and have some of the loose stones re-set. I was hoping to surprise you with it, but I didn't realize being without it would distress you so much. I'm sorry, Charlotte."

I blinked.

"It's not lost," I said simply, mind reeling, emotions condensing like clouds before rain.

"It is not."

"Monsieur Honoré didn't pilfer it while we were dancing, which would have made me the worst sort of spy," I confirmed.

"Spy? Or agent?" Antoine said, covering a smirk at our inside joke. "No, *mon amour,* he did not steal it from you."

"You took it—because you wanted me to have a Christmas present?"

He nodded, wincing slightly. "I'm sorry."

Relief, elation, and compassion washed over me and I leaped from the tub, toppling Antoine onto the plush carpet. I cried even harder than before, but they were tears of joy.

"You wonderful, wicked thing," I sobbed between kisses. "How could you torment me so?"

I felt the low vibrations of his laugh through the fine lawn of his shirt. "Next time, I'll try not to be at death's door for Christmas. Perhaps I'll have more time to come up with a better gift that doesn't involve driving you mad."

"I should get that in writing," I mumbled, tugging at the falls of his breeches, desperate to undress him. "But for now, it's only fair that I return the favor."

"You're going to give me a gift?" he teased. "Or you're going to drive me mad?"

I grinned. "Oh, *chéri*—isn't that the same thing?"

THE END

NIGHT OF THE HUNT
A VAMPIRES IN VERSAILLES STORY

AUTHOR'S NOTE

This extra spicy bonus epilogue takes place after the events of Long Lost, but before the events in the original epilogue.

BONUS EPILOGUE
CHARLOTTE

February 14, 1768
Château de Ruisseau Magdelaine

If you're going to turn your fiancé into a werewolf, you'll want to clear your social calendar.

There are countless changes in your body when you suffer from the blood plague, but perhaps the most unexpected is your advanced supernatural senses intensify when you're in proximity to those of your bloodline. And if you turn someone you're already quite enamored with, any kindling desire becomes a rather dangerous conflagration.

Actually, I turned Antoine before he proposed, but that was neither here nor there. And it had very little bearing on my current issue—the pervasive fitfulness that hung over our château like a miasma of ill humor. Since our supernatural condition was rather new, it was impossible to say whether it was due to our changed state of being, the approaching full moon, or the fact that it had been far too long since we'd satisfied our insatiable sexual appetites. I felt like I was going to crawl out of my skin with agitation, and it was making me a frightful dinner companion.

"You're certain you don't mind skipping the Saint Valentine's *fête* at Versailles this evening?" Antoine asked, frowning.

"I'm certain," I insisted, exasperation adding more bite to my tone than I'd intended. "We shall stay in tonight."

"Charlotte..." he began, setting his silverware down.

"You've asked me three times already, *l'amour*. This is always my least favorite ball, Daphne and Étienne won't be attending, and we've both been so busy lately, I feel as though I haven't spent more than an hour in your presence in weeks," I replied, devouring the last bite of raw mutton from the dish in front of me. It was the first meal we'd shared in far too long without one of us having to rush off for other obligations: wedding planning, Antoine's new conscription, my work with Daphne for *les DD* and social calls with Dr. Van Helsing. Considering our privileged, aristocratic life, our leisure time had been limited to frenzied bouts of lovemaking in the small hours of the dawn, and even that had waned in the face of our exhaustion. Anxiety had begun to needle me and grim thoughts sowed doubts in my mind. Antoine had only been turned in December. What if this wasn't the vision of immortality he'd agreed to?

"It's just...I don't think I've ever known you to turn down a party," he pointed out. "You'd tell me if something was amiss, wouldn't you, *petite*?"

"*Bien sûr*," I responded, not bothering to hide my petulance. "I just don't feel like going. Why are you so concerned? Do *you* wish to attend?"

Antoine snorted a laugh and rolled his glowing jade eyes. I watched the tendons in his neck stretch as he rolled out his shoulders. My teeth ached with the salacious urge to bite him there—*hard*.

"If I ever agree to prance around a ballroom with a court full of smelly aristocrats instead of bedding my delicious fiancée until she passes out from pleasure, you'll be obliged to cut off my head."

I sucked in a breath, lascivious excitement coiling deep in my gut. My skin felt too hot and stretched too tight over my flesh—sensations that often plagued me before I shifted into my lupine form. Despite my kindling desire, my concerns lingered in the front of my mind.

"So, truly, you have no regrets?" I asked, forcing levity into my tone. His gaze snapped to mine. Sharp as he was, he immediately sensed my question was about more than the declined ball.

"I have many regrets in my life, Charlotte. Loving you is not one of them. Perhaps the only regret is that we've both been so busy working to build our future that we haven't had as much time to enjoy our present. But everything is a season, my love. We'll weather it and more," he said, tilting his head contemplatively. "Is this what's been on your mind?"

I could've denied it, but my emotions stuck in my throat. I nodded, chagrinned.

"You've been like a caged animal these last weeks, and all because you fear I resent you for turning me? Or maybe you think I've changed my mind about committing my immortality to a beast—a monster?" he asked. Candlelight glinted off his lengthening fangs.

His ability to see through my artifice and bluster had always unmoored me, and even now I found myself regarding him with wide eyes and a trembling lip.

"Perhaps you need reminding that you are mine, Charlotte," he said in a low tone, laced with heat. "I chose you just as much as you chose me. You have a magnificent talent for engineering the world to be as you see fit, but you must give me some credit. You are my fiancée, my lover, my very heart. You brought me back from the grip of Death but I would not have come if you hadn't been waiting for me on the other side."

My heart stuttered—metaphorically speaking. *Dieu,* how I loved this man. I wiped the tears that had gathered in my eyes and sniffed.

"You wish to remind me, then?" I said with a small smile.

Carnal hunger sparked in Antoine's gaze and a dangerous smile danced upon his lush lips.

The remainder of our mid-evening meal lay forgotten between us, having become far less appealing than the handsome face and muscular body of my soon-to-be husband. His nostrils flared and his eyes darkened—he'd scented my arousal with his supernatural senses.

"It seems you have something in mind, Comtesse."

"You know," I began, slowly rising from my chair. "The full moon is only four nights away. I've been feeling a little restless. Haven't you?"

"I'm always restless in your company," he said, tracking my movements with tethered intensity.

I came around the shining oak table and perched atop his lap, twining my arms around his neck. His body went rigid beneath me, fingers gripping the arms of his chair. Long claws sprouted from his fingertips and left deep grooves in the wood of the chair.

"Do you remember our first night together?" I murmured, feathering kisses along his sculpted, shadowed jawline.

Antoine's brow rose, pulling at the white moon-shaped scar on his face as regarded me skeptically.

"When I kidnapped you?" he asked with sarcasm.

"You were protecting me," I said with a smirk. "But yes."

"What about it?" he uttered, inhaling at the crook of my

neck. His hands trembled and his thick thighs flexed beneath me—he was losing our little game, the battle not to touch me despite how much I teased him.

"Would you have continued to chase me if the *bêtes* hadn't caught up to us?" I asked.

"Of course," he answered, confusion evident as he paused sowing small kisses along my throat. "*Dieu*, you smell so good—it's maddening."

I nipped at his ear and he moaned, the sound more erotic than a litany of prurient words.

If my heart could still beat, it would've been pounding.

"Do you think you could catch me?" I whispered.

"Well, I..."

Before Antoine could finish his sentence, I bolted for the front door. Once outside, I tugged at the belt of my dressing gown and let it fall to the ground, the white muslin landing like a puddle of pale moonlight on the gravel path. I didn't slow my stride as I tugged my chemise up over my head, and as I tossed it behind me, I heard the unmistakable sound of wood splintering and fabric tearing, followed by the blood-curdling, guttural howl of Antoine shifting into his werewolf form.

Like me and the man in black, Antoine wasn't a graceful natural wolf. The first time I'd seen him transform, I'd had to fight to keep my screams down, even though I'd been the one to turn him. With limbs longer than a wolf's, charcoal-colored fur, red eyes, and massive claws and teeth, he looked more like Hell's approximation of a wolf than the animals roaming the countryside. He was as horrifying as I was, and it was unbearably erotic.

Even without turning, I could sense he wasn't far behind me, so I banked quickly to the left toward the patch of woods skirting the estate. I could shift at any time and increase the distance between us, but the thrill of being chased ignited something primal in my blood—something other than fear. *Excitement. Heady lust. Possession. The need to be run down and claimed by my mate.*

I became the winsome young woman running for my life, determined to protect my soul and my chastity. *I snorted a laugh at that.* Threading my way through the dense undergrowth and towering trees, I looked back at the way I'd come. I was deep enough in the woods to block out the lights from the château. Bare branches stretched spindly black shadows against the nearly full moon above. The snow from last week's storm had all but melted, but the night was still clear, crisp, and laced with frost. It was a blessing I could not feel the chill.

Crouching low to the ground, I listened, waiting for the telltale sounds of panting, monstrous breaths and the crunch of decaying leaf litter beneath heavy paws. An owl hooted in the distance, and with my supernatural senses, I could hear the scurrying of rabbits and field mice beneath the ground, but I did not hear Antoine stalking me.

I tipped my nose up and inhaled deeply, trying to catch his scent in the frigid night air. In my haste and excitement, I'd foolishly run upwind and was unable to smell his telltale fragrance of apples, earth, leather, and horseflesh. Perhaps he was trying to wait me out and let me make a mistake that would give away my position.

After another two breaths, I sensed him just at the edge of my awareness. He was still some distance away, crawling through the forest on steps more silent than Death. In this position, I didn't think he could see me, but he certainly would be able to smell me. It wouldn't be long before he pinpointed my exact location, and I wasn't ready to give in just yet.

I hefted a melon-sized rock and threw it as far as I could in the opposite direction. Antoine was after it like a shot and I seized my chance to make for the folly at the other end of the grounds—the perfect place to hide with its massive stone columns and Grecian statues.

I hadn't had a chance to show the faux ruins to Antoine yet, but it was one of my favorite places in my family's estate. My father had constructed the reproduction of Aphrodite's temple for my mother, who spent ages coaxing pink roses and climbing vines around the chipped marble. Now that it was winter, the thick foliage had died back, leaving bare tendrils and sparse branches clinging to the walls. Fortunately, there was enough to conceal me for a few moments, and I hid in the small central courtyard encircling an ice-choked fountain, waiting for my dangerous wolf.

It wasn't long before I heard him coming—slow, deliberate steps in the soft mud. As he neared my hiding place, I saw he'd shifted back to an almost human form. He was so beautiful—completely naked, visibly aroused, his corded muscles flexing beneath delicious, scarred skin. Long claws tipped his fingers and his impressive fangs appeared to glow in the moonlight.

"Come out, come out, wherever you are," he growled in a half-human, half-monstrous voice. "I can scent your desire, *petite*. You've done very well keeping me at bay, but I know you're in here. Your body is mine to claim." He rolled his neck and sniffed the air, stalking toward me. If I didn't know him—hadn't turned him and promised him my eternity—I would've been terrified. As it happened, I was nearly mad with lust.

A flood of arousal gathered between my legs and as soon as it did, Antoine's head whipped in my direction. A predatory grin stretched across his lips.

"*Bon soir, petite,*" he chuckled, meeting my gaze through the leafless vines.

I returned his smile and stepped around the low wall where I'd been crouching, crooking a finger in his direction. His eyes widened, his nostrils flared, and he pounced.

The fall wouldn't have hurt my supernatural body, but Antoine rolled me on top of him before we hit the ground, anyway.

"Did you enjoy the chase?" I asked, leaning down to press a scorching kiss to his lips.

"Mm," came his response. His claws dug into the soft flesh of my ass and I gasped—the pain sharpening the edges of my pleasure. "I always enjoy eating what I hunt."

He pulled my hips forward until my thighs bracketed his ears and my sex covered his mouth. There was no delicacy to his manner—his fangs scored the lips of my pussy and he sucked at the peak of my pleasure like the Devil come to devour my soul.

"This sweet cunt has been so neglected lately," he rumbled. "Poor thing. What a feast I'll make of you tonight."

My legs shook and I worried about crushing him, but the moment I tried to lift myself up off Antoine's face, he dug his claws in further and snarled.

"Don't you dare, Charlotte," he warned, eyes flashing. "You stole my breath long ago and I would drown in you if I could. Give me your weight, *l'amour*. Do not hold back—ever. I've come for your pleasure and now you'll come for mine."

Obediently, I leaned forward. When his hot tongue speared me, I swore and let out a sound between a scream and a wolf howl.

"I'm so close, *chéri*," I panted, grinding against Antoine's ravenous mouth. On a satisfied groan, he slid his thumb forward to rub small circles at the apex of my sex—his claws gently pricking the lips of my pussy.

"*Oui, l'amour!* Don't stop—don't stop!"

He unleashed a growl that vibrated up through his throat and tipped me over the edge, hurtling headfirst into a brutal explosion of bliss. Waves of pleasure crashed over me, loosening some of the tension I'd been feeling over the last few weeks. Incandescent and temporarily satiated, I threw back my head and howled. Antoine answered with a rumbling growl and deftly lifted me to roll us onto our sides, cushioning my head from the damp ground with his substantial bicep.

"That was spectacular," I sighed.

"I wanted to do that to you ever since I saw you naked in that godforsaken inn outside Versailles," he admitted, pulling a twig from the snarled mass of my hair. "You spent so much time running from me—and then running circles around me, it was rather enjoyable to lead the chase for once."

"Well, I'd say I was the one leading the chase this time. After all, I led you right where I wanted you," I preened, running my hands down his muscular chest.

"If that's what you wanted all along, I beg you to simply ask me next time. I'm happy to hunt you down and claim your exquisite body over and over again," he chuckled.

My hands had drifted over the small line of dark hair trailing down his hard abdomen to his still hard cock. Already, my body burned for him again.

I quirked a brow at him. "Oh? I'd hardly call it a claiming."

Antoine narrowed his eyes and sucked on a fang. "Who said I was finished?"

"Well, I assumed since we're just lying on the ground here..."

"I'm giving you a moment to recover," he said darkly. "This is all the chivalry you'll have from me tonight. Once I start in again, I don't think I'll be able to stop."

The warning in his words sent a fresh wave of desire through my veins and I reached down to wrap my fingers around his thick length. He sucked in a breath and tensed beneath my touch.

"Charlotte, do not test me," he ground out. "I do not wish to hurt you."

I leaned forward to take his lips in an eager kiss, stroking his erection with a firm hand. His harsh breaths became deep whimpers, then morphed into feral growls as he found his beast form again.

"Come on, then, my love—I've been yours from the start. Let loose your monster and let it have its way with me," I breathed, heating the scant space between us.

No sooner had I issued the challenge than Antoine laughed —a dangerous, wild sound—and he whispered in my ear.

"Run."

Up I jumped, ducking through the bare trees and rushing past the folly. This time, I didn't make it far before he barreled into me, knocking me forward into the soft grass and slick mud. I hardly had time to catch my breath, and I shivered with lust-filled anticipation when his clawed fingertips parted the delicate folds between my legs.

"Still so wet for me, monster than I am," he grunted, the words sounding far less human than moments before.

My own claws and fangs lengthened in response and I lifted my hips to meet his explorations.

"Monsters that *we* are," I reminded him, digging my lengthening fingers into the dirt.

When he dragged the tip of his cock through my wet entrance, I howled, my humanity forgotten. In answer, he slid forward, pounding into me with the perfect exquisite, hellish rhythm. One fingertip circled the bud of my pleasure and stars danced along the edges of my vision.

"Mine," he demanded, repeating the word on each delicious thrust. "You will be my love, my wife, my monster. Every part of you—every shade of you—*mine.*"

"Yes," I cried out, feeling my half-human, half-werewolf

body draw up tightly with the onslaught of possessive words and unrelenting pleasure.

When my orgasm crested, this time Antoine followed me over the edge, clinging to my hips and slumping forward to drop kisses and fierce little nips up my spine toward my neck.

"Was that enough of a claiming for you?" he panted.

"For now," I chuckled. "That was a much more enjoyable chase than our first one outside Versailles."

"I would've much preferred our first encounter to end thusly," he said, finally catching his breath and shifting back to his human form.

"I would've preferred our first encounter to have *begun* so," I agreed. "Think of all the time and heartache we would've saved."

"Neither one of us were monsters then, though," he admitted, picking me up to carry back inside our home, where I knew he'd take infinite care in cleaning the mud from our naked bodies. For now, our beasts were sated, but the night was still young.

"How absurd!" I scoffed. "I've always been a monster. I'm only newly a werewolf. And you know, with an eternity of nights like that in our future, I've rather come around to the idea."

With a smile that would've tempted the Devil himself, Antoine winked at me.

"So have I."

THE END

ACKNOWLEDGMENTS

Once again, this book would not exist without the support of a few of my favorite people in the world. My Discordant Owls—where would I be without you? Susan, you kept me sane and grounded in a world that feels increasingly bananas. Huge heartfelt thanks to my family and friends for supporting me—you all keep me going, even when the going is tough. Love to Finn, Zoe, Michelle, Dad, Mary, Cassie, Alisa, Brian (I can't believe you edited my books TWICE, I truly owe you), and everyone else who has helped me get from book one to book two. And always to Heather for believing in me from the start and helping me put my words out into the world. Thank you.

OTHER BOOKS BY LILY RILEY

Vampires in Versailles series:

The Assassin and the Libertine

The Agent and the Outlaw

COMING SOON: The Doctor and the Devil

ABOUT THE AUTHOR

Photo by Kara Brodgesell

Lily Riley is a romance novelist currently focused on books that feature a little bit of cheek and a lot of steam.

The Agent and the Outlaw is the second book in the *Vampires in Versailles* series, which begins with *The Assassin and the Libertine* and will conclude with *The Doctor and the Devil*.

When Lily isn't writing about dreamy, supernatural beings in 18th century France, she enjoys sipping champagne, eating cake, and dancing naked by the light of the full moon. To sign up for her newsletter or read more about her upcoming projects, visit: www.authorlilyriley.com